ST. MARTIN'S

MINOTAUR

MYSTERIES

MORE . . .

CONSPIRACY THEORY

Jane Haddam

St. Martin's Paperbacks

CONSPIRACY THEORY

Copyright © 2003 by Orania Papazoglou.
Excerpt from *The Headmaster's Wife* copyright © 2004 by Orania Papazoglou.
Jacket photograph by Kiyotsugu Tsukuma.

Library of Congress Catalog Card Number: 2003040637

ISBN: 0-312-99000-6

Printed in the United States of America

St. Martin's Press hardcover edition / July 2003
St. Martin's Paperbacks edition / May 2004

St. Martin's Paperbacks are published by St. Martin's Press, 175 Fifth Avenue, New York, NY 10010.

10 9 8 7 6 5 4 3 2 1

This book is for

RAM

rec. arts. mystery

and everybody on it—especially the

Australians, who send TimTams.

ACKNOWLEDGMENTS

First, I need to thank Norma Frank, her husband, Bob, and all the people from Mystery Books on Lancaster Avenue in Bryn Mawr. It was a great mystery bookstore—it's closed now, but it should have been declared a historic treasure. Norma and company have been of invaluable help in setting me straight about all things Bryn Mawr. If I've taken their excellent information and made a hash of it, it's my fault.

Second, I'd like to thank Vicki Ball, who spent several weeks gamely attempting to write messages from RAM to the Federal Bureau of Investigation protesting their investigation of Father Tibor Kasparian—then I changed the plot and couldn't use the stuff and left her hanging out to dry. I apologize, and note that she runs an excellent on-line source for mystery books: Books 'n' Bytes at www.booksnbytes.com. If you're looking for mysteries, or for information about your favorite mystery writers, start there.

Third—I'd like to thank all the people I work with, who make it possible for me to write books that don't sound as if I've just sat down at the computer to spout gibberish before I've had my serious caffeine: Don Maass, my agent; Keith Kahla, my editor; and Teresa Theophano, the world's greatest editorial assistant, who's now left to go off and get another degree and do real work in the real world that will actually help people and, and—no! no! I'm not hyperventilating. I'm not. I'm fine. It's not like she deserted me. It's—no, really, it's . . . nah. Good luck, Teresa. I miss you.

Finally—a note about the Web sites. By now, I've had dozens of people read this manuscript, and all but one of them have said the same thing: You made those Web sites up, didn't you? No, as a matter of fact, I didn't. If a Web site is mentioned in this novel, it existed on the Web at the time I wrote this manuscript, and maybe still does. Go try them out. For people who know nothing about conspiracy theories, or about the people who are committed to conspiracy theories, they're quite a revelation.

Of necessity, the conspiracy theories and the conspiracy theorists used here are mostly American, British, Canadian, or Australian—but there are a lot more of them worldwide, and a lot more variations on them than I could cover here. There are secular, Protestant, Catholic, and Muslim varieties, to start with. There are wholesale conspiracy theories, where *everything* is a plot, and partial conspiracy theories, where it's just the Republicans trying to get the Democrats or the Democrats trying to get the Republicans, or . . . well, you see what I mean.

I don't like conspiracy theories, much, and I don't respect them, and it worries me that there are so many of them alive in the world right now. But—check them out if you dare.

—*Litchfield County, Connecticut*
September 2001 to January 2003

THE HARRIDAN REPORT

November 7

This week, Philadelphia will be host to one of the most important, and most sinister, gatherings of the Illuminati on the planet—and most of you won't know it. Like all the best secrets, this is a secret hidden in plain sight. Open your copy of the mind-controlled mainstream press on the morning of November 9 and take a look at the pictures spread out across the "society" section. You've probably seen pictures like these before: young girls in ball gowns; distinguished-looking men in tuxedos; stately dowagers in beaded dresses and four strands of pearls. Philadelphia's social season has begun, and the shadowy leaders of the Illuminati have done their work so well, most Americans see nothing odd—or dangerous—about the process. After all, what is so awful about giving a few formal parties to raise money for charity?

If you're tempted to fall for this line, I suggest you try a little experiment. Try to get tickets to the Around the World Harvest Ball, that supposedly "open" event that anybody can buy a ticket to, if they have the price of admission. The price of admission is not cheap: 25,000 dollars a table, meaning 2,500 dollars a seat. Even if you could come up with the money, or more, you couldn't crack your way into that exclusive enclave. Most of the tickets were already taken long before they were advertised for sale. The few left were handed out only to carefully vetted supplicants, who had to pass muster with an invitations committee made up of women from the most important Illuminati families. Chairwoman of the event is Charlotte Deacon Ross, a Rockefeller on her mother's side and married to a collateral member of the House of Morgan, who also happens to be Anthony van Wyck Ross, head of Lessard Cole, one of the world's biggest and most important investment banks. Vice chairwoman is Bennis Hannaford, a member of the notorious Duke family. The Dukes founded Duke University in North Carolina, the only university in the United States that funds academic "research" into the occult. Their most famous member, Doris Duke, once known as the richest woman in the world, was ritually murdered in 1993 to keep her from exposing the family's involvement with Satanism and the New World Order.

If all that isn't enough for you, consider the event's purpose: to raise money for UNICEF, the United Nations International Children's Emergency Fund. You remember UNICEF. If you were like me, you probably carried little orange-papered milk cartons around on Halloween, collecting money to "help" children in the poor nations of the world. But UNICEF doesn't help children anywhere, and the fact that it collects its money on the Illuminati's only sacred holiday is no accident.

The purpose of UNICEF is now, and has always been, to separate children from their parents so that they can be raised by the state as mind-controlled slaves for the New World Order. That's why UNICEF supports such radical political measures as "children's rights," including the "right" of children to be "vaccinated" against "diseases" that will supposedly kill them otherwise. You and I know that those "vaccinations" are really implants, the means by which the Illuminati and their forces get the necessary microequipment into the bodies of children, the better to control their behavior for the benefit of the corporations—and the banks—who really run this world.

The important thing to remember is that the Illuminati

never get together in public unless they have to. Something is up. Philadelphia is the heart of the vortex of the New World Order this weekend. Something will be decided here. Something will be launched. Something will come to fruition. We may not know what until it's far too late.

Check back next week for the Harridan Report's *firsthand account from the belly of the beast.*

PROLOGUE

The American Constitution has been called "the finest document ever written by the mind of men!" The American people have been taught that it was written to restrict the power of government, and to protect their God-given inalienable rights to life, liberty and property.

But Ralph Epperson has discovered the evidence that the men who founded this nation were not God-fearing patriots as we have been told, but occultic practitioners of a secret worship on this earth. In fact, he will discuss the evidence that our founding fathers created two separate governments in the Constitution at the same time, and ONE OF THOSE GOVERNMENTS WAS GIVEN ABSOLUTE TYRANNICAL POWER! And that this is the government ruling America today!

—PROMOTIONAL COPY FOR *AMERICA'S SECRET DESTINY* BY RALPH EPPERSON (TUCSON, ARIZONA: PUBLIUS PRESS, 1977) AT HTTP://SYNINFO.COM/EPPERSON/#B17

1

It was on November 8, one year and some weeks after the September 11 attacks on the World Trade Center and the Pentagon, that Father Tibor Kasparian received the letter—and realized, without much shock, that he had spent a decade living in a fantasy. Maybe, he thought, sometime in the middle of the afternoon, when his head was pounding so badly that he would have willingly cracked it open on a brick wall, maybe all of America was a fantasy, a kind of Brigadoon, outside space and time, outside reality. Father Tibor's own reality had begun fifty-five years before on the flat dirt floor of a back room in a midwife's house in Yekevan, Armenia. There were hospitals in Yekevan, and doctors, but his mother hadn't trusted them. Those were the days before—just before—the Soviet occupation, but she hadn't trusted them anyway. She hadn't liked the condescension of the medical staff, who seemed to think women knew nothing about giving birth. She hadn't liked the soldiers in the street, who belonged to one side or the other, but never hers. Most of all, she had wanted a priest, a real Armenian priest, from an Armenian church, willing to give baptism on the spot just in case the worst decided to happen. All these years later, *that* was the one thing about his mother that Father Tibor Kasparian had not been able to accept. He could not fully love anyone who thought so little of God as to think that He would send an infant into eternal hellfire simply because it had happened to die before someone had been able to baptize it.

I have become Americanized, he thought—but it didn't bother him, because he was a little proud of it. Some people grew up wanting to be doctors or lawyers or astronauts or spies. He had grown up wanting to be an American. The first time he had ever risked his life, he had done it to see a movie. It was 1962, and he was fifteen-years-old. The movie was *The Parent Trap*, starring Hayley Mills. He had no idea how the two young men who ran the floating American movie concession had gotten hold of their copy. They were students at the university, and people said they were traitors. At least, that's what they said publicly, but by then everyone knew the doublespeak that went on where the authorities could hear. Patriots were traitors. To be Armenian was to be a traitor. To be anti-Soviet was to be a traitor. To be caught in a cellar watching contraband American movies was to risk jail, or worse. For the two young men whose names he had never known, the result had been worse, in the long run— two years after the night on which he had seen *The Parent Trap*, Tibor had watched one of them gunned down in the street and the other captured when the police had raided a showing of an Elvis Presley movie called *Fun in Acapulco*. Hayley Mills, Elvis Presley—it seemed incredible to him now that they could have taken it all so seriously, studying the films as if they were ancient sacred texts, the secret of the universe, the meaning of life. When he'd first come to America for real, many years later, he had made a point of seeing all those movies again. He'd been shocked at how awful most of them were, something that had been masked at his first viewing by the fact that they had been shown in English without subtitles—where were two university students going to find American movies subtitled in Armenian? Or even Russian?—and by the further fact that they had been completely incomprehensible. People talked about culture shock, but they didn't understand what it meant. He could still see himself in the dark of that small room, sitting next to Anna Bagdanian without the courage to take hold of her hand, wondering in bewilderment why, if the girls were attending the obligatory patriotic training camp, nobody ever sang patriotic songs or marched with flags.

Stupid, he thought now, but not about himself, or even about Hayley Mills and Elvis Presley. He was feeling a little light-headed, and had been, ever since the mail had come at 10:35 this morning. It was now almost six o'clock, and cold for this early in November. Outside the door of the small apartment he lived in behind Holy Trinity Armenian Apostolic Christian Church, in the little bricked courtyard, wind was blowing leaves and stones into gutters. On any other day, he would have been headed down Cavanaugh Street to the Ararat Restaurant, to meet Bennis Hannaford and Krekor Demarkian for dinner. Tonight, they were on their way to some party a friend of Bennis's was giving to benefit UNICEF, and he was on his way to do a little business for the church. If the letter hadn't come, it wouldn't have mattered. It was only because he knew that he needed advice, and needed it desperately, that he felt so completely at sea. Or maybe not, he thought, irritated at himself, and at everything about himself. He looked around his living room at the stacks of books that lined all the walls and cluttered most of the furniture, at the carpet that he should have replaced a year ago, at the big framed poster of the World Trade Center Twin Towers lit up at night. He did the same things over and over again these days. He saw the same people. He read the same books. He had this small church in his charge, to be pastor of, to celebrate the liturgy in, out in the open, without fear. He had more food in his refrigerator than he would be able to eat in a year. He published his articles about theology in good journals and was asked to conferences to sit on panels with people whose names he had once known only as the authors of banned books. He knew that if he sat down and tried to write out all the things he had wanted when he was still in Yekevan and Anna was still alive and his wife, he would have achieved every single one of them with the exception of a life with Anna herself—but he was sure he had come to terms with that years ago. He didn't know what was wrong with him. He didn't know what it was he wanted that he hadn't wanted a week ago. He only knew that he was suddenly ill at ease, and unhappy in his own skin. The world inside himself felt flat. The world outside himself felt dangerous and deliberate. Maybe reality was something that slept, and now it had woken up.

Don't dramatize, he told himself. Then he went into his vestibule and got his long good coat out of the closet. There was a time and a place for wearing hair shirts, and Philadelphia on a cold winter night was neither. He started to button the coat from the bottom and then stopped. He put his hand in under the coat and felt around for the inside pocket of his jacket, where the letter was, wadded up so many times that it felt like a stone. He ought to leave it here, where it would be safe. If he got mugged while he was out in the city, the muggers might take it, thinking it was cash. When they found out it wasn't, they might rip it up. He left it where it was and buttoned his coat the rest of the way to his chin. He got his gloves out of his coat pockets and put them on. He got the Stewart plaid muffler he had been given for Christmas last year and wound it around his neck. The muffler was cashmere. The gloves were leather and lined with cashmere. He wasn't a rich man, or even close, but he had rich things. Maybe that was part of what was wrong too—but that was worse than stupid, because he was as nearly oblivious to what he ate and what he wore as it was possible to be without going naked and starving. He was just mixed up, tonight, that was all; mixed up and frightened to the bone, and there was nothing he could do about it.

He checked his pockets for change for the bus and then stepped out his door into the courtyard behind the church. He pulled the door shut and looked at the brass knocker, shined so flawlessly it glowed gold in the light from the streetlamp. When he and Anna were first married and he had just been ordained, he had celebrated a liturgy in a cramped little apartment on a side street in Toldevan, a godforsaken mining town in the middle of nowhere, full of people whose names no one else on earth would ever have been able to recognize. It had been a cold night then too, and November, but he hadn't had a coat that would protect him from much of anything. The apartment had heat only between midnight and six in the morning. It was eight in the evening. The only warmth came from a paper-fueled fire the grandmother of the family had lit in a large can that had once held lard. You had to be careful with the cans. Some of them melted more quickly than you'd expect. Fires broke out that way all the time, and whole apartment blocks went down in flames. At this liturgy there was himself, Anna, the family, and three other families from the same building, carefully chosen, part of the elect. Still, that had made nearly forty people, and the room they were in was very small. There were no lights in the room. Electricity was expensive, and he was expected to know the liturgy by heart. It was dangerous to carry liturgical books, or books of any kind that had not been published by government publishing houses. His hands were cold. His fingers were stiff with the beginning of premature arthritis, brought on by too many nights consorting with the cold. He had given communion to everyone in the room and felt relieved. He had promised to return to perform a wedding on the third of June. The room smelled of urine, and worse. The only facility was down the hall and not working very well. The people in the apartments used tins, like the one with the fire in it, so that they wouldn't have to go down the hall in the middle of the night.

"Listen," the grandmother had said to him, in a sibilant whisper, snaking her thin hand around his wrist as he started to pack up. "Listen. God made evil, just the way He made the good. Never forget that."

"God didn't make evil," he said, a little too loudly. Anna looked up from the other side of the room, alarmed. "God could not make evil. God is all-good."

"God made evil," the grandmother said again, and then she smiled, the worst smile he had ever seen, worse even than the smiles of the secret police ten years later when they murdered Anna. The old woman had had a stroke. One of her eyes was half closed and out of control. The "good" one was rheumy and full of water. Her clothes were crusted over with dirt. She stank. Tibor thought she was decomposing in front of his eyes, except that her grip was so strong. He couldn't get his wrist away from her.

"God made evil," she said again—and then, suddenly, she let go, and he staggered backward, into something soft, someone not expecting him.

"God made evil," he said now, coming back to the present, staring still at that brass door knocker. It had his name engraved on it, in script. He unbuttoned his coat again and checked the inside pocket of his jacket again. The letter was still there. That was the worst smile he had ever seen in his life, but that wasn't the only time he had seen it. He had seen it twice more, and in only the last few weeks. He had seen it just a few hours ago, today.

Somewhere out on the street, around to the front of the church where he couldn't yet see, two women were talking. Their voices were high and light and giggly. Their steps on the pavement were sharp, as if they were wearing very high heels. *I should have worn a hat*, he thought, superfluously. He didn't own a hat.

Then he turned around and did something he had never done before on Cavanaugh Street.

He locked his door.

2

All the way back from New York in the car, Anthony van Wyck Ross had been considering the advantages of poverty. It wasn't sentimentality. He had no use for Hallmark card emotions, or Lifetime movie epiphanies, or those Great Morals taught by shows like *Leave it to Beaver* and *Dawson's Creek*. He only knew what Hallmark and Lifetime were because, unlike most men in his position, he had taken the trouble to find out. But then, Tony Ross was not like most men in his position, and his unlikeness had been evident almost from the beginning. "He's a throwback," his mother used to say, vaguely, to the sort of people who came to their lodge in Maryland for the hunting. He'd liked hunting the way he later found he liked all blood sports. He had a natural instinct for the kill. What he couldn't stand were the hunt breakfasts that came afterward, the long dining room lined with buffet tables, the longer ballroom with its doors propped open to let in the cold damp of the spring morning, the endless Bloody Marys. He sometimes amused himself, idly, by trying to pinpoint the exact moment when he had realized that at least half his parents' friends were almost drunk almost all the time. It was like walking around among people who lived permanently in a mist—and what worried him was that, if they were anything like his mother, they might live in that mist even when they *weren't* drunk. By the time he was ten-years-old, stupidity enraged him. There was some part of him that could not believe it wasn't deliberate. By the time he was twelve, he had mapped out his life with the kind of precision and attention to detail that would have done credit to a general of the army in the middle of a major war. That had been the last straw in a long history of straws between himself and his mother. She had always disliked him. When he entered puberty, she started to hate him, and the hate lasted—hot and resentful and mean—until the day she died, at eighty-six, of a ruptured appendix. She was in the house at Bryn Mawr at the time. He was in London, at a private meeting with the prime minister, the American ambassador, the Belgian ambassador, and two representatives of the Rockefeller banking interests in Europe. When the call came, he'd seen no reason to take it.

The reason he was considering the advantages of poverty, at the moment, was that he wanted to murder his wife. He wanted to do it right here, right now, as they sat, without having to think twice about the implications of the scandal that would follow—or even of the possibility of any scandal at all. The car was bumping along the roadway in the right lane, moving carefully, staying within the speed limit. It wouldn't do to be stopped for speeding, and it was always necessary to be careful with other drivers on the road. Resentment was out there, just beneath the surface, waiting to erupt. Charlotte was playing with the pearls she always wore around her neck during the day. It was an atavistic custom that belonged more to their parents' generation than their own, but Charlotte was nothing if not atavistic. The skin along the edges of her jaw sagged. Celebrities and jet-setters got face-lifts, but women of good family from the Main Line did not. The single square-cut diamond on her left hand and the plain gold wedding band behind it were the only rings she wore. No woman of her background would wear more, just as no woman of her background would wear earrings that dangled. In traditional religious orders before the travesty of Vatican II, there were nuns called "living rules," women whose behavior so perfectly conformed with the order's rule of life that it could be re-created just by recording the things they did and how they did them. Charlotte was a living rule for the Philadelphia Main Line, the part of it that wasn't supposed to exist anymore, the part of it that wasn't supposed to matter. She did not live under the delusion that she was an anachronism.

She was waiting for him to say something. Tony was aware of that. He was also aware of the fact that he would not say something. It wasn't to his advantage, and there wasn't any point. The privacy shield that cut them off from the driver was closed. The windows of the car were tinted darkly enough so that nobody on the outside would be able to see in unless they pressed their faces directly to the glass. Tony looked down at the copy of *Civitas Dei* he had in his hands and wished he'd brought a book light. It was rude to read in front of other people, but he never cared if he was rude to Charlotte.

"I'm not going to shut up and go away," Charlotte said, the words coming out in that nasal Society whine that made his teeth grate. You'd think, after years of listening to Bill Buckley and Katharine Hepburn, that women like Charlotte would know better. "I'm not going to drop the subject," she said. "This has gotten completely out of hand, Tony, and you know it."

"I know no such thing. The only thing that seems to be out of hand is you."

"You can't expect me to just sit still while you . . . well. While you make it plain to everybody we know—"

"It's been plain to everybody we know since the day we were married. More than plain. Nobody on earth was fooled, not even you."

"You think it was plain to everybody we knew that from the day we were married you couldn't stand to fuck me?"

"Where do you get the language, Charlotte? Sometimes I listen to you and I think I'm hearing the boys at the YMCA."

"You don't go to the YMCA."

"I don't, no. What's your point?"

Charlotte shifted in her seat. Her fingers were long and thin, but not as long and thin as his own. Her nails were covered in clear polish. "It's one thing to have the sort of mistress they all do," she said carefully. "Actresses. That sort of thing. I do understand that sort of thing. But that's not what you're up to, and you know it."

"I'm not actually up to anything. There is no other woman. I am not having an affair. I'm too damned busy to do a mistress any good."

"Maybe you just hate sex. All kinds of sex. That would be amusing."

It was already dark outside. The car lit up every time they went under one of the tall arched lamps that lined this part of the Pennsylvania Turnpike. Tony toyed with the idea of telling the driver to keep driving, to miss their exit, to head for the mountains and Lehigh and that long stretch of road with no exits at all.

"I don't think you heard me," Charlotte said.

"I heard you. I don't consider this discussion worth having."

"You didn't always hate sex, though. I should know."

"Should you?"

"You've managed to father four children."

"At least. I should think that would be enough. I should

think that would be enough of me for you, to be precise. What is it you really want here, Charlotte?"

"I want you to give it up."

"Give what up? You haven't discovered anything I'm doing that I could give up. There isn't anything to discover. And you can't want me to go back to sleeping with you. You barely stood it the first time."

"I want you to give *him* up."

"David?"

"Yes, David. I want you to give him up."

"Why? Or do you now imagine that I'm sleeping with David? God only knows when he'd have the time, considering the fact that he's sleeping with half the debutantes in Philadelphia and three-quarters of the debutantes in New York. At last count. And he's completely in control of the Price Heaven mess, which is a mess, and which is likely to get messier very soon."

"I don't see why you stick up for him," Charlotte said. "He's not just in charge of Price Heaven now, he set that whole thing up to begin with. He's managed it from day one. And what did you get? There's going to be a bankruptcy any day now and you know it. I can't stand the sight of him. He makes my skin crawl."

"Why?"

"How should I know why? He's insidious. And I don't care who his family is. He's not—right. I don't know how to put it."

"You never did have much of a talent for words."

"I don't need that kind of thing from you now, Tony. I really don't. I need him out of my life. At the very least you can stop inviting him to where I am."

"David is my confidential assistant. We're in the middle of a major crisis. You're behaving like a spoiled brat."

"You're always in the middle of a major crisis. To hear you tell it, there's nothing in life but major crises. The story of American banking."

"Often, yes."

"Get rid of him, or I'll get a very public divorce."

"Nonsense."

"Maybe I'll do something better. Maybe I'll leak it to the press. Not the press you own, the other kind. The tabloids. I'll say you are sleeping with David Alden. You know they'll believe it."

"The tabloids aren't interested in me. Their readers don't know who I am, and wouldn't care if they did."

"Maybe I'll leak it to that man. Michael Harridan. The one with the Web site."

"Michael Harridan is taken about as seriously as Bugs Bunny."

"You don't take me seriously. And that's a mistake, Tony. I promise it is."

"We're getting off the turnpike," Tony said. "We'll be home in less than twenty minutes."

Charlotte turned her face away, her long neck straining against the stiff white collar of her linen shirt. She was too thin, the way all these women were. The muscles in her neck looked like ropes. He was not afraid of her. There was nothing she could do to him, and nothing she would really want to do, once she thought about it. She made him tired, so that all he could think of was sleep, endless sleep, black sleep, the kind that was supposed to come over you when you drowned in the waters of Lethe.

Still, if he'd been somebody else, somebody poorer, somebody less hedged in by security and position—he would have wrapped his hands around her neck and ripped her windpipe out.

3

There was a single short moment, at almost exactly six o'clock, when Anne Ross Wyler considered staying home for the evening. She had that priest coming over, for one thing. Lucinda had printed his name in block letters on a three-by-five card and tucked the card in her mirror, so that she could practice pronouncing it: *Father Tibor Kasparian.*

It seemed ironic as hell to her that she had managed to give up almost everything about her former life, but this. She still could not pronounce "foreign" names with anything at all like grace. Tony would probably tell her she was insane, that there was nothing about life with the family that could have made her tone-deaf to Eastern European cadences—or maybe he wouldn't have, because, in his own way, Tony was as odd and contrary a person as she was. Whatever it was, though, she couldn't do it. Even Italian names threw her, and by now it was practically an Old Philadelphia tradition to be Italian. Every once in a while, she would veer to her mirror and try the name out, stretching the syllables, worried that she was getting it more wrong every time she tried to say it. She was only grateful that she had so many other things tucked into the mirror's edges and hanging over its top and sides that she couldn't see herself at all. There was one thing she did miss about the way she had been when she had still been part of All That. She missed the fanatical discipline of the body. God only knew, she didn't do anything for herself when she was left to herself. She was fifty-five-years-old, and she looked it. "Stumpy," one of the newspapers had called her once. One of the local television stations had described her as "the once elegant Mrs. Kendrick Wyler." She ran her hands through her very thick grey hair and felt it stop abruptly in midair. This last time, she had cut it off herself with a pair of pinking shears one afternoon when she'd been busy and it had gotten in her way. Other women, millions of them, managed to live sane lives in the world without turning themselves into poster children for bag ladies, but with her it was like the "foreign" names. She couldn't seem to manage it.

The other reason she had considered not going out was that it was cold, as cold as she could ever remember it being in November in Philadelphia. Down on the first floor, there was ice along the edges of the windowsills. If they ever got enough money together, they would have to replace those windows. Surely it made sense that, in weather like this, the girls would not be out on the street where anybody could see them. That was what she would have thought, her first year at Adelphos House. Before that, she had never even wondered what whores did when it got cold. They could have gone to Florida for the winter, and it would have made sense to her. She hadn't ever wondered who the whores were, either, or where they came from, and if she had, she had probably thought that they must be black. That was what you saw in the movies, when you went to that kind of movie. She couldn't have said what you saw on television, because at that point in her life, she had never owned one, and never watched one except on trips to Europe, in those five-star hotels where every mechanical convenience was provided for Americans who were assumed to be mad for technology. God, she had been such an incredible, unbelievable snot. Worse, she had been a happily ignorant snot, and there was nothing more evil on this planet than happy ignorance.

The whores would be out tonight, in the cold. They would stand together in tight little huddles near parking meters, wearing fake-fur jackets that shed when they walked, and too much makeup, and fishnet stockings that left huge patches of the skin on their legs bare to the cold. The johns would be out tonight too, but they would be in cars.

She got a black jersey turtleneck out of her wardrobe, to go with her black pants. She would find a black sweater to put over that. She considered pinning her *Freedom FROM Religion* button to her sweater, and decided against it. There was no point in antagonizing Father Kasparian, who was not representative of the kind of religion she wanted to be free of, at least as far as she could tell. She ran a brush through her hair and then ran her hands through it, ruining everything. It had been weeks since she had had a full day to herself, and she was exhausted.

The johns would be out, in their cars the way they always were. With the cold this bad, they'd sit well back in their seats. They wouldn't stick their heads out the windows. That would make it all the harder to get pictures of them, which meant she would have to rely on the pictures of the license plates, which was always problematic. Hell, even when she got a picture of money being passed with the john's face as clear as it would have been for a video dating service, it was nearly impossible to get the police to do anything. It didn't matter that the girls were mostly under sixteen or that there had just been a raid on a child porn ring on the other side of the city. She wondered what that meant, that the police jumped right in to protect boys, but looked the other way when it came to teenaged girls, and there were no other kinds of girls on the streets of Philadelphia. Whores might get old in New York and Los Angeles, but here, they seemed to disappear as soon as they hit eighteen. Maybe they just died.

She found the sweater she was looking for and pulled it over her head. She shoved her feet into good black leather sneakers. She felt like James Bond, sometimes, except that she either walked or took the bus. She'd long ago decided it was too expensive to keep a regular car. A couple of centuries ago, her family had come to this part of Pennsylvania as dissenting Quakers, pacifist and dour, with a streak of asceticism in them that some of their neighbors would have considered extreme in Puritans. *That* was a part of the family legacy she'd hung on to with both hands. "You'll never be really happy unless you start flagellating yourself," Lucinda said, whenever she went on a streak of self-recrimination and self-denial—and it was true, but it was limited, because she would never allow it to interfere with her work. Maybe that explained what all those women were doing, like her mother, when they starved themselves into their size twos. Maybe it was just Puritanism come back to haunt them, disguising itself as snobbery.

She took twenty dollars and her driver's license out of her wallet. When she hit the street, she carried neither her purse nor any significant amount of money. She took the gold chain off her neck and left it on top of her vanity table. The table seemed badly named, since the mirror was unusable and there was no sign of makeup on it. She brushed the hair out of her eyes again and vowed, for the thousandth time in the last two years, to let it grow out long enough to be held back in a rubber band. The three-by-five cards stuck into the mirror's sides shuddered a little in the draft allowed by the fact that the windowpane here had a crack in it and three tiny pieces missing. *Freedom from Religion Foundation: http://www.ffrf.org,* one of them said. *Lucinda's birthday, June 26th,* said another. Anne looked at the one with Father Kasparian's name on it, said the name three times in her head and once out loud, and then gave the whole thing up.

Out in the hall, the rest of the house felt deserted. It probably was. Six o'clock on a Friday night was not usually one of their busier times, although with the cold this bad it would get busy later. They'd start lining up outside the front door, looking for shelter, somewhere around ten. She looked at the drawings Lucinda had put up on the walls without really seeing any of them. They had a woman come in once a week who worked with the girls with what she called "art therapy." Anne didn't think she was doing any good, but she didn't think she was doing any harm, and the girls seemed to like it. She got to the stairwell and went down. Nobody was in the foyer, and there was no sign of anybody on the porch. She checked her watch, a plain steel Timex she'd bought at Kmart for seventeen dollars. When she was seventeen, her mother had given her a gold dress watch from Tiffany's. It had cost 1,500 dollars and she had lost it one day playing tennis at the Coach and Racquet Club. She had had it for less than two months.

At the bottom of the stairs, she turned toward the back of the house. The walls here were lined with drawings too, a lot of them faintly obscene. The girls liked art therapy, but they laughed at the therapist, who always reminded Anne of the woman who had taught her dancing in kindergarten. Everything was cheerful. Everything was obvious. She got to the back of the house and pushed open the swinging door to the kitchen. Lucinda was sitting at the table with her feet propped up on another kitchen chair. The television was on, as it always was whenever Lucinda was near it. When they'd first met, Lucinda had announced, without embarrassment, that if she were rich, she'd have a television in every room in the house, including the bathrooms. It had taken Anne a while to realize that that feeling she had, as if all the air had been knocked out of her lungs, was culture shock.

Lucinda looked up as Anne came in, her enormous black helmet of hair bobbing vigorously above her thick neck. She had a Holy Bible on the table in front of her, unopened. Lucinda took a Holy Bible everywhere she went, but Anne hadn't seen her open it yet.

"So what's it you're doing?" Lucinda said. "Trying out for a part in *The Matrix*?"

"Which one is *The Matrix*?"

"It's the one with the red pill and the blue pill. Never mind. It's a movie. We ran it here about a month ago. You came."

"I get distracted."

"Don't I know it. Seriously, though, you ought to wear some kind of reflective clothing. You're going to get killed out there one of these days."

"Maybe," Anne said, "but not in a car accident. Isn't there something called vehicular homicide?" She opened the refrigerator and looked inside. There was a bucket of fried chicken. It was probably a good three weeks old. There was a package of celery, half-used. She closed the refrigerator door. Lucinda had a big piece of Swiss cheese on the table, with a knife and crackers. Anne sat down and started on those. "I take it there's no sign of our visitor," she said.

"He's not due for half an hour, Annie, relax. There's not going to be anybody out there cruising yet."

"They cruise all day."

"Not most of them, they don't. They like the dark. You ever notice that? That's what you should do, instead of taking pictures of their license plates. You should buy a whole bunch of big spotlights and set them up down there. That'd drive them off faster than anything."

"They'd only move to another street. The city's already tried that."

"The city got bought off."

"Probably. What are you watching?"

"*Mother Angelica Live*. I know she's a Catholic, but she's a good woman. Had a stroke, kept right on going. Reminds me of my grandmother."

"The queen of England reminds you of your grandmother."

"Well, you know how those things went, back in the colonies. Maybe we're related."

Anne tried the cheese. It was hard as a rock. One of the things she would never be able to understand was why, now that she lived in a place where the food was both erratic and awful, she weighed so much more than she had when she'd been able to get the best food on the planet, simply for the asking. At least she'd rid herself of that prejudice about the lack of discipline and self-respect that so often made poor people so fat. Obviously, it just happened, even when you didn't eat much of anything.

She cut herself another piece of cheese and wrinkled her nose at it. She put the cheese on a Saltine cracker and hoped for the best. The television program went to commercial, except it wasn't really a commercial. It seemed to be a public service announcement about some kind of novena. She wished Father Kasparian would get there, so that she could do what she had to do in the way of greetings, and then disappear. She was beginning to get hyped-up and adrenalized, the way she always did when she went out. In some ways, it was like a drug. By the time it was over, she'd be so pumped up she wouldn't be able to sleep for hours. She wouldn't even be able to think straight. That was when she would hit the Net and the Web sites she'd come to rely on—the Freedom from Religion Foundation; the World of Richard Dawkins; the Marbles game—so that she could keep her mind occupied enough so that she wouldn't think. When she did think, she thought about what it would feel like to do something real about this. She imagined herself chasing them down on foot, pulling them out of their cars, beating her fists into their heads until the skulls cracked and the skin broke open to spill blood.

"Oh, one thing," Lucinda said. "Your brother called."

4

At first, Kathi Mittendorf had been shocked to realize how easy it was to join America on Alert—easier than it had been to join the Girl Scout troop in Marshford Township where she grew up, where nobody got a chance to wear a green uniform unless Mrs. Davenport okayed it. Kathi missed Mrs. Davenport daily. She didn't miss Mrs. Davenport's daughter, Katy. It was hard to miss somebody who was so obviously destined to become one of the anti-American liberal elite. Kathi had known what *they* were when she was only ten years old, although she wouldn't have been able to put a name to them. She thinks she's *so* much, people used to say about Katy Davenport, and it was true too. She thought she was just wonderful, because she always got the best grades in school and because she read things from New York like *The New York Times* and *The New Yorker*, instead of the things everybody else read, which Kathi had to admit wasn't much. Still, that was suspicious in itself. Good people didn't read all the time, and they certainly didn't read things that made them argue with the teachers about what America had been doing in Vietnam, or why the electoral college should be abolished. Now that Kathi understood the way things worked—the way the Illuminati carefully chose from among the regular people, handpicking the ones who would be allowed to "succeed," so that it wouldn't look as if they were running the world the way they really were—she found she was a lot less angry with Katy Davenport. That was a good thing, because for a while there she had been caught up in an anger so deep and implacable that she sometimes found herself sinking in it. It had started on the day that the notice had gone up in front of the guidance counselor's office, saying that Katy Davenport had been accepted to Yale. She remembered herself standing in the hall, staring at the little card with Katy's name on it, and on all the other little cards, the kids who were going to Penn State and Swarthmore and Concordia and Duke. It had felt as if she were the only one in school who wasn't going somewhere after graduation. Her shame had been so deep, it had wormed its way into every atom of her skin. She wanted to run away from home before graduation day. At the very least, she wanted to do something that would get their attention for once, instead of being the one whose name nobody would ever remember when the time came around for reunions, which she wouldn't go to, because she wouldn't want them to see that she was still in town and working at Price Heaven, when they were off being Important.

Of course, the truth was, they would have remembered her. She hadn't realized it then, but everything the Illuminati did, every single shudder in the military-industrial complex, was directed against people just like her, and nothing at all like Katy Davenport. This was one of the first things Michael had taught her when she'd gone to her first lecture, almost two years ago.

"They make you think you're nobody," he said—not just to her, of course, but to all of them, sitting in a big huddle in the small side room of the Holfield Meeting Hall in South Philadelphia, his voice coming out of a speaker, and blasting out at the crowd. Everybody had drawn a little closer, moving their metal folding chairs silently along the linoleum, hungry. Even then, Michael was in far too dangerous a position to appear in person. "If you think you're nobody, you think you're powerless. You don't do anything. You don't even try to stop them. And they know that. They know the only force on earth capable of stopping them is real Americans, just like you, and that's why they know every one of your names."

If Kathi had been running America on Alert, she would have gone about it differently. She would have made sure there were requirements for membership, maybe even an investigation into each and every person who wanted to come to meetings and join the organization and vote. No matter what Michael said, there was always the danger that the Illuminati would infiltrate them the way they had infiltrated so many other organizations, and good ones too. The John Birch Society was nothing these days if not an Illuminati front. They kept playing the same old record about "communism," when it was obvious that the Illuminati weren't interested in communism anymore. It had been a straw man right from the beginning. The real danger was far more insidious, made up of people who thought they were better than you were, smarter than you were, more—more *worthy* than you were. It had taken Kathi a long time to come up with that word. It contained everything that had ever bothered her about Katy Davenport and all the Katy Davenports she had met since: the politicians she saw on TV; the smug-suited "authors" who flickered by on *Booknotes* on C-Span; the supervisor at Price Heaven who sent his contributions to the ACLU from the office, brazenly, not caring at all that it would be a red flag to any good American on his staff. The supervisor Kathi Mittendorf worked under was a Jew. She'd found that out the very first week. She'd been ready to quit on the spot, but Michael had stopped her, because according to him *some* Jews were good Americans, a very few of them, the ones who did not think of themselves as citizens of Israel first. She thought she had known from the contributions to the ACLU that Mr. Goldman wouldn't be one of those, but there was virtue in vigilance. The longer she stayed, the longer she could keep her eye on the things Mr. Goldman didn't expect anybody to be looking for, like the ways in which he helped the Price Heaven corporation pump drugs into the air at the store so that the employees and the customers would be more easily bent to the Illuminati's plans. As far as Kathi could tell, two-thirds of the population of the United States of America was drugged to the gills every day of their lives, programmed and brainwashed to do exactly as they were told. The programming came through their television sets.

Now it was very nearly zero hour of her first important operation, and Kathi found that she was sweating. She had no idea if the nervousness was legitimate or provoked. They got to you in the strangest ways, when you weren't expecting it. You turned around and realized you'd been caught. The only thing she could do about it was work through it. She went into the bathroom and rinsed her mouth out with water from the big glass tub she got delivered from Crystal Stream twice a week. Crystal Stream was an America on Alert company, owned by one of their oldest members, so you could be sure the water was pure. Tap water in Philadelphia had fluoride in it. Then she went back into the living room and watched Susan checking the switches on the main receiver set. Susan looked worried, but Susan always looked worried. She was in love with Michael, but Kathi didn't care about that. Every woman in America on Alert was in love with Michael, one way or the other. He had more sense than to fall for any of them.

"I wish he'd call in and tell us where he was," Susan said. "I don't like the thought of him wandering around out there in enemy territory. They're bound to realize he isn't anything at all like them."

"He's done it before," Kathi said. "I don't see why there should be anything to worry about now. Have you checked the explosives?"

"I don't like handling the explosives. I know they're supposed to be disconnected or whatever it is, but I can't stop thinking about that time in Greenwich Village in the sixties. Do you know about that time in Greenwich Village in the sixties?"

"I wouldn't know anything about Greenwich Village no matter when it was," Kathi said. "Why would I have to know about Greenwich Village?"

"Some people had explosives there. They blew up a building. By accident. They were making a bomb and blew it up by accident. We ought to keep that stuff someplace else, where it couldn't hurt us."

"It can't hurt us here," Kathi said. "Calm down. Are you getting anything yet?"

"Just people talking about food." Susan turned back to the receiver. The headset sat across her over-blond head like a snake. It made the color seem even falser than it was. Kathi's own hair was the same color blond, but for some reason she liked the color better on herself than she did on Susan. What really mattered was that they colored their hair at all. Lesbians never colored theirs, and never wore jewelry, and never wore makeup, either. Once you understood how it worked, you could see all kinds of clues, all around you—the conspiracy at work.

Kathi leaned over Susan's shoulder and turned up the volume. A high, nasal female voice came pounding out, affected and obnoxious, superior. "I don't care what the caterer told you, the ice swans do *not* go on the main buffet table. How we're ever going to get through this, I really don't know. There isn't any *room* on the main buffet table. You have to put the ice swans with the rest of the pâtés."

"See?" Susan said.

Kathi stood back. It made her stomach feel odd to know that she had just heard one of Them, a real one of Them, at home and in private, when she thought she wasn't being watched. They always put on a mask for outsiders. Michael had told them that. Now there was no mask, and this woman seemed—

Stupid, Kathi thought. She wiped the idea out of her head. The Illuminati weren't stupid. They only wanted you to think they were. Maybe this woman wasn't really in private. Maybe she was putting on a show for whoever she was talking to. Susan turned the volume back down.

"I'm recording everything," Susan said, "just like Michael told me to. But so far, this has been all there is. Food. And music too. There are going to be bands. Do you realize there are going to be thousands of people at this thing?"

"Only fifteen hundred," Kathi said. "Michael has the guest list."

"Still. Fifteen hundred is a lot. Maybe we should take those explosives over there tonight and set them off. That would get rid of a lot of them, wouldn't it?"

"You're crazy."

"Maybe I'm crazy," Susan said. "But it seems to me that it would make more sense than what we are doing. If they really are evil people who want to take over the world, why don't we just get rid of them? We wouldn't get them all at once—"

"We wouldn't get the most important ones," Kathi said. "Can't you see that? The ones who run the really big banks, the ones in Europe. They won't all come to something like this. Only the Philadelphia ones will. And then the rest of them will be on their guard. And they'd find us. And then what would happen?"

"Maybe we'd wake up the rest of the country. Michael is always saying that most Americans would agree with us if they only understood what was going on. Maybe this would be the way we could tell them what was going on."

"Did Timothy McVeigh tell them what was going on?"

"Michael said McVeigh doesn't count. He wasn't really one of us. If he was, he wouldn't have blown up a building with a lot of babies in it. He was a plant. That's how the Illuminati work. They close off all the avenues of action. They pre-opt everybody. This would be different."

"You think blowing up a lot of women in evening gowns would be different?"

"It would really be blowing them up," Susan said, stubborn. "I don't understand what goes on here sometimes. You all say you're patriots, and you all worry nonstop about how the Illuminati have taken over the country, but you won't do anything about it. You don't do anything but give speeches and sit around here and—"

"We bugged them tonight. And we have to give speeches. We have to convince the American people—"

"You're the one who says the American people are all brainwashed. And I believe it. I believe it. If they hadn't been brainwashed, they'd never have believed all those things about the World Trade Center and the Pentagon. They'd have seen in an instant that a bunch of Stone-Aged Arabs couldn't have done anything like that, but—"

The receiver cracked. Kathi leaned forward and turned the volume up again. This time, the voice coming through was neither high nor nasal, although it still had that accent she thought of as "snobby." They all had that accent. It was as if they had all been taught to speak by the same computer program, and maybe they had.

"No," the voice said. "It's all right. Put the rose center-piece with the swans, just the way the plan calls for, but put them all with the pâtés, and that way we don't have to worry about Charlotte having another fit. And don't cry. It's useless to cry about the way Charlotte behaves. She's a spoiled brat."

"Charlotte," Susan said. "That's Charlotte Deacon Ross. She's right there. And Michael is there too. We could have sent a nice little package in with him, and nobody would have known—"

"Of course they would have known," Kathi said. "They probably have X-ray machines, out of sight, so that the guests don't notice. They probably have all kinds of security."

"Maybe we should just gag Charlotte and lock her in a closet," the voice on the receiver said. "God only knows, that's the only way we're getting through until midnight without my killing her. Or worse."

Kathi turned the receiver down, again. "We're supposed to make a transcript. We'll make a transcript. Michael is supposed to find out what they're going to be up to next. Maybe we'll get lucky, and they'll have a ritual right there in the open, and we'll get it all on tape."

"I don't care how reasonable you think you are," Susan said. "You're going to have to use them sometimes. You can't just keep them here in your living room forever."

"Make a transcript," Kathi said.

Then she retreated into the front hall, where it was quiet, a claustrophobic space not even large enough to hold a little table. Michael had warned them all about people who tried to push the organization into ill-considered violence. They were almost always enemy agents, pilot fish for the shock troops whose only purpose was to destroy little groups just like this one. If Susan was a pilot fish, they would have to find a way to get rid of her—move the meeting places, change the phone numbers, hide the mailing lists. They wouldn't hide the literature, because as far as Michael was concerned, the more people who saw the literature the better. Even some of Them might be convinced, or enlightened, or deprogrammed, by reading the truth about who and what they were.

Still, no matter how enormously satisfied Kathi would be if it turned out that Susan was one of Them, the fact was that she was telling the simple truth. They would have to use the explosives some day. They even intended to, and there were a lot more of them than Susan realized. In this house alone, there were at least two-dozen small cluster bombs, made of dynamite and grenades bought on the military hardware black market, any one of which could destroy a store the size of an ordinary 7-Eleven in a couple of seconds flat. There were other things too, bits and pieces of things that could be put together to make a bigger bang than any single piece could do, if you didn't care too much about precision or accuracy or being able to recognize the target when the mission was over. Then there were the weapons, the ones Michael had shown Kathi how to shoot: Soviet military issue, most of them, bought over the Internet, sent to an address without a real name attached to it, stockpiled in another state. Timothy McVeigh had been an idiot to rely on a fertilizer bomb. He could have done three times the damage if he had known how to go about doing what he was doing.

If the World Trade Center attacks had been for real, instead of for show, they wouldn't have been carried out with commercial airlines, and they wouldn't have left those buildings standing for an hour after the explosions went off. The Illuminati were sly. They knew what frightened people. They knew how to make people behave.

Kathi opened the front door and stepped out onto the sidewalk, the cold, the dark. In the middle of the city like this, it was impossible to see the sky. Someday, they would level all the cities. They would flatten all the tall buildings and grids of wires that shut out the stars and the sun and kept them all docile and ready for the kill, and America would be America again, perfect as it had been on the day it was founded, cleansed of all the evil that had come upon it since, the paper money, the multinational corporations, the bureaucrats with their agendas of "health" and "sanity" and tyranny and control.

All that would be gone, and Katy Davenport would be gone with it.

5

Ryall Wyndham had never understood how anybody, anywhere, could go about life haphazardly. It wasn't just a question of money, although money counted. He could name two-dozen people in his class at Brown whose approach to money was a lot like their approach to cheeseburgers: Eat it up fast, before it had a chance to get away. None of them seemed to be able to wrap their minds around the idea that someday they would be old. They lived in a continuous present, and that present was filled with enough in the way of alcohol and drugs to addle God himself on a bad day. They were that way about women too, and that was worse. Ryall could remember a time when men worked very hard not to marry. Now they married all the time, for no reason at all, because it was Tuesday. They married women with money and women without it. They married women with background and women without it. Mostly, they seemed to marry women their parents wouldn't approve of, as if that, and that alone, was enough to qualify a human female to be the mother of children. Ryall Wyndham did not have a wife, and he did not have children, and he did not expect to acquire either until the time was right. The time would be right when he could get one of these silly debutantes he escorted to all the best places to fall hideously, ridiculously in love with him.

The problem, he decided, checking out his tie in the mirror, was that the women he knew did not seem to go about life as haphazardly as the men he knew. Even the really ugly debutantes realized they were sitting on gold mines, and not just their crotches, either. God, he would love it, one day, to go in to one of those places and use a word like *crotch*. Or *cunt*. *That* was a good one. They really hated that one. They'd use words like *crotch* every once in a while just to show how down-to-earth and unaffected they were, but they'd never use a word like *cunt*, because it smelled of real vulgarity. The only people who could get away with real vulgarity were members of the Blood Royal. That was what all these people wanted to be, even though they'd never say so out loud. That was why they sent their children to those schools where the teachers worked overtime to instill true liberal guilt. The rich in America hate the poor everywhere in the world. The people of the Third World want only to rise up and throw off their capitalist oppressors and take on the mantle of vanguard communism for the new millennium. The real problem with this country is the Consumer Mentality. Oh, yes. Groton and St. Paul's, Exeter and Choate. All those places positively despised the Consumer Mentality. It was just so damned tacky, and bad for you. McDonald's hardened your arteries and ruined the landscape in pristine wildernesses from Maine to California. Television was a drug, meant to take your mind off Really Serious Things and keep you stupid and happy. Wal-Mart was the worst, because it not only did everything morally wrong, from refusing to carry emergency contraception to resisting the formation of workers' unions, but it killed the very heart of America, the American small town. America had been a much better place when people had been forced to pay very high prices for bedsheets and electronics on their very own local Main Streets. Ryall was sure these people had seen a Main Street or two, once or twice in their lives. There was one in Stowe where they went to ski. There was another in Bar Harbor.

Tacky, tacky, tacky, Ryall thought. Then he closed his eyes and put his forehead against the mirror's glass. He was very revved up, and he hadn't even taken anything yet. He hated to medicate himself before he absolutely needed to. It was getting harder and harder for him to keep his mind on the subject when he went to one of these affairs, and yet everything—his whole life—depended on his remembering what he had seen and *not* writing it down until he was safely in the car and on the way home. Of course, he could cheat a little. He could find his way into the bathroom a couple of times every night and take out his notebook then, getting the details down before they disappeared forever from his head. It wasn't as good as having the nearly total recall he'd had when he'd started, but it helped. The problem was that it had its natural limits. If he started hitting the bathroom every hour, rumors would be in full swing by the end of the night. They'd have him half-dead of AIDS or addicted to crack before he'd had a chance to file his column in the morning. That would be the end of everything. Reliability was the key. The women really weren't as addled as their men. They kept their heads, and they kept their eyes on the main chance, and they weren't about to jeopardize the only thing that mattered to them to hold on to a pudgy little dork whose only amusement value lay in his ability to get their names in the papers. There was a contradiction for you. The men really did things. They ran banks. They determined the economies of nations. The women did nothing but go to parties, and they were the ones with their names in the papers.

Ryall stepped back, reached around on his bureau top for his tape recorder, and switched it on. He really was pudgy, in the way unathletic teenagers are pudgy. He was round and white and soft, like something that had lain for a long time in the water and bloated. He rubbed the side of his face. His fingers were stubby too. It didn't make much of a difference that he was always careful to keep them very well-manicured.

"This is Ryall Wyndham reporting from the Around the World Harvest Ball, Philadelphia's most talked-about event of the preChristmas social season."

He switched the recorder off. *Christ,* he thought. He sounded like a Walter Winchell imitation in a forties movie. What was *wrong* with him these days? If he'd had more money, he could have been married ages ago. The problem was, he could never understand how to get money, and that in spite of the fact that he was very good at keeping it. He tried to imagine himself going in to work every day as a banker, and all he got was an image of Porky Pig in a bow tie. He had actually tried law school—at Georgetown, acceptable but not stellar—and lasted less than a month. He could still hear his old English teacher at Canterbury—one more time, acceptable but not stellar—telling him that he just didn't have a knack for respectability. *Respectability.* He ought to go into one of these things wired sometime. *That* would blow the game to pieces in no time at all. He could just imagine the look on Charlotte Ross's face when she heard her voice coming out of a little black box, screeching, *"I'm not going to have some goddamned car salesman spilling drinks on me all night just because he's got his own foundation."* Car salesman. That's what Charlotte Ross called the Ford, who didn't have the right kind of money.

Ryall got his cell phone, and switched it on, and punched in the numbers for his office. He hated to say that he "dialed" the cell phone, even though everybody did, because he so obviously *didn't* dial it. A dial was round. He listened to the ring and checked out his cuff links while he waited. They were good gold cuff links, engraved, from Tiffany's. In the position he was in, he could not afford to settle for the fake. *They* settled for it, though. It wasn't only Barbara Bush who wore faux pearls in the daytime.

The phone was picked up on the other end. "Marilyn?" Ryall said. "You have a minute?"

"I thought you were supposed to be at that party."

"The car is due in about fifteen minutes. Don't worry. I won't miss it. Did you do that thing I asked you to, about the records? You didn't call back—"

"I haven't had time to call back," Marilyn said, sounding cross. "And yes, I did do it. I made triplicate copies too, in case you start losing them, which you always do. I don't know why you bother to do research, really. You can never hang on to anything for longer than a day or two at a time. You're really pathetic."

"Yes. Well. I'm sorry to cause you so much distress. Did you happen to notice anything that was in the records?"

"No. Why should I? I'm not a gossip columnist, Ryall. I don't really give a damn what these people do. I don't think anybody does. I think the paper just keeps the column on because those people are investors, or something, and they like to get some publicity. I know I never read that stuff. Or *Town and Country*, either."

"Yes." You had to be patient with Marilyn. She was a very good assistant. She kept the appointment book meticulously. She did whatever research she was asked to do. She answered the phone without sounding as if she wanted to bite somebody's head off. It was just that she was a . . . cunt.

"I don't see what your problem is anyway," she said. "I can't figure out if you're obsessed with Anthony van Wyck Ross or with his wife. And neither of them are anything to be obsessed about. I mean, really."

"Anthony van Wyck Ross is one of the most successful bankers on the planet," Ryall said. "Get your head out of the social columns for a moment. He's got more money than God. He determines monetary policy for half the world. Oh, not officially, of course, officially we've got all these government agencies. But in reality, that's how it works."

"Maybe. Who cares? And what do you need his transcripts from Yale and Harvard Law School for? I mean, truly, even if there was some kind of huge scandal, who would care? It's not as if he's Steven Spielberg."

"You don't think anybody would care if one of the most important men on earth was involved in something less than honest?"

"No. I don't even think they'd be surprised. Well, they might be interested if he killed his wife, or she killed him. I don't suppose you could arrange for that?"

"If they wanted to kill each other, they'd hire hitmen. And not the kind who get caught."

"Nobody cares about those people anymore. They're not

relevant to real people's lives. And don't give me that thing about running the world, because it doesn't matter if they do. They don't run *my* world."

"You wouldn't think that if they took it into their heads to shut down the newspaper and you were out on your ear looking for a job."

"I don't think anybody would just take it into his head to shut down the newspaper. That's not the way it works, Ryall. Come into the real world for a time—pretty funny, considering your name. Do people make that joke on your name all the time?"

"No," Ryall said. "And we've had this conversation before. Never mind. As long as you have the material. I'll come in tomorrow and look it over. Although God only knows, I hate to come in to the office after one of these things. I always have a hangover."

"It's like that Enron thing," Marilyn said. "It was a big scandal, and a big deal in all the newspapers, and it was on TV for months, but nobody really paid attention. Why should they? It's just a business thing. It's not as if they're—"

"—Steven Spielberg—"

"—Madonna."

"That's the car," Ryall said. "As long as you have them. Put them somewhere safe. I don't want them getting lost."

"I never lose anything," Marilyn said, which was true. She never forgot appointments, either. Ryall was sure that, if she had been alive at the time, she would have been the one person in her class who would have remembered all her homework on the day after the Kennedy assassination. He knew for a fact that the events of September 11 hadn't fazed her for a moment.

"They'll be in your private drawer," she said. "I've even taken the care to lock it, since you've been so paranoid. But if you ask me, you're behaving like a lunatic."

"The car," Ryall said. Then he switched the cell phone off and put it down. The car wasn't really here, not yet, and wouldn't be for a while. He still had to find all his paraphernalia: his money clip; his wallet; his card case; his key ring; his Swiss army knife. The Swiss army knife was made of sterling silver and accented with gold. It was the kind of thing that impressed people like Marilyn.

"Crap, crap, crap," Ryall said to the air. He didn't want to spend the night at this party. He didn't want to file a story about it with the paper and then with *Town and Country*. He didn't want to *feel* like Porky Pig anymore, so that right in the middle of any moment when he was able to think of himself as winning, the image would pop up on the back of his eyelids like a computer virus and there he would be, squat and round, with a little curly tail sticking out of the back of his best tuxedo pants.

"Crap, crap, crap," he said again. Then he swept all his things off the top of his bureau and headed out his bedroom door and down the stairs.

6

Lucinda Watkins had been born and raised a Baptist in a world where the most exotic "other" religion belonged to the Catholics at St. Mary of the Fields, and there weren't many of them. "The preachers say they worship the Devil," Lucinda's grandmother had said, "but I don't believe it." And because Grandma Watkins hadn't believed it, Lucinda hadn't believed it, either. In the end, everything that had ever happened to Lucinda had come down to Grandma Watkins, who had taken their residence in Mount Hope, Mississippi, as a kind of purgatory come early, except that she hadn't believed in purgatory. God was getting them ready for something special. She believed in that. The long back roads that got so hot in the summer they were nothing but dirt, the "schoolhouse" that was nothing but a shack at the edge of a cotton field that had been leached clean of nutrients before the Home War, the good jobs cleaning up in the brick houses along White Jasmine Drive that went to black people and not to them—it was all preparation, all rehearsal, for something they were supposed to do later.

"They think they're rich, the people in those houses," Grandma Watkins had told Lucinda one afternoon when Lucinda had come to walk her back after a long day's work at the diner. "It isn't true. I've been to Atlanta to visit my cousin. *Those* are the rich people."

Lucinda hadn't had the faintest idea what Grandma meant. The people on White Jasmine Drive looked rich enough to her. Not only were their driveways paved and their houses made of brick, but they had cars parked out front and black people to clean up after them. Lucinda held on to the thought anyway. She never lost the conviction that Grandma Watkins was right about everything, from rich people to heaven, and she never would. It was why she didn't talk slang, like everybody else she knew, not even in front of other poor people. Grandma wouldn't say *ain't* to save her life. Even at work, where white trash were supposed to play an elaborate ritual straight out of a bad MGM screenplay and central casting, Grandma Watkins sounded like she'd just been graduated from Miss Hellman's School for Young Ladies. Sometimes she didn't even sound southern.

"You go north," Grandma Watkins said. "Not that they're much better in the north, but they've got different rules than they've got here. There's a little more room to make your move. You go north and you can go to college."

Now Lucinda stood up from the kitchen table and picked up the coffee cups and little plates she'd used to serve Father Tibor Kasparian. There were times when she became extremely self-conscious about her life story. She knew how it was supposed to end—the bad MGM screenplay version, the one from central casting. She was supposed to go north to college and do brilliantly. She was supposed to become famous and go back to Mount Hope in a limousine. Or something. Whatever it was, it hadn't worked out that way. She wasn't athletic, like Larry Bird. She wasn't a brilliant writer, like Truman Capote. She wasn't ambitious and dedicated, like Julia Roberts or Helen Gurley Brown. In the end, she had had to face up to the fact that she was a bright, hard-working girl, but not a superstar, and not the material from which media stars are made. She'd gone north, the way Grandma Watkins wanted—but to Gettysburg College, not to Vassar or Smith. She'd found her room to make her move, first into a master's of social work at Penn State, then into a doctorate in sociology at Temple. If she'd had a different personality, she might have ended up on the faculty of some small college somewhere, happily settled into a routine of teaching and giving little dinners and pottering around her own brick house, only just far enough from the campus so that she wouldn't have to do what she hated most in the world, drive in bad weather. She had a fantasy about that life that was so real, she almost felt she'd lived it. The problem was, it made her feel ashamed even to think of it. She did *not* have a different personality, and because she did not, she had landed here, at Adelphos House, where, no matter what else she was doing, she was providing some help to the girls who lined the darker side streets of the inner city. Most of them were younger than sixteen. Most of them were addicted and sick at the same time. All of them were angry, so that helping them was a matter of getting past that barrage of invective that was their first response to anything but a john offering money, and was sometimes their response even then. Through it all, Lucinda kept waiting for something to happen, she wasn't sure what.

If there was one thing Grandma Watkins had been dead right about, it was that thing about the rich people. The white people on White Jasmine Drive had barely been middle-class by Main Line standards. They'd had the kind of houses you saw in the neat little suburbs for factory workers, the ones that ringed the city close. The real rich people were far-ther out, and Lucinda could still remember the moment she had first seen one of those houses, spread out across a hill in Radnor like a movie-set castle. Her gut instinct was to call it an institution, a school, a mental hospital, anything. It was impossible that a single private family could have enough money to live in that house. Then there had been other houses, whole big lots of them, some tucked back behind gates and out of sight, some right where anybody could stare at the windows and doors, the long curving drives, the vast stretches of green lawn that nobody ever played on. That was when her own anger had started, white hot and hard. How could people—*lots* of people, a hundred of them at least, she'd seen the houses—how could all those people have all that money at the same time that the girls walked the side streets for twenty bucks a blow and got AIDS and died before they were twenty-four? How could all those people have big green lawns at the same time that the schools in Philadelphia didn't have enough books for all the students, and didn't have enough plumbing, either, so that the toilets backed up into the halls at least once a month and the walls themselves were disintegrating under onslaughts of ooze from broken pipes that nobody had the money to fix? It hadn't helped, much, that when she'd first come to Adelphos House, Annie had taken her out to Bryn Mawr to see her brother and his wife. They were looking for money, and the brother had money. He had also had a butler, three maids in uniforms that Lucinda had been able to count, and a wife so intensely, poisonously bitchy that Lucinda had come very close to stabbing her with a butter knife. It was harder to make the brother out. He seemed to hate being where he was, but Lucinda had the impression that he felt that way everywhere, and with everyone.

It was, Lucinda thought, a good thing that she was both too old and too young for Power to the People and the Weather Underground. If she'd been born a couple of years earlier or later than she was, she would have armed herself to the teeth and died in a bank robbery without having the faintest idea what she was hoping to accomplish. Or maybe she wouldn't have, because Grandma Watkins would definitely not have approved. Grandma Watkins was dead now, of course—if she was alive, she'd be a hundred and thirty—

but she'd lived long enough to see the New Left, and she hadn't been impressed.

Lucinda considered doing the dishes, and decided against it. It was the first thing the volunteers went for when they came in in the morning. Lucinda more and more often thought she ought to let them at it. She'd spent her entire childhood washing dishes. These girls had spent their entire childhoods visiting the Museum of Fine Arts and having French lessons. She washed her hands under the tap in the sink and dried them on the clean dish towel she always left hanging from the refrigerator door. Sometimes she wondered what the people of Mount Hope, Mississippi, would think of Philadelphia, where there were more Catholics than anything else, and the Catholics weren't the strange ones. She knew what they would have thought of Annie's atheism, if they could have been convinced that Annie was an atheist at all. People in Mount Hope tended to think that everybody really believed in God, deep down, even if they said they didn't. She knew what they would have thought of Father Tibor Kasparian too. They would have been purely convinced that he worshiped the devil.

She went to the swinging door that led to the hall and stuck her head out. The hall was empty, but it almost always was at this time of night. She had been hoping to catch Father Kasparian on his way out.

"There anybody out there listening?" she called.

There was a rumbling somewhere in the distance and a blond head appeared halfway to the foyer. "I'm here, Miss Watkins. I'm doing some paperwork on the lunch project. Can I do something for you?"

"I was just wondering if Father Kasparian was still around somewhere."

"Oh, no. Should we have held on to him? I mean, nobody told us to. And Mrs. Wyler was here to say good-bye to him—"

"Annie's back?"

"She came in about ten minutes ago. Really, he hasn't

been gone long. You could probably catch him if you ran. He must be headed toward the bus stop. You know you can't ever catch a cab on this block. You could just—"

"No, no. It's all right. As long as he got that package I made up for him—"

"Oh, he did, he did. Mrs. Wyler made sure. I didn't know that Armenians had their own church different from everybody else's. Did you? I thought they were just Catholics, like the Greeks."

"The Greeks aren't Catholics."

"They're not?"

"Never mind," Lucinda said. "Where did Annie go? Is she all right?"

"She went to her room. I think she's a little upset about something, although you really can't tell with her, can you? She's always so quiet. My mother says the Rosses have always been like that, very odd really, and nothing at all like most people, but—"

"Excuse me," Lucinda said.

Then she retreated into the kitchen, backing up so quickly she bumped into a cabinet on the way. She blamed the private schools. They took these girls with nothing in their heads and gave them social consciences that were more social than conscience, and then Adelphos House got stuck with them. Community Service Internship Interval. It was awful.

It was also awful that Annie had come back early, and upset. Lucinda counted to thirty, long enough for the blond girl to retreat to her papers, then went back out into the hall and up the stairs. When Annie came back early, it could sometimes be good news. The girls weren't out tonight or the johns weren't buying. When Annie came back upset, it was usually the start of a major catastrophe.

If we're about to go to war with the mayor again, I'll just spit, Lucinda thought—and then she mentally erased the *spit,* because Grandma Watkins wouldn't have had the kind of fit that is only available to goddesses and ice queens.

7

David Alden checked through the last set of spreadsheets in the file, clicked back to make sure he had looked at everything he was supposed to look at, made a note to himself to find out just how exposed the bank was in the mess that was about to become of Price Heaven, and gave the command to print. That was something he'd learned during the first week of his first real job. No matter how extensive your computer files, no matter how well you'd backed them up with copies and disks, you must *always* make a hard copy. If you didn't, some fifteen-year-old slogging his way through a yahoo high school in Dunbar, Oklahoma, would come along and wipe you clean. David always wondered why the CIA and the FBI didn't hire these kids to make sure their computer records had been sanitized. Hell, he wondered why the bank didn't—except that he didn't really wonder, because he knew. The bottom line about the bank was that it kept all records, no matter how damaging, no matter how obscure, and it kept them forever. If they were ever to get hit with a scandal or a meltdown, there would be no point in shredding documents, because there would be far too many of them to shred, and far too many independent computer networks to clean out, and far too many hard copies in far too many file cabinets in far too many home offices. Human beings had a mania for documentation. They took pictures of themselves doing nothing at all. *Here's Uncle Ned, drinking lemonade at last year's VFW picnic.* They kept birth certificates, First Communion records, Confirmation scrolls, high school diplomas, marriage licenses, driver's licenses, family Bibles, school pictures, postcards. David imagined the average American house as a stockpile of paper, the closets filled to overflow with souvenirs and mementos, the basements and the attics stocked with brown cardboard boxes going to mold and mildew, keeping the faith. Or maybe not. David was sometimes acutely aware of the fact that he had never been in an average American house, not once in all his thirty-six years, not even on a visit to the families of college friends or business colleagues. In the circles in which he moved, nobody would be caught dead with four bedrooms and two-point-five baths on half an acre in New Jersey. No matter how well they played the game of being a friend to Working Americans—the bank's own television commercials sounded like hymns to *Good Housekeeping* and *Better Homes and Gardens*—there was a river of distaste running through the upper echelons of every business he knew, and the distaste was for all things suburban and middle-class. Especially middle-class. There was a reason why they sent their children to private kindergartens that cost in tuition more than most public school teachers made in a year, and it wasn't just for the prestige, or for meeting the right people. It took work to build an adult who never watched television, never listened to pop music and didn't even know the way to the local mall. It took something more than that to make sure your children would be instantly recognizable, and distrusted, by outsiders. Cocoons are not comfortable things. Nobody ever stayed in them unless they had to.

The printer was finished printing. There was a pile of paper in the well at the top of the machine. David thought he was getting a headache. He sometimes loved his job and sometimes hated it, but he did truly and always hate the peripheral obligations, of which this evening would be one. It helped a little, but only a little, to know that Tony wasn't any happier about this than he was himself.

He got the papers out of the well: three collated hard copies, one for his desk, one for his file, and one for the attaché case he carried with him everywhere. The rule was the more important the man, the fewer the papers he carried. Only middle-management nobodies without a chance in hell of rising in the hierarchy schlepped two reams of paper with them every time they headed for their cars. His attaché case wouldn't have held two reams of paper if he'd wanted it to. He felt almost guilty giving it this single thin file, but there was nothing he could do about it. He had to talk to Tony about the numbers and he had to talk to him tonight. It would at least help pass the time at this idiotic party if he could spend a few minutes talking reality among the potted palms. The whole mess made him wish he would never have to marry. There were only two choices, in marriage, for people like him. Either he got married to a woman like Charlotte, or he got married to one of those women for whom ambition was more important than plastic surgery. In either case, he would be miserable.

He dropped one of the copies in his attaché case and closed up. He picked up the other two to leave on Adele's desk when he passed it. He had his own assistant, but in this case it made more sense to give the work to Tony's, since she had been coordinating this particular project from the beginning. Maybe Adele lived in an ordinary American house, or had, when she was growing up. David knew she went out to Delaware on holidays to visit her sister, who lived there, doing David did not know what. His own family had been reduced over the years to his mother and his two sisters—and nowhere near enough money to keep any one of them. His mother lived in Paris, on the Avenue Hausmann, in a "small" apartment that had a reception room large enough to stage a cocktail party for five hundred, if she should ever want to stage a cocktail party. She wouldn't. His sisters were both married to investment bankers and living on the Main Line, in houses exactly like the one they had all grown up in. He was here at the bank, finding out, firsthand, how impossible it was to live decently and amass a safety net at the same time.

He turned off the lights in his office. There were cleaning ladies who came through and turned the lights off, but for some reason he felt guilty for making them do what he could easily do himself. He went down the hall to Adele's big desk and dropped the copies there. He went back out and down to the reception area, pulling his gloves on as he moved. It had been cold for a week and it was going to get colder.

"I know what's bothering you," Anne had told him, when he'd gone out there to take her to lunch last month. "You've been there and done that. Your life looks exactly like your father's. You're drowning in boredom and at the very, very bottom of your soul, you think you're going to hell. And I don't mean that figuratively."

No, David thought, he didn't mean it figuratively, either. There was a circle of hell Dante had failed to notice. It was the one full of old boys from Exeter and Hotchkiss and St. Paul's, who had never for a moment thought beyond their own small circle of self-doubt, and yet who were constantly in danger of falling out of it, of not having the resources, of not being able to keep up.

The phone began to ring almost as soon as he was in the elevator. He took it out of his pocket and switched it on.

"Yeah," he said. "Is something wrong?"

"Just a little nervousness on my part," Tony said, "and the simple fact that I'm ready to kill Charlotte, which is nothing new. What's the word?"

"All bad."

"How bad?"

"You're looking at eight to fifteen thousand layoffs, more likely the latter. In the month before Christmas. As soon as possible."

"It can't be pushed back after the first of the year?"

"Not if Price Heaven expects to survive. Which it shouldn't, because even with the layoffs, they're going to be on very shaky ground."

"How exposed are we?"

"We've loaned them a total of two and a half billion dollars—not too bad, but not chump change, either."

"How much of it do we lose if Price Heaven goes West?"

"Pretty much all of it. Oh, we do have some secured loans in the bunch, but not nearly enough. We've bought into way too much of their paper. I told you last July—"

"I know, I know. Crap. The logic of this escapes me. Does the logic of this escape you?"

"Not really," David said. "It's not the 1950s anymore. People have more money. They don't want to buy discounted crap all the time—"

"Some of them must. Not all of them have more money. We've got, what, nearly fifty million people who can't afford health insurance? They have to buy their clothes somewhere. They can't be going to Laura Ashley to do it."

"There's Wal-Mart. And Kmart. And Kmart has been in trouble for a long time. If you bring the prices down low enough to matter, you don't have the margin you need to make any money. If you don't bring them down, the people you need to draw never come into the store. And the ones who can buy Laura Ashley won't come in just because your prices are a little higher than Sam Walton's."

There was a long, exasperated sigh on the other end of the line. David felt the elevator bounce to a stop at the lobby level. The doors opened. He walked out. The security guard was on duty in front. Nobody else was around. He had worked past everybody else's quitting time, again. He sat down on the edge of the big marble planter in the foyer's center and stretched his legs out in front of him.

"Tony?"

"I'm here. Sorry. Charlotte is having some kind of tantrum about the ice swans. Ice swans. Never mind. How the hell does a company lose thirty million dollars in eight months and not even have a record of where it went? How can anybody be that disorganized? And now we've got—what? Is it just layoffs? Are we going to have to push for closings?"

"I think so. I don't have a complete plan just yet. That's going to take till the middle of next week. But at the minimum, I think they're going to have to close down at least a fifth of their stores, maybe a quarter. Anything in direct competition with Wal-Mart, certainly. Maybe some of the smaller places that aren't doing much volume."

"Anything right here in Philadelphia or on the Main Line?"

"I don't know for sure. Off the top of my head, I'd say yes. There's going to be trouble with all the city stores. Philadelphia, New York, Boston, Hartford. They've all got the same problem, which is terrific overhead. The real estate taxes alone are crippling."

"Crap again. So they lay off eight to fifteen thousand right before Christmas, and those heavily concentrated in central cities where there's practically no other work for their people to find. I can see the headline in *The Nation* now."

"Yes, I know. But I don't see that there's anything else we can do."

"Maybe not. But you're not the one who's going to be called an 'Apostle of Greed' by David Corn. Or maybe, God help us, by Gore Vidal."

"Yes, I know. We need to get this done over the weekend if we can. It would be best if we could do it informally. Do you want me to make the phone call, or will you?"

"No, I'll make it. It'll give me another excuse to avoid the ice swans. Are you coming out to this thing?"

"Wouldn't miss it."

"I would. Forget it. I'll talk to you here. We'll disappear into the cloak room for half an hour and I'll read through the sheets. Crap, crap, crap."

"Yes," David said again, but Tony had already hung up. David shut off the cell phone and folded it up and put it back in his pocket. Suddenly, the world just outside the bank's tinted glass doors looked worse than cold. It reminded him of that Robert Frost poem: *some say the world will end in fire, some say in ice*. He had no idea if he was quoting that correctly. He hadn't paid much attention to literature classes when he was at Exeter. He hadn't paid much attention to anything in all the long years of his education, not at Exeter, not at Yale, not even at the Harvard Business School. He was beginning to think he should have.

"Here's the deal," Annie had said, hunching over the big plate of linguine with white clam sauce that she hadn't even touched. "Once you've started asking yourself questions, you've only got two choices. Either you do what Tony does and learn to live with the alienation, or you get out. I don't think you're the kind who can learn to live with the alienation."

"I don't think I'm the kind who can get out," he'd said—and then he'd downed his entire glass of wine in a single gulp.

He got off the marble planter and went out the bank's front doors, into the cold that was even more frigid than he had been expecting it to be. If there had been any moisture in the air, it might have snowed. He couldn't remember a time when it had snowed this early in November. He stuck his gloved hands in his pockets and stepped off the curb to hail a cab.

The real sad thing about this thing tonight was that Annie wouldn't be there. Charlotte wouldn't invite her, and if Charlotte did—and hell froze over—Annie wouldn't come. David wondered when it had gotten to the point that having money meant never being able to do anything you wanted to do.

8

It was eight o'clock, and Charlotte Deacon Ross was in a state of high piss-off unmatched in all her fifty-two years on earth, except maybe by the time that Marietta Hand had shown up at her own debutante ball in a black dress. Charlotte's mother had put that particular tantrum down to "Charlotte's sensitivity to nuance," by which she meant she thought Charlotte was afraid a black dress would bring bad luck. It wasn't true. Charlotte did not believe in luck. She did believe in the divine right of kings—and, more to the point, queens—but she saw that as predestined, the way her solidly Presbyterian forebears had seen their election to heaven as predestined. God chose, before the start of time. Charlotte was one of the chosen.

Charlotte had been angry at Marietta Hand because she hadn't thought of that black dress first. Forever more, when people wrote those over-illustrated histories of Society in its prime, it would be Marietta, not Charlotte, singled out as the daring innovator that nobody could stop talking about. It gave Charlotte a great deal of satisfaction to remember that Marietta had eventually married an impecunious nobody she'd met at college, only to have him fail in one business after the other until Marietta's money was gone, or nearly gone. Marietta hadn't had to go to work, of course. She probably had ten million dollars left. Still, ten million dollars wasn't enough to live like *this*, or even approximate it. Now, when Charlotte saw Marietta, it was only by accident, at parents' day at one of the schools, where Marietta's children were proving to be just as stupid as her husband had been. Really, the whole thing was ridiculous. Anybody with a brain would have known better. If you're going to marry poor, you wait to see how he'll turn out. You marry somebody like Steven Spielberg or Steve Jobs. You don't pick some intense brooder in your Introduction to Philosophy class and decide that he's a genius.

Marietta's husband had committed suicide, in the end. It was the kind of thing people like that did. Charlotte had no idea what Marietta did with herself. Now she looked around the longest of the buffet tables, counting china crocks of beluga caviar, and feeling so worked up she almost thought steam might be coming out of her ears. There was the danger of television, and of all entertainment like it. Once the vulgar images got stuck in your head, you could never get them out again. She counted the crocks again. She took a deep breath. She considered blasting the caterer and decided she couldn't risk it. If he walked out this late, there would be a disaster. She was, she thought, willfully misunderstood, by everybody around her. She wanted only what was best for everybody. She wanted only perfection.

She counted the crocks again. She counted the plates of sliced salmon. She counted the canapés set out in slanting rows on a long silver serving tray. She was nearly six feet tall and, even at this age, and in spite of the Main Line prejudice against plastic surgery, a magnificent-looking woman. Her neck was long and thin. Her eyes were huge and blue. Her hair was as thick as the evergreen bushes that comprised the topiary garden at the bottom of the terrace. She had no idea why she was so angry she could barely see straight, but she had been this way most of the evening, and she was going to be this way for as long as she had to stand here listening to twaddle from people who pretended not to know all the things she knew. Charlotte had never believed all that talk people put out about how different everything was now than it had been in the fifties. Nothing was ever different. Blood will tell. And what it told was the story of the necessity to keep people properly sorted out.

There were exactly as many canapés as there were supposed to be. There were exactly as many china crocks of caviar as there were supposed to be. There were probably as many crackers as there were supposed to be, but she hadn't counted those, because there were too many of them. She wanted to do something physical, to get the poison out of the veins of her arms, to cause destruction. People would be arriving any minute and, of course, now that it was too cold to open the doors to the terrace, there wouldn't be enough room.

She looked to the other side of the ballroom and saw Tony deep in conversation with that man Bennis Hannaford had brought. Leave it to Bennis to hook up with some godawful immigrant wreck who couldn't even look comfortable in a dinner jacket. The man reminded her of Henry Kissinger, although he was better-looking, and a lot taller. It was the tone. You could always tell the ones who were trying too hard. They *strained*, and the strain radiated out of them like an aura. Charlotte believed in auras, in just the way she believed in reincarnation, and in predestination too. The best people were always the same people, culture after culture, time after time. They'd just been transported from one body and one place to the next ones, and as they shifted, the fate of civilizations shifted too.

Charlotte made a signal in the air, just as Tony was looking up. She saw him freeze momentarily, then lean toward Bennis's foreign-looking friend, then straighten up again.

He did not look happy, but Charlotte did not much care if he was happy. He came toward her.

"Well?" he said, drawing up next to the buffet table.

"Let's go out to the foyer for a moment," Charlotte said. "I do think it would be in better taste if we didn't have full-blown arguments in the middle of the ballroom with Bennis Hannaford and her pet Italian for an audience."

"He's not an Italian," Tony said patiently. "He was born right here in Philadelphia. He graduated from Penn. And from the Harvard Business School. Which is what we were talking about, before you decided to drag me away for no purpose."

Charlotte was moving, slowly but inexorably. When they got to the ballroom door, she edged into the foyer and watched Tony edge with her. "He's some kind of foreigner," Charlotte said, "and not the right kind, either, and you know it. He looks Jewish."

"He looks like Harrison Ford, who is about as Jewish as New England boiled dinner. And I'd lay off the nonsense about who's Jewish. These days, it's likely to get you into a lot of trouble, and not with the journalists, either. It would be a fairly intelligent idea if you didn't offend the people at Goldman Sachs. What's all this about, Charlotte?"

Charlotte opened the front door and went out. It was freezing cold out there, and her gown was both backless and strapless, but she didn't care. She couldn't have stood being in that stuffy house one more moment. She felt as if she were suffocating to death.

"There's nobody from Goldman Sachs here," she said, looking down at the lights stretched along the edges of the drive to guide the cars. A man from the caterers was walking along the edge of the walkway, wearing white tie and tails and white gloves, to open the car doors as they came up. There would be somebody around to park the cars too. Nobody was coming in yet. The invitations said eight, but nobody would show up exactly on time, because nobody ever did. This was the part of the evening she always hated most.

She wished people would grow up. All this not wanting to be the first to arrive. It was behavior unworthy of ten-year-olds.

"Charlotte?" Tony said.

"I just had to get out of the damned house. Look, there's a car. Maybe it's one of your people from Goldman Sachs. I've got a headache. If he isn't Italian, what is he?"

"I told you. He's American. He was born in—"

"Philadelphia. God, I hate Bennis Hannaford. I always did. Everybody always did. She was always such a—"

"I always thought she was very beautiful."

"I'll bet anything you want she's shacking up with him," Charlotte said. "It's just the kind of thing she would do. She was in *People* magazine, did I tell you that? As if she were some hopped-up pop star pushing a record."

"She was a novelist pushing a book."

"She's not a novelist. She's not like Jonathan Franzen or Anne Tyler. She writes—well, I don't know what you call them. Pulp. About elves."

"Fantasy," Tony said.

The car that had been coming down the drive pulled to a stop at the curb. The man in the white gloves leaped forward to open the door in the back closest to the curb. If the car had been an ordinary sedan, driven by whomever owned it, the car-parking man would have come out to take the keys, but it was a limousine—rented, Charlotte could tell from the license plate—and the driver would take it wherever it had to go. The man who stepped out onto the drive was heavyset and tired-looking. The woman who followed him was tired-looking too, but so thin it seemed as if there was nothing at all between her skin and bone. Tony frowned. This was Henry and Delia Cavender. Tony hated them.

"*Charlotte*," Delia Cavender said, pecking at the air the way she'd seen somebody do in a movie once. Maybe she was reading the novels of Dominick Dunne. Charlotte pasted a smile on her face and did her best.

"Delia, what a wonderful jacket. You're the first ones here, except of course for Bennis and her gentleman friend. Henry, you look wonderful."

"Henry," Tony said.

"Tony," Henry said.

Charlotte could not, for the life of her, remember what Henry worked at. He was some kind of lawyer, but she didn't remember what kind. It was like it was in that Hamilton cartoon. Everybody was a lawyer.

Another car was coming down the drive, and right behind it there were two more.

"I'm going into the house," Tony said. "There's no point standing around out here. That's what we hired the extra help for. You ought to come in yourself before you catch the flu and lay yourself out for a couple of weeks."

"Oh, for God's sake," Charlotte said.

And then, everything got strange. The new car pulled up at the curve. The next two queued behind it. The sky was very clear and very black. People began getting out, women in ball gowns, men in dinner jackets. Tony turned his back to them and headed for the front door.

Charlotte felt light-headed and sick to her stomach. *Maybe I'm coming down with something already*, she thought, and then Tony twisted backwards and he was in the air. His feet came right off the ground. One of the newly arrived women put her hand out to steady him. It was as if he had slipped on some ice and needed to be protected from a fall. Tony put his hand out too, but not to the woman, not to anybody, just out into the air and the dark and the cold and the nothing at all.

A second later, Tony Ross's face exploded into a mess of blood and skin and bone, and everybody started screaming.

9

At 8:15, Father Tibor Kasparian got off the bus at the corner of Cavanaugh and Welsh, pulled his collar up around his neck, and started walking the five blocks home. The bus stop was not on what he thought of as Cavanaugh Street proper. The real neighborhood didn't begin for another block, although it might, someday, with the way they'd all been expanding. He put his hands in his pockets and chided himself for not taking a cab. He always had enough money for cabs these days, and taking the bus one time would not give him enough spare change to really help out at Adelphos House. Besides, he *was* helping out at Adelphos House. He had just committed himself, the church, and the Ladies Guild to one thousand hours of volunteer work, manning phones, packing and delivering food baskets, serving in the soup kitchen, organizing mailings. It was hard to know what else he or the women of Cavanaugh Street could do. He was impressed with Anne Ross Wyler's forays into the red-light district. He remembered a time in his own life when he had been willing to go places and do things that put him in direct physical danger, and thought nothing of it, because what he wanted to do was so very important to the world. Now he did not feel that way about anything, and it made him guilty. *How can they live the way they do and not be ashamed of themselves?* he had wondered, back in Armenia, when all he'd really known about America was what he saw in the movies. Now he knew the answer. He wasn't ashamed of himself either. It was easier than he'd ever realized to drift through every day unaware that there were people hardly an arm's-length away who needed more than you had to give. They got too complacent, Americans. Now that he was an American, he got complacent with them. He wrapped his arms around his body and told himself not to be ridiculous. He might be rich by Armenian standards, but it was nothing here. Most Americans would consider him a relatively poor man—"middle class" the way they all were, but at the lowest rung of middle class, without a home he owned, without a car. It wasn't the luxury that had gotten to him but his age, and it did no good to tell himself that Anne Ross Wyler was no more than two years younger than he was. Maybe he just wasn't making sense anymore. Maybe he should give up the superfluous things, the walk-in shower, the good coat, the hot and cold running water, books that lined every wall of his apartment. Maybe he should just accept the fact that he was not a saint, and that Anne Ross Wyler was, in spite of the fact that she had a sign up in her bedroom that said Freedom *From* Religion. He'd lived long enough to know that saints came in every conceivable package, including atheist ones.

The newsstand on Lida and Gregor's block was still open. Father Tibor had to remind himself that it wasn't even nine o'clock. The night was so dark, it felt later. His heart was dark too. He went in and said good evening to the incommunicative man who was the only person he had seen inside this store in the six months since Michael Bagdanian had sold it and moved to Florida. He'd tried a few times to strike up a conversation, to find out the man's name and where he came from, but he'd never been able to do it. Even Lida hadn't managed to do it, and she'd brought a huge plate of honey cakes for bait. Tibor got some change out of his pocket and picked up a bedraggled copy of *The New York Times*. He got the Philadelphia papers delivered every day. He didn't much like news magazines, because they were too preachy. Lately, he didn't much like CNN, either, because it seemed to have become one long commercial for pop music. Why was it that Americans had so many television stations and all of them were alike, more commercial than content, as if life was about nothing but buying things? Tibor had actually liked commercials when he'd first come to the States. He'd spent so long living in a place where there was nothing to buy and no point in advertising it, commercials had been a novelty. Now it was not so much the commercials he minded as the noncommercial commercials that ate up everything else: the five minutes of every half hour on *Headline News* devoted to movies and CD albums; the incredible clutter of hype on AOL's version 7.0 that was one flashing huckster cry after another; the "sponsorship" announcements on PBS that were commercials in everything but name. Even the advertisements in newspapers and magazines had gotten bigger and brighter and worse. He had only been a United States citizen for four years, but he had been careful to vote in every election he was eligible to vote in. He knew that the United States government could not ban advertising, because it would be a suppression of free speech. He still thought he'd vote for any candidate that promised to do something about it, if only to provide every citizen with special viewing glasses that would block out the box of Kellogg's Corn Flakes on the breakfast table in the latest sitcom and the banter about Coke and Pepsi in the hot new dramatic series that everybody praised for its "realism." *Seriously*, Tibor thought, *in real life, people do not argue about Coke and Pepsi.* Maybe he ought to stop watching television and change his ISP to something that did not belong to a company that not only owned half the planet, but was trying to sell it.

He put his newspaper down on the counter next to the cash register and said good evening. He put his money down on top of the cash register and waited. The man behind the counter said nothing, and didn't look up. Grace Feinman said he made her nervous, but everybody made Grace nervous, especially the audiences she played for in the early-music quintet she had come to Philadelphia to join. Hannah Krekorian said he made her think of evil, but Hannah had written a fan letter to *Buffy the Vampire Slayer*. To Tibor, he just looked like a man, too heavyset for his own good, with hair that somebody cut for him at home. He took the two dollar bills and made change. Tibor put the change in his coat pocket and said thank you. There was a country-music station playing softly in the background: Garth Brooks.

"Have a good evening," Tibor said, suddenly hyperaware of his accent, which was very thick, and always would be. The man grunted and Tibor went out onto the street again. The windows at Lida's were dark. The windows at Bennis and Gregor's were dark too, although, these days, the windows at Bennis's were always dark, because Bennis was never there. He tucked the paper under his arm and walked another block up. If he went one block more, he could go to the Ararat and have some coffee. There would be somebody there to talk to, even if it was only old George Tekemanian, who showed no signs of wanting to move to Florida. The spotlights outside the church were lit up, which was how he had left them. Part of him hoped that homeless people would find out the church was unlocked and move in at night to get out of the cold, the way they did at that Catholic church downtown. Maybe Cavanaugh Street was too far off the beaten path as far as homeless people went. Whatever the reason, none had ever shown up. Tibor considered going back to his apartment, but didn't want to. He considered going in to the church and checking things out, but he didn't want to do that, either. He felt restless and dissatisfied in every possible way. Maybe when he got himself sorted out, he would sit down with St. John of the Cross's *Ascent of Mount Carmel* and make himself feel perfectly guilty by witnessing the life of a real ascetic. These days, he could barely make himself give up coffee for Lent.

He went up to the next block, until he was directly across the street from the Ararat. Gregor was always warning him against jaywalking, but he could never take the warnings seriously. There was never any traffic to speak of on Cavanaugh Street. He crossed the street and tried to get a look into the Ararat's big plate-glass front windows at the same time. They'd gone to candlelight and wall-dimmers already. It was hard to see anything or to know who was inside. Halfway across the street, he looked back over his shoulder at the church, reflexively. He was always checking to be sure it was there. For some reason, a vision popped into his head of that pastor in New Mexico who had burned a lot of Harry Potter books. *When,* he wondered, *did we get to the point where we stopped understanding that witches aren't real?* At least, those kinds of witches, the Harry Potter kind, weren't real. He started to turn back to the Ararat, to finish crossing the street.

That was when Holy Trinity Armenian Christian Church exploded. At first it was just a light, an inexplicable light, blinding, like Saul on the Damascus road. Tibor half thought he had been granted a vision from God. Then the noise came and suddenly the air was full of stones and bricks and glass. They were everywhere. Noise was everywhere. Fire was everywhere too, and in the heat and madness, Father Tibor Kasparian passed out cold.

PART ONE

I reveal how a global secret society called the Illuminati (the "Illuminated Ones" as they call themselves) have been holding the reigns of power in the world since ancient times, expanding their power out of the Middle and Near East (and other centres) to control first Europe and then, thanks to the British Empire and other European empires, to take over in the Americas, Africa, Australia, New Zealand, Asia, and elsewhere. When those empires appeared to withdraw from these regions, the Illuminati left behind the secret society networks and the Illuminati bloodlines and these have continued to control and orchestrate events ever since.

—"WHO REALLY RULES THE WORLD?"
BY DAVID ICKE AT HTTP://WWW.
DAVIDICKE.COM/ICKE/VISITOR.HTML

ONE

1

In the first few days after the explosion, Gregor Demarkian found himself getting up in the middle of the night to look at what was left of Holy Trinity Armenian Christian Church. It wasn't easy. Even in the days when the church was still standing in the ordinary way, even when it was decorated top to bottom by Donna Moradanyan Donahue on one of her periodic holiday enthusiasms, it was still more than a block away and set back from the sidewalk to make room for the three shallow steps that led to its front doors. Gregor had never had any idea what the steps were for. Maybe the men and women who built the church believed that people should ascend on their way to talk to God. Maybe the church had been built before the sidewalk and the street paving had been put in, and there was some worry that without a few steps to wipe their feet on, people might track mud into the church. None of these thoughts made any sense at all, and none of them mattered, but Gregor found it hard to look up the street without thinking about something besides the obvious. It was a good thing the bomb had not been as big as it had sounded to Tibor on the night it went off. There was some of Holy Trinity Church still left, even if it wasn't of much good to anybody. Even more importantly, only the buildings directly next to the church had been in any way damaged. According to the bomb expert sent out by the police on the morning after, and according to the bomb expert at the FBI, for whom Gregor had pulled in a few markers for him to come out and look at the scene, much more firepower and all the buildings on the block, on both sides of the street, might have suffered "structural damage." Gregor had heard the words *structural damage* a thousand times before without knowing what they meant, or even wondering. Now he knew. They meant that the ground had rattled so much, it had made the foundations of the buildings disorganized and unsafe.

Now it was not the middle of the night, but the early morning—6:45 in the morning on November 13, to be exact. Gregor finished shaving in front of the enormous vanity mirror Bennis had installed in his bathroom and reached for the toothpaste and his toothbrush, feeling as disoriented as he ever had in his life. He could still remember, with perfect clarity, the first time he had ever seen a dead body that wasn't laid out in a casket for a wake. It was his first year at the FBI and he was the junior partner on a kidnapping detail, the kind of thing that usually required nothing more from the agents but sitting by a phone and recording ransom demands from half-demented fools who hadn't realized how difficult it would be to actually collect a large amount of money in small bills. That was why he had been assigned to that particular case. You didn't send brand-new agents out of Quantico into one of the nastier situations, even if you thought you had no choice. This time, though, the half-demented fool had been a manic-depressive, or maybe stoked out on the kind of drugs that made mood swings behave like roller-coaster rides. Every time he called to give instructions about the ransom, he got crazier—and unlike most kidnappers, he called a lot, over and over again, apparently heedless of the fact that it was going to be possible, eventually, to trace those calls. Still, that was a long time ago and the technology hadn't been as good then as it was now. He might have gotten away with it if his only problem had been a desperate need to talk. Instead, he'd also had a desperate need for validation, or absolution, or *something* that was so mixed up in his brain he couldn't put it into words and he couldn't live without it. During the fifth phone call his voice began to squeak and soar. The experienced agent on the case was as tense as Richard Nixon at a press conference. The kidnapper was losing it, and even Gregor had been able to understand that. He might have been inexperienced as an agent, but he'd spent his time in the army. He knew the sound of panic when he heard it. He also knew the sound of gunfire when he heard it, and that was what came next. The explosion was so loud that the woman whose daughter had been kidnapped screamed and dropped the phone. A second later, she was holding her ear, doubled over in pain. Gregor held his breath. If the phone went to dial tone, it would mean the child was dead. The phone did not go to dial tone.

They found the child, and the kidnapper, two and a half hours later. With the phone line open and nobody to hang it up, it was easy to trace. The child was locked in the bathroom, sitting in the bathtub in tears, but not otherwise hurt. The kidnapper was lying half-on and half-off the big double motel bed he'd been sitting on when he made the call and put the gun to the side of his head. If you're going to shoot yourself, never shoot yourself in the side of the head, Gregor's instructor at Quantico always said. Shots to the side of the head often didn't work, and what happened was that you were left alive but worse off than before, brain-damaged, immobile, a walking vegetable. In this case, the man had been lucky, if you could call it that. He was most certainly dead. The side of his skull on the far side of the shot had exploded outward, splattering blood and skin and bone all over the motel bed's bedspread and the window in the wall beyond it. His eyes were wide open and caught in a paralysis so profound, Gregor couldn't shake the feeling that they were trying to communicate something. It was the first time he'd realized that the newly dead did not look dead so much as hyperalive. Their eyes tried to catch and hold you. If you were there at the critical moment, their arms reached out for you. Gregor had always wondered if they were trying to hold on to life or trying to drag you into the tunnel along with them.

He wiped the froth of toothpaste off his mouth. He washed his face again. He gave a little consideration, but not much, to Bennis's suggestion that he might look good with his hair cut short enough to almost look shaved. He put the towel back on the rack and went down the hall to the living room. Bennis was standing at the big front window, doing what he himself had been doing during the night for days: twisting sideways to see if she could see what was left of Holy Trinity. She was as "dressed" as she was going to get for the day, meaning a turtleneck and flannel shirt and jeans. She was having no more luck than he did when he tried to see the church. In the first two days after the explosion, crews had come out from the city to clean up the mess. The entire façade of the church was gone. What was left was something like a stage set, with the pews and aisles and altar exposed to anybody who wanted to come by and see what they were like. Bennis had her arms wrapped around her body so that she could twist more easily against the glass. If this had been a year or two ago, she would have been smoking.

"It doesn't work, you know," he told her. "I try it all the time. We never could see Holy Trinity very well from here, even when it was standing."

"It's still standing," Bennis said. "All except one wall of it. Yes, I know. You don't have to bring it up again. It will have to come down."

"It was an old building, and it was built by people who didn't have the kind of resources you need to put up something solid for the ages to begin with. It would have had to come down anyway, eventually. Tibor's said so, more than once."

"I don't think this is what he meant, do you? Although I've got to admit, it's going to put a crimp into Howard Kashinian's lectures about how the church is solid as a rock and it would just be a waste of money to build a new one. I gave a little money to the rebuilding fund, did I tell you?"

"No. Everybody else on the street told me. That was a rather dramatic gesture."

"Yes, well. I make all this money and I never spend any

of it. I mean, let's face it. I don't like jewelry. I don't take elaborate vacations. I do have the car, but at the rate I drive it I'm still going to have it in the third millennium. Does it make me a bad person that I'm not more upset about Tony Ross?"

"I don't think so," Gregor said. "Are you coming down to the Ararat with me? I know you don't like talking to John Jackman, but in this case you might—"

"No," Bennis said. "That's all right. I don't mind talking to John anymore. All emotions wear out. Did I ever tell you that my sister Myra tried to marry Tony once? This was back the year she was coming out. Tony was, I think, a year older than she was, still at Yale or wherever, but you could see even then that he was going to be something extraordinary. And Myra being Myra, she was determined to marry something extraordinary. But Tony didn't seem to be interested."

"From what you've told me about your sister Myra, that might not be surprising."

"It wasn't." Bennis stopped twisting in the window. "You really can't see it. I never noticed that before. Maybe I never tried to see it before. God, what a mess. Tibor's coming home from the hospital today. Did I tell you that? Donna and I are going to go pick him up."

"Yes, you told me that. He's all right, you know, Bennis, he wasn't really hurt. It was mostly shock and precaution."

"I was thinking we could put him in my apartment. I never use it these days anyway, and he can't go back to his place. It's still standing, but it isn't safe. God, what's he going to do about all the books? He won't let them get plowed under. You know how he feels about books."

"I know how he feels about books."

"Of course, it will mean he won't be able to pretend not to know we're living in sin, or whatever it is we're doing. Do you think he thinks that, that we're living in sin?"

"I don't know. I doubt it. Tibor doesn't usually think things like that."

"I don't really know how Tibor thinks," Bennis said. "We treat him like a pet, or at least I do. We find him endearing.

But that isn't what he's about at all, I don't think. It really was a bomb, wasn't it, Gregor? I mean, the bomb squad couldn't be mistaken. It couldn't have been a gas explosion or something like that."

"The church has electric heat. And no, I don't think the bomb squad was mistaken, although we've still only got a preliminary report."

"It just seems so awful to me that anybody would deliberately try to bomb Holy Trinity Church. Awful and ridiculous. Does that make sense to you? It makes sense to me that somebody might want to kill Tony Ross. He was rich as hell and he was the head of a big investment bank and he made decisions all the time that affected people's lives. But this is Holy Trinity Church. It's a little Armenian church on a side street in Philadelphia that isn't important to anybody at all except the people who live here. It isn't even in one of those categories that the hate groups go after. It's not a black church. It's not a synagogue. Tibor doesn't mix in politics except for voting in every election. It doesn't make any sense."

"It will when we find whoever did it. Probably."

"Probably?"

"Let's just say it will make sense of a kind, no matter what," Gregor said. "Sometimes the rationale for these things is not necessarily contaminated with linear thought. Get your shoes on and come to the Ararat with me. John may not have anything to report, but he'll be good to talk to. And you can see everybody and commiserate with them. Again."

"Linda Melajian told me yesterday that the Ararat is full for every meal these days but it's like being at a wake. Everybody just . . . sits there."

"You should know. You haven't eaten at home since it happened."

"You can't eat here, Gregor. I can't cook, and you think stocking the refrigerator means buying two boxes of Dunkin' Donuts and putting them on different shelves."

"You can eat the Dunkin' Donuts," Gregor said.

Bennis marched away from the window, past the long

black leather couch, into the foyer. A moment later, Gregor heard the sound of clogs against hardwood and reached for the jacket he had left over the back of a chair.

"Now I'm ready and you're not," she called. The clogs went back and forth across the hardwood, back and forth, back and forth.

Gregor considered telling her that it was obvious she'd been crying, but in the end that did not seem to be a sensible thing to do. It would only get her started talking about Emotions, which she could do all day, in intimate detail, and he couldn't do at all. He not only couldn't talk about them, he often couldn't recognize them. He had only two labels for what he felt most of the time, "good" and "not good." He had one more label for use in emergencies—"scared"—but that one was rarely necessary. Even now, when every muscle in his body was fighting urgently for paralysis, for collapse, for anything at all that would release him from the necessity of walking down Cavanaugh Street in front of that bombed-out church—even now, he wouldn't call what he felt "scared." He didn't know what it was.

"*Gregor.*"

He threw the jacket over his shoulders and went out into the foyer, where Bennis was waiting for him. It was cold as hell outside, but she was not wearing her jacket, and wouldn't if he asked her to. He got his own coat off the rack and put it on. She walked away from him and out the door onto the landing.

There really had been a time, he thought, years ago, before his wife had died, before he'd retired from the Bureau, before he'd moved back to Cavanaugh Street, when he hadn't had anything more complicated to think about than the paperwork required to document the interstate tracking of serial killers. He was not Bennis Hannaford's lover, or Tibor Kasparian's friend, or the man a lot of people looked to to make sanity prevail in a thoroughly insane world. He did not remember the change coming over him. He could not pinpoint the one moment when he had begun to be someone he had never been before. He couldn't even tell if he liked this version of himself better than he liked the other.

What he did know was that, no matter how much he wanted to talk to John Jackman and find out what the police had on both the bombing and the murder out in Bryn Mawr, he'd be content to be ignorant for the rest of his life if it meant he didn't have to walk past the front of that exploded church. He *had* walked past it, two or three times a day, every day since it happened, but he wasn't used to it, and he didn't think he ever would be. If he'd been a different kind of man, he would have packed everything he owned into a couple of suitcases and taken off for a place where nobody had ever heard of Holy Trinity Church. Unfortunately, it would be impossible to go anywhere where nobody had heard of Tony Ross.

2

Oddly, it was much less difficult for Gregor to actually walk down the street in front of Holy Trinity Church than it was for him to think about doing it. The church always looked far less damaged than he had imagined it was, and he was able to ignore the fact that he knew it looked far less damaged than it actually was. The police had cordoned off the sidewalk directly in front of it. Anybody walking down Cavanaugh Street on that side now had to cross the street to continue. They had put a guard there the first two nights. The guard had disappeared on the third morning, far sooner than Gregor thought appropriate. In an FBI investigation, it would have taken far longer than this to gather the necessary evidence. He was determined to keep his disapproval to himself. John Jackman was now commissioner of police in Philadelphia. He was here because he was taking a personal interest in this case, and that at a time when all the police departments from the city down the length of the Main Line had been pressed into emergency service in the murder of Tony Ross. And it wasn't just the police departments. You could see the problem was that the media had started out only vaguely interested—oh, murder at one of those fancy estates in Bryn Mawr; good for a week or two; yawn—and then woken up to what had really happened. One of the most powerful men in the world, one of the men who ran the banks and dictated policy to governments, had been killed by a sniper with a silencer on the front steps of his own house. At any other time, the destruction of Holy Trinity Church would have been big news in Philadelphia. There would have been an outpouring of support and a concentration on the human angle. There might even have been a fund to rebuild the church. Gregor found that he resented, more than a little, that none of that was happening. It didn't matter that Tibor wouldn't need a fund to get the church rebuilt. People on the street would give what they could, and in some cases that was plenty. It mattered that nobody was paying attention. This had to be the worst hate crime in the history of the city. Nobody was noticing.

John Jackman was standing at the door to the Ararat up ahead, bent over old Marta Varnassian, who seemed to be lecturing him. Since old Marta Varnassian lectured everybody, usually on the perfidy of all Turks everywhere, this was not surprising, but Gregor found it both hopeful and incredible that Marta was talking to John at all. There was a time when Marta would no more have had a conversation with a black man, even about the Turks, than she would have made love to the president of Turkey on the church steps at high noon. Maybe it was John's two-thousand-dollar suit. Maybe it was just that John had been around so much in the last few years, Marta now thought he was Armenian.

"There's John," Bennis said.

"Looks good, I think," Gregor offered, neutrally. Once, back when he and Bennis had first met, he was fairly sure that Bennis had had an affair with John Jackman. It was something they never talked about, just like they never talked about any of the other men she had had affairs with, including the governor of a large western state and a member of the Rolling Stones. In their case, it was Bennis who had had wild oats to sow.

"John always looks good," Bennis said. "It's that goddamned bone structure. Doesn't it bother you that you can see all the pews and they're still there and nobody has bothered to move them to someplace safe."

You couldn't see the pews at all, from there. They had walked past the church and the building on its right side, which had had to be evacuated. The building on its left side had had to be evacuated too. At this point, there was no way to know if those buildings could be repaired or if they would have to be torn down. Gregor worried more about the fate of the people who had lived in them than he worried about the fate of Holy Trinity Church.

John Jackman shook Marta Varnassian's hand, gravely. She patted him on the arm and made her way through the doors of the Ararat to whomever was waiting for her there. Marta would not eat breakfast in a restaurant on her own. That meant at least one of the other Very Old Ladies must have come with her. John straightened up and waved to them. He was staring, slightly, at Bennis, but she was not staring back.

"Hi," he said, when they reached him. "Interesting woman, that was. Mrs. Varnassian. Did the Turks really invade Armenia this morning?"

"It was in 1915," Gregor said.

"Oh."

"Hi, John," Bennis said.

"I caught Linda a second ago," John said. "She's saving us a table, but not the one at the window. Do you know what she's talking about?"

"Yes," said Gregor. The window table was the one where he usually sat with Tibor and old George Tekemanian and whomever else wanted to join them. Today, Tibor was in the hospital, and old George was out on the Main Line staying with his nephew Martin, whose wife Angela had decided that Cavanaugh Street was not a safe place for him to be.

They went into the Ararat. Linda waved them toward a table along the far wall, marked out from the rest by a big black-and-white *reserved* sign stuck into the metal sugar packet holder.

"That's subtle," John said.

Gregor sat down. "There's not a hope in hell that it will be private. You know we'll have people coming over here as soon as we get settled. They want to know."

John sat down too. Bennis waved to Linda for the coffee and then curled into a chair like a sick cat. John looked her over quickly, and only once, and then looked away.

Linda Mclajian arrived with the coffee and three cups. She put one down in front of John Jackman and said, "I hope you're going to do something about whoever did this. I hope you don't have your mind all messed up by debutantes on the Main Line."

"John loves debutantes on the Main Line," Bennis said.

"Behave yourself," John said. He reached for the little metal pitcher of cream. Linda knew better than to bring nondairy creamer to *his* table. "We're doing everything we can. It might be less than you'd like."

"Somebody planted a bomb, for God's sake. There must be some way to send him to jail. Or something worse."

"We'll do our best," Jackman said.

She marched off without taking their order. Jackman watched her go. "Well," he said, "I suppose that's not all that odd. Everybody's upset. Everybody deserves to be upset."

"Part of it's just that there's no way to stop thinking about it," Gregor said. "The church is out there with the whole front wall blown off, practically. Everybody has to pass it every day."

"I wish you'd left the guard there longer," Bennis said. "Whoever it was could come back. And even if he doesn't, children could get into there and hurt themselves."

"At the moment, we've got practically every cop in the city and four of the townships working on the Tony Ross murder, or guarding somebody or something connected to the Tony Ross murder. I know that sounds unfair to you, but under the circumstances it makes sense. I don't know if you realize it, but the first lady of the United States was in a car not more than a mile from Ross's front gate when the shooting started. Another five minutes, and the place would have been lousy with secret service officers."

"And the shooting would never have happened," Bennis said.

"Not necessarily," John said. "Considering how cleanly whoever it was got away, what might have happened was a couple of more people dead. That is, assuming this turns out to be politically motivated, or domestic terrorism, which is what the FBI thinks it's going to be when they finally get it figured out."

"Do you agree?" Gregor asked.

John shrugged. "It seems likely. That had to be a professional, the guy who got Ross. That whole thing was just too damned clean for it to have been anything else."

"There's always dumb luck," Gregor said.

"Not often. And not right between the eyes," John said.

Bennis looked away. "Do you notice what happens? Whenever anybody starts talking about the church, they end up talking about Tony Ross. Even we do it."

"I thought domestic terrorism meant homemade bombs and the militias," Gregor said. "That doesn't sound professional."

"Things have changed a lot since your day," John said. "Lots of the guys in the militias are ex-military and lots of them are good at what they do. God only knows they can buy whatever they want in terms of weapons and ammunition."

"So what happened to the church?" Bennis said.

Linda Melajian came back. Bennis ordered fruit and cheese. John Jackman ordered fruit and cheese. Gregor ordered three scrambled eggs, a side of hash browns, a side of sausage, and some buttered toast.

"Still suicidal, I see," John said.

Bennis waved it away. "What *about* the church?" she said. "You've had four days, you disappeared after two, there's a big hole in the street, there must be something—"

"There is something." Jackman pulled a small notebook out of the inside pocket of his jacket. "First, it was a small bomb—"

"Small?" Bennis said.

"Very small," John said. "Bennis, if that had been a bomb of any significant size, it would have taken down the whole church and the buildings next to it and destabilized all three blocks. It doesn't take much. That's why they've got all that special architecture in California to handle even tiny earthquakes."

"So what kind of a bomb are we talking about?" Gregor said. "Dynamite? Remote-controlled? What?"

"We think, from what we got out of the rubble, that there were three small pipe bombs. Very small. Plastic explosives, the kind you can pick up on the black market for cheap. Nothing particularly fancy. This, by the way, is the kind of thing most people associate with the militias. Somebody could store the materials for this kind of thing in their basement, and nobody would know a thing about it. That's just what the militias do, really. They've got their stuff stashed in basements, in rec rooms, in the backs of SUVs."

"But why would a militia want to blow up Holy Trinity Church?" Bennis asked. "It doesn't make sense, does it? They blow up government buildings, and that kind of thing."

"I'm not saying it was a militia," John Jackman said. "I'm just saying the method used corresponds to what we used to associate militias with, oh, maybe ten or fifteen years ago. What interests me, and what interests the police in Bryn Mawr, are the connections."

"The connections between what?" Gregor asked.

"Between the bombing here and the murder of Tony Ross."

"Oh, for God's sake," Bennis said. "You can't honestly tell me that just because I was at that party and Gregor came with me and we both live on Cavanaugh Street that somebody went around killing Tony Ross and blowing up Holy Trinity Church on the same night to, to—to do what? What would be the point?"

"I have no idea what the point would be," John said, "I'm just letting you know what's going on. And it's more than that you and Gregor were at that party. It's what Father Tibor was doing the night of the explosion. He was at Adelphos House. Do you know about Adelphos House?"

"Of course I do," Bennis said. "It's an outreach house for child prostitutes. The church is involved in some kind of volunteer thing with them, or it was going to be. Are you trying to tell me that Tony Ross was seeing child prostitutes?"

"No, I'm trying to tell you that Adelphos House was founded by and is run by Tony Ross's sister."

"What?" Bennis looked truly shocked.

John Jackman flipped through a few pages of his little notebook. "Anne Ross Wyler," he said. "A year older than her brother. Came out at the Philadelphia Assembly. Graduated from Wellesley College in 1971. Married Dutton Wyler in 1980. Divorced him in 1985—"

"He was one of those people," Bennis said. "They never do anything. They get born rich and they go to parties."

"Not what the Ross siblings were into, I take it," John said. "Anyway, the details of her life between '85 and '96 are sketchy at best, but in '96 she went to work for a settlement house in New York. She stayed there two years. Then she came back to Philadelphia and opened Adelphos."

"I think Bennis's original objection still stands," Gregor said. "That's a very tenuous connection. How would Tibor's interest in doing something to help Adelphos House connect to Tony Ross's murder?"

"How would *anything* connect to Tony Ross's murder?" John said. "It's not like we know what we're doing here, and the FBI doesn't know either, no matter what they try to tell me. The point is that the connections exist, and we have to follow them up."

"Even though the two methods seem to be so at odds with each other?" Gregor asked. "Professional quality in the murder of Tony Ross. Amateur fun with explosives in the bombing of Holy Trinity Church."

"We've got to start somewhere," John said, "and that's true with the problem with the church as well as with the murder of Tony Ross. Look, we found pieces of the bombs. We might be able to trace some of the materials. It's a long shot, but we might. In the meantime, do you have any information besides the connections to the Ross murder that might help us out? Has there been any vandalism? Nasty words spray-painted on the church, or on Tibor's apartment? Hate mail?"

"Of course not," Bennis said. "This is Cavanaugh Street, for God's sake."

"What about the people who live here?" John asked. "And don't tell me it's Cavanaugh Street. Has anybody had an argument with Father Tibor? Has he been riding anybody's case, come down on sin a little hard lately, had a dispute with a tenant, anything?"

"He doesn't have any tenants," Gregor said, "and the church doesn't either."

"What about that stuff he writes?" John was being patient. "Has he been writing letters to the editor about politics lately? About Armenia? About September eleventh?"

"I don't think he writes letters to the editor," Bennis said.

"How about the Internet?" John tried again.

Gregor looked quickly at Bennis, and then away. He always forgot about the Internet, because he used it so seldom himself. "I forgot about the Internet. He does talk politics on the Internet, but not the way you'd think. He goes to this chat room—"

"It's not a chat room, it's a newsgroup," Bennis said. "A Usenet newsgroup. And it's not about politics, it's about mystery stories. Rec.arts.mystery."

John Jackman took out his pen. "Repeat that for me, please. WWW . . ."

"No," Bennis said. "It's not a Web site. There's no *www*. It's a newsgroup. I'm not sure how you get on it usually, but on AOL you do *control-K*. Then you type in *newsgroups*. Then you can find it by clicking on *search all newsgroups* and asking for it. I'm probably not making much sense. I could show you if we got to a computer."

"Don't worry about it. We've got guys in the department who know all about this stuff. Rec.arts.mystery."

Bennis spelled it for him. "It's his favorite thing to do when he isn't reading."

"Mystery stories doesn't sound like what we're looking for," John said.

"Oh, they discuss everything," Bennis told him. "And I do mean everything. Mystery stories, and theology and, yes, politics sometimes. I've forgotten all about it. He's been in the hospital for days, and nobody's told them. They get all involved with each other. They'll be concerned."

"One of them could be something else than concerned."

"I suppose." Bennis did not look happy. "It would be terrible if all this ended up being connected to RAM."

"What?" John said.

"RAM," Gregor repeated. "Rec.arts.mystery. RAM."

"Oh."

Linda Melajian was coming back with their breakfasts. Gregor's took up two-thirds of the tray. John and Bennis each had a small round plate with a pear in the middle of it. The pears were stuffed with Danish blue cheese. Bennis stared at hers and went back to her coffee.

"Well," John said. "There's no use worrying about it now. Let me look into this stuff. Then I'll get back to you. And don't the two of you forget. You're going out to Bryn Mawr to talk to Frank Margiotti. I don't care if you talk to the FBI or not."

TWO

1

Lucinda Watkins had been working with Anne Ross Wyler for six years, and never once in all that time had she been able to forget the differences between them. It was not, at all, the way she had expected it to be. Annie didn't sound Upper Class, the way that fool William F. Buckley did on that television program Lucinda had once found as fascinating as a disaster area. Annie didn't use a lot of big words or dress up no matter what the time of day or night, either. It was usually Lucinda who ended up fussing about clothes, because Annie quite literally didn't notice what she wore. She was more than capable of going into the living room to meet a reporter dressed in baggy jeans and an oversized T-shirt that said *Bite the Wax Tadpole* in big red letters. The worst was when she had shown up at a Congressional hearing on child pornography wearing a T-shirt that said *Friends Don't Let Friends Vote Republican*, and Lucinda had only had forty-five seconds to exchange blouses with her so that she didn't end up alienating the entire United States House of Representatives. Later, Annie had lectured her endlessly on the fact that the *entire* United States House of Representatives was not Republican, but Lucinda had stuck to her guns that time, and with good reason. They were in enough trouble, on a day-to-day basis, without offending Newt Gingrich.

Where Lucinda saw the difference, and couldn't avoid it, was in things. Annie did not have a lot of things, and she didn't seem to care about having "nice" ones, but what she had she was entirely indifferent to. Lucinda couldn't break a plate or stain a tablecloth without experiencing deep feelings of guilt and panic: guilt because she had ruined something that she had had the responsibility of taking care of; panic because such an accident almost always meant an expenditure that would be difficult to make and injurious to the family budget. She could still remember her grandmother sitting down at the kitchen table working out the figures with pen and paper. So much out of the grocery money; so much out of the bus money; so much out of the money put aside each week to buy the papers: all this, just to get enough together to replace a toaster or a dress that was supposed to last the whole school year but that Lucinda had ripped on the playground the very first day. Life was counting, addition and subtraction, rigidity. A broken milk pitcher was a week with two days of greens, no meat. A ruined pair of shoes was a month without snack money for school and the two meatless days a week on top of it. The only money that never got cut was the money for books. Grandma Watkins insisted on buying them all a book a month, a real one, not from the racks at the drugstore but from the one bookstore in Jacksonville that the owner wouldn't look down on her in. That had been a ritual as solemn and unbending as the rituals of the Catholic Church, which they did not belong to because the Catholics did not praise the Lord with enough joy, and because it was bad enough being poor in Mississippi without being Catholic on top of it. Lucinda had never, in all her life, ruined a book, and she couldn't imagine herself doing it. Even the ruin of really bad books made her ill. She had tried and failed to join the Progressive Conference of Philadelphia, because at her first meeting a man had stood up and ripped apart a copy of *The Bell Curve*. Once, finding a copy of *A Wake Up Call for the White Race* getting rained on on the ground just next to a bus shelter, she had picked it up and wiped it off and put it in a dry, although suitably out of the way, place. It was not that she did not understand the power of hate, but that she felt the power of books more strongly, and the power of the need to preserve all things and waste nothing, against the day when you had nothing at all.

Annie's basic attitude to things was not to notice they were there. If they broke, and she had to notice them, she got annoyed at them and threw them away. Then she went out and bought another of whatever it was. Lucinda had known, from the beginning, that Annie was rich, but this approach to possessions had startled her from the beginning, and still did. It was bad enough when Annie swept away a load of broken crockery that had been smashed on the dining room floor—the girls, when they came to stay, were often angry; they screamed; they ranted; they broke things—and drove down to Price Heaven to buy three or four more sets of dinner plates or coffee mugs. At times like those, Lucinda could tell herself that she was being neurotic. A rich woman like Annie didn't have to worry about the price of a few cheap plates. When it came to the cameras, Lucinda could not convince herself so easily that she was the one who was crazy. Cameras cost money. The cameras Annie bought cost hundreds of dollars, in one case over a thousand, because they were equipped to take night shots without an ordinary flash, to take shots at odd angles, to do all kinds of things that an ordinary off-the-shelf camera couldn't do. Annie was no more careful about the cameras, or worried about their breaking, than she was about the plates. At least twice a month, she came back with one of the cameras smashed. The johns hated being photographed. If they thought they could get away with it, they leaped out of their cars and chased her. Sometimes it was the cops who took the cameras and ruined them. "Never underestimate the power of a cop on the take," Annie always said, and Lucinda had come to understand that this was true. Lord only knew, Annie was right to say that the wholesale prostitution of twelve- and fourteen-year-olds would not continue to thrive if *somebody* wasn't looking the other way.

Standing at the door to the darkroom, Lucinda hesitated. The red light wasn't on, which should mean it was okay to go in, but Lucinda had the feeling that Annie wasn't always careful about the lights. Finally, she knocked. There was the sound of metal things being moved around—what went on in a darkroom Lucinda didn't know—and Annie said, "Come in."

Lucinda went in. Annie was sitting on a swivel stool. Print after photographic print was spread out on the long, wide worktable in front of her. She had her retractable art light trained right over the ones in the middle. Lucinda closed the door behind her. In spite of the art light, the room was dark.

"Well?" she said.

Annie shook her head. "Ambiguous. Far too ambiguous, unfortunately. And yet I know it was him. I recognized him as soon as I saw him."

"I still don't understand why that isn't enough."

"It isn't enough because he's got friends in high places and they're not about to let him go down in a way that will make him look bad. Even if he really isn't one of our own."

"This is the Main Line stuff you're always talking about? One of our own?"

"Something like that."

"I'm beginning to wish you hadn't taken the car that night. If you hadn't taken the car, you wouldn't have been able to follow him."

"It was too cold a night not to take the car," Annie said. Then she pushed her stool back until she could reach the switch on the back wall and turned on the overhead lights. In the now bright light, Lucinda could see that Annie was wearing that *Freedom FROM Religion* button she'd taken to putting on since the national prayer service after September 11. "Crap," Annie said. "I don't know what to do about this at all."

"I don't suppose you could let it drop."

"No," Annie said. "I saw the man pick up a thirteen-year-old girl and pay her twenty dollars to blow him. You know who it was? It was Patsy Lennon."

"Good Lord," Lucinda said.

"Yeah, I know. That kid has more issues than *National Geographic*. She's a complete mess and an addict besides.

But there he was, and there she was, and all I got a picture of was Patsy's head and his hand on top of it. Maybe I'll go looking for a telephoto lens. Maybe if they think I'm not there and can't see them, they'll go back to being out front about what they do."

"It's too bad you didn't take pictures later, when you got to that party. It seems like everybody in the world is looking for whoever it is who shot your brother."

Annie sighed. "I was invited to that party, did you know that? Oh, Charlotte's never been able to stand me, I'm everything she hates about everything, but Tony always insisted. I've got the invitation upstairs. I should have gone. I could have stood around at the buffet table buttonholing political hotshots and financial wizards and reciting chapter and verse about their forays onto the Strip. Except that I wouldn't have gotten anybody but the second-raters. Did you know that? The people who really run things, the people like Tony, know better than to even try something like this."

"He's not one of the people who run things?"

"No," Annie said. "He's—" She let her hands flutter in the air. She looked, Lucinda thought, incredibly tired. "I've often wondered if some of them don't indulge, anyway. I know the attraction exists. Maybe what people like that do—" She pointed at the photograph in front of her. Lucinda couldn't see anything in it but blur. "Maybe what they do is find suitable companions for the people who can't find them for themselves. Can't because they don't dare. Can't you see the headlines? *Presidential Friend Linked to Child Prostitution. Head of International Bank Arrested for Soliciting Sex with Minor.* The major papers wouldn't run them, but the rags would. Thank God for the *National Enquirer*."

"So?" Lucinda said. "Does it go on?"

"I don't know. On one level, it seems to me inevitable that it would. On another, it seems to me just as inevitable that it wouldn't."

"And I thought you'd know, growing up with those people," Lucinda said.

Annie laughed. "In my day, there were some things they

didn't tell daughters. There probably still are. I just wish I knew what all that was about. There's only one reason to rush off for a quickie blow job from Patsy Lennon on the way to the biggest charity ball of the season, and that's because he's got the bug and he's got it bad. He has to be completely out of control. Which poses a lot of interesting questions."

"Maybe your brother knew about it," Lucinda said. "Maybe your brother was going to make a public stink about it. So this guy—"

"Shot him? Over that? I doubt it."

"Somebody shot him," Lucinda pointed out. "And you were there. I mean, Annie, think of the timing. You were *right* there. You must have seen whoever it was go right through the gates in front of your nose."

"I know."

"And he went through the gates, before your brother was shot. Didn't he?"

"Yes."

"Well, then," Lucinda said, but she didn't know what she meant by it. Well, then, you should go to the police and say something about it. Well, then, you should start tracking this guy and see what else you can find. Well, then, you should take care of yourself and butt out. Annie was staring down at the best of the prints, the one with Patsy's head with the hand on top of it.

"Well, then," Lucinda said again. "You might just consider covering your ass. Go to the police and get this over with. Because if you don't, and somebody noticed you there, you're going to get yourself in a huge amount of trouble."

Annie sat up a little straighter in her chair. "I've got a better idea, better than going to the police. I should have thought of it before. Do you have a volunteer that can cover for you this morning?"

"No," Lucinda said. "Not until this afternoon. Why?"

"I want you to go with me. We'll go this afternoon. I should have thought of this before."

"Thought of what?" Lucinda said, but it was no use. Annie was packing up her prints, bustling around, cleaning up, as if nothing more unusual had happened in the last several days than that one of the johns had actually been arrested. It was impossible to talk to Annie when she was like this. At least, this time, whatever she had on her mind was unlikely to cost a great deal of money.

Annie put the prints in a big manila envelope and the envelope in the locked top drawer of her filing cabinet. Lucinda went out into the hall and thought about calling child protective services to let them know what Patsy Lennon was up to, again. There were some people who never seemed to be doing anything but learning to be dead.

2

Kathi Mittendorf had been holding her breath ever since the night Anthony van Wyck Ross was murdered, and since she'd known about that murder long before most other people in the city, she was beginning to feel light-headed.

"You know what they're like," Michael had said when he'd called, his voice sounding muffled as always and surrounded, this time, by wind. "They're going to look for the first likely candidate to pin it on, and we may be that candidate. We've got a lot of literature out there. We've been making a lot of noise."

More to the point, Kathi thought, there was the problem of all the explosives, and of the guns and ammunition in the basement. She had no idea what kind of a gun Anthony van Wyck Ross had been murdered with, but she had some of nearly everything on the premises, each piece bought separately and by seemingly unconnected people over a period of nearly three years. Even with warning, she knew she wasn't going to be able to get rid of it all on short notice. There was the problem with the licenses too. Everything she had was licensed—except, of course, for the explosives, which were straightforwardly illegal—but none of it was licensed to her, and no two pieces of it were licensed to the same person. It was easy as cake getting around the licensing laws if you knew what you were doing, which Michael did, but it was not so easy explaining where you'd gotten everything if you got caught. There was also the problem that one stockpile led to another. They tried very hard to construct the kind of organization the Illuminati themselves had pioneered, with small cells isolated from other small cells, nobody knowing more than three or four of the others, most hermetically sealed off from the rest, but it hadn't worked out. They needed each other too much. It was hard being among the very few who knew what was really going on in the world. It was too easy to panic when you realized what you were up against: the assembled forces of the great in the world, the banks, the foundations, the armies. Even now, after all this time, Kathi found herself waking up in the night in a cold sweat, sure as hell that every noise she heard was one of *them* tapping his way into her house, bugging her phones, filling the air of her living room full of hypnotic gas. The one thing Kathi feared more than any other was that she'd become like those people who drifted into the movement and then drifted out again. Either they saw the truth and didn't want to believe it, or they were gotten to, nobody knew how or why. Kathi thought it was a little careless of them to hold their meetings in public and to advertise them, even if only in the little local weekly papers. *They* were everywhere, and *They* did not take chances. America on Alert was so open, it almost had to be infiltrated. Someone in the membership had to be working for Them.

"Timothy McVeigh was set up," Michael Harridan had told her, the first time she spoke to him. "Never forget that. It's the best protection you have against being set up yourself. *They* want the American people to believe that *we're* the ones who are dangerous, that *we're* a bunch of kooks who'll blow a bunch of babies to hell just because of our paranoia. That's their word for us. Paranoid. That's what they said about Randy Weaver and David Koresh. But they weren't paranoid. They were right."

Kathi had wanted to put up a little shrine to all of them, a long line of framed pictures, on the wall of her bedroom, but eventually she had decided against it. If she got arrested, or blown away by the enemy, they could use those pictures to "prove" that she was insane and dangerous. If you were insane, they could do anything they wanted to you. You didn't have any rights, the way you did if they arrested you in the ordinary way. Michael said there were hundreds of people, maybe thousands, locked away in mental institutions whose only real crime had been to understand what the Illuminati were doing and tell other people about it.

"*Paranoid* is a wonderful word," Michael said. "They call it a disease. The symptoms are anything they want them to be. One minute you're on the street, getting people to really look at what has happened to America. The next minute, you're in the loony bin, and the only way they'll let you out is if you agree to stop talking about what you know."

The problem was to strike a balance between being clean and being careful. Kathi couldn't help herself. Her nerves were shot. She wasn't Michael Harridan. She wasn't a professional on a mission. She was an ordinary forty-five-year-old woman, a little dumpy now at the beginning of middle age, easily tired at the end of a long day. She was only important because she knew what she knew, and because Michael trusted her. When the call came, she got Susan and went to work hiding the things they had to hide. They put the explosives in big black trash barrels in her basement and covered them with clothes that were so badly mildewed it was hard to be in the same room with their stench. They put the rifles in odd places that only women would think of: in the old washing machine that hadn't worked in all the time Kathi had rented this house; at the back of the cedar closet behind a cracked panel that opened into the hollow wall. All the walls in this house were hollow. It was a house that would be considered very shabbily made even today. It had probably been considered a gimcrack mess in 1894, when it was built. The Illuminati were operating here in those days too—in fact, George Washington himself was a tool of the Illuminati, a thirty-third-degree Mason who was head of his local lodge—but it took a long time for a population to be habituated to the internal rot the Illuminati had decreed for all human lives.

"They think in centuries," Michael always said. "Most people think in days, or maybe weeks. They take their time. If they didn't, people would catch on, people would get frightened. Instead, it all looks normal. We make fun of the kind of people who talk about how things aren't as good as they used to be. We treat them like cranks."

Kathi had not been able to give up all the guns. She could probably have hidden everything she had and hidden it well, but if she had, it would not have been available to her if something drastic happened. She hadn't been able to shake the feeling that something drastic was going to happen any moment now. There was a homeless man who rummaged through the garbage cans on her street every morning. He looked a lot more alert than he ought to, and lately he'd been staying closer than ever to her door. There were all the security cameras at work. Price Heaven photographed everything, even the ladies' changing rooms. There wasn't a moment when management couldn't zero in on anybody anywhere in the store. There were the transcripts she had made of the recordings from the party where Anthony van Wyck Ross had been killed. She still had them, the original and five copies, in the bottom drawer of the desk she kept in a corner of the dining room so that she could do her bills every month. She was sure they had been disturbed more than once while she was away from home, and that the desk had been moved too. It made her feel sick to her stomach to think of somebody coming into her house while she was away and going through her things. She'd rather have SWAT teams storm her front door.

The bottom line was this: Kathi no longer felt safe going anywhere, even to the bathroom, when she wasn't armed. She had therefore armed herself, out of the huge cache in the basement, as soon as Susan had left for the evening and she was alone with the nightly news. By then, of course, there were news bulletins flashing by every few minutes. CNN and

CNBC were reporting the story as if it were a political assassination, which it might well be. Kathi knew nothing about pistols. She couldn't have recited the name of any to save her life. She'd simply picked out the biggest, blackest one in the pile, passing by the smaller "ladies' guns" that might have fit more easily into her everyday purse. She was sure bigger guns would pack more of a wallop than smaller guns. Bazookas and howitzers were huge, and they packed more of a wallop than rifles. It took her nearly an hour to get the gun loaded. She didn't know what any of the terminology was supposed to mean. She didn't know how to match the gun with the bullets that belonged to it. Some bullets didn't fit into the chambers, so she discarded them. Some bullets fit but were wrong for reasons she could not divine. Every time she found what she thought was the right ammunition, she took the gun up to her bedroom and fired into a big stack of pillows she used to prop her head up when she did *Penny Press* Fun and Easy Puzzles before dropping off to sleep. The gun kicked back against her hand painfully. She'd had no idea that firing a gun could set your bones on fire. Some of the bullets didn't fire at all, though, and there was no pain then. Some of the bullets seemed to half explode inside the chamber. Eventually, she discarded any bullet that did not fit exactly. Too loose a fit, she decided, was just as bad as too big to fit at all. It was only when it was all over, and she had the bullets she needed, that she wondered if she could have done herself some real damage by experimenting the way she had. Maybe one of the bullets that rattled around too much could have made the gun blow up in her hand. She had no idea. She only knew it hadn't happened.

It wasn't until much later that it occurred to her that she might have been heard by somebody in the neighborhood. All the houses here were very close together. When neighbors heard gunshots, they didn't come over to check, but they did sometimes call the police. She sat down on her couch and waited for three hours to see if somebody would come to the door, but nobody did. Maybe none of her neighbors were home. Maybe none of them were paying attention.

Kathi had a vision of them all sitting in their living rooms, glued to their TV sets, listening to the first reports of the shooting. By then, CNN had camera crews on the spot. Kathi could see the tall wrought-iron gates that closed off the house. CNN must have had a helicopter too, because there were aerial shots of the house itself with dozens of police cars parked in front of it. People came and went on the ground: women in evening gowns; policemen in uniform; men who might have been guests or detectives or FBI agents.

"All men wear uniforms," Michael always said. "That suit and tie that men wear to work is a uniform. So's the T-shirt and jeans they wear on the weekends. The trick is to narrow choices without letting you realize they've done it. They don't like individuality, those people. Individuality is dangerous to them."

Kathi should have been at Price Heaven right this minute. Ten to six was her usual shift—but only four days a week, because Price Heaven didn't hire anybody full-time if it could help it. She had called in sick today, in spite of the fact that, being part-time, she would not get paid for being out. She had put the gun, fully loaded, into the big canvas tote bag she'd taken to carrying instead of her purse. There were laws against carrying a concealed weapon on the streets of Philadelphia, but they were the Illuminati's laws. One of the first things the Illuminati tried to do was to disarm the population. A disarmed population was unable to fight back.

The bus was bumping along on streets she didn't know. Like most people, she rarely left her own neighborhood except to go to work, and then she had a fixed routine for travel. She kept the tote bag on her lap with her hands wound through the handle. She had to physically prevent herself from reaching in to touch the gun. It gave her that much reassurance. The houses were nicer here than they were in her part of town. Most of them were brick. The people seemed to be better-dressed too. Either they had good dark coats that went all the way down past their knees, or those quilted-looking parkas people bought from L.L. Bean. Katy Davenport had had one of those parkas when they were together in school.

The bus pulled up to a stop. Kathi consulted her three-by-five card—she always wrote notes to herself on three-by-five cards; they were harder to lose than Post-it notes—and realized she was at her stop. She got up and waited for the bus's back door to open. She had the impression that people who got out the back door were less conspicuous than people who got out the front. On the street, she looked around, checking the street signs. In the rich towns out on the Main Line, there were sometimes no street signs at all. If you didn't know where you were, you didn't belong there.

"There are people who think they're well-off," Michael said, "but they only think that because they don't know how really rich people live. Really rich people live as far out of sight as they can. They don't want people to know how much they really have."

Kathi consulted her three-by-five card again. She had no idea what she was going to do now that she was here. Maybe there would be a diner where she could get a cup of coffee and some toast. It was just about all she could afford if she expected to have enough money to take the bus home. She folded the three-by-five card in half and put it in the pocket of her jacket, which was nothing at all like an L.L. Bean parka. *Cavanaugh Street*, she repeated to herself, in her head. Then she turned in the direction of the yellow police barriers that had been set up along the sidewalk two blocks down.

3

Ryall Wyndham had been waiting most of his life to be famous, and now that it had happened, he didn't know what to do with it. It wasn't that he minded the attention. There were people who got rabbit-caught-in-the-headlights syndrome, but he wasn't one of them. It hadn't occurred to him, at first, the kind of capital he would be able to make of this. He'd only wondered if he was going to be in for endless hassles of

a legal nature, because there he was, just a few hundred feet
away, and there was that prick Tony Ross exploding into
pieces *right* in front of his face. The problems of a legal nature that he had envisaged were strictly of a procedural kind.
It hadn't hit him until much later that he might be considered
a suspect, not only because he'd been on the spot but because he'd been so public about the fact that he'd loathed
Tony and all of his works. Of course, a lot of people loathed
Tony Ross. Anybody in a position like that made enemies,
without even trying, and on top of that Tony had the whole
class thing: good-looking in an emaciated, English sort of
way; tall and lean; good at sports; good with women; intellectually accomplished. Intellectually *snobbish*, that was
what Ryall thought, but there was no way to fight that manner when you were confronted with it, unless you had it
yourself. Ryall was one person who never misquoted that
line from *Hamlet* that most people mistakenly thought said
"to the manor born." It wasn't "to the manor." It was "to the
manner," and that alone convinced Ryall that Shakespeare
was a genius. There was something there he could write a
book about some day. If you told a woman like Charlotte
Deacon Ross that you thought Shakespeare was a genius,
she'd think you were a middlebrow hick, and that would be
the end of your invitations to her "intimate evenings." The
only way you could redeem yourself would be to give a lot
of money to one of her projects. Ryall did not have that kind
of money. Charlotte herself gave 150,000 dollars a year
to the opera alone. Women who wanted invitations were
known to give a fifth of that, first time out. For Ryall, there
was no substitute for staying an insider. He might consider
Shakespeare a genius, but he'd never say so where anybody
could hear him, and he would always know the name of the
literary genius of the moment. The literary genius of this
particular moment was Cynthia Ozick, who wrote excruciat-
ingly thin little novels about alienation and spiritual disloca-
tion, laced through with Yiddish folklore. Charlotte liked
Cynthia Ozick because Cynthia Ozick had once been
quoted, in *Esquire*, saying, "I am not entertained by enter-

tainment." It was the kind of thing the queen of England would say. Charlotte liked that, in spite of the fact that she thought of the queen of England as hopelessly bourgeois.

I am now making no sense whatsoever, Ryall thought, staring into the small screen of his television set. The very chicest thing was to have no television at all, and Ryall hadn't had one until three days ago, when he realized he wanted, passionately, to see himself on all these television programs he was doing. He wanted to see himself when the show aired, and he wanted to see himself on the videotape they gave him a day or two later, like a souvenir. He'd had to buy not only the television set, but a VCR as well, and that had left him not only dangerously out of pocket but upset as well. Apparently, nobody was buying videotapes anymore. They were buying DVDs. The clerk in the Radio Shack Ryall had gone to had been as disdainful as Charlotte Ross when confronted with a tourist from Topeka who "really loved art." Ryall didn't care. He only wished he'd bought a bigger set, so that he didn't have to scrunch up his eyes to see himself on the screen. In a couple of days, he was supposed to be on *Larry King Live.* Practically everybody watched *Larry King Live* except those women who were too chic to own a television set, and their children watched it. He had no trouble imagining himself at the next big fundraiser—when one of those women had the guts to give one—with all those college kids hanging off his elbows while he talked about what it was like to schmooze over coffee with Jesse Jackson and Barbara Ehrenreich.

The tape had come to its natural end. All he could see on the screen was fuzz. The cell phone he had plastered to his ear was humming. Nick Bradenton was lecturing him, again. He stepped forward and hit *rewind*. He wanted to watch the tape again. He wished he had bought a bigger set. He wished even more than he hadn't lost the remote for this one. The tape finished rewinding and he hit the *play* button again.

"Are you *listening* to me?" Nick said. "I talk and I talk, but I don't think you ever listen to me."

"I'm listening to you."

"I'm your editor," Nick said. "I'm responsible for you. And you're behaving like an ass."

"I seem to be doing all right," Ryall said. On the screen, there was a sudden sharp picture of himself, only a few seconds long, being introduced to the viewers. He *did* look like Porky Pig. He half-expected the camera to pan around to his behind and catch a view of a curly little tail poking out from the seat of his trousers. God, it was embarrassing.

"You're making yourself suspect number one in the biggest shooting of the year," Nick said. "Or maybe of the decade. You're plastered all over everything from the *National Enquirer* to *Crossfire*, and the only thing that ever comes out of your mouth is just how close you were when the bullets hit."

"I *was* close when the bullets hit," Ryall said. "I saw his face explode in front of my eyes."

"Save it for cable. You know and I know that if you really had been that close, you wouldn't have stood there watching Tony Ross's face explode. You'd have dived under the nearest table and done your best to be invisible."

Ryall sniffed. "Maybe you underestimate me, Nick. Maybe I'm not just some poof society gossip columnist."

"Have I ever called you a poof?"

Ryall didn't answer.

"Shit," Nick said.

If Ryall had had the remote, he would have been able to freeze frames to study what he was doing wrong. He was too jumpy. He talked too fast. His face was too animated. You wanted to be larger than life when you went on television, but not too larger than life, because then you looked—cartoonish.

"Try to pay attention," Nick said. "I don't give a flying fuck about your sex life, your social life, or your sexual orientation. I do care about having my office invaded by a bunch of FBI agents who need a quick fix and think they've got one in my least retiring regular columnist. This is not a game, Ryall. Got that? Tony Ross wasn't just Charlotte Ross's husband. He was the head of one of the world's most influential investment banks. He's had dinner at the White

House as a matter of course for the last four administrations. The first lady was on her way to his front door when he got offed, and the offing looks a lot like a professional hit. This might, just *might*, have some connection to international terrorism, if only because of Ross's exposure on the globalization issue. So when you go around telling everybody and his cat that you looked right into Tony Ross's eyes at the moment he was hit—"

"I *did* look into his eyes."

"—a few people, like those FBI agents, and the Bryn Mawr cops, get to thinking that the reason you knew enough to be staring at Tony in the first place was because you were either in the process of shooting him or because you had prior knowledge that he was going to be shot. And when you put that together with the fact that this mess has been the biggest boost to your career since the day you first learned how to use a computer, *some* people—"

"That's ridiculous," Ryall said. "Nobody would shoot anybody just in the hopes that it would give his career a boost. Nobody would even think of it."

"People think of everything."

"Besides," Ryall said, "you already said it. It looks like a professional hit. I couldn't carry out a professional hit if I wanted to. I can't even hit skeet."

"Somehow, I don't think that's going to be the kind of argument that impresses anybody. Look, Ryall, for God's sake. I'm just trying to save your ass. You've already got them so focused on you they can't think about anybody else. Tone it down a little."

"I don't have any reason to tone it down a little," Ryall said. He sounded constipated, even to himself. "I'm only telling the truth."

"You're only saying what you have to say to keep getting asked back to those programs," Nick said. "This isn't going to work, Ryall. You're not going to be the next Greta Van Susteren."

"I'm only telling the truth," Ryall said again. Then he pulled the cell phone away from his ear and switched it off.

He could hear Nick's voice coming out of it right to the very end. He didn't care. He could always say they'd been cut off. Nick wouldn't believe it, but he wouldn't press the issue. It happened with cell phones all the time.

On the little screen, a tiny, overanimated version of himself was jumping and squirming on the padded seat of a guest chair. He hadn't understood how the camera would catch and magnify his every mood. He didn't just look like Porky Pig. He looked like Porky Pig on amphetamines, sixty seconds before a serious psychotic break. Nick was wrong. He *would* be the next Greta Van Susteren. He had been plucked out of relative obscurity by the crush of great events and a major news story. By the time it was over, he would be familiar to everyone in America. It astonished him to realize just how much he wanted this. It went deeper than any other emotion he'd ever known. It brought him bolt upright in the middle of the night and made it impossible for him to sleep for more than four hours at a time. It was the miracle he'd been waiting for, and he hadn't even known he'd been waiting.

God, he thought. *What I wouldn't do to be rid of every last one of them.* It was too bad that this wasn't a case of serial murder, so that he could watch them dying in agony one by one. He would reserve a very special death for Charlotte Deacon Ross, who looked down on the English royal family and thought that Ryall Wyndham existed only to provide an uncontroversial escort for women temporarily unaccompanied by their husbands—that, and just the right amount of just the right kind of publicity, when she decided she wanted publicity.

The tape had run its course again. It had only been a half-hour talking heads show. Ryall pushed *rewind* and waited for the tape to scroll back to its beginning. He pushed *play* again and pulled up one of the chairs as close to the screen as he could manage. It was a question of studying and working and thinking and planning. If he did everything right, he would be released.

THREE

1

These days, the trip out to Bryn Mawr was like taking no trip at all. If you went by car—and Gregor was going by car, because Bennis was driving him—it hardly looked as if you'd left the city. The nicer parts of Brooklyn, that's what it reminded him of. The buildings were lower and set further back on the road than they were in Philadelphia proper. There was grass along the edges of the sidewalks. There were more gas stations and sit-down fast-food restaurants in small ponds of parking lots. It was not the Bryn Mawr he remembered from his childhood, when he used to come out here with friends just to drive through the winding streets and look at the big houses behind their gates. The big houses were still here. He had first met Bennis in the one that had belonged to her father, which also happened to be one of the oldest and biggest in the township and a landmark of railroad robber-baron excess. Tony Ross and his wife had their house here too. From what Gregor had seen on the night of Tony Ross's murder, that one was big enough to be a boarding school. Still, there was something about Bryn Mawr experienced the way he was experiencing it now. It was as if it had somehow, inexplicably, shrunk.

Bennis was bouncing along a widish, two-lane main road with too many cars parked at the curb on both sides. Every once in a while, she swore. Every once in a while, she slowed to a crawl so that she could read the signs on the cross streets. They were no longer in Bryn Mawr, which was fine, because Bryn Mawr didn't actually have a police station. Lower Merion did, in Ardmore, which covered Tony Ross's house. Both Bennis and the Lower Merion detective who had approached him at the Ross house after the murder had explained all this in detail, but it made his head hurt.

"Looking at you," Gregor said, "nobody would ever guess you grew up here."

Bennis shot him a sour look. "It's not my part of town. I got you to Tony and Charlotte's the other night without having to pause for anything but stop signs. Besides, I never came back here as an adult if I could help it. Before my mother got sick, I used to have her come into the city and I'd meet her there."

"You were living in Boston."

"It was too difficult for her to come to Boston. My father, as you know, was a professional bastard."

Bennis paused again, at another side street. The car behind her honked. She ignored it. "Here," she said, turning right. "I think we got a little off the track the directions said we were supposed to be on. You've been here before. How did you get here?"

"John Jackman drove me. He was chief of police here at the time."

Bennis let the subject of John Jackman's career drop. She went down a block and made another turn. She went down another two blocks and made another turn. Gregor had been here before, but he had never paid much attention to his surroundings, and now he found himself surprised that there was this sort of area in Bryn Mawr at all. It wasn't poor. The small storefronts were well-tended and the sidewalks were free of debris and street toughs propped up against buildings trying to look like they were concealing weapons. It was *modest*, that was the word Gregor wanted. He saw a small store with plate-glass windows making up almost the entirety of its sidewalk-facing wall. When he looked inside its windows, it seemed to go back forever in a narrow line, like those old railroad flats in New York. It sold mystery books. Gregor saw a copy of *Blindsighted* in the window, which he recognized because Bennis and Donna had both been reading it. Farther along, the stores got more ambiguous. One looked like a hardware store, except for the riot of wicker baskets taking up one window. One looked like a pharmacy, except that its main window had a display of what looked like hair dryers. The side streets they crossed now led to small houses set in small square lawns. Like the mystery store and the hardware store and the pharmacy, they all seemed to be made of brick.

"Here we are," Bennis said, turning into a parking lot that looked as confusing as a puzzle. There was a lot of it, but it did odd things, and seemed to accommodate too many people. There was the police station, and the township building, and a Chinese restaurant that gave an entirely new meaning to "upscale." Then there was more parking, in the back, marked only for police, which was where Bennis took them, since they'd been told to "consider themselves official" for at least this visit.

"I'll bet you anything they've got a first-class drug problem here," Gregor said. "I know the signs. They've got population. They're close to the city."

"I thought you said every place had drug problems these days," Bennis said. "Even small places that aren't close to cities."

"There are drug problems and *drug* problems," Gregor said.

Bennis was carefully locking up the car. It was a custom-painted, tangerine orange Mercedes two-seater convertible. Gregor had warned her about the color. It was like putting a strobe light on your vehicle and running a tape screaming: *Slash my tires! Crack my windshield! Run your keys through my paint!*

A door opened in the side of the building and a man in a brown wool suit looked out. Gregor looked back. The man nodded to himself and came down the small set of side steps and started across the narrow lot to them.

"Mr. Demarkian," he said. "Miss Hannaford."

"Are we late?" Bennis said. "I was trying to keep track of the time—"

"No, no," the man said. "I'm Detective Lieutenant Frank Margiotti. I don't know if you remember. We met briefly the other night—"

"I remember," Gregor said.

"We talked mostly to that other man," Bennis said.

"Marty Tackner, yes. Marty's inside waiting. We were just, ah . . . It's been a little stressful here these last few days."

"I'm sure," Gregor said.

"And then there's the FBI." Frank Margiotti paused and looked quickly back at the building. He shook his head slightly. "I mean no disrespect, mind you, but I'm not so happy with the FBI. You were an agent, weren't you?"

"An agent and later an administrator."

"Well, I really do mean no disrespect. He says you're something of a legend at the FBI. Invented the method they use to catch serial killers."

"Hardly," Gregor said.

Frank Margiotti looked back at the building again. He was a short man, no more than five foot eight, and thin the way some Italian-American men are thin, wiry and hard. Gregor did not think he was normally a nervous man, but he was nervous now, rocking back and forth on the balls of his feet, making and unmaking fists.

"It's always a pain in the ass—excuse me, Miss Hannaford—it's always a pain when we've got a crime with one of these people involved. Even people a lot less important than Tony Ross. We had the United States Secret Service out here the other day, did you know that? He did something or other with the International Monetary Fund. Tony Ross did. I'm not even sure what the International Monetary Fund is."

"It loans money to poor countries," Bennis said. "I think."

"Christ," Frank Margiotti said.

Gregor cleared his throat. "Maybe we ought to get inside and talk to whoever we're supposed to be talking to."

"We should," Frank said. "We should." He didn't move. "Did John Jackman tell you that we won't be able to officially use you as a consultant? Technically, you're a suspect in the case. Because you were there, you know."

"I know," Gregor said. "It's all right. It's quite proper, really."

"Yes, well. Nobody really takes you seriously as a suspect. Not just because you're you but because you were in at that buffet table when the shots were fired, so obviously you weren't firing them. And, uh, we did check with the FBI about your marksmanship record."

"Oh, God," Gregor said.

"It's freezing out here," Bennis said.

Frank Margiotti balled his hands into fists and then unballed them. He looked at the sky. He looked at his feet. He did not move in the direction of the building. "The thing is," he said. "Marty and I were talking. It *does* look like a professional hit. Everything the papers have been saying in that direction is true. And the FBI guy is insisting on it. Go after the professionals. And that makes sense."

"But?" Gregor said.

"For some reason, to me, it doesn't make sense," Frank said. "It just feels like bullshit. Sorry, Miss Hannaford."

"Don't worry about it," Bennis said. "I can swear like a pimp in Elvish."

"Do you have a reason for why it feels like bullshit?" Gregor asked.

"No," Frank Margiotti said.

"You want me to give you one?" Gregor asked.

Frank brightened. "Is there one? Marty feels the same way, but the FBI guy keeps telling us we're both acting like assholes. Excuse me, Miss Hannaford."

"I give up," Bennis said.

"Look at it this way," Gregor said. "Tony Ross was a very important man. An *internationally* important man. You hire a mercenary to kill him, you've got a man out there who knows who you are and who's got about as much compunction about committing another murder as you've got about having a second cup of coffee at breakfast. Which puts you in an extremely sticky situation, long-term."

"All right," Frank said. "That's good. But—it doesn't seem like the kind of thing that one of the guests could do, does it?"

"No," Gregor said. "If I were you, I'd be looking for some kind of organization. Something with a high commitment factor where the members have access to professional training. Islamic fundamentalists. One of the separatist groups, Basques, that kind of thing. Maybe the militias, but only maybe. They like to think of themselves as professionals, but they're mostly good ol' boys with delusions of grandeur."

"Timothy McVeigh's delusions of grandeur killed a hundred sixty-eight people," Frank said.

"With a fertilizer bomb," Gregor said, "not a high-powered rifle with a silencer fired at a distance in the dark at a target standing in a group of people, all of them both moving and standing close enough to him to turn into collateral damage at the least mistake in aim. Has any group tried to take credit for this?"

"Oh, hell, yes. Dozens of them. We're checking them out, but—" Frank shrugged.

"I'm going inside before I freeze to death," Bennis said. "Or he starts apologizing to me for saying *hell*."

She walked off. Gregor looked after her. Frank Margiotti looked after her too.

"Beautiful woman," Frank said. "Something of a handful and a half, I'd think."

Gregor thought about agreeing with him, but under the circumstances he thought it would be redundant.

2

The special agent's name was Walker Canfield, and Gregor Demarkian hated him on sight. Bennis had gone off somewhere in the building. Since this was an official meeting, and there was no possible way to designate her as anything but an ordinary suspect, they had to maintain at least a pretense of protecting their information, even if they knew Gregor would tell her at least some of it as soon as he got back into her car. Bennis didn't seem to mind. There was a plate of doughnuts and a coffee machine in a little room on the same corridor as the conference room. Officers and administrative personnel used it when they had a few minutes to relax in the middle of the day. Bennis walked into that, took the only available chair—a metal folding chair with a wooden seat that looked like it had been treated to sneak attacks from a buzz saw—and took out her book and her glasses. Gregor gave her a long wistful look before he allowed himself to be swept up by the official investigators. He had spent more than twenty years of his life in meetings like this one. It wasn't until he retired and moved to Cavanaugh Street that he realized how much they bored him.

Marty Tackner, Frank Margiotti's partner, turned out to be an African American who looked eerily like Sidney Poitier playing Mr. Tibbs, right down to the three-piece pinstripe suit. He also looked out of sorts and something beyond fed up. Frank introduced them. Marty nodded. Then Marty and Frank both looked at the other man in the room. That was when Gregor realized they were all in for trouble. He had spent twenty years of his life in the Bureau. He knew special agents. This one gave every indication of being the kind Gregor had always found most useless both when he was in the field and when he was working as an administrator. He had complete and utter disdain for local law enforcement. He thought he knew more about policing than the battle-scarred veterans of inner-city gang warfare. He went by the book and if the book was wrong, he'd never know it, because he'd never consider the possibility that he should have done things differently than exactly the way he had been taught at Quantico. He had no instincts. He came close to having no personality. Gregor couldn't help thinking of the line from *Men in Black: We in the FBI have no sense of humor that we know of*.

"This is special agent Walker Canfield of the Federal Bureau of Investigation," Frank Margiotti said, sounding as if he'd been coached.

Gregor had to work hard not to wince at the name. Walker Canfield: a kid who'd been born in the Midwest to a mother who had desperately wanted to send him East to college, but hadn't had the money. Walker Canfield was holding out his hand. Gregor took it.

"Mr. Demarkian," Canfield said. "I asked around about you in Washington. You've got quite a reputation."

"Do I?"

"Jack Houseman said to say hello."

"I hope he's well," Gregor said.

Walker Canfield shrugged. "It's because of him you're here. It's highly unusual, calling in a civilian to consult on a case like this. Apparently the locals do it all the time, but it's not how we operate in the Bureau. But you know that."

"I also know that the Bureau doesn't investigate much in the way of murder," Gregor said. "National parks, Indian reservations, maybe the assassination of a federal official— but none of that covers this case. So what are you doing here?"

Canfield blinked. "Lending a hand to local law enforcement."

"Uh, huh. Lending them a hand in what?"

"In the investigation." Canfield rubbed the flat of his hand against the side of his face. *Good,* Gregor thought. *I've got him nervous.*

"In the investigation of what?" Gregor asked him.

Canfield was now visibly squirming. "In the investigation of the murder. The Bureau helps local law enforcement with murders. You know that. You headed up a whole department that does that. You invented it."

"The Behavioral Sciences Department provides a clearinghouse for information in serial-killer cases with known or possible interstate implications. Do you expect that the person who killed Tony Ross is a serial killer?"

"It's the interstate implications. That's what it is," Canfield said. "Anthony van Wyck Ross was an important man. We think the killer, uh, left the scene and then left the state."

"And that's enough for the Bureau to assign a special agent full-time to the investigation? And only one?"

Canfield started rubbing his hands together. "This is a big case. Local law enforcement needs all the help it can get. The director felt—"

"Bullshit," Gregor said pleasantly. "I had lunch with the director not two months ago. He's sane." Gregor turned around and looked at Frank Margiotti and Marty Tackner. They were standing so still they were barely breathing. Gregor knew they were both fascinated and a little smug. He could just imagine how Walker Canfield had been behaving since he got here. "Would you mind?" Gregor asked Frank and Marty. "I'd like to talk to Mr. Canfield here in private."

"Anything you want," Marty said, pushing himself away from the wall he'd been standing against and heading for the door.

"We'll go get some coffee," Frank said.

Gregor waited for them to leave and shut the door behind them. Walker Canfield waited too. He had gone beyond nervous. His eyes were darting around in his skull. The palms of his hands were sweating enough to leave visible marks on the knees of his pants when he rubbed them. *Oh, fine*, Gregor thought. *No instincts, and no nerves, either.*

When the door shut, the click sounded as loud as a cap gun going off in a playground. Gregor sat down on the edge of the conference table.

"Now," he said, "let's make some sense. What is it exactly you're supposed to be doing here? And don't hand me that crap about helping law enforcement one more time."

"I do have a brief for confidential agency business."

"More crap. Try again."

"You aren't an agent of the Bureau any longer, Mr. Demarkian. You know as well as I do that it is entirely against the rules for me to divulge confidential agency business without first getting a green light from—"

"You want a green light? Fine. Let's get a green light.

There's got to be a phone around here somewhere. I'll call the director himself and we'll—"

"No," Canfield said.

"No? Why not? If this is confidential agency business you're on, the director will know about it. He has to know."

"He does know," Canfield said. "I mean, he knows in general."

"Then why not ask him?"

"It's not that simple." Canfield had calmed down, but it wasn't a good kind of calm. His palms were still sweating, and now so was his forehead. His face looked like it was covered with water. It was not a good face under the best of circumstances.

Gregor got a chair and sat down on it, straddling it, resting his chin on its back. "So," he said. "If it's not that simple, what is it?"

Canfield sighed. "I had a partner. On this investigation."

"The investigation of Tony Ross?"

"No, no. We were here a long time before that happened. Months, to tell you the truth. He went undercover and I did backup."

"Undercover as what?"

Canfield gave Gregor an odd look. Then he reached into his jacket and pulled a wad of papers from his inside jacket pocket. "Here," he said, flattening them on the conference table. "Take a look at these."

Gregor looked. *THE HARRIDAN REPORT*, the page at the top said, in bold italics. That page was stapled to three others. Then there was another set of stapled pages, the first one with the same logo. Then there was a third set. Gregor picked up the first set and scanned the text. He picked up the second and did the same. He stopped midway through the second page.

"Do you know who this is?" he asked, pointing to the name.

"Bennis Hannaford," Canfield said. "We checked her out. Comes from one of those old money Main Line families, railroad money and then steel, I think. Went to Vassar. Tends to be a little pink, to use an old-fashioned word. Writes science fiction. I don't remember everything else. I'd have to check my notes. She—"

"She's sitting down the hall eating doughnuts. She drove me in from Philadelphia today."

"What?"

"I hate sloppy work," Gregor said. "She and I have been plastered all over *People* magazine more than once. It's not like it would have been hard to find out."

"We weren't interested in her," Canfield said defensively. "She wasn't our target."

"Who was? This Michael Harridan?"

"Yeah," Canfield said. "Sort of. It's this whole organization he runs. America on Alert. You heard of them?"

"No."

"We got word about six months ago that they were buying weapons. A lot of weapons, and explosives too. So they sent us down to check it out."

"And?"

"And," Canfield said, "it was true. They weren't even being cagey about it. These two women, Kathi Mittendorf and Susan Hester, they went to gun shows. They bought on the street. They bought on the Internet. They used false ID, of course, but not good false ID. And they just kept stockpiling the stuff. They put it in Kathi Mittendorf's living room, as far as I can tell."

"Fine. We're making progress. At least we're finally talking about something the Bureau really does investigate. What about ATF?"

"We got a guy at ATF we're feeding information to, yes," Canfield said, "but we're trying to be careful. These conspiracist groups are paranoid as hell. They think there's an agent of the New World Order behind every bush. We didn't want to land a bunch of agents in their lap all at once, if you see what I mean."

"Yes," Gregor said. "I do see. So you played backup, and your partner went undercover. Undercover as what?"

"As somebody interested in joining the movement."

"And that's possible? How do you make an approach in a case like that?"

Canfield got up and started to pace. "It's not like those Islamic groups, where you've got cells and nobody is supposed to know anybody else in the cells. The conspiracist groups are much more open, if that makes any sense. They give lectures that are open to the public, they sell books, like that. We sent Steve to one of the lectures."

"Steve was your partner?"

"Steve Bridge, yeah. We went down to Price Heaven and got him a pair of chinos and a cheap polo shirt. He really looked the part. And he went to a couple of their lectures, and after a while he started getting asked to meetings."

"And?"

"And nothing, really," Canfield said. "He went to meetings, but they didn't trust him right off. They wouldn't. So he tried to be helpful and he tried to sound like he'd gotten religion, so to speak, and they seemed to be buying it. He got the names of the members, the real ones. We did some background checks."

"Why didn't you raid them? You had the weapons violations. You knew where the weapons were. ATF should have been able to go in there and clean them out."

"We wanted to get a line on Michael Harridan himself."

"And did you?"

"No," Canfield said. "He didn't come to meetings, at least not in the flesh. And he didn't give lectures or attend them. We were pretty certain that the women had met him at some point, because they were always talking about him and the things he said and the things he did, but we weren't able to figure out when they saw him or where."

"Did it occur to you that there might not be any him to see?" Gregor asked. "Maybe the two women invented him for reasons of their own—because the kind of men who join this kind of movement don't take too well to leadership by women, or something like that."

"We thought of it, but we knew it wouldn't fly," Canfield said. "It really wouldn't. Neither of them had the technical skills to produce the newsletter, for one thing. And it was more than that. At one point the group had a remote bug with a satellite relay planted at the offices of the City Planning Commission in Philadelphia. Not one of those deals where you had to have a van parked practically out in front of the place, but a real relay—"

"You must be joking."

"I'm not. And it worked too. Steve sat in Kathi Mittendorf's living room and listened to the feed for half an hour. He said the quality was lousy, but the thing worked. Neither of the women could have done that. Whoever this Michael Harridan is, he knows what he's doing and he's good at it. He's also smart enough not to show his face."

"So Steve never actually saw him," Gregor said.

"Not as far as I know," Canfield said.

"Which means what?"

Canfield looked at the floor, frowning. "Meaning, Steve might have seen him. Back at the beginning of last week, maybe three or four days before the Ross shooting."

"What makes you think that? Did he say so?"

"No. He didn't say anything. That's the point."

"I'm not getting the point," Gregor said.

Canfield sighed. "That's when Steve went missing. Poof. Gone. Disappeared. That's the last time I saw or heard from him."

"Jesus Christ," Gregor said. "He's *gone?*"

"I didn't think anything of it at first," Canfield said desperately. "It wasn't all that unusual for me not to hear from him for a day or two. We really were being very careful to keep him undercover. But then the Ross thing happened, and he didn't surface—"

Gregor took a deep breath. "You haven't told the Bureau," he said. "You haven't told anybody that he's gone."

Canfield cleared his throat. "I didn't know there was anything to tell," he said carefully. "And then the Ross thing happened and I was distracted—"

"Jesus Christ," Gregor said again. "I walked in here and took one look at you and thought you were the kind of idiot who couldn't imagine ever doing anything except by the book, and here you've got a special agent, your own partner, missing for—what?—ten days now? And you haven't called anybody. You haven't notified anybody. Have you done anything sensible? Have you searched the morgues?"

"I couldn't do that without—"

"Never mind," Gregor said. "Let's get the two of them back in here and start making phone calls. Your career just died."

"There's something else," Canfield said.

"What?"

"Well, you saw that newsletter. Harridan already had his sights set on that party at the Ross's. The last thing Steve told me the last time I talked to him was that there was supposed to be another feed. At the party itself. Harridan was going to bug the party and the women were supposed to sit somewhere and take notes and make tapes."

"Did you do a sweep of the house for bugs?"

"Of course I didn't. The secret service might have done a sweep for bombs and that kind of thing, though. Because the first lady was coming. We did inform the Bureau that America on Alert was interested in that party."

"Thank God for small favors."

"I'm not anywhere near as stupid as you're trying to make me out to be," Canfield said. "What I did made perfect sense, whether you're willing to accept that or not. When somebody's undercover, they often have to break off communications for short periods of time. It's not unusual. I didn't want to do anything that might blow his ID."

"Right," Gregor said.

Then he got off his chair, opened the door to the conference room, and called down the hall for Frank Margiotti and Marty Tackner to come back in.

3

Usually, Gregor Demarkian told Bennis Hannaford everything he was thinking. She was one of those people who made it almost useless not to, when she focused herself on you. Tibor sometimes said she had X-ray vision. This time, he was silent most of the way back to the city in the car, and she did not seem inclined to question him. The ride back was depressing in too many ways. Gregor hated this time of the year. What vegetation was visible from the highway was either dead or pinched. The evergreen trees looked as if they'd had all the sap drained out of them. There was far too much concrete. Gregor knew nothing about highway design, or about who designed them. He did know that in some places the highway didn't block out all evidence of normal life, but that here it did. *Government incompetence* were the words going around in the back of his skull, but he wasn't about to say them out loud. He hated those old men who had nothing to talk about except how much more awful young people were today than they had been back when they themselves had been young, and the government too. What bothered him was that he couldn't keep his mind off Canfield and what he'd done, or not done. The fact of it was stuck in his brain, and he knew that in spite of the phone calls he'd made from the Bryn Mawr police station—and that he'd made Canfield make—he'd do some calling on private lines as soon as he got to his phone at home. Maybe all the complaining older people and conservatives did had some basis. Gregor couldn't imagine anybody he'd been at Quantico with pulling a stunt like this. Then he thought about it some more, and decided it wasn't true. He hadn't heard of anybody doing exactly what Canfield did, but he had heard of them doing some pretty strange and stupid things, and sometimes when the stupidity was especially high, people were killed. For some reason, it was always worse when Bureau agents got together with agents from Alcohol, Tobacco and Firearms. Gregor could remember Jack Houseman the first time they'd had to deal with ATF in the flesh.

"What the hell do these idiots think it means?" Jack had said. "Drink, smoke, and shoot at stuff?"

They were off the highway and in the city. They must have been there for some time, because the neighborhoods were beginning to look familiar. Gregor suddenly remembered that Canfield had always spoken of Steve Bridge in the past tense. He'd done it right at the beginning: I *had* a partner. Gregor was not one of those people who pined for the glory days of the FBI. He had come in at the tail end of J. Edgar Hoover's reign, and as far as he was concerned, the old man had been a raving psychopath. A raving psychopath with power was not a comfortable thing. Still, there were levels of minimum professionalism, the least to be expected code of conduct, something, and Canfield had passed all those things on his descent into absurdity. Gregor was still convinced that a man with a mission was the most dangerous man on earth, and that a man on a holy mission carved a special place for himself in hell. He now thought that a man who took nothing seriously might be almost as bad.

They were on Cavanaugh Street. Gregor had no idea how they'd gotten there. He looked around and saw nobody he knew, and not much of anybody he did not know. Bennis had pulled up to the curb in front of the brownstone house where their apartments were.

"Aren't you going to park in the garage?" he said.

"I've got to go pick up Tibor at the hospital," Bennis said.

"I thought you and Donna were going together and using her van."

"We are, but I don't have the time to put this in the garage now, so I thought I'd leave it here. Are you all right?"

Gregor reached in through his coat and jacket and came up with the folded wad of papers that were the copies he'd made of Canfield's copies of *The Harridan Report.* He opened the wad and rifled through it. He found the one he wanted and handed it over.

"Halfway down the page," he said. "Tell me what you think of that."

Bennis checked the car clock out of the corner of her eye, but she took the papers and scanned them. "Oh," she said. "Look at this. 'Chairwoman of the event is Charlotte Deacon Ross, a Rockefeller on her mother's side and married to a collateral member of the House of Morgan, who also happens to be Anthony van Wyck Ross, head of Lessard Cole, one of the world's biggest and most important investment banks. Vice chairwoman is Bennis Hannaford, a member of the notorious Duke family.' "

"Is that accurate?" Gregor asked her.

"About what?" Bennis said. "Charlotte's mother wasn't a Rockefeller, she was only a second cousin or something. Not that you weren't made to know that, Charlotte being Charlotte. Although she was good. You could never tell just how she got it across."

"What about what it says about you?"

"It's crap. Not only aren't we members of the Duke family, my father wouldn't talk to them at parties. The whole thing with Doris, you know—I mean, she was my father's generation. One of the things about the old Main Line, and the people like them elsewhere, is that they have an incredible number of rules about how to bring up children, because you do have to worry about it. If you don't give the child a decent foundation, he's going to get hold of a forty-million-dollar trust fund when he's eighteen or twenty-one or whatever and go completely nuts, which is what Doris did. My father thought that she'd been left to run wild as a child and not taught proper morals, which considering what he was like is something of a laugh. Of course, Doris wasn't brought up in Philadelphia, but that wasn't supposed to matter."

"Was she really," Gregor checked the newsletter again, " 'ritually murdered in 1993'? What does that mean, exactly, 'ritually murdered'?"

"It means that Doris has been prime meat for tabloid journalism for most of a century. She did die in 1993. She was eighty, for God's sake. And there was some suggestion of foul play, but mostly because Doris did the one thing every old money family has nightmares about, and that was leave a ton of money to her butler. I forget his name. People said he and a doctor had deliberately given Doris an overdose of morphine but, for goodness sake, how could anybody tell? She'd been drowning herself in alcohol and drugs since her teens, and in men too. Hot and cold running affairs all her life, and she was rich enough so that in the end she could buy what she couldn't attract, and from all indications, she did just that. One of her cousins wrote the nastiest book about it about ten years ago."

"So what is this about 'ritually murdered'?"

Bennis sighed. "You ought to spend more time on the Internet," she said. "These guys are all over the place. Your basic choice is between the religious ones and the secular ones, but even the secular ones go on about satanic ritual abuse, which is supposed to be going on everywhere, right under our noses, and the reason we never find any of the bodies of the tens of thousands of infants supposedly murdered in rituals every year is that the Illuminati eat them, or something."

"What?"

Bennis pulled down the visor over the steering wheel and got one of the deposit receipts she kept there. She checked the date, then reached for the pen in the cup holder. Then she put the deposit slip on the steering wheel, wrote something on it, and passed the slip to Gregor.

"There," she said. "While I'm out getting Tibor, get online and go to that. It's an ad for tapes and things that they're selling but if you scroll down, you'll find complete descriptions of what's on the tapes, and that should give you a pretty good idea of what is going on."

Gregor looked at the slip of paper. Written on it was a single line in dark red ink: http://home.inreach.com/dov/cdlcons.htm.

"While you're at it," Bennis said, "you might do searches for David Icke and Cisco Wheeler. Icke is supposed to be an 'investigator.' They all give themselves these titles, you wouldn't believe it. Anyway, he's got nothing in the way of serious journalistic credentials, but he does run a Web site. Cisco Wheeler is even better."

"Who is Cisco Wheeler?"

"She's a lecturer on the one-world conspiracy, satanic ritual abuse circuit. She *claims* to have come from one of the richest and oldest families in the country and to have been ritually abused as a child because, she says, that's what these families do to their children to make sure they're mind-controlled."

"Okay." Gregor was beginning to feel as if his head was about to explode.

"But the thing is," Bennis said, "*I'm* from one of the country's richest and oldest families and trust me, we all know each other. If we haven't met directly, we've got connections through aunts and uncles and cousins and grandparents. We go to the same schools. We go to the same dancing classes. We go to the same camps. We're in each other's weddings. And as for Cisco Wheeler, not only have I never heard of her, neither has anybody else I know. It's remarkable what kind of bull you can throw just because most people don't know what it takes to get into the *Social Register*."

"What does it take?"

"Not a whole hell of a lot," Bennis said. She grabbed her coat from the seat behind her—for some reason, Bennis couldn't stand to drive wearing a coat—and popped open her door. "Listen," she said. "This stuff is everywhere. We're in the midst of a vast conspiracy to bring about a One World Government that will end freedom as the United States has known it. The conspiracy goes back to the Merovingian dynasty—"

"The what?"

"Ask Tibor. Back to the early Middle Ages. The very early Middle Ages. Anyway, it looks like people rise and fall in the hierarchies of the world, but it's all a smoke screen. It's all the same thirteen families, and then every once in a while they pick some talented kid from a poor background to advance. That's just so that the rest of us won't catch on that the game is always rigged. They picked Bill Clinton, for instance. They established contact with him at an early age and have been training him ever since. The Rhodes Scholarship program is actually a training ground for Illuminati operatives. The UN is an Illuminati institution, and any minute now it's going to take over the whole world and impose One World Government on us. Then it will outlaw Christianity, and we'll all be MKUltra mind slaves, which most of us are already, because the CIA has been brainwashing us through our television sets and the chemicals in fast food for years—"

"Wait," Gregor said.

Bennis got out of the car. "Go look it all up on the Web. I've got to get Tibor or he'll probably have a meltdown. The bed's already made up in the second-floor apartment. Grace is going to come down and ask you for the key. She made Tibor something or other and she wants to leave it on the counter in the kitchen. And don't worry about this *Harridan Report* thing. There's a ton of stuff like that out there. It's harmless, it's just completely nuts."

"Timothy McVeigh wasn't harmless."

"Most of these guys are nothing at all like Timothy McVeigh. They're people who are profoundly disappointed in their lives, and this gives them a way to feel important. They're not unsuccessful cogs in a big machine run by people who are smarter and more ambitious than they are. They're the last defense of freedom against an enemy so vast and so secret, most people don't even know it's there. But they know. They can see what other people cannot. They're *smarter* than practically anybody. And that's all they need."

Bennis was all the way out of the car. She slammed the door shut. Gregor thought that her description would have fit Timothy McVeigh perfectly well, except that McVeigh had needed more than just to feel how smart he was. And there was the Posse Comitatus, whose members were accused in at least one murder of a federal officer in the eighties. Gregor was sure he had read something about the Posse Comitatus being opposed to One World Government. He opened his door and got out onto the street, feeling as if he was climbing out of a deep well. When Mercedes offered bucket seats, it meant *bucket* seats. He shook out his coat and then leaned back in to lock Bennis's door. He locked his own and shut it. He had no idea what time it was, but the air was grey and dark and felt wet even though it wasn't raining. If it did anything today, it would probably snow.

He went around to the sidewalk and then into the front

door of his building, hearing the sounds of Grace's harpsichord pounding down from the fourth floor as soon as he walked into the foyer. Maybe he should spend more time on the Internet. He had never paid much attention to conspiracy theories. The few he'd run into had been about the FBI, and they'd gotten so many of the details wrong that he hadn't had the patience to take them seriously. He looked at the slip of paper Bennis had given him. Maybe, when he was finished calling the director and Jack Houseman both and letting them know how he felt about Walker Canfield, he'd brave the Internet on Bennis's computer and go looking for David Icke and Cisco Wheeler and all the rest of them.

He started up the stairs, and stopped. He turned around, walked back through the foyer, and went out the front door. Standing on the low stoop there at the top of three shallow steps, he could just see the front sidewalk-lined edge of the place where Holy Trinity Church still was, sort of, almost. The yellow warning bands were still up, and probably would be for months, even after reconstruction started. He put his hands in the pockets of his coat and wished he didn't feel so hollow. The world had done very odd things to itself in the years since he'd been a child on this street. The big picture was bad enough: wars and police actions and terrorism. It was the small picture he truly hated. The whole country was descending into reflexive madness. When had people stopped knowing that witches who did magic were just pretend? When had superstition and book burning become respectable hobbies for small-town mayors who wanted to make the world safe from Halloween and Harry Potter? When had these people—he looked down at the slip of paper he still held crumpled in his hand—when had this sort of blatantly hysterical irrationality found a following large enough to impinge on the everyday world?

He stopped trying to get a look at Holy Trinity, turned around, and went back into the building. Grace's harpsichord was as loud as he'd ever heard it. Maybe she had her door open, waiting to hear Tibor or Bennis or Gregor himself come home. Gregor went up the stairs passing by the door of old George Tekemanian's ground-floor apartment. Usually, he liked visiting with old George. Today, even if George had been there, Gregor had nothing to say.

FOUR

1

No one had to tell Charlotte Deacon Ross how to behave. Even her mother, who had been widely considered to be the last of the old-line Main Line grande dames, had been in awe of her. The key to civilization was self-control and personal responsibility, Charlotte always thought, and then she went about doing what mattered immeasurably not only to herself but to the small world she lived in. It was a world that had not changed in many generations, although the people in it had washed in and out much faster recently than they had when Charlotte was a girl. There was still a tight little world of people who owned and ran the banks, people who owned and ran the major law firms, people who owned and ran the largest corporations—or at least sat on their boards; nobody wanted to be exposed, legally, the way a chief operating officer was in this age of regulation. There was still that solid phalanx of people whom the public never saw, deliberately obscure for their own protection. They still all knew each other and sent their children to the same half-dozen prep schools and the same half-dozen universities, and—contrary to public opinion—those things still mattered. They still lived in ways that most ordinary people would find odd and alienating. Charlotte could always tell, when one of her girls brought friends home for the weekend, which were the ones who would last and which were the ones who would not. The ones who would not kept looking for a television set, as if somehow a house was incomplete without it. There was a television set in Charlotte's house, but it was in the big common room in the servants' wing.

Now she sat in the big wing chair in the morning room, her embroidery in her lap, and looked out at a late afternoon as grey and depressing as the one on the day Tony died—on the day he was *murdered*, she amended, because part of taking responsibility was calling things what they really were. The word had no resonance in her mind. *Murdered murdered murdered*, she thought, and she might as well have been saying *kumquat*. She kept waiting to feel something besides cold and clearheaded and calm. If she had had a tape of the scene as it had happened, she would have watched it: Tony standing so close to her; Tony's body jerking backwards; Tony's face exploding. It had been nothing at all what she had been led to expect from her favorite detective writer—in fact, the only detective writer she read—P. D. James. She might have seen something similar if she'd gone to certain kinds of movies, but she didn't. The few movies she saw were Italian or French, and usually had to do with the deaths of marriages. That was a concept Charlotte didn't understand. Marriages did not die, in her opinion, unless they had been improperly made to begin with. Marriages were not about happiness, or compatibility, or sex. It fascinated her to watch people, even fictional people, who seemed to think that getting divorced was like giving back a boy's fraternity ring, something trivial that you did because your emotions were shallow, or because you were bored and wanted to do something else for a while.

The oddest thing about what had happened when Tony died was the blood. There had been so very much blood. It had come spurting out of his face as if his head were a grapefruit and somebody was squeezing it. There was blood on the slate that lined the edge of the drive. There was blood on the hedges that made a buffer between the slate and the house. Then Tony had turned and taken a step toward her and there was blood on her dress, running down the front of it in rivulets.

On the other side of the room, Charlotte's oldest daughter, Marianne, stood leaning on the white molded mantle of the fireplace. She had been crying, but all that was left of that was the red bloating around her eyes and mouth. Marianne was a brilliant girl, but not pretty. Charlotte looked away from her to the small Chippendale desk where Miss Parenti had piled the stiff white linen cards she would use to write thank-you notes to the people who sent flowers. She would do every note by hand, and Miss Parenti would provide her with a log that told her some little something about those people she had actually met on one occasion or another. A lot of the flowers would come from people who knew Tony professionally, or who worked at the bank, or who had some other ceremonial reason for marking his passing, and she could acknowledge those formulaically. She had come to hate the flowers that had piled up in her foyer these last few days. She hadn't expected people to refrain from sending them, even though she had placed one of those notices in the paper—the family would appreciate donations to the Philadelphia Women's Hospital in lieu of flowers—but she hadn't anticipated how overwhelmingly awful they would smell. She no longer went out to the front of the house unless she had to, and she never had to. She was grateful for the gates that kept the reporters from pressing their noses against her windows and going through her trash.

Marianne was a senior at Harvard. If this didn't throw her completely, she would graduate summa and go on to Oxford in the fall. Tony had been tremendously proud of her. The other three girls were more along the lines they were expected to be. Julia was a sophomore at Colby Sawyer, majoring in Dartmouth boys. Cordelia and Sarah were still at the Madeira School in Virginia, dreaming of coming out in the way that debutantes had come out in the thirties. Charlotte had no idea if they were thinking of their father. They weren't crying openly, as Marianne was, but that said less than it might have in another kind of family.

Marianne shifted from one foot to the other. She was tall and thin, as Tony had been, and she had Tony's great hooked beak of a nose that had made him look English to people who didn't know who he was. It made Marianne look lopsided.

"I still don't understand what you think you're doing," she said. "You don't know anything about the bank. How can you possibly take over where Daddy left off?"

"I don't intend to take over," Charlotte said. "I wouldn't dream of it."

"Then why do you want to sit on the board?"

"Because I like to look out for my own interests. In my mother's day, women never did that kind of thing. Even when I was growing up, the policy was to keep the girls in the dark and train the boys to take over. But the world changes. Sometimes it even changes for the better. I want to keep an eye on things. I don't trust David Alden."

"David won't take over at the bank," Marianne said. "He's too young. It'll be one of the vice presidents or something, or they'll bring in somebody from the outside."

"David will still be there, and he'll still be in an important position. No matter how the board feels about him—and, by the way, I think the board likes him. Your father liked him—but no matter how they feel, David knows more about what your father was doing and what needs to be done in the wake of his death than anybody else. Sheer prudence will make them keep him on, and I do not delude myself that I'll be able to change their minds just because I decide to sit on the board. I still think it makes sense to be careful. Your father always thought you might like to go into the bank one day."

"Go into the bank," Marianne said. "You sound like Dickens."

"Of course I don't. Dickens was a vulgar writer, far more vulgar than that silly man, who was that, Henry Miller. One of the Biddle women gave a party for him back in the days when his books were banned because they were supposed to be pornography, and everybody was incredibly impressed with how avant-garde she was. Even I was impressed, and I was only a child. We were more easily impressed in those days."

"Wouldn't it make sense to talk about it?" Marianne said. "He died, for God's sake. Somebody blew his face off. He was assassinated."

"Don't exaggerate."

"I'm not exaggerating. That's what the papers are saying. He was assassinated. Some terrorist group killed him because they oppose globalization, or something, and he was one of the chief architects of globalization. You should see the British papers. My roommate had her mother send them to me."

"The British papers are always foul. There's no reason to pay attention to them."

"And then there's this delay," Marianne said, as if she hadn't heard. "It's been almost five days. It's going to be six at least before we have the body back, and then we'll have a wake and a funeral with something that's—that's—decomposing."

Charlotte picked up her embroidery. She didn't embroider in any serious way. She only liked to have it with her to give herself something to do with her hands. "The casket will be closed for the wake," she said, "and the embalming will take care of the smell, if that's what you're worried about. The delay is unpleasant, but there isn't anything I could have done about it. The law requires an autopsy in cases of violent death, and in this case there were other considerations pertinent to the investigation—"

"You sound like a press release."

"—that held up the return of the body to us. There's no point in making a fuss, especially in public. You know what happens. The papers fill up with op-ed columns deploring the way in which the rich expect special treatment not available to ordinary mortals."

"Well, don't we?"

"Not where it can be reported on in the newspapers, Marianne, no."

"Doesn't it bother you? Somebody hated him enough to kill him, somebody he probably didn't even know, at least not personally."

Charlotte put the embroidery back in her lap. The truth of it was, she hated embroidery, just as she hated needlework, just as she hated almost all the things her mother had taught her in the way of "ladylike pastimes," as if the mere fact of having a vagina made it incumbent on her to prick her fingers with needles. Besides, she was bad at it, and she'd never had much patience for what she was bad at.

"Most people," she said carefully, "do not care who your father was, or what he did. Most people care only about celebrities, and your father made it part of his lifework never to be a celebrity."

"He's certainly a celebrity now," Marianne said. "And you know there are going to be hundreds of people at the funeral. Onlookers. People off the street. And the press. And the police. He's not going to be able to stay obscure in the midst of all that."

"It's not like we're movie stars," Charlotte said. "It's not like we're the Kennedys. If we maintain a solid policy of noncooperation, it will all blow over in time."

"Someone will right a book about it."

"Probably. But he won't get any help from me."

"Maybe they'll make a miniseries of it," Marianne said. "Isn't that a wonderful prospect? People are fascinated by these nuts, you know, they really are. Timothy McVeigh. All those people."

"Timothy McVeigh murdered one hundred sixty-eight people and obliterated most of a block in Oklahoma City. You're exaggerating again."

"I'm trying to get you to *react*," Marianne said. "God, you're impossible. You're worse than impossible. You're living in a fantasy world."

"No," Charlotte said seriously, "the one thing I'm not doing is living in a fantasy world."

Marianne ran her hand through her hair. It was too long and too thick and too haphazardly cared for. Then she turned around and walked out of the room. Charlotte listened as her footsteps receded down the hall, heavy thuds of expensive running shoes landing on carpet. When Charlotte was sure Marianne was gone, she leaned over and pulled a small folded sheaf of papers out from under her. She'd been reading them when Marianne first came in, but she'd known, instinctively, that she shouldn't be caught at it. She leaned over, pulled up the ottoman, and put up her feet. Then she flattened the papers on her lap.

THE HARRIDAN REPORT, the first one said, at the very top, as if whoever had desktop published this did not want to waste paper. *The Reptilian Connection.*

Charlotte ran one delicate fingernail—polished clear, not too long, not too sharp—along the side of her nose.

One of the few things we know for certain about both the Deacon and the Ross families is that they're part of the reptilian bloodline. They look human, and people who have been brainwashed by the system believe that they are just lucky: lucky to have been born rich; lucky to have been born talented; lucky to have been born better than the rest of us. Well, they were born better than the rest of us, with powers of intelligence and concentration no ordinary human being could possibly attain. They are the descendants of the intermarriage of humans with something the ancients called "gods," the Serpent Race described in the holy books of every culture from Sumer to Rome. From this hybrid race came the ruling families of all the countries of the world, first in the Middle East and Europe, and then, through the conquests of the British Empire, in Asia, Africa and America.

If you don't believe me, check for yourself. All forty-two men who have been presidents of the United States can trace their lineages back to Charlemagne, just like the British nobility and the great royal houses of the Bourbons and Saxe-Gotha. This is the "divine right of kings" so vigorously defended for centuries and only apparently abandoned in the tremendous pressure of the world's peoples for freedom from reptilian rule. The rule did not end, however, and has not ended to this day. It only changed its public face. Now we are presented with "choices" between possible rulers. We can pick between George W. Bush or Al

*Gore, or between John Major and Tony Blair. The real-
ity is too far under the surface for most people to notice. There is no choice. Bush and Gore are descended
from the same bloodlines. So are John Major and Tony
Blair. So is the Pope. So is Gorbachev. All our
"choices," between "capitalist" and "communist," between "democracy" and "dictatorship," between "liberal" and "conservative," between "religious" and
"athiest," all of them are false choices, because in
each case we are offered nothing but what the Illuminati want us to have. The Illuminati do not care if we
call the system we live under "free market" or "social
democratic." They only care that they rule.*

*We are coming upon a time of great persecution.
Anthony van Wyck Ross was not murdered by men and
women like us, who know the truth and want to expose
it to the world—but by the Illuminati who will do everything in their power to make it look as if we are at fault,
to brand us extremists, terrorists, and lunatics. Anthony
van Wyck Ross was murdered by the same people who
destroyed the World Trade Center on September 11,
2001. In other words, he was murdered by his own, by a
CIA operative on the direct orders of George W. Bush.
Long powerful and reliable in the corridors of power,
Ross had begun to disintegrate mentally in the last
months of his life, the results of alcohol and drug
abuse brought on by his attempts to ease the painful
memories of the sexual abuse that was the foundation
of his training as a member of the Illuminati. It was
feared that he would no longer be able to keep the secrets he had been entrusted with. The most dangerous
secret, the one thing the Illuminati cannot allow the
public to understand at just this point in time, is that
the September 11 massacres were carried out on the
orders of the United States government, with the help
of the British, French, German and United Nations
power elites. Ross was himself involved in the planning*

of those massacres. If he couldn't shut up—and he couldn't, not any longer—he would have to be silenced.

Charlotte licked her lips and folded the sheaf of papers in half again. It was like being trapped inside the mind of a lunatic, imprisoned in his skull. She had no idea where this thing had come from, or who had put it squarely in the middle of her desk here in the morning room, so that it would be the first thing she would find. She had no idea who *had* been leaving them here, for months. She was sure Miss Parenti had had nothing to do with it. She was not sure the servants had not. The idea that somebody who worked for her read this . . . *thing* . . . on a regular basis made her feel as if she had been turned to ice.

She got out of her chair and took the sheaf of papers with her. She should turn them over to the police. She should outline the entire incident, the way they were lying right on top of her green felt ink blotter, where she couldn't miss them. She should make out a list of the people in her service and the people who had been to visit during the day. She did none of these things. She threw the sheaf of papers in the fire and stood by to watch them burn. She counted the seconds until the flames had turned the papers to ash.

Then she left the morning room and walked down the hall to the small powder room near the back stairs. She needed to throw up.

2

It would have been better if there had been someone on the street when Father Tibor Kasparian got home—not a big welcoming committee; he wasn't up for that, and he had a feeling he'd get it whether he wanted it or not in an hour or two—but just someone familiar, bringing home groceries, buying the paper, moving a car that had been parked too long at the curb. Sometimes you needed the ordinary and the everyday. They were all that took the edge off the frightening and bizarre. He thought ahead to the crush that would develop as soon as word got out that he was home. Lida Arkmanian was probably watching from the big plate-glass window in her living room right this minute. When it started, it would be inexorable. People would drift in to Bennis's old apartment, scrupulously *not* talking about why it was free for somebody else to move into for a month or two, bringing food. Eventually, the women would ignore him and drape themselves over all of Bennis's furniture to talk about who was getting married and who was getting divorced and who was going to graduate in the spring from what really fancy college in Massachusetts. Paper plates and plastic forks would accumulate on tables, brought in by whichever one of them realized that the last thing he'd want on his first day home was a lot of dishes to do. Books would accumulate on the coffee table in the living room, wrapped in tissue paper and tied with grosgrain ribbon. His suitcases would be laid out on Bennis's freshly made-up bed. He had no idea what he would do when they were all gone. It hadn't occurred to him until just this moment that he hadn't been alone for a single minute since the explosion had ripped through Holy Trinity Church.

There was a cold wind coming down the street as he got out of the car, blowing stray pieces of paper along the gutters. He turned in the direction of the church and tried to get a look, but Bennis was right. There was nothing to see from here. It was too far up, and the church had been set back a little from the sidewalks.

"I think I only imagined I could see it all that time," she'd told him, while they'd still been at the hospital. "I knew it was there, so I thought any dark space in the vicinity must be the church and I must be seeing it."

Tibor did not point out to her then, or remind her now, that at the beginning of last week the church had been much closer to the sidewalk than it was now. It had had an extra wall. At least, that was what the news programs had said when he'd watched them on television in the hospital, even though the doctor hadn't been sure he ought to be allowed. There had been one clear photograph of the front of Holy Trinity in daylight, the wall mostly gone, the vestibule destroyed, the long rows of pews covered in rock and sand. It had been taken from too far back for Tibor to be able to tell what had happened to the altar. It made him nauseated to realize that he had not seen the actual church since the explosion had happened. He hadn't been there to see it. He thought he would have gone crazy in his hospital bed if he'd had to listen to nonstop news reports about the explosion, but there weren't any. The explosion was not big news. The death of Anthony van Wyck Ross was.

He went up the steps to the tall stone house where Bennis and Gregor lived, along with old George Tekemanian on the ground floor and Grace Feinman on the fourth. As soon as he stepped into the foyer, he could hear Grace's harpsichord above him. She was playing Bach. He turned toward the mailboxes and stopped. His mail would not be here. It would be down at the apartment behind the church, where he was not allowed to go because of the structural damage caused by the blast.

"What do they do with my mail?" he said to Donna and Bennis coming up behind him.

"They leave it at your apartment," Bennis said. "Donna and I went over and got it and brought it to you in the hospital, except for what are obviously condolence cards. We left them here."

"I thought nobody could go into the apartment."

"That was only the first couple of days," Donna said. "While they were working things out. We've been going over there all the time, since. Bennis has been packaging up your books."

"Don't worry," Bennis said. "I've been classifying them and labeling the boxes. There's a crack in the wall of your bedroom and a leak in the roof there now. That's the wall the apartment shared with the back of the church vestibule and the first part of the church room, the—"

"Sacristy," Tibor said.

"That, yes." Bennis looked relieved. "Anyway, there's a crack there and the roof is damaged. That's why you can't go back right away. But it's not like the church itself. You could go over there and look through things when you feel stronger."

"Where are the books you put in boxes?"

"In my back room," Donna said. "Don't worry. Russ is terribly impressed. He said he never realized you had such a range before, like with the science books."

Tibor could have told her that he didn't really understand the science books, which was true. He read Richard Dawkins and made notes on his books, but he found the details impossible to assimilate into a brain that had been trained from adolescence in literary explication. Instead he started up the big swing-back flight of steps that went to the second floor. At the landing, he paused and looked out the window. There was nothing to see but the wall of the building next door. He went up the rest of the flight and paused politely before Bennis's front door.

"Stay as long as you like," Bennis said, brushing past him with a suitcase and pulling him along with her as she went. "I've got no need for this place at the moment, and I won't have for a while. Spread out. My cleaning lady will be in twice a week. If you leave your laundry out on the bed, she'll do it for you. There's enough food in the refrigerator for a week, and there will be more. You know how that works—"

"Stop," Tibor said.

"We're making him tired," Donna said. "Maybe we should let him take a nap."

"I don't need a nap," Tibor said. "I'm fine. I was always fine."

"You were so fine, they kept you in the hospital for observation for over four days," Bennis said.

Tibor shook his head. "They kept me in the hospital because you guaranteed the bill."

"Did you really?" Donna said.

"Better safe than sorry," Bennis said. Then she looked

away. "God, I've started talking in clichés. I thought disaster was supposed to bring out the best in people."

Tibor moved into the apartment, through the foyer, into the living room. Bennis's papier-mâché models were everywhere, lunar landscapes next to verdant green hills, knights and ladies leaning into each other next to castles with outsized towers that looked tall enough to rival Babel. This was what Bennis used the apartment for, now that she spent all of her private time with Gregor. She wrote here, and she built her models so that she'd be able to see the landscapes she was inventing. Tibor sat down on the long sofa and looked out the window at Lida Arkmanian's living room. No one was in it.

"Are you sure you're all right?" Bennis asked, sitting down in the big overstuffed chair that faced the couch. The coffee table was huge and square and—if you really looked at it—in the shape of a gigantic antique book lying on its side. Donna stayed standing in the back, moving from foot to foot, restless.

"I'm fine," Tibor said. "I need to talk to my bishop. There was no liturgy here on Sunday, because I was in the hospital "

"Some people went over to Radnor," Donna said quickly. "It was all right."

"It was not all right," Tibor said. "We will have to do something about the coming Sunday. I will have to get permissions. There are details to be worked out. Then there are the other things. The insurance. The rebuilding. If we're going to rebuild."

"Of course we're going to rebuild," Donna said. "We've even got a committee going on the project already."

"Mmmm," Tibor said. "Do you know that this was not built to be an Armenian church? It was built for the Greeks, and then they moved out of the neighborhood and we took it over. That was before my time, of course. It was before Gregor's time, unless he was an infant, and maybe not even then. Anyway, when we rebuild, we'll be able to fix the things we could never fix before. The iconostasis can be replaced with a veil. The pictures can be adjusted. I never minded it the way it was, though. It seemed—ecumenical."

"Oh," Donna said.

Tibor got up off the couch and went to the window. Pressing his face against the glass and twisting the side of his body almost 180 degrees, he could just see the black hollow where the front of the church should have been—or maybe he couldn't. Maybe that was an illusion too. He went back to the couch and sat down. He looked at the things that had been left on the coffee table: *Vanity Fair*; *National Geographic*; a Swiss army knife; a flashlight; a book of matches, untouched. He was not doing anything intelligent, and he was beginning to shake with cold the way he had on and off in the hospital. "Panic attacks," the doctor had called them, but Tibor was sure that wasn't what they were.

"I'm going to go make some coffee," Donna said, heading out for the kitchen.

Bennis leaned forward on her chair. "You're shaking again. And sweating. You should have let the doctor give you some sedatives."

"I don't need sedatives."

"You need something."

"Will I interfere with you here? Do you need the apartment to do your work?"

"No. Tibor—"

Tibor waved her away. "It doesn't matter." That was true too. It didn't matter in any way she would understand, and he didn't have the words he needed to explain things to her. He could have explained them to Gregor, but Gregor was not in sight. It wasn't just the church. It was everything. People said that the change had come because of the events of September 11, but that wasn't true. September 11 was an effect, not a cause. The change had come long before that, and it had less to do with violence than with—what? He wished he could get more interested in what had happened to Anthony van Wyck Ross.

"Where is Gregor?" he asked.

"Upstairs in the apartment, as far as I know," Bennis said. "I'm surprised he isn't down here already. Do you want me to go get him?"

"No, no. Maybe he is taking a nap. It would be good for him."

"Do you want *anything?*" Bennis said.

Tibor fluttered his hands in the air. "When I first came to America, I lived in St. Mark's Place, in the East Village, in Manhattan. Did you know that? I didn't have a church then. I had a part-time job translating for a publishing company. Every week on Monday I would go in and get my projects. The rest of the time I would spend in my apartment working. Except that every day in the late afternoons I would walk a long way to have coffee in a big café where other immigrants went, but only in the afternoons, because at night the same place was full of young people. I was the only one from Armenia. A lot of the rest of them were Russians."

"And?"

"And," Tibor said, "nobody was crazy. And from what I remember, nobody was crazy in the rest of the country, either. People didn't think that magic was real. They weren't looking to burn witches. They weren't looking for Satan under every bedspread. Do you know what Satan is, really?"

"The most favored angel of God who took up arms against heaven and was defeated by St. Michael and sent to Hell," Bennis said. "I remember from my course in Milton."

"Satan is willful ignorance," Tibor said. "Satan is superstition. Satan is what we all do when we take the easy way out and look for magic and potions and plots to explain life to us, and now we all seem to do it. The president of the United States does it. They think it's religion, Bennis, but it is not. It wasn't when we burned witches in the Middle Ages and it isn't now. It's a kind of brain disease."

"You think the explosion in the church had something to do with burning witches?" Bennis looked at sea.

Tibor waved it away. "Maybe I will give a homily on Satan the next time I celebrate the liturgy. Except that I don't know if I could make sense. I wish people were better than they are."

"So does everybody."

"I wish people were more like people," Tibor said.

Bennis got up. "I'm going to run upstairs and get Gregor. He wanted to know when you got back. And don't tell me I can't wake him up."

"I do not believe in witches," Tibor said. "And I do not believe in UFO abductions. Or conspiracies. Or miraculous healings at prayer meetings held in auditoriums where the healer is on a stage. Or that God put fossils in the earth to deceive people of little faith into believing that evolution had occurred. But I do believe in God. And I do believe in evil."

"If I hurry, I can get Gregor down here before the crowds arrive," Bennis said. "Lida and Sheila and Hannah made you something for a coming-home present. They want to present it to you personally."

"You think I've become as insane as I think they are," Tibor said.

"No," Bennis said. "I think you're still incredibly upset. Give me a moment. I'll find Gregor."

She crossed the room and went behind him, into the foyer. He heard the apartment door open and then close again. Donna came back in from the kitchen with a big mug of black coffee that she put down in front of him on the coffee table.

"There," she said. "That should help. I made the Turk— ah, the Armenian kind, although how you can drink that much caffeine without going into cardiac arrest, I just don't know."

Tibor looked into the mug. The coffee was as thick as mud, the way it was supposed to be. He did sound as crazy as the people he was talking about, who probably didn't sound crazy at all to most people most of the time. They did their shopping. They went to work. They paid their mortgages and mowed their lawns. They just thought that it was really true that people rode around on broomsticks and shape-shifted themselves into ravenous wolves and stole children through the pages of fantasy books.

He put his hands inside his jacket and felt the thickness of paper in his inside breast pocket. It had survived the blast, and the hospital stay, and been there for him to find when he got dressed to wait for Bennis early this afternoon. He'd half-forgotten about it.

"Tell me," he asked Donna. "Do you believe there is a guardian angel always watching over you and everything you do?"

"I've never thought about it," Donna said. "Am I supposed to believe it?"

"Never mind," Tibor said.

He picked up the coffee mug in both hands and took a drink so long it made his throat feel scalded and raw.

3

For David Alden, it was the worst week he could remember, ever, in his entire life, and all he really wanted was to get out of the New York office and back to Philadelphia. In another time, on another planet—back before Tony was murdered; back when all he had to worry about was getting the data on the Price Heaven mess in place on time—he would have taken off for the rest of the week and only resurfaced when he wanted to, or thought he could no longer get away with it. Now there was no time, and that was true even though he was not Tony's heir apparent. He knew Charlotte thought he was, or at least thought he intended to end up at the head of the bank, but the idea was laughable. He was far too young, and he'd had far too little experience. If he did everything right, he might curry enough favor with whomever the new man would be to stay on there. He might not. It was less than pleasingly sentimental, but he'd updated his résumé and FedExed it to a headhunter less than two days after Tony was pronounced dead at the scene at the Around the World Harvest Ball. Ever since, he'd had one ear trained for the sound of other banks looking for talent.

He did not sit at Tony's desk when he worked. It would

have made sense if he had, in terms of efficiency, but it gave him the creeps. He did not make calls from Tony's phone, either, although he answered the ones that came in. He had taken up residence in the office's corner sitting area: a couch, two chairs, and a coffee table bordered on two sides by floor-to-ceiling windows that looked out on Wall Street and lower Manhattan. When the World Trade Center had collapsed in 2001, they had been forced out of these offices for nearly two weeks while inspectors made sure there was no structural damage to the building and window installers replaced the windows on every floor of the side that faced the disaster. Then the cleaning women had had to come in, to sweep the broken glass and the other debris from the floors. Tony's Persian carpet, flown in from Iraq in the days before Saddam Hussein was supposed to be Evil Incarnate, had been destroyed. David Alden did not understand politics in the way politics was played by people like Hussein and the Trade Center bombers. War seemed, to him, so obviously counterproductive. It destroyed economies, and in destroying economies it destroyed markets. David understood markets, and had since he was in high school—although he resisted using the words *high school*, because in his case, they were so clearly affected. Groton was not a "high school" the way anybody who had gone to a public high school would understand it, but David didn't like *prep school*, either. That sounded worse than affected. That sounded deliberately off-putting, as if he were not only an elitist— which he was—but a snob. America could be a very schizophrenic place to live, if you were the kind of person he was. He had tried to get that across to a British girlfriend he'd had for a while, but it had gone right past her. To Rosamund, being someone who went to famous schools and had been required to dress for dinner in a jacket and tie since you were eight years old was just a fact of life, and if other people resented it, it was because they lacked both character and proportion.

The Price Heaven documentation was spread out in front of him in variegated stacks of paper, freshly printed out this morning so that he could get a physical sense of what was happening there. Actually, there was no doubt what was happening there. Price Heaven was in free-fall. Even the drastic measures David had outlined to Tony might not suffice to correct it. If they didn't, Price Heaven would file for bankruptcy—real bankruptcy, David thought, not just Chapter 11—and then the shit would truly hit the fan, because the bank was exposed on this one big-time. David had done the calculations a dozen times. There was no way around it. In all, the bank had loaned Price Heaven something close to a billion dollars outright, and provided spot financing and stock-price support in a myriad of small ways. The small ways were adding up.

The door to the office opened. David looked up from where he was sitting—on the floor, with his legs spread out in front of him and his jacket tossed onto the couch behind him—and saw Paul Delafield coming in. Paul Delafield was executive vice president in charge of development, a fancy way of saying the man who found new projects for the bank to invest in, the man who had brought Price Heaven to the bank. Paul Delafield looked pale, as he had been looking pale for weeks. If he was mourning Tony's loss, there was no evidence of it on his face.

Paul came over to the little sitting area and dropped down on one of the chairs. "Well?" he said. "Should we all batten down the hatches?"

"At least." David thought about getting up, but didn't see the point. There were people he had to fear in the bank, but Paul Delafield wasn't one of them. "The good news is that it's not Enron. There's no evidence of accounting fraud."

"And the bad news?"

"We're going to be lucky as hell if they don't implode completely. And I mean completely. Chapter eleven bankruptcy. Public liquidation."

"Shit."

"I agree." David bent over the papers again, but he couldn't keep it up. He didn't have his heart in it. He already knew what was here, and now that he'd spent a few hours making the reality physical—turning it into stacks of physical paper so that he could visualize it—he had a knowledge of the internal workings of Price Heaven far more complete than its own directors ever had had. Which was a good part of the problem. Price Heaven might not be in the mess it was in if its directors knew what they were doing. It completely amazed him that so many people rose to the heights of American business with IQs in the single digits, and not because they were hereditary legacies, either. The chairman of the board of Price Heaven was Jerry Poldawicz, who grew up in Levittown and did his undergraduate degree at SUNY New Paltz. The CEO was Tom O'Hay, whose father had been a bricklayer and mother a nurse. There were probably a dozen Price Heaven employees running cash registers in Price Heaven outlets who could have done a better job of managing a company than either of those two.

"So," Paul said. "Where do we go from here?"

"Don't ask me," David said. "I just make recommendations. I have no power at all over what recommendations the board will decide to follow."

"What recommendations do you intend to make?"

David sighed. "All the layoffs we discussed last week, before Tony—before Tony. Then we need to close at least a third of the stores. They've got stores in the oddest places, small outlets that have been doing next to no business for years. It's bizarre. Once they opened a store, nothing could get them to close it. And I do mean nothing. So they've got little hole-in-the-wall places in small towns off the highway that nobody can get to because nobody knows they're there, but that nobody would want to get to even if they knew, because there's nothing at the end of the ride but a kind of mom-and-pop novelty place with not much to buy. Some of them were opened in the 1940s. They should have been closed or moved to malls years ago. It's insane."

Paul Delafield looked away, out those big windows that looked over lower Manhattan. He didn't seem to be seeing anything. David had always found it interesting to see who was and who was not emotionally affected by the World

Trade Center collapse. Some people—Paul Delafield—seemed to live in an emotional vacuum.

"She's not going to like it," Paul said.

"Who isn't?"

"Charlotte."

"She'll just have to live with it, then," David said. "There's really no way around this. We should have done something a long time ago. We're sickeningly exposed, and we don't have the excuse we have with governments, where we can say we loaned Argentina all this money to make sure nobody starved or their economy could keep running. This is Price Heaven. It's an old but mostly derelict company that under other circumstances would have been run underground by Wal-Mart long ago."

Paul turned around in his chair, put his elbows on his knees, and leaned forward. "She's been on the phone to me all morning, Charlotte has. She thinks it looks bad, laying off all those thousands of people right before Christmas."

"Everybody stages layoffs right before Christmas. That's the end of the fiscal year. It's that or your paper looks awful when the accounting gets done."

"She says she thinks it's that kind of thing that got Tony killed. She got something in the mail, some piece of literature, she called it. Something that said that Tony was ripping off the proletariat, or something like that."

"Somehow, I can't imagine Charlotte reading Communist propaganda."

"Still." Paul Delafield was stubborn. "She's going to be able to sit on the board, you know that. She's going to have control of a tremendous amount of stock, both her own and whatever Tony's left her—"

"Tony may have left the estate to his daughters. Or to the oldest one. It isn't as if Charlotte is in any need of money."

"Even with just her own stock, she could make a lot of trouble. Wouldn't the daughter side with her? Or is it one of those Greek tragedy things?"

"I don't think I'd go that far," David said, "but I don't think the daughter and the mother see eye-to-eye on much.

Marianne, that's what her name is. Sorry. My mind goes blank sometimes."

"Charlotte says it looks bad when companies lay off thousands of workers right before Christmas, like they're all interested in being Scrooge. She thinks we should wait until after the first of the year."

"Price Heaven can't wait. If it tries, it will collapse completely."

"There's the Christmas buying season. We're right in the middle of that. That could help them instead of hurt them."

"Christmas is in five weeks. The only things that make that kind of money in five weeks are fantasy movies. Too bad Price Heaven didn't produce *Fellowship of the Ring*."

"It does look bad," Paul said. "I can see her point. And don't think the public doesn't know the banks are behind those things when they happen. Then all the stories come out. Tony Ross made thirty-two million dollars in salary and bonuses last year, and what he got the bonus for was making sure Price Heaven laid off a bunch of minimum-wage salesladies who aren't going to be able to go on making the payments on their daughters' medical treatments. And then it will come out that Price Heaven hired practically everybody part-time, so most of their workers didn't get health insurance, not even crappy HMOs, and at the same time the Price Heaven executives and us here at the bank all have top-of-the-line fee-for-service plans that pay for everything from extracting ingrown toenails to having yourself cloned."

David sat back, curious. "So?" he said. "What about that? That's the way the system works, isn't it?"

"Of course it's the way the system works."

"Do you want to change it?"

"Of course I don't want to change it." Paul Delafield looked disgusted. "The system does work. You know that. People have to expect a few dislocations. They have to expect—"

"What? Working seventy hours a week at two different part-time jobs and bringing down three hundred and fifty dollars gross before taxes and no benefits?"

"That's not my fault. They should have stayed in school. They should have learned useful skills for the marketplace."

"Just as a matter of curiosity," David said, "what do you think would happen if they all *did* stay in school and learn some useful skills for the marketplace? What do you think would happen if they all went to Harvard and Wharton?"

"Don't be ridiculous," Paul said.

David laughed. "Tony was smarter than you are about these things. At least he got the point."

Paul Delafield looked like he was pouting. "Still," he said. "She's got a point. With all the things that have been happening. That out there." He jerked his head in the direction of the window, in what he thought was the direction of the rubble of the World Trade Center. "And Tony dying. Being murdered. There's a lot going on. People are . . . restless."

"What's the matter, Paul? Are you expecting someone to shoot you in your bed?"

"Maybe we ought to give that possibility more consideration than we do," Paul said. "It doesn't hurt to be intelligent about the way we go about things. It doesn't hurt to be careful."

David looked across the stacks of papers on Price Heaven. All of a sudden, he felt as if his head were going to explode. Paul Delafield was a profoundly stupid man. All the years he'd spent at all the right schools—Hotchkiss, and Yale, and Wharton—had left no mark on him at all. He might as well have been born ten seconds ago with a program tape playing in his head and nothing else alive in him but the instinct for self-preservation. Suddenly, David had to get out of there, out of the bank, out of New York, out of his life. He pushed aside the stack of papers he'd been working on and stood up. He wished he were taller than Paul Delafield. For some reason, he thought that that would be a moral victory.

"Charlotte isn't going to like it," Paul repeated.

David turned his back to him. "It doesn't matter what Charlotte is going to like," he said. "I'll take care of Charlotte."

FIVE

1

Gregor Demarkian had intended to be home when Tibor came back from the hospital. In fact, he'd been planning Tibor's arrival for at least two days, going over and over in his mind what he wanted to say and what he didn't, how to impart news of the investigation without saying the most pessimistic thing—which was that, since the police had the Tony Ross murder to worry about, they weren't going to spend too much time on one little bombing that would surely turn out to be the work of a small-time brain-dead fanatic who committed hate crimes for the fun of it. Gregor wasn't much in favor of singling out "hate crimes" from other crimes, or giving them harsher sentences, but he knew one when he saw it. Still, the simple thing was, the Philadelphia police had bigger things to worry about, even if Tony Ross had been murdered in Bryn Mawr instead of in the city. The feds were descending in droves, and so were the reporters. To paraphrase Bette Davis, it was going to be a bumpy ride.

He was getting out of his tie and finding a sweater in the mound of sweaters the top of his bureau had become—Bennis, the most organized person in the world when it came to her work, went at the job of putting clothes away in drawers like a dyslexic Tasmanian devil on amphetamines—when the doorbell rang. He thought it was Bennis, home early, and for some reason he was able to get down the hall, across the living room and into the foyer without realizing that if Bennis was home this early, she'd been traveling at the speed of light, or faster. He had a sweater in his hand, but his shirt was unbuttoned halfway down his chest. He reached out to straighten the framed square picture of flowers he kept above his mail table next to the front door. Then he opened up, and found himself confronted by the most nondescript middle-aged woman he had ever seen in his life. She was shortish, no taller than Bennis. She was thickish, not exactly fat, but not slim, that odd solid that some women got at menopause. Her hair was grey and cut short. She was wearing no makeup. Her clothes looked like they'd been picked up at Price Heaven, but Gregor was willing to reserve judgment on that. These days, it could be very tricky to judge clothes. She held out her hand and said, "Mr. Demarkian? I'm Anne Ross Wyler. I'm Tony Ross's sister."

Actually, now that he knew, the resemblance was easy to see. She had the same high forehead and narrow Grecian nose. To go along with them, she had enormous almond-shaped blue eyes. Gregor thought she had been pretty once, when she was young. She would be pretty still, if she took care of herself, which she obviously didn't bother with. He stepped back to let her in. She walked into the foyer, shed her coat, and handed it to him. That's when he saw the big round pin on her knit tunic, placed up near the left shoulder: *Freedom FROM Religion*.

She saw him looking at the pin. "Does it offend you? If it does, I'll take it off. I don't usually, but I've come to ask a favor. And I'm actually not quite so militant as all that."

"No, no," Gregor said. "That's fine. I'm used to people who need to make statements, so to speak. I didn't see you at the party the night Mr. Ross died, did I? I know we weren't being introduced to each other at the end, and there was quite a crush, but somehow I think I would have noticed you."

"Because of the clothes? I have very decent evening clothes in the back of my closet somewhere. I was debutante of the year the year I came out, according to some magazine or other, I don't remember which. I probably still wouldn't be wearing makeup, though." She looked around the foyer. "Do you mind if I come all the way in? I've got a little problem and I don't know what to do about it."

"Does the problem relate to your brother's murder?"

"It might."

"Then you ought to go to the police with it," Gregor said. "There are two excellent officers on the case, Frank Margiotti and Marty Tackner. I could get you their phone number."

"I'd like to talk this out first, if you don't mind. My instinct, under the circumstances, is to keep my mouth shut. Not because I give a rat's ass about the gentleman involved, you understand, but because I'm afraid it might jeopardize my work, and my work—"

"Your work is what?" Gregor asked. "What do you do?"

Anne Ross Wyler looked surprised. "I'm sorry. I thought everybody knew. You must read even fewer newspapers than I do. I run a safe house for child prostitutes. Adelphos House."

Gregor straightened up abruptly.

"You *have* heard of it," Anne said. "We really do get a lot of publicity, on slow news days. It is almost impossible to find anybody who hasn't at least run across our name."

It wasn't that, Gregor thought. Of course he'd heard of it before. He just hadn't made the connection. From the first moment he'd heard of the explosion at Holy Trinity Church, hours after it happened, because when the church blew up he was busy witnessing the murder of Tony Ross, he'd been trying to find a connection, and now, out of the blue, here it was.

"I've heard of it around here," he said. "One of the church groups was going to do volunteer work there. I'm not sure of the details."

"And Father Kasparian came to see us on the night Tony was murdered, yes," Anne said. "We're always desperately in need of volunteers. We've got children living in the house. We've got a whole contact and ID thing going. We have to contact the families, even though many of them are abusive. Then we have to protect the girls when the families want them back."

"Girls?"

"Most child prostitutes are girls between the ages of eleven and fourteen, yes. They learn to make themselves up in a way that the johns can make the excuse that they certainly looked eighteen. Although the johns know, of course. I'm sorry. I'm afraid I tend to lecture. Most people think of child prostitutes as eight-year-olds, and there is some of that, but not as much as the media might make you believe. Do you think we could go somewhere and sit down? I'm afraid I've had an exhausting few days."

Gregor waved her toward the living room. She went in and looked around, without seeming to take much in. This was a woman who did not waste time on appearances. "Sit where you like," Gregor said. "Would you like some coffee?"

He had those coffee bags that worked like tea bags. Bennis had bought them for him so that he could offer coffee to people while she was out, and not be in danger of killing somebody.

"I'd prefer tea, if you have any," Anne said.

Gregor went into the kitchen and got the Red Rose. Then he put the kettle on to boil and took out two cups with saucers. If Bennis were here, she'd put the whole mess on a tray and bring it in like a maid.

Anne Ross Wyler appeared at the kitchen door. "Why don't we just sit in here? You won't mind, will you? I spend all my time at Adelphos House in the kitchen."

"I won't mind," Gregor said. He was actually relieved.

Anne sat down at the kitchen table and looked around. "Very nice. We have a mutual friend, don't we? Bennis Hannaford."

"You know Bennis?" The kettle was already whistling. Gregor poured water into cups.

"She knew Tony better than she ever knew me," Anne said. "I was better acquainted with her sister Anne Marie. That was a mess, wasn't it? I do manage to read the papers some days. Maybe my problem is that I always read them on the wrong ones."

Gregor put the cup with the tea in it in front of her place at the table. He put the cup with the coffee in it in front of a chair on the other side. He put down cream and sugar and spoons. He didn't think Bennis could have asked any more of him, although Lida could have, and would have, if she hadn't taken over the enter tea ceremony herself.

"Well," he said. "Why did you come here instead of going to the police? And you do realize I'll send you to the police, eventually. If you've got some information, you have to talk to them, whether you like it or not."

"Oh, I know. And I do have some information, although possibly not the kind of information they've been looking for. One of the things I do, at Adelphos House, is take pictures of the johns."

"The johns actually come to Adelphos House?'

Anne shook her head. She was going to let the tea steep until the water was black. "No, of course not. Some of the pimps do, to try to get the girls back, but not the johns. I go downtown, to the streets where the girls walk, and take pictures there. Of men at the doors of cars. Of men getting into cars. Sometimes even of men getting blow jobs in cars. I've got a telescopic lens, and I've got some equipment that's supposed to make it possible to take pictures in the dark without a flash—which doesn't work too well, for some reason, maybe because I don't really understand how to use it. I can't use a flash because it tips them off, and then they chase me."

"I'll bet," Gregor said. "Have you been doing this for long?"

"Three years."

"Then I'd say it's a damned miracle you haven't been killed."

"I don't believe in miracles," Anne said. She took the tea bag out of her cup, tasted the tea, and nodded. "Red Rose. Excellent. Where was I? Oh, yes. I don't believe in miracles. I don't believe in faith healing. I don't believe in God. But most of all, I don't believe in politicians who'll talk for two hours about their deep commitment to religious faith and never say one concrete thing about what they're going to do if they're elected. I've made it my mission to get one politician in this city to come right out and say, 'We're going to start arresting the johns and prosecuting them.' If he says that, I'll sit still and listen to how his life turned around when he accepted Jesus Christ as his Lord and Savior."

"Had a bad year with Philadelphia politics, did you?"

"With Philadelphia politics and the national kind, both. Don't even get me started on the national prayer service after nine-eleven. Or faith-based social services, unless you're talking about Catholic Charities. And yes, I know what the Catholics got caught doing less than five years ago. But then, I could go on and on about the fashion magazines and the movies too. Do you know what we've done, Mr. Demarkian? We've redefined beauty in women to mean a body type only found in human females at the start of adolescence. Grown women don't have tiny waists and narrow hips, not usually. Eleven-year-olds do."

"Right," Gregor said.

"I'm ranting." Anne stood up. "Give me a second here."

Gregor watched her as she went back into the living room. She fussed with her coat, which she'd left on the couch, and came back carrying a small manila envelope.

"Here," she said, throwing the envelope down on the table. "Take a look at these. I took them the night Tony was killed."

Gregor opened the envelope and drew out a thick stack of color photographs. They might as well have been black and white. He saw a car. He saw a girl who looked the way actresses did when they tried to look like children. He saw bits and pieces of a man's body. A leg. An arm. Once or twice, he got the side of a face, but the pictures were blurry. He couldn't make out the man's features.

"The girl's name is Patsy Lennon," Anne said. "We first found her on the street about two years ago. She had just turned eleven. We've handed her off to child services half-a-dozen times. She hates foster care and runs away, or they try to reunite her with her family, which is a disaster. Her mother is a drug addict who turns tricks for dope, and she's always got a pimp who wants Patsy peddling her ass. Patsy runs away and finds a pimp of her own."

"The pictures of the man aren't helpful," Gregor said.

Anne laughed. "No, they're not. I told you I was a lousy photographer. But I saw him with my own eyes. I saw him get into that car with Patsy Lennon. I saw him get a blow job from Patsy Lennon—"

"And you didn't try to stop it?"

"I couldn't have stopped it. I know. Back when I started, I wasted a lot of time trying to stop blow jobs. I got beat up a couple of times. But I saw him do it. And then he put Patsy back on the street and took off, and I followed him. I had the Adelphos House car and I followed him all the way out to my brother Tony's house. Not that that was difficult, by the way. He wasn't exactly tearing up the road."

"Who is he?"

"His name is Ryall Wyndham. Or he says it is."

"And you don't believe him?"

Anne shrugged. "There are dozens of people like Ryall Wyndham all across the country, all across the world, maybe. They worship Jackie O. They desperately want to be part of Society, as if Society still existed in the way it did in the thirties. Oh, I'm not saying that it doesn't exist at all. There are still 'in' people and 'out' people, and there is still 'social standing,' if that's the kind of thing you're interested in. They're interested, so they change their names and find some way to connect to the people they think are important—people like Charlotte, to be frank about it."

"But why question the name?"

"Because Ryall is a family name. It's a New York family name, not a Philadelphia one, but still. We all know each other. If he was really a Ryall, I would have heard of him."

"All right," Gregor said. "He paid a prostitute and then he drove out to your brother's party and you followed him there. Which means he must have had an invitation to your brother's party. Or am I being dense? Was he going to gate-crash?"

"No," Anne said. "He definitely had an invitation. Charlotte wouldn't leave him out. He's a social columnist. He writes a column once a week, invoking the spirit of *The Philadelphia Story*."

"And?"

"And nothing," Anne said. "He went through the gates and I didn't. I could have. The guard was Tony's regular one, with some reinforcements in the background. He would have known who I was. I just, I don't know. I didn't want to be part of the fuss. When Ryall went through, the place was pretty close to deserted except for the guards, but then I sat there for a while and all sorts of people started showing up. There were a lot of cars on their way in. It was a huge ball. Charlotte was fund-raising for the UN. And then something odd happened. The guards closed the gates, even though there were cars there. Later on, I thought that that must have been when Tony was shot. At the time, I thought it might just be the first lady. I've been through security lockdowns like that, in my former life. I didn't see any point to being part of it, so I took off. I came back to Adelphos House, and Father Kasparian had just left."

"This Ryall Wyndham. Was he driving himself, or was he being driven?"

"Oh, he was driving himself. I don't think anybody would let his driver take him to a prostitute. Or maybe they would. To me, it's like asking to get convicted. You're giving the prosecution an eyewitness."

"I see what you mean," Gregor said. He hadn't touched his coffee. By now, it was probably cold. "Do you think this is connected? Ryall Wyndham's encounter with a prostitute and your brother's murder?"

"I have no idea. At first, I wondered if Wyndham was what Hemingway called a pilot fish, one of those people who scope out the territory so that the rich people won't have to take too many risks. That maybe one of the people in that group was looking for fresh meat, so to speak. And maybe that's it."

"Do you think it was your brother Tony?"

"Good Lord, no. It's not sisterly affection, Mr. Demarkian, it's just that I knew Tony. He channeled his sex drive into his work. He was one of those people. Charlotte used to complain about it, but always in code. God, all those people talk in code."

"You're one of those people."

"True," Anne said. "But I made my escape. Anyway, I just wanted to tell somebody this, and I'll tell the police if you want me to. I really don't understand the relevance it has. I'm only sorry I didn't get better pictures. The police won't arrest the johns, and as long as they don't, the prostitution will continue. Sometimes, if you get evidence against somebody prominent enough, you can get it into the media and then the police have to pay attention, at least for a little while. My Holy Grail is a crackdown on the johns only. I'm not going to find it."

She gathered the pictures up in a stack again. Gregor looked at the face of Patsy Lennon, who was supposed to be thirteen-years-old. She didn't look thirteen-years-old. She looked forty-two. Anne put the pictures back in the manila envelope.

"They get old fast," she said. "Patsy will have to move on to rougher trade in another year. I'm not kidding myself that I'm somehow going to save her. Most of them don't get saved."

"Then why do you do what you do?"

"Because it called to me," Anne said. "And don't ask me to explain it, because I can't. I just woke up one morning next to my husband, who was a perfectly nice investment banker who'd become completely convinced that poor people were delinquent adolescents who had nobody to blame for their misery but themselves, and my entire life suddenly seemed completely ridiculous. Then about two days later, I found myself paying twenty-thousand dollars for an evening gown to wear to the April in Paris Ball in New York, and the whole thing was so asinine, I couldn't keep a straight face. I had to have them messenger the damned dress to me, because I couldn't stand to touch it. So I hacked around for a little while and landed back in Philadelphia and started Adelphos House. You can do a lot of things with trust funds."

"Obviously."

"I've got to go," she said. "Write down the names of those detectives and I'll call them."

2

Gregor Demarkian waited until he saw Anne Ross Wyler emerging from his own front door onto Cavanaugh Street before he admitted to himself that he was just too jumpy to sit still, and then he spent two straight minutes trying to talk himself out of doing what he had been thinking of doing for the past four days. Crime scenes had to be kept clean, he knew that. The question was whether or not Holy Trinity Church was a crime scene. The church board had been given permission to go in and look around. Plans were already underway for rebuilding, if you could call tearing the place down and putting up something entirely new on the same spot "rebuilding." Whatever. At least it would be a church and not a new apartment building or a water-treatment plant or whatever it was they committed urban renewal in the name of nowadays. Cavanaugh Street didn't need to be renewed. It didn't even need to be cleaned. At least once a week, the older women and the women who had just come from Armenia went out and hosed down the sidewalks. It wasn't the famous scrubbing the Swiss were supposed to do, but it did insure that debris didn't collect in the gutters and that the sidewalks were clear of the sort of stains dogs left in spite of the pooper-scooper law. He was, he thought, avoiding the issue, as he almost always avoided the issue these days. He found it much easier to deal with the death of Tony Ross than he did the destruction of Holy Trinity Church. The death of Tony Ross was both sensible and explicable. At the end of the day, they would find one of the usual suspects: a disgruntled employee; a jilted lover; his wife. Maybe his wife had hired a hitman. From what Gregor had seen of Charlotte Deacon Ross, he wouldn't put it past her.

He got his coat out of the foyer and went downstairs.

Tibor still wasn't back from the hospital, and nobody was in Bennis's old apartment on the second floor. Grace was still playing upstairs. This time, it was music he couldn't identify at all, although since she played with a chamber group that specialized in Baroque, he expected it was some of that. He got down to the first floor and saw that there was a note on old George Tekemanian's door asking the old man to call Sheila Kashinian as soon as he got in. That was new since Bennis had dropped him off. Gregor wondered what Sheila Kashinian wanted, besides a new fur coat every fall and a vacation in the Bahamas every winter. It was remarkable how predictable people got as they got older. He wondered if it had happened to him as well.

Out on the street, he didn't feel depressed, or pessimistic, or frightened. *If you face your fears instead of run from them, they'll be easier to bear,* his mother used to say, when he was growing up on this very street, in the days when the buildings were all divided up into tiny apartments and most people's parents spoke English badly and never at home. He turned up the street toward the church and the Ararat. He still went to the Ararat for breakfast every morning. That meant he'd been passing the church at least twice a day since the explosion happened. He'd been passing it on the other side of the street, deliberately, in a way he never would have only a month ago. It was too bad he hadn't been on the bomb investigation squad at the Bureau. He'd had the standard training in explosives, but that had been in his training year, and after that he'd never had any cause to use the information. Use it or lose it. Bennis said that about something other than information.

He got to the church and crossed the street so that he could stand on the sidewalk directly in front of it. The yellow barrier tapes were still up, warning him of danger and the illegality of trespassing. He stepped over the one nearest to him and walked up the shallow steps to what used to be Holy Trinity's front door. That was gone, and so was the wall that had divided the vestibule from the sacristy. He could look right down the center aisle to the altar. The pews were covered with junk. The roof was only half standing. Near the front to his right, it had caved in entirely. Toward the middle on the left side, there was a large hole like a ragged skylight. Rain had come through it and spread water stains across the pews.

He was thinking that it would not be ridiculously dangerous if he walked up to the altar and assessed the damage for himself, when he realized he was being watched. There was somebody behind him, staring at him. In the worst-case scenario, it would be a reporter—but there wasn't really any danger of that. As long as the Tony Ross case was front-page news, very few reporters would bother with coming down here. In the best-case scenario, it was somebody from the street, maybe one of the Very Old Women, waiting to lecture him on taking foolish chances. He turned around to see who was stalking him and stopped, confused. The person standing on the sidewalk in the place he had just left was nobody he had expected at all.

The man who was standing behind him was very tall, and very broad, and very tired—tired in the way only immigrants are tired, with that bone-weary defeatedness that comes from struggling every day to do the very simplest things. Gregor was sure he'd seen him before, but he couldn't for the life of him remember where. He was sure he wasn't one of the new Armenian refugees Tibor and the women of Holy Trinity found room for every week. The man saw Gregor watching him and shifted slightly on his feet. He was wearing a heavy jacket that was worn at the hems and the elbows but still serviceable, the kind of thing that had been expensive once because of its utility, not its elegance. Gregor cocked his head.

"Yes?" he said. "I wasn't going to disturb anything, if you were worrying about that. I was just looking around. I suppose I shouldn't have been."

"You are Mr. Gregor Demarkian?" the man asked.

"That's right." The accent was indecipherable, Gregor thought—not Armenian, surely. Possibly Russian. Possibly from one of the old Soviet Republics. "Can I help you?"

"I am Krystof Andrechev," the man said.

Gregor thought—*yes, right, Russian*.

"I have now the store there." The man jerked his head down the road.

Gregor brightened. Now he knew where he'd seen him before. "The newsstand? The one Michael Bagdanian used to own?" Gregor never went in there. He had his paper delivered, and he didn't read magazines unless Bennis subscribed to them or he got stuck in an airport.

Krystof Andrechev shifted again. "Yes. I have bought this store from Mr. Bagdanian. I have—you will come with me, please? I have now in my store something, something—" Gregor didn't know if he was straining for words or for courage, but whatever it was, he didn't find it. "I have now in my store a very large problem, a difficulty. You will come with me, please, and see this thing?"

"Sure." Gregor came back down the front steps and stepped back over the yellow barrier onto the sidewalk. "Are you all right? You look—"

"I am upset," Krystof said. "I am also angry. I do not know what to do about this, and I am being afraid it will make me—make me—" He threw his hands into the air, frustrated. They were walking down the street toward the newsstand. Gregor could see some of the women looking out their windows at what was going on—after all, Krystof was their mystery man at the moment. They all said he never talked, and wondered who he was, and where he came from. Now that they'd seen Gregor with him, he'd never get any peace.

"I am hearing that in this country you trust the police, but I am not sure this is sensible. I am not sure. You understand?"

"Yes," Gregor said. "I do understand. If you want my opinion, you should usually trust the police, but you should always make sure you've got your ass covered."

"Ha." Krystof smiled, and stopped moving. They were at the front of the store. It was shuttered as if he had closed it for the night. It was also locked. "Covering my ass, yes. This is what I was looking to do. I was not sure how it could be done. I go for a walk. I see you standing there. You are an investigator, no?"

"No," Gregor said firmly. "I work as a consultant for police departments on homicide—murder—cases, when I'm asked."

"Fine. You know the police. They know you. Everybody here—" Krystof looked around Cavanaugh Street. "Everybody here thinks you are a good man. So with you I cover my ass. I do not know who this woman was. I never see her before. Come inside."

Krystof finished unlocking the door and swung it back on its hinges to let Gregor in. When they were both in, Krystof shut the door and locked it again.

"I do not want somebody coming in," he said. "It would be dangerous. See there on the counter next to the cash register."

Gregor went to the counter. Even in the gloom, it took no time at all for him to see what Krystof Andrechev was worried about, and to think that, if it had been him, he would have been worried too. The gun in front of him was enormous, black and polished and deadly-looking—a .357 Magnum, possibly, or one of the knockoffs that had flooded the black market a few years ago.

"Good God," he said. "What are you doing with that thing? Do you have a permit for it? Having something like that in a neighborhood like this can be—"

"No, no. You do not understand. This is not my gun. I own no gun. This she left here, this woman who came today. I have not touched it. Not once. Not even with a handkerchief."

"What woman?"

Krystof shrugged. "An old woman. Nothing much. Past the time of being pretty but not, what do you say, not hunched over. Not near dead."

"Middle-aged," Gregor said.

"She comes in maybe two hours ago. There is nobody in the store. She comes up to me and asks me if I know what is going on in this neighborhood. Of course I know what is going on in this neighborhood. The women are bringing food to each other all the time, up and down the street, day after day. It is very strange not everybody here is very fat."

"That's a point," Gregor said.

"I do not answer her," Krystof said, "except I make a noise, you know. I do not say words. I do not like to talk much because my English is not good and my, what do you call it, my voice—"

"Accent."

"Accent, yes. It gives me away. I did not know, when I came here, that everybody would be from Armenia."

"They're not. Most of them were born in the United States. What do you have against the Armenians?"

"I have nothing against anybody. But I am from Russia, and Russia and Armenia have not always been, what is it? Allies."

"True enough. I doubt if anybody here will care." This was not exactly accurate. The Very Old Ladies might care, but they might not, since their enmity was still fixed on the Turks.

"So," Krystof said. "She comes, and I say nothing, and she talks. She talks for a long time. About how here on this street they worship the Devil. They worshiped the Devil in this church up here where the explosion was. I know this is not true. This is only an Orthodox church. I think she is very stupid and very ignorant, and I wish her out of my store, but I say nothing. Even hello and good-bye I mostly do not say to the people who come here."

"Yes," Gregor said. "I'd heard about that."

"It is no wish to be unfriendly. I am only ashamed of the way I talk. So I do not talk, and this lady hands me these things." Krystof went around behind the counter, rummaged underneath it, and came up with a stack of papers and magazines.

Gregor recognized the paper on the very top. It was another copy of *The Harridan Report*. Gregor wondered which one it was. Krystof handed the stack across to him, and he took it. Right under *The Harridan Report*—an edition he hadn't yet seen, he was sure—was *America Fights Back*. Gregor would have thought it was one of those hyper-patriotic throwaways that had been everywhere after the

September 11 attacks, except that under the title there was smaller lettering: *Against the New World Order.*

"You know what these things are?" Krystof said.

"I've seen similar things, yes," Gregor said.

"I have looked them over," Krystof said. "After she left and I locked up the store, I sat down to think for a while and then I looked them over. I read a little. They are insane."

"Yes," Gregor agreed. "They are insane."

"We have something like this in Russia after the government falls. Everything is a plot. Everything is the KGB. But nothing like this—reptiles. Thinking people are reptiles."

"What?"

"So she puts them on the counter, and then next to them she puts this gun. There is nobody else in the store, you understand? There is never anybody in the store at this time of day, and now she is there and she puts the gun on the counter and the first thing I think is she is trying to rob me, but I am not afraid. She is a small woman. I do not think I will have trouble getting rid of her."

"And?"

"And she says I should not be afraid, the gun is for me. To protect myself. Against these people here on this street, who worship the Devil, or think they worship the Devil, because she knows that I know it is really something else. They are really agents—spies—for something else. It's not a word I have heard before."

"The Illuminati?" Gregor suggested.

Krystof's face cleared. "Yes, that is it. You know this? It is not a word that makes sense to me. This is an organization of terrorism you have here a problem with?"

"No," Gregor said firmly. "This is a paranoid delusion some people obsess about. I'm sorry. I didn't mean—"

"If you could maybe talk a little slower," Krystof said.

"Yes, I am sorry. She just came in here and laid down the gun? Just like that?"

"I am afraid the police will not be believing me," Krystof said, "but that is what she did, yes. She is talking the whole time, about this word I don't remember again, about the New

World Order. I know that. We have that in Russia. About how this here on this street is full of spies or saboteurs or, I don't know. She talks and talks."

"And she leaves the gun."

"Right there," Krystof said. "I did not touch it. Not even one time. Not even with my little finger. I just leave it there and then I lock up and try to think what to do. Then I go out for a walk to go on thinking because of the air, and I see you in the church, and I think you will know. I have read about you in the *People* magazine."

Gregor did not want to discuss *People* magazine. He looked at the gun again, wishing he was better at identifying firearms. That was another sort of information he hadn't had much use for after training, and had no use for at all since his retirement, even when he worked as a consultant. That was why police departments had crime labs.

"I think," Krystof said, "that if I do not do the right thing, I have much trouble. There are many who believe that all Russians are gangsters. Yes? We are not the Mafia, but people think so. So I think I have to do something smart, and then I see you. I go out after I locked up, but I do not see this woman anymore. She is not a woman from the street here that I know. She is never before coming into the store."

Gregor looked down at the stack of material in his hands. There was a publication from something called *Conspiracy Digest* entitled "The Bush Crime Family." There was material from something called *A-albionic*, whatever that was supposed to mean. The A-albionic material looked as if it had been printed out from a Web site. "Origins of the Modern Conspiracy to Rule the World," it said and "Mystery of Masonry's Origins Solved?"

"Freemasons," Krystof said wisely. "We have too, in Russia, people who are afraid of the Freemasons. Here, I meet many Freemasons. They are nice men. They ask me to join their lodge, because I am now a member of the community. This is not for the United States, do you understand? This is nonsense for backward people."

"We'd better call the police," Gregor said. "If you've got a phone, I can—"

Krystof reached under the counter and came up with a phone. Gregor put the magazines and publications down and took the phone instead.

"It is only to prove," Krystof said, "backwardness and ignorance are everywhere. Stupidity is everywhere. There is no escape. But I do not touch the gun. I am not an idiot."

3

Four hours later, Gregor was finally free of the newsstand and Krystof Andrechev. If it hadn't been for the help of John Jackman, it would have taken much longer, and been accompanied by the kind of public circus that brings crowds out of their apartments at every hour of the day or night, little knots of people gathered across the street or down the block from the immediate action, huddled against each other because they forgot to bring their coats, intense. With John's help, he got an unmarked car and two detectives who were probably assigned to the case. It startled him to realize that he hadn't paid enough attention to know who was handling the explosion at Holy Trinity Church. He had John Jackman to ask for information. John got him better information that he would ever get out of the officers in charge, unless he had been hired on as a consultant, which he would not be in this matter. He wasn't really a suspect in the murder of Tony Ross, in spite of the fact that he'd been at the party. Tony had been killed by a bullet from someplace down the drive and into the night. He'd been behind in the big ballroom with a crystal bowl of paté in his hands. He could be a suspect in the explosion of Holy Trinity Church. He lived here. He knew these people. For all the police knew, he could be carrying grudges, harboring resentments, going crazy.

By the time the detectives were ready to go, it was dark. The streetlights were on all up and down Cavanaugh Street.

When Gregor walked out onto the sidewalk, he could see the glow that meant the Ararat was all lit up and streaming light out its plate-glass window. In a little while, the lights would be dimmed and candles would be set out for dinner. The Ararat liked to exude "ambience" in the evenings. He looked back at Krystof calmly locking up and the detectives getting back into their unmarked car, the gun nowhere in sight. One of them was checking something in his notebook. The other was staring out into space, making eye contact with nobody. Gregor remembered that from the Bureau. It was what you did when you were gathering evidence or arresting someone while being watched by a hostile crowd.

Gregor had been free to go half an hour before. He had only hung around to make sure Krystof was all right. Gregor was not somebody who assumed that the police in every city were automatically corrupt or automatically racist, but he had been around long enough to know that some of them were both. These two had turned out to be only efficient. They had insisted that Krystof Andrechev give them his fingerprints. They had not insisted that Gregor give them his, but only because Gregor's were already on file with the department. At least they hadn't panicked, or arrested anybody. Gregor had a hard time understanding who they would have arrested or for what, but when cops got spooked, it could have been anybody for anything.

Gregor went back down the street to his own building. This time, he did not crane his neck and twist his body around to see if he could see what was left of Holy Trinity Church. He went up the front steps and into the vestibule. He made note of the fact that the door to old George Tekemanian's ground-floor apartment had no light coming out through the peephole and remained firmly shut. Sometimes, when old George was at home, he left the door open a crack so that he could catch anybody coming in from outside. Old George was not worried about burglars. He was worried about company. Gregor paused to listen, but Grace was no longer playing the harpsichord way upstairs. He wondered if she had a performance this evening. Bennis and Donna had taken him once—and Russ too—to one of Grace's groups performances. It had been held in an enormous pseudo-Gothic room in a university downtown, and Gregor had found himself both enjoying the music and being annoyed by the setting. He hated "college Gothic," the way he hated Tudor houses on the Main Line. Neither the Goths nor the Tudors had ever had anything to do with America. They certainly hadn't left buildings there. *Why*, Gregor wondered, *did people so often choose to be fake when it was actually easier to be authentic?*

He went up the stairs to the second floor, to the apartment he still thought of as Bennis's. He raised his hand to knock, but before he could, the door opened in front of him and Grace Feinman was standing before him, looking flushed.

"Mr. Demarkian," she said. "We've all been wondering where you'd gone. It's just Father Tibor here now. And me."

"Where did Bennis go?" Gregor stepped into the apartment's foyer and looked around. It was exactly like his foyer, one floor above, and exactly like Grace's, one floor above that. This building had been converted into three identical floor-through condominiums with a fourth, a little smaller, on the ground floor. It was not the kind of place Gregor normally thought of as "condominiums." "Condominiums" sounded like modern, concrete things with too many hard primary colors and shiny surfaces pretending to be modern art.

"She went to park the car," Grace said, closing the door behind Gregor as he walked in. "She left it parked somewhere or other again, and she had to put it back in the garage. If I had a car that expensive, I'd probably bronze it and not drive it at all. Except that I'd never buy a car that expensive. If I got that much money in place, I'd buy another harpsichord, or have one made, or maybe I'd buy an antique. It would be wonderful to have one of the really important harpsichords, like the pieces we use when we make disks."

Gregor had gone into the living room, which was covered with Bennis's papier-mâché models of Zed and Zedalia. Everything in the room was Zed and Zedalia. Bennis owned

the original art from all her covers. She also owned the sign-
ing posters from all of her book tours. All these were framed,
and on the walls. Tibor was sitting in an enormous black
leather chair next to the big window that looked out into the
street, and directly across to Lida Arkmanian's second-floor
living room. The coffee table was piled high with food.

Gregor walked around the back of the couch and sat
down, close enough so that Tibor wouldn't have to raise his
voice too far to be heard. Tibor did not look well. He didn't
look ill, exactly. Gregor knew there was nothing physically
wrong with him. The brick that had hit Tibor on the night of
the explosion had only grazed his shoulder. It had created a
nasty bruise, but no lasting or serious damage, like a concussion. Tibor had been passed out cold when the police
reached the scene, but the doctors thought that was shock. It
wasn't an injury to the head. There hadn't been a trace of
hematoma anywhere on his scalp.

"So," Gregor said, patting Tibor on the knee. "You look
terrible. Were the women too much for you?"

Tibor shrugged. "The women were the women. They
brought food."

Gregor and Tibor both looked at the huge mess spread
across the coffee table.

"They brought more than this," Tibor said. "It is in the
kitchen, in the refrigerator and on the counters. They even
brought Pringles and Cheez Waffies."

"What on earth are Cheez Waffies?"

"They're the round ones with the two waffle-looking
wafers making a sandwich with the fake cheese," Grace said
helpfully.

"It doesn't matter what they are," Tibor said. "You
wouldn't like them. I'm just tired. I can't get over being
tired. The doctor said this is probably psychological."

"It probably is," Gregor said.

"Yes. Well, Krekor, psychologically I am tired. And we
have the Sunday coming up. We need to celebrate the
liturgy. I do not like the idea of this neighborhood going to

another church on Sundays. It might give the bishop the idea that we don't need a church here."

"If you don't want them to go, they won't go," Gregor said.

Tibor nodded. He did not ask Gregor why Gregor had not been at the apartment to meet him. He did not make an effort to see what was going on in Lida's living room, or on the street. He just sat, and the longer he sat, the more alarmed Gregor became.

"You know," he said, "it doesn't make much sense to brood on it. The world is full of nuts. It really is. There's not much any of us can do about it. Oh, I know, every time there's a disaster people start insisting on precautions. Look at what happened after September eleventh. Half the country was willing to shred the Bill of Rights to be safe from terrorists. You can't make them understand that nothing will ever make us safe from terrorists. Or from nuts of any kind. Even the Israelis aren't completely safe from terrorists, and they take the best and most sensible precautions on the planet—"

"No," Tibor said. "There's something else."

Gregor took a deep breath. "What?"

Tibor glanced at Grace. She had her back to them, fussing with something on the occasional table that sat against the narrow piece of wall between the foyer and the living room's entry to the kitchen. Maybe there was food there.

"Grace," Gregor said. "Do me a favor, will you?" He reached into the pocket of his pants and got his keys. "Run up to my place and get my copy of *Anderson's Guide to Forensic Pathology*. It's lying on the desk in my room, under some other things. To the left of the computer. Look around and you'll find it."

"Oh, all right," Grace said. She took the keys. "Are you sure I'll need the keys? I never lock up anymore except when I'm leaving the building."

"I've got the door on automatic lock," Gregor said.

"Why do we need this book about pathology?" Tibor asked, as Grace rushed through the foyer and out onto the landing. They both heard the door *snick* shut behind her. "I do not much like forensics in any form, Krekor. It makes me ill."

"It gets her out of the apartment for a good five minutes, which is what it's going to take to unearth that thing," Gregor said. "So tell me what's wrong."

Tibor reached into his suit jacket and came out with an envelope. It was an ordinary white envelope, "business-sized" as they used to call it when Gregor was in school. Tibor put it down on the coffee table between them, balancing it against a big bowl of tiny meatballs with toothpicks in them.

"There was this that came the day the explosion happened," he said. "It is not the first one. I threw the other ones out."

Gregor picked up the envelope and took the letter from it. It was a very short letter, typed on a computer, a little smeared by a printer that seemed to be malfunctioning.

Priest of Satan, the letter said. *Don't think we don't know what you are. Don't think we don't know what you're doing. We've seen the bodies of the infants you killed. We know you cremate them in the basement of that hellhole you call a church. We know that you fuck children there night after night, stick your filthy prick up their anuses until they scream. We've heard their screams. We won't let them go unrevenged.*

Gregor stopped reading. "What the hell?" he said.

Tibor shrugged. "They came for three weeks. At first a few days apart. Then almost every day."

"And you didn't tell anybody?"

Tibor slammed his palms on the arms of his chair. "I do not want to sound like a fool," he said. "It's not the first time. We have had such letters before, Krekor, they come on and off, people don't understand what we are. They don't know about the Orthodox churches. They know only about Protestants and Catholics. So they get confused."

Gregor looked down at the letter again. *Don't think*

you're going to get away with it forever. We're watching you. We know how to put an end to the evil you've brought to this city and this country. We know how to put a stop to you, and we aren't too timid—or too cowed by the law that you've got in your own Satanic pocket—to take the measures we need to take to stop you. We are coming."

"This," Gregor said, "is a threat. It's an immediate threat of imminent physical violence."

"Yes, Krekor, I know. I should have done something about it. I should have showed it to you. I didn't want to."

"Why ever not?"

"Because I didn't want you to go to the police." Tibor shook his head. "Krekor, please. It did not occur to me that anybody would actually commit any real violence. You see this sort of thing on the Internet all the time. Mostly, it does not get physical—"

"Except that this wasn't on the Internet. This was sent directly to you."

"Yes, I know. But still. And then I worried about the obvious. That people would believe what these things said."

"Believe that you were sacrificing infants to Satan?"

"No, Krekor. Believe that there was some truth in the other things. That there was sex going on at Holy Trinity. That is not so far-fetched an accusation, is it? Think of what happened with the archdiocese in Philadelphia, and then in Boston too, hundreds of children, dozens of priests, all involved in—in—"

"Those were the Catholics," Gregor said firmly.

"It doesn't matter," Tibor said. "It doesn't matter that you and I know that nothing like that has ever gone on at Holy Trinity. It doesn't matter that the whole neighborhood knows. The mud would fly and the mud would stick, out there, in the city, no matter what we did to clean it up. And then I thought that maybe that was the point. That whoever sent this expected me to go right to the police, and then when I did the contents of the letters would be aired in the press, and the reputation of the church would be destroyed. So I threw them away."

"Okay," Gregor said.

"Now I am thinking that maybe I brought this on us myself," Tibor said. "That if I had done what I was expected to do and gone to the police, the church would still be standing. That they only blew up the church because the other thing, the thing with the letters, was not working. It was very wrong of me, Krekor. It was a matter of self-regard, and self-protection, and that is not what a priest with a congregation should do."

"Okay," Gregor said again, trying to think. "But you kept that one. Why did you keep that one? Why didn't you throw it away?"

"I—it was different. More abusive. And by then they were coming every day, and I thought I should now maybe show them to you. That one frightened me. It used, what do you call it? Not curse words. Anglo-Saxonism, you know. Bad words like that, where the others hadn't. And there was the direct threat. And I couldn't make myself throw it away, so I put it in this pocket and I went out to Adelphos House and when I got back to Cavanaugh Street it was still there. And then the church blew up."

Gregor got up. His head hurt. Tibor was not entirely wrong about what would happen to the church's reputation, or his own, when the contents of this letter got out—and they would get out. "You can't throw that one away," he said carefully. "Not now. It's evidence in a crime, or it might be. Maybe I can take it straight to John Jackman and see if he can keep the contents private, at least for the time being—"

"Oh, Krekor."

"The time being may matter a great deal. If it turns out this whole thing was orchestrated by one of the nut groups, the press will concentrate on the nut group. And I should think it's inevitable that that's what happened. The next most likely thing is that this was the act of a single deranged individual. All we have to do is to show that he's made similar threats to other people before. The public isn't completely cynical, Tibor."

"Not cynical, no," Tibor said, "but jaded. And you can't

blame them. Those things did happen, in the Catholic archdiocese, and in other churches as well. Sometimes I think that is the only religious news I read anymore, the sex molestation cases. Except for the politics, you understand, where some pastor somewhere is burning books. It's as if the whole world has gone insane, and not just since September eleventh. People no longer have common sense."

Gregor thought that people never had had much in the way of common sense. In his experience, common sense was less common than genius, because even geniuses didn't usually have it. He folded up the letter, put it back in its envelope, and put the envelope into his own jacket pocket.

"I'll call John about this right away," he said, thinking that John Jackman was going to start regretting the fact that he'd given Gregor his private cell phone number. "We'll do this the very best way we can. But for goodness sake, if you get any more, don't throw them away."

Tibor smiled slightly. Gregor stood up, thinking it made as much sense to call from the phone here as to go upstairs. Bennis wouldn't be charging Tibor for the phone bill. Gregor got around the edge of the couch and headed for the bedroom. Bennis also had a phone in her kitchen, as he did himself, but for some reason that felt far too public for a call like this. Tibor had gone back to looking out the window, but not looking, the way he'd been staring at everything since Gregor had first seen him in the hospital after the explosion.

"It's not just that people no longer have common sense," Tibor said. "It's that so many of them want to see evil with a capital *E*. It's not enough anymore that there are people in the world who do bad things. It must be some big plot, some ultimate war against the forces of darkness. But I never thought the forces of darkness were like that. I always thought that Armageddon, when it came, would happen in a civil servant's office, and most people wouldn't even notice."

"Well," Gregor said, unsure where to go from there.

The door to Bennis's apartment slammed open and Grace came running in. "Mr. Demarkian," she said, breathless. "There's a man on the phone and he says he has to talk to you right away, because Charlotte Deacon Ross is dead."

PART TWO

Title: SEPTEMBER 11, 1990—PRESIDENT
BUSH [Senior] PRESENTS SPEECH TO CON-
GRESS, "TOWARD A NEW WORLD ORDER."
SEPTEMBER 11, 2001—MIGHTY BLOW
STRUCK TO BRING ABOUT NEW WORLD
ORDER—PRECISELY 11 YEARS LATER TO
THE DAY. BUSH [Junior] PRESIDENT.
Subtitle: Since "11" can rightly be thought of as
the New World Order Number, this double "11"
is most shocking. It seems to confirm the
complicity of both Bush presidents and their
CFR advisers in this most shocking of terrorist
attacks. The number "11" simply surrounds the
attacks and for very good additional reason: it is
a primary number in Mind Control.

> —FROM THE CUTTING EDGE AT
> HTTP://WWW.CUTTINGEDGE.ORG/NEWS/
> N1541.CF

ONE

1

The good thing, if there could be said to be a good thing, was that this time Gregor Demarkian's status in the investigation was far less ambiguous. Nobody could say that he was a suspect in the death of Charlotte Deacon Ross because, as far as he could figure out, he had spent the time of the shooting talking to two Philadelphia police detectives in Krystof Andrechev's store. The worst thing of many bad things was what this death would do to the elaborate theoretical construct Frank Margiotti and Marty Tackner had made of the death of Tony Ross—or Anthony van Wyck Ross, as they called him, formally, whenever they launched into their theory about the case. All the way out to Bryn Mawr in the cab, Gregor thought about those two detectives and what they had considered self-evident about the shooting on the night of the charity ball. Gregor could not decide if he, himself, had thought the same things. He had always found it very difficult to get his mind around the existence of people like Tony Ross, even though he'd spent much of his early career working with them. That was what you did on kidnapping detail. You put in your time with the rich. Tony Ross, though, was more than rich. He was the kind of rich that most people never see and wouldn't understand, because he made it a point to be both obscure and opaque. It was unlikely that any of his children would ever have been kidnapped. Potential kidnappers wouldn't know that the name

"Ross" meant anything—unlike a name like Rockefeller, or Vanderbilt, or Gates—and they probably wouldn't find the Ross daughters all that rich-looking. Clothes from J. Crew and L.L. Bean and Abercrombie and Fitch, ten-year-old station wagons to get around town in, jewelry limited to sterling-silver hoops in pierced ears—no, these people were nothing at all like "rich" as it was defined in the celebrity press. They simply had more money, and more influence, and had had both for generations back in time.

Of course, Gregor thought, Charlotte Deacon Ross was something else again, a matron from an earlier brand of matrons, somebody who not only expected to look rich but expected other people to notice. Even so, a potential kidnapper spying her in a store in Philadelphia or New York would probably put her down as one of the second or third rank, a Society woman manqué. Understatement in everything, Gregor told himself, even understatement in in-your-face hauteur. Charlotte would have been completely obvious only to her own kind and the climbers who followed them. That would have been her point.

The front of the Ross estate was awash in searchlights. There were the regular security lights, but also new ones, brought by the police, meant to help in the combing of the area. Gregor sat back in the cab and tried to think. If they were combing the area near the gates, then they must expect that somebody had come in that way. The murder had not been committed by somebody already in the house. Or had it? It was not so easy to make that sort of determination. Gregor was a little concerned that Frank and Marty were so invested in their theory that they would still assume the truth of it in the face of a death that couldn't possibly be part of that particular puzzle. Gregor leaned forward and tried to see out the windshield. The drive wound and curved and zigzagged, as if whoever had put it in was really trying to make an obstacle course for go-carts to race down.

They pulled up in front of the house itself, a long Gothic pile stretched out a good two hundred feet along the drive, 50,000 square feet, 100 family rooms. A uniformed police officer came toward them, waving. At the last moment, he saw Gregor sitting in the backseat and waved the cab on. The cab pulled as far forward as it could, which wasn't much. There seemed to be dozens of vehicles parked near the front door: police cars, a forensics van, an ambulance, unmarkeds. It looked as if everybody in this corner of the Main Line had decided to come down here and get in on the action.

The cab pulled to a halt. Gregor glanced at the meter, took his wallet out of his pocket, and threw enough money into the front seat to be sure that the driver would get not only his fare but a tip. He got out into the cold dark air and looked around. Frank Margiotti was standing in the arched front doorway, talking to someone Gregor did not recognize. A moment later, the unrecognized someone took off for the interior of the house, and Frank looked up and saw Gregor.

"Thank God," he said, running down the front steps to where Gregor was still stymied by the maze of equipment laid out along the walk. "Sorry to pull you away from whatever it was you were doing, but we need some help here. And we didn't want to ask the FBI."

"Not that particular agent of the FBI, no," Gregor said. "Is he still here?"

"We don't know," Frank said. "We didn't call him. We've got—ah. This is a mess. They just got the body back. Tony Ross's body. They were in there getting ready for the wake."

"And Mrs. Ross was where when she died?"

Frank Margiotti waved his hands down the drive. "Out there. It was nearly exact, really. She must have been doing what Tony Ross was doing on the night he was killed, going down the walk for some reason—"

"Tony Ross was greeting somebody," Gregor pointed out. "There were people arriving that night, a lot of them. Were there people coming here tonight?"

"No. Not until tomorrow. Tomorrow is the wake." Frank Margiotti looked around. "I've been on the Main Line most of my life. I've lived with these people. I still can never get over them. Who would want to have a wake in their own house?"

"It's a big house," Gregor said.

"Yeah, yeah. It's a dead body. A very dead body. I wouldn't want a dead body anywhere near where I sleep. They're all in there in the something or other. Morning room."

"Who?"

"The daughters. Four of them. And this guy named David Alden. Like Miles Standish and John Alden, except I didn't say that, because I'm not crazy. Come on in. Marty is expecting you. And we're all completely strung out."

Gregor looked back over his shoulder to the walk on the other side of the door and saw that the chalk marks of the body were indeed down, and saw a barrier to make sure that nobody stepped on them or entered the immediate scene while forsenics was working. Then he followed Frank into the entrance hall. It was an entrance hall on a grand scale, built by a Robber Baron to accommodate delusions of grandeur that might have been less delusionary than many people supposed. It must have been remarkable to be newly rich in an age like that, when so many other people were becoming newly rich along with you, and nobody laughed when you brought back entire walls of English castles to install in the Pennsylvania suburbs.

The entrance hall led to another wide hall that Gregor remembered was called the gallery. There were paintings on the walls, but not important ones. The Rosses had a serious art collection somewhere. Gregor wasn't sure if it was on the grounds or outside them. Maybe they had endowed a museum. Toward the end of the gallery on the right side, doors were open and people were wandering in and out of them, but not many people, and not very often. Gregor noticed an enormous portrait of a portly man in formal evening dress with a monocle in his left eye. He looked less imposing than uncomfortable.

Frank went all the way to the end, to a swinging door that had been propped shut with a wastebasket. He turned right into the nearest room and said, "Here he is, Marty. Got here as soon as the cab could get him here."

Marty Tackner stopped talking to a tall young woman without makeup and came over. "Mr. Demarkian. We're glad to see you. Nobody has the faintest idea what happened—"

"I do," the young woman without makeup said. She strode over to them, looking angry. What she really looked like was Tony Ross, right down to the thick eyebrows that arched almost to a point at the center. "Somebody killed my mother, that's what happened."

"Marianne Ross," Marty said, apologetically.

Marianne Ross ran a single large, spread-fingered hand through her hair. "You're—who? I've seen you before."

"My name is Gregor Demarkian."

"I remember. You handled the Hannaford case out here a few years ago. God, that was a mess. I thought my mother was going to choke. My mother was the kind of woman who had hysterics about publicity. I suppose she'll get publicity now. I suppose there won't be any way to avoid it."

"No," Gregor said. "I don't think there will be."

Marianne Ross looked away. "You've got to wonder what's wrong with these people. Don't they have anything else to do? It isn't as if my parents were the Beatles, or whoever it is these days. It's not as if they were jumping around in front of television cameras every chance they got. They were very private people."

"Dominick Dunne says that nothing is as fascinating as rich people in a criminal circumstance."

"I can't stand Dominick Dunne. He's a throwback. And there's nothing criminal here. My parents didn't do anything but walk out their own front door and become the targets of a crank. He'll turn out to be an escaped mental patient or a member of the Symbionese Liberation Army."

"I'm not sure the Symbionese Liberation Army is still in existence," Gregor said.

Marianne Ross snorted. "It doesn't matter what they call themselves. It's all the same. They're all obsessed with money and they want to be famous and we're available. I don't understand why the police don't just round them all up and lock them away instead of waiting for somebody to be killed. It's the craziest thing I ever heard."

It was also in direct contradiction to the U.S. Constitution and to dozens of laws meant to safeguard the rights of people to express their opinions and receive due process in the criminal justice system, but Gregor didn't tell her that. Marianne Ross wasn't really listening. The rant was automatic, what she did instead of crying in front of a lot of people she didn't know.

"I've got to go talk to my sisters," she said. "They're upset as hell. We were all here to bury our father."

She turned on her heel and walked off. Gregor watched her go. Frank Margiotti and Marty Tackner watched her go too.

"She's something else," Marty said. "She's like a locomotive. I think we've just talked to the first woman president of the United States. Maybe we talked to the first woman Pope."

"I don't think the Pope can be a woman," Frank said.

"If she wants to be Pope, she'll fix that," Marty said. Then he turned to Gregor Demarkian. "Sorry, Mr. Demarkian. We're still in crisis mode here. Did Frank tell you anything about what's going on?"

"Not really," Gregor said.

"That one," Frank jerked his head to indicate the departed Marianne, "says she saw her mother go out onto the front walk a little after four."

"And was that usual?" Gregor asked.

"No," Marty said. "It wasn't. She said she had no idea what her mother was doing, but she didn't really think anything of it, because why would she? They were in their own house. Her mother could go out the front door and look around if she wanted to."

"I agree. Then what?" Gregor asked.

"Then," Frank said, "she—this is Marianne, now—she went down this hall to the den, which is about two doors closer to the center than this one. The rooms are pretty big.

That's a fair ways down. Marianne went into the den and she was there when she heard the shots."

"Why did she go into the den?" Gregor asked.

"She didn't say," Marty said. "Look, we're still in the middle of the crime scene. The body just left. I know it's best to get as much information as you can as soon as you can, but I think that under the circumstances—"

"No, no," Gregor said. "It's all right. I wasn't criticizing you. I was just trying to work things out. Marianne went into the den. Somebody else was here too, though, what's his name? Alden?"

"David Alden," Frank said.

"Who is David Alden?"

"He was Tony Ross's right-hand man at the bank," Frank said. "Not that he puts it like that, and not that anybody else does, either, but that's what it comes down to, I think. The guy who could pull the strings when Tony Ross wasn't there."

"The man who will take over now that Tony Ross is dead?" Gregor asked.

"I don't know," Frank said.

"So, okay. Let's see where we are. There were, in the house, Charlotte Deacon Ross herself. There were her daughters, Marianne and more—how many more?"

"Three," Marty said. "They're in the main living room, or whatever they call it."

"Fine. There was David Alden. Why?"

"We don't know yet," Frank said.

"All right," Gregor said. "What else? Who else? Servants?"

"About a dozen all told," Frank said. "That's the permanent, full-time staff. Most of them don't work in the house, though. This place has about a hundred acres and it's apparently mostly lawn. They keep it up."

"But they were in the house at the time Charlotte Deacon Ross died?"

"In their rooms or in the common room in the back wing," Frank said. "There's a back wing. This place is insane."

"Was there anybody else in the house?" Gregor asked. "Anybody at all? Visitors? Anybody?"

"No," Frank said. "Not that we know about. And that's it for the immediate family. Those are all Tony Ross's children."

"I don't think you have to worry about who was in the house," Marty said. "I've talked to the M.E. He can't be sure until all the tests are run, but it looks like this was another rifle hit, somebody off in the trees somewhere. We might be able to rule out anybody who was actually inside the house at the time Charlotte Deacon Ross died."

"Yes," Gregor said. "We might be able to do that." Then he went around the perimeter of the morning room. He looked out the big windows. They opened on the drive and the front walk too. He looked at the small, framed flower prints that lined one wall. He looked at the big Chippendale secretary that somebody—Charlotte Deacon Ross, most likely—had used as a desk.

He came to a stop in the middle of the room and looked at the carpet under his feet: not only Persian, but good Persian.

"Do you think this David Alden would talk to me if I wanted him to?" he asked.

2

He found David Alden in what the butler—there was no other word for him, he was a butler; Gregor found himself feeling like a character in *Remains of the Day*—called the living room. Why it was a living room when the half-dozen other rooms they had passed on the way to it that seemed to contain the same sort of furniture were not, Gregor didn't know, but this was the part about working with rich people that he had not been comfortable with even when he was with the FBI. That was one of the reasons why he had been so pleased to become an administrator. It was all well and good to write heroic-sounding novels about the integrity and farsightedness of the dedicated investigator in the face of the bureaucratic timidity of the timid administrator. In real life, the dedicated investigator spent his time uncomfortable in one way or another. Either he was hiding in bushes while the rain fell on his head, or he was sitting in "living rooms" with people who spoke a language less comprehensible than Martian. It was not the same with public officials. The White House did not make Gregor Demarkian nervous, and neither did the houses of senators if their names weren't Kennedy. He would have had a hard time putting words to the distinction, but he knew what it was, and he wasn't the only one. Every agent in the Bureau had hated having to work with "those people," and that was in spite of the fact that "those people" often took care to be relentlessly "nice."

The "living room" was an immense space, fourteen feet high, with a fireplace along one wall big enough to cook a side of beef on a spit. The fireplace surround was marble, and well taken care of. The Caravaggio on the wall was a real Caravaggio. The man Gregor presumed was David Alden was standing at one of the windows that looked out on the front walk and the drive, holding a drink in the air in one hand as if he were James Bond. It was only the attitude that worked, though. He was the wrong physical type for a Bond, too broad in the shoulders, too tall in the wrong way. If David Alden had gone to public schools instead of private ones, the other boys would have called him "string bean."

The butler cleared his throat. David Alden turned around. "Oh, yes," he said. "You must be Mr. Demarkian. Wardrop can bring you some coffee if you need it. Or tea. Or a drink."

"I don't think so," Gregor said. He made a mental note of it—David Alden felt enough at home here to tell the servants what to do. That could be true familiarity, or cheek. At the moment, he had no way of knowing.

Wardrop inclined his head slightly and went out. David Alden watched him go as if it really mattered to him. Then he shook his head slightly and turned his attention back to Gregor.

"Excuse me. My head is full of wool. We were in the same room for a while, you know, the night Tony was killed."

"I think I was in the room with half of social Philadelphia."

"Oh, no. It only felt like that. Most people weren't even close to arriving. People are like that. They like to be late. I've never understood it. Tony didn't either, but then, when the person waiting for you is the king of Saudi Arabia, being late is not an option, even if you're Tony Ross. You keep company with one of the Hannaford girls, don't you?"

"Ah," Gregor said, thinking that Bennis would climb the walls to hear herself described that way. Or maybe she wouldn't. He had to wonder why Bennis herself didn't make him nervous the way the people in this house did. "Yes," he said finally.

"Maybe I should say the last of the Hannaford girls. God, that was an awful thing. I'm sorry. I'm dancing around the subject. You came here to talk about Charlotte. *Can* you have a drink? Or is it true that policemen aren't allowed to drink on duty?"

"I'm not a policeman," Gregor said.

"No, of course not. You're a—consultant. I never know what that word means, even in business."

"In this case, it means you don't have to talk to me if you don't want to," Gregor said. "Most of the consulting I do does not concern talking with witnesses, although I like to do it when I'm able. Usually I stick to patterns of criminality and the structure of investigations. If you'd prefer not to, though, nobody can compel you."

"Hardly. I'd much rather talk to you than to them. Most of us would. You *are* keeping company with one of the Hannaford girls. We won't seem like alien life-forms to you. With them it's like talking to zookeepers, sometimes."

Gregor decided to say nothing at all about his recent reverie on the alienness of people like David Alden and houses like this one. "You'll have to talk to them eventually. They've got things to do at the moment, but they will insist. And anything you say to me here, I will report."

"Yes, of course." David waved it away. "I know that. I don't object to talking, although my lawyer will probably have a fit when he hears I have. They don't like you to talk to anybody, no matter how innocent a bystander you might be. The point is one of approach, and of understanding. It's very easy to fall under suspicion for behaving in an unorthodox way when there's nothing unorthodox in the way you're behaving. It's just a different set of customs, and expectations."

"Fair enough," Gregor agreed. "I don't really know that I understand the customs and expectations any better than you do, though. I came in because I've been thinking about a piece of information I received from someone a little while ago. She said that all of you, all the people connected to the ball last week, I suppose—I should have pinned it down, but at the time, it didn't seem important—that all of you belong to some kind of shooting club—"

"Oh, not all of us," David Alden said quickly, "but quite a few, yes. Marksmanship practice. That kind of thing. A lot of us took it up as a sport when we were children."

"Children with rifles?"

"Supervised, yes, of course, why not? It was offered as a team sport when I was in school, starting in about third form—fifth grade, I think. When we were ten-years-old."

"And you did this?" Gregor said. "You belonged to a marksmanship team when you were ten?"

"Absolutely. It was that or baseball in the spring, and I've never been able to stand baseball."

"Did your family insist you play sports?"

"My family?" David looked blank. "Oh, no, although it's expected of everybody, even now, that you'll participate in athletics in some way. Squash. Handball. It keeps you in shape. It was the school that insisted, though, of course. There were two hours at the end of every day when everybody had to take part in sports. I don't suppose it was the most comfortable thing for people who weren't good at it."

Gregor thought it sounded like hell on earth. "So you learned to shoot early. Did you learn to shoot well?"

"Very well," David said drily. "I was champion of my prep school and my college teams."

"Are you still that good? Have you kept up with it?"

"Of course." David smiled. "Don't think I'm giving anything away. You can check with my club. They keep records. Ryall Wyndham and I were the two best shots in the place except for Charlotte herself, and nobody is ever going to be better than Charlotte. Than Charlotte was. It's hard to wrap my mind around the fact that the reason we're standing here is that she's a bloody mess on the front walk and it isn't just Tony who's dead."

"Ryall Wyndham didn't learn to shoot at private school, though, did he?" Gregor asked. "His background is ambiguous."

David shrugged. "There are always people like Ryall around. All this matters to them. They do what they have to do to be close to it. I don't see that it matters. If you meet them in business, all you really care about is how good they are at what they do. If they're very good, you adopt them. Ryall isn't very good at business that I can tell. He writes a gossip column."

"About people who say they don't want to be gossiped about."

"That's all right, Mr. Demarkian. Ryall doesn't print the kind of gossip people like Charlotte don't want to see in the papers, and I'm not sure he could if he wanted to. It's not the thirties anymore. People don't care about debutantes and Society parties the way they used to. You couldn't make *The Philadelphia Story* now."

"People care about the banks," Gregor said. "They care about layoffs, and companies that pull up stakes and leave communities high and dry."

"True, but Ryall doesn't know much about any of that. He does know who's had to go off and have an abortion this month, and who got sent down from Foxcroft for sneaking a boy into her room at midnight, and who had to have a marriage annulled. It's odd to think that sixty years ago, that would have been big news in the local papers. Now, you'd practically have to hump Britney Spears under the Liberty Bell to get the papers to take any notice."

"You could kill somebody," Gregor said. "That gets the papers to take notice."

"True." David put his drink glass down. It was empty, except for the remains of two ice cubes at the very bottom. All the liquid was clear. "Before this, I was sure we had a political sniper. One of the antiglobalization people. One of the conspiracy people. We do watch them, you know. We're not idiots. Most of them are perfectly harmless, just a little cracked. Some of them are dangerous."

"And you think the murder of Charlotte Deacon Ross rules out any participation by conspiracy groups?"

"Well, it would have to, wouldn't it?" David said. "Why would a conspiracy group want to kill Charlotte? I wanted to kill Charlotte. Most of the people who knew her did. She was that kind of woman. I'm sometimes surprised at the fact that Marianne has managed to go this long without denouncing her mother in a tell-all book, but Marianne was Tony's favorite. She wouldn't have done anything to pain him. But a conspiracy group? The only thing Charlotte ever conspired at was fixing the invitation list for the Philadelphia Assemblies."

"It doesn't bother you that you've just admitted to having wanted to kill a woman who's just been murdered?"

"It doesn't bother me to admit to anything that's a matter of public record," David said, "and besides, you know as well as I do that I wasn't admitting to wanting to actually kill her. Don't be ingenuous."

"I'll try not to be," Gregor said. The lights coming through the front windows were changing. The strobe effect was getting fainter. Maybe one of the marked police cars was leaving. "Tell me," he said. "What are you doing here? You worked with Mr. Ross at his bank, didn't you?"

"Yes. I was his confidential assistant, which is a nice way of saying his hitman and his spy. A man in Tony's position has to have one."

"And the bank is where? The physical building, I mean. Where you work."

"It's in New York."

"What?"

"It's in New York," David said patiently. "It's in the financial district. We're only a few blocks from what used to be the World Trade Center. We were both at our desks when they evacuated the area on September eleventh. We had to close down for almost three days."

"Do you live in New York?" Gregor asked.

"I live in Philadelphia," David said. "I have a town house in Society Hill."

"And you commute from there to New York? Every day?"

"On and off. Sometimes I stay in New York for days. Sometimes I go back and forth. It's not all that odd," David said. "Lots of people do it. Tony did it. You can get in by Amtrak express in no time at all. Or you can do what Tony did, and have a driver. The commute is no worse than to the outer suburbs in Connecticut. And I grew up here."

"Every day," Gregor said again.

"The bank keeps an apartment in town. I stay over if I have to work late. My family is here. My friends are here. And New York can be a pressure cooker if you don't have someplace to go to get away from the insanity. Like I said, lots of people do it. Go up and down the road here and talk to the people in these houses. See how many of them include men who commute to New York."

Gregor filed it away for future reference. "Did you come here today from New York?"

"Yes," David said. "I worked up until about three-thirty and then I packed up my things and came on out. I was intending to work at home this evening."

"Why did you come here?"

"To see how Charlotte was getting on, and what the arrangements were about the funeral. The bank will bring people down on the day. We'll hire buses. But even yesterday, we weren't sure when the body would be released. There was no way to plan. I wanted to know."

"You could have called."

"I could have, yes, but I thought this would be more considerate. I'm sure Charlotte was sick of phone calls."

"Did you come down from New York on the night of the party?" Gregor asked.

"I did," David said, "and so did Tony and Charlotte."

"Wasn't Charlotte supposed to be supervising?"

"She was supervising. By cell phone. She had caterers in. They had something on for the night before that Charlotte couldn't miss, and then Tony had business in the city. It's this Price Heaven disaster. That was happening even then."

"Did they bring you down with them?" Gregor asked.

David shook his head. "No, not at all. I worked a lot later than Tony did that day. I had to, and it was Tony's obligation to be here for Charlotte, not mine. If I'd ended up missing the party or being an hour later, it wouldn't have mattered. If Tony had done either of those things, he'd better have had a damned good excuse in Charlotte's terms, and I'm not sure what that would have been. The end of the world and the Last Judgment might have qualified, but I wouldn't place bets on it."

"So," Gregor said. "You came down from New York on the night of the party, and you came down from New York today. And when you got here—what? There are gates, aren't there? And there's somebody guarding the gates?"

"There's somebody, yes," David said, "and he's a lot more competent than you think. Tony had a security service. They're armed. And they're good."

"He had this all the time, not just for the party? I thought security was reinforced because the first lady was expected to be here."

"It was," David said. "But security around here is always tight, or at least as tight as it can be. What happened the night of the party was that they tried to close off the bridle paths."

"Bridle paths for horses?"

"Right." David walked over to the windows and looked out. "All these places, all the properties along this road and the properties behind them, are connected by bridle paths. They have been for over a hundred years. People keep horses. And there's the Hunt Club, which is on the circuit too. It's what's been bothering me for months."

"Bothering you how?"

"Well," David said carefully, "Tony had the guard at the gate, armed. And on the night of the party, the secret service closed the bridle paths and patrolled the grounds closest to the house on foot. But Tony didn't have security people patrolling the grounds every day. Charlotte said it made her feel as if she were in jail, and Tony wasn't too happy at the idea either. But even if they had had people patrolling the grounds, it wouldn't have mattered, because the bridle paths would have to have remained open even now."

"What do you mean, open?"

"The bridle paths are rights of way," David said patiently. "They go between the properties, and they're rights of way. People on horseback have the right to use any of them at any time. That's been a condition of the deeds out here in this section of Bryn Mawr for a century. One of them comes right up close to the house about a hundred yards up the drive. One of them comes around the back near the terrace. You're sitting back there or standing out here and people you've never seen before come lumbering through on horseback. Of course, mostly they *are* people you know, but you see what I mean. It made a joke of any security Tony installed. Except for the night of the party, anybody could come barging onto this property at any time. It wouldn't be legal to try to stop him."

"What do you mean the secret service tried to close them off?"

"I mean it would have been impossible. Most people in these houses don't even know where they all are."

3

By the time the mobile crime lab was ready to leave, it was cold in the way it can only be if the wind is high and strong. The night was so black that looking beyond the security lights onto the lawn was like staring at tar. Gregor went out to the front steps and watched as Frank and Marty bent their heads together over a pair of notebooks. There was no point in being inside. Not only did the house still make him uncomfortable—and there was a good question: What made him so uncomfortable about the house?; from what he remembered, Bennis's father's house hadn't bothered him at all—but there was nobody to talk to. David Alden had sunk into a deep interior space. He responded to comments only when prodded. Marianne Ross was off somewhere in the private rooms with her three sisters. They would have been trained from birth not to come out in public during a situation that threatened their privacy. The really remarkable thing was that there was no press there. That was the good of having a gate near the road. Well, Gregor thought, the press would be here soon enough. It wouldn't take long before one of them found out about the bridle paths. Then they'd be on the doorstep, and there would be very little the family could do about them. In fact, at least one of them probably knew about the bridle paths already—Ryall Wyndham. From what Anne Ross Wyler had said about him, Gregor was surprised he hadn't shown up already, in the guise of a friend of the family.

Gregor went down the steps to where Frank and Marty were standing. The chalk marks were still clear on the sidewalk, but there seemed to be no barriers up. If this was a crime scene, it was one that was going to be neglected, at least in the immediate future. You could throw a family out of their little raised ranch for a week or two while you went over the evidence. You couldn't do that with a family like the Rosses or a house like this. Gregor made a face.

Frank and Marty looked up as he came over.

"We got more of them," Frank said, shaking a sheaf of papers loose from behind the paper in his notebook. "Found it in the morning room, the one where they all were when we got here. Look at this."

Gregor looked. It was *The Harridan Report* again, yet another edition from the ones he'd seen. He scanned the first page and raised his eyebrows. "Reptiles?"

"I wonder how she got it," Marty said.

"I'd expect somebody sent it to her," Frank said.

"Yeah, but you wouldn't expect any of the people she knew to know about it." Marty shook his head. "You know the people who are into that kind of stuff. They just got laid off at a mill someplace, or they've worked forever at a convenience store."

"Maybe it was one of the servants," Gregor suggested. He tried to shake off the feeling that there was something ridiculous about talking about the servants. He felt as if he'd been taken hostage in an English novel. "I wonder how they decide to employ the people they employ. They live on the premises, don't they?"

Marty checked his notebook. "About half of them do. According to the big one—Marianne?—it's hard to get people to live in these days, except immigrants, and they have nothing against immigrants, but there aren't enough of them to staff a house this size. When it's running optimally, it takes twenty-five people on full-time, fifteen of them in the house itself."

"How big is it?" Gregor asked.

"One hundred twenty-five rooms, plus servants' quarters." Marty shook his head. "It's not a house, it's a hotel. For God's sake. I've lived all my life on the Main Line. I know what it's like. But this is insane. If I hit one of those three-hundred-million-dollar lotteries tomorrow, I wouldn't want a place like this."

"They're used to places like this," Frank pointed out. "This is the way they've always lived. They probably wouldn't feel comfortable in your place. They'd be too cramped."

Gregor tried to pull the conversation back on track. "The first thing you need to do is to find out what kind of background checks they do on the people they hire to work here, and especially the ones who live in the house. The ones who don't still matter, though, because the chances are they'd be able to get through that gate any time they wanted to, because whoever is guarding it would regard them as having legitimate business here. Then you need to talk to the whole lot of them one by one. I'm not in love with the idea that this will turn out to be a case of 'the butler did it'—"

"*That* butler didn't do it," Frank said. "He's a waxwork saint."

"—but we have to at least check it out." Gregor was imperturbable. "If there does turn out to be some connection between these murders and *The Harridan Report*, if there does turn out to have been some kind of domestic terrorism involved—"

"Terrorism?" Frank looked blank. "I don't think this has anything to do with terrorism. There aren't any bombs involved. Nobody blew up the Liberty Bell."

Gregor shook his head. "Terrorism isn't always the World Trade Center or Timothy McVeigh. Terrorists commit targeted murders all the time. It's part of the equation in the Middle East all the time. And think of the Unabomber."

"I understand why people like that might want to kill Anthony Ross," Frank said, "but what would be the point of killing his wife? Let's be reasonable here."

"I agree," Gregor said. "We do have to be reasonable. And the first thing we have to be reasonable about is those flyers, or newsletters, or whatever we're supposed to call them. They seem to be everywhere, and they're all about this family. Or all the ones I've seen have something to do with the Rosses."

"We have a few more down at the station that don't," Marty said. "We've collected maybe fifty different ones, all told. A lot of them are just general. There's a big plot afoot to destroy the Constitution and bring the United States into a One World Government ruled by the UN. Bill Clinton was in on this plot. So is George W. Bush. So was Bush Senior. Kennedy was murdered in a plot run by the CIA, the Kremlin, and the Vatican. All the presidents of the United States are related to each other, and they're really descendants of Martians, or the Devil, or something. I can never wrap my mind around that part. The world's thirteen richest families have been the same since the something dynasty, but they 'change their names so people will think change is happening when it isn't."

"The Merovingian dynasty, from the early Middle Ages," Frank said. He shrugged. "I had Jesuits."

"Fine," Gregor said. "We need to go over them, one by one. We need to find out how many of them directly mention any member of this family. We need to figure out if there's anybody else they mention on a regular basis and what's happened to that person or persons. We might be looking at another murder down the road. We might be looking back at a death that either wasn't originally thought to be a murder, or that was tagged as a murder but was never solved. Then we need to find this Michael Harridan. Do we have any idea who he is?"

"We know who his organization is," Frank said. "That's what those FBI guys were working on, America on Alert. Steve what's-his-name was going to their meetings. Before you nailed his ass, Walker whoever was giving us chapter and verse. Where they meet. Who goes to meetings regularly. I've got it written down."

"Good," Gregor said.

"Do you really think it's going to turn out to be America on Alert?" Marty asked. "I mean, I suppose it could be, but it doesn't feel right to me. Maybe I'll feel differently when I meet them, but right now, I just can't see how somebody who believes all that stuff"—he pointed to *The Harridan Report* Gregor was now holding—"I don't see how somebody like that could be mentally integrated enough to pull off a pair of murders like these."

"Timothy McVeigh—" Frank started.

"Yeah, yeah," Marty said. "Timothy McVeigh. But this wasn't Timothy McVeigh. It wasn't the September eleventh attacks. All those people had to do was be stupid, be obvious, and be bold. This sucker took precision. What do you think, Mr. Demarkian?"

"I don't know." This was the truth. Gregor really didn't know what to think at the moment, and the more he tried to work it out in his head, the more confused he got. This was not the way it was supposed to work. "I would," he said, "be careful not to close off other options. For instance, we need to get a reading on the will, who benefits. We need to know if Tony Ross or Charlotte Ross had any life insurance policies. That's doubtful, but not impossible, especially when it comes to Charlotte. Then we need to look into the daughters. Do we know if they were here for the party, or expected to be here?"

"No," Frank said.

"We need to find out," Gregor said. "And we can't fail to remember that those girls could have gotten on this estate at any time they wanted, even on the night of the party, even without an invitation, even with the extra security all over everything. They'd have been cleared. The same is likely true of Anne Ross Wyler."

"Who?" Frank said.

"Tony Ross's sister," Gregor said. "She runs an outreach program for young prostitutes in Central Philadelphia—"

"I know her." Marty straightened up. "Annie Wyler. She's famous. Especially with cops. She keeps trying to get them to arrest the johns, and you know they're not going to do that in Philadelphia, not when the john's in a Lexus or a Mercedes. She takes pictures and sends them to the newspapers. Sometimes they get printed in one of those alternative press things. She's Tony Ross's sister?"

"She is," Gregor said. "It might be a good idea to check into her background too. If she has any money of her own. If she needs any. What her relationship with her brother and sister-in-law was. Ask the same questions about David Alden back there, especially about his relationship with his boss. Was he secure in his job? Had something happened recently that might make it likely that he'd get fired? Has there ever been any hint of embezzlement, or recklessness? Look into both of the Rosses' close personal friends. Find out if any of them are in the will. Find out if any of them have money problems. Find out if any of them had reason to think that the death of one or both of these people would be an advantage to them. Most of the time, it comes down to money."

"Yeah." Frank looked relieved. "I can handle money. I understand money. This other stuff—" His body shook and he looked away. "I don't like nuts," he said. "They're wild cards. They're too unpredictable. You can't get inside their heads."

Gregor grunted, which might have been agreement, or might not have. On one level, he didn't think the nuts were hard to understand at all. They were like a record with only one song on it. The song played over and over again. There was no room for deviation. The problem was that the song didn't follow any of the accepted rules of composition, so that if you didn't know what was coming next, you couldn't necessarily figure it out. Still, there was this about nuts—they were relentlessly, unswervingly logical. *A* was followed by *B* was followed by *C*. Neither emotion nor self-interest was allowed to interfere. Unfortunately, reason wasn't allowed to interfere either. *A* could be that Martians were kidnapping eggplants from farmers' gardens from one end of the country to the other—and that was the one thing they would not question, and that they would not allow you to question, either.

It was too cold to be standing outside like this. The wind was too harsh. Gregor snapped up the collar of his coat and put his hands in his pockets.

He wanted to make copies of all the *Harridan* newsletters and read them in as close to chronological order as he could get them. He wanted to do that tonight.

TWO

1

There were police everywhere. Kathi Mittendorf had seen them, or the traces of them, tucked out of sight in the bushes that marked the edge of the little park at the end of the street, slipping into bathrooms in the small branch of the public library where she went to get her romance books. She had been very careful, since the death of Anthony van Wyck Ross, not to look too dedicated to the cause of America on Alert. She knew the way the Illuminati could make the sanest, most ordinary citizen look like a "fanatic." She was even a little proud of herself. She had always wondered what would happen to her if the Illuminati began to put the pressure on. She hadn't really imagined that she would ever be important enough for them to bother with. America on Alert was dangerous to the Illuminati and their plans for a One World Government. Michael was dangerous to them. Kathi saw herself as a foot soldier for the movement, one of those absolutely necessary people who filled the ranks behind the leaders who knew what the score was and how to negotiate it. Her newfound importance had come on her very suddenly. It was the result of a combination of factors, no one of them individually significant: that she lived in the house where they stored the weapons; that she was the one who had picked up the phone when Michael needed to talk; that she had been the only one to be really friendly with Steve. Things came together and you used them. You used every advantage you could find. They were few and far between. Kathi didn't care that she was an accident. Sometimes she found herself stopping in the middle of the day, caught and startled by the way her life had changed, and it was almost like being drunk—almost, because Kathi didn't get drunk. She'd tried it once back in high school and ended up sick and embarrassed in the back of somebody's pickup truck. She wondered what would happen to her now that she had become the focal point of an entire operation. She did not expect to live through it, or to become somebody like Michael. She couldn't see herself as a seasoned leader with a history of operations to her credit. What she hoped for, in the long run, was what Timothy McVeigh had accomplished—not the bombing, but the martyrdom. She'd be smarter about it than McVeigh had been, though. She wouldn't keep her mouth shut. She'd talk to every reporter who asked for an interview. She'd tell them everything she knew about the Illuminati, and the way the world's secret power elite was manipulating events behind the scenes to destroy the freedoms Americans had won for themselves in the Constitution and to bring the American government and the American people under the control of the United Nations. She'd tell them the truth about Timothy McVeigh and the World Trade Center bombing. She'd expose the CIA and the Bildebergers and the Trilateral Commission and the Rhodes Scholarship program and the way they were all run by the same people and working together to accomplish the same thing. It didn't matter that not many people would believe her, some would. It didn't matter that the press would make her sound like a psychiatric case, the way they had with David Koresh and Randy Weaver. There were people out there who didn't know the truth but expected it. There were other people who only knew that things were terribly wrong and they were terribly unhappy. Those people would hear her in a way the brainwashed people wouldn't. That was the way it worked. When the FBI and the Bureau of Alcohol, Tobacco and Firearms destroyed Koresh and the Branch Davidians, and the footage was played on television for the world to see, *some* people began to realize that it was not paranoid to believe that America was run by a secret government that hated the Bill of Rights. It was only sensible. When the FBI and the Bureau of Alcohol, Tobacco and Firearms killed Randy Weaver's wife and son with high-powered rifles because the Weavers wouldn't let the evil agents of the illegitimate secret government onto their private land, *some* people began to wonder if the things they'd heard about the FBI—those uncorruptable agents of law and order—were nothing but propaganda. What kind of a government engaged in propagandizing its own citizens? It was like a gigantic jigsaw puzzle. Until you'd fit at least some of the pieces together, it made no sense at all. Kathi had seen the puzzle almost complete. That was what Michael Harridan had done for her, and she would never be able to thank him enough.

The truth of it was that she was more than a little excited at the thought of becoming a martyr. It made her happier than she had ever been, and the thought of herself being interviewed on *60 Minutes* by a somber-faced Ed Bradley made her feel as if her body were expanding endlessly, ballooning into space. There was always the possibility that the Illuminati would get wind of what she was doing and shoot her instead of taking her alive. There was an even better possibility that they would make sure she died in prison, and early, in one of those prison murders the authorities always claimed it was impossible to solve. She would have to be careful about both those things.

At the moment, she had to be careful to be as normal as she always was, a middle-aged woman who worked at Price Heaven and wasn't even a supervisor, although women half her age who had been working at Price Heaven far less long had advanced that far. She had checked and rechecked the guns and the explosives. They were safely in place in the hollows between the walls, under the floor in the basement, disguised by wads of yellowed newsprint in the old woodstove nobody had used for as long as Kathi could remember. It was not the arms she was worried about. Nobody could claim she was about to shoot anybody any time sooner. It would take a good half hour to unearth anything useful. She wasn't worried that the arms would be confiscated, either, because of course this was not the only house where they kept weapons and explosives. There were houses all around the city, and only Michael knew where they all were. Everything was ready. Everything had been carefully planned. If the need arose, America on Alert—or at least the core of it—could be out of sight and undetectable in an instant. What worried her was the police, slithering as they were in bushes and bathrooms, staying out of sight. Something was about to happen. She could feel it. She didn't know what it was. It was one thing to wait in expectation for martyrdom. It was another to just wait, not knowing what would happen next, not being sure what you were supposed to do.

It was seven o'clock in the morning. Her shift started at ten. She had taken her shower, and eaten her breakfast, and gotten dressed in plain black slacks and a white blouse. Later, at the store, she would put on the green apron she was required to keep there and be in full uniform. The uniform bothered her to no end. For one thing, she had had to buy it, or rather the slacks and blouse, from Price Heaven itself. She had been told she was being given an "employee discount," but there was no way to prove that. Price Heaven didn't sell its uniform pieces to the general public. The pieces weren't out on the floor with price tags on them so that she could check to see if she was getting any discount at all. For another thing, there was the simple fact that it was a uniform. That was what the Illuminati liked to do to people. They liked to turn them into cogs in a machine, ciphers without individuality. Ending individuality was one of the things they cared about most.

She did not have a television set. She'd thrown out the one she had at the end of her first month in America on Alert. She'd finally understood how that set was destroying her, because it was sending out the signals that brainwashed her into passivity while she thought she was just watching *Golden Girls*. She didn't get the newspaper, either, because she didn't want the newspaper delivery man coming to her door. Everybody knew that newspapers were one of the greatest bastions of evil in America. Even people who would say that America on Alert was full of kooks knew that. Kathi didn't want to give the newspaper a chance to plant a bug on the premises. As it was, Michael came in once a month while she was at work and swept the place for bugs and did whatever else had to be done to make sure that any bugs he didn't catch wouldn't work. She knew he'd been there because he always left a little box of four Russell Stover chocolates on the dining-room table for her to find. She was restless and a little upset. She could read *The Harridan Report*, but she'd read all the issues of it she had. She could look through the longer literature America on Alert put out for the public, but she'd read all that too. She could recite some of it by heart. This was how she knew television was an addiction. It had been years, but the simple fact that the set wasn't in the house for her to turn on to pass the time made her the next best thing to panicked.

The phone rang. She had call-waiting—Michael paid for that; she couldn't have afforded it herself, since Price Heaven paid not much better than minimum wage and never gave anybody enough hours to be "full-time"—and she raced across the dining room into the living room to look at the numbers on the little screen. Sometimes she just turned the ringers off on all the phones and left the machines on. If it was somebody from America on Alert, they would said "bloody wrong number" into the machine and then hang up. She would turn the ringer on on one of the phones and then wait until it rang. Nobody from America on Alert would leave a real message on an answering machine, of course. It was virtually impossible to erase an answering machine tape, at least in any practically useful way. That was the kind of thing that showed up in evidence at trials and, worse, got used to track down the members of an organization when one of their number was captured but would not talk. She wished she had kept just one of the guns out for herself to use. She understood why Michael got upset at the very idea of that—if she had a gun on her, they could shoot her dead and claim she had shot first. They could claim that even if the gun was in her purse and her purse was lying on the ground next to her—but she would have felt safer if she had been armed. She found it hard to sleep knowing that there was no longer a loaded Luger on her nightstand next to the glass-based table lamp with its sky blue polyester shade.

The phone number on the screen was not one she knew. She stood still and waited. The answering machine kicked in. A moment later, she heard Michael's voice say, "bloody wrong number." The *bloody* was a work of genius. It didn't mean anything. It was some swear word people used in England. It wasn't the kind of thing anybody in America would use. Unless, of course, the Illuminati got wind of what was going on. Then they could use it to try to trick her into betraying herself, or Michael. In this case, though, Michael's voice had been clear and unmistakable. She turned the ringer on and waited.

The phone rang. The bell was harsh and overloud. The call-waiting screen flickered. Kathi picked up.

"Yes?"

"Have you seen the news today?" Michael asked.

"No." Kathi bit her lip. She didn't want to defend herself. It made her feel small. Michael should know by now that she never saw the news before she went out in the morning, and then she only saw it, or heard about it, secondhand.

"Go out and buy yourself a paper," Michael said. "Don't read just the front page."

"What I'm looking for isn't on the front page?"

"Some of it is. Read the business section too. The really important thing is in the business section."

"Is there something in particular in the business section?" Kathi hated this part. She hated the business section. It always seemed written in code.

"Don't worry," Michael said. "You'll see what it is as soon as you lay eyes on it. And you'll see the other thing too.

On the front page. The small thing they're going to pretend is the big story. Go now. I'll call you back at eight and we can go over what our response should be. Can you get hold of Susan?"

"Yes." Kathi didn't want to.

"Good. Get hold of her and have her at your place at eight. Turn on the speaker on the speakerphone. We'll have a conference call. Now I've got to go."

"But—" Kathi said.

The phone had gone to dial tone in her ear. She hated that sound. She hung up. Her coat was lying across the couch that wasn't really a couch. It was too small. A "love seat," people called them. She made a face at it and at the worn spots in what had once been fake velvet but now looked like matted mush. She put her coat on and took her wool hat out of the left-hand pocket. Her gloves—wool gloves, not leather ones—were inside the hat. She hated going out before she had to. Being outside was different from being at home. You were much more exposed. Somebody could shoot you and take all your identification, and even your best friends wouldn't know for weeks that you were dead.

She went out and locked the door behind her. She had triple locks on all the doors, although she wasn't in the least worried about ordinary, garden-variety burglars and rapists. She went down the front steps and up the block. This was not a good neighborhood, although it was not one of the worst, either. Here, the houses were interspersed with dry cleaning stores and candy stores and hardware stores. None of the big chains had bothered to venture here except for McDonald's and Dunkin' Donuts. To go to the bookstore, to go to Starbucks or Radio Shack, you either had to go to better neighborhoods or to the Main Line to the malls.

There was a candy store at the corner that served as a newsstand. The newspapers were out front in a wire rack. There were lots and lots of copies of *The Philadelphia Inquirer* and a few of both *The New York Times* and *The Washington Post*. The headlines in the *Times* and the *Post* were about something President Bush was doing that involved Attorney General John Ashcroft. The headline on the *Inquirer* said:

WIFE OF SLAIN FINANCIER MURDERED

Kathi picked up a copy, found some change in her pocket, and went into the store. The picture of Charlotte Deacon Ross was a posed one that had been taken in a studio. She was shown only from the shoulders up, looking as if she were wearing nothing but pearls.

The newsstand owner took her money and grunted. Kathi ignored him. She thought he might be a spy, but Michael didn't agree with her. In the long run, it probably didn't matter. She had tried to give him some of America on Alert's pamphlets, and he had called her a lot of unpleasant names.

Out on the street again, she stopped and began to page through the newspaper, looking for the business section. She was not very interested in the death of Charlotte Deacon Ross. It might mean that the police would have to back off on America on Alert, since there was no reason at all why patriots would want to harm a silly Society woman who spent her life planning parties, but the police could always find some way to justify doing what they wanted to do. Besides, she was prepared for everything and anything to come of the murder of Tony Ross, which had been carried out in the way it was carried out precisely because that would make it possible for the authorities to "do something" about the threat that America on Alert posed for them. Nothing was an accident. Nothing was a coincidence. Everything was planned.

She got to the business section and saw, immediately, what Michael had been talking about. The headline reached across most of the page, something she'd noticed that newspapers tended not to do on any page except the very front one.

PRICE HEAVEN FILES FOR CHAPTER ELEVEN

REORGANIZATION CALLS FOR CLOSING OF 300 STORES

Suddenly, her throat felt very scratchy. Her stomach felt raw. There was a bench in a little shelter where the bus stopped. She went to that and sat down, the paper still open in front of her face. She wasn't reading the story. She knew what it would say. Michael always pointed out that this was the Illuminati's most treasured tactic. They wanted the people to be prosperous, but not sure of their prosperity. If people began to feel that there was nothing to worry about, they'd always be able to find work and enough to eat and enough to have the things they wanted, they would stop being docile. That was what happened in the sixties, when everything began to go completely out of control. Now they were more careful. They made sure there were always downturns and layoffs. They threw some of their least important companies into bankruptcy. They cut jobs right before Christmas and placed the news very prominently in the newspapers and on the television news—but never on the front page, and never as the lead story. The trick was to let people know at the same time you had them distracted by trivialities. That way they'd become uneasy and afraid, but not be able to figure out who was the cause of either, or what to do about it. The wind around her legs was very cold. She hadn't noticed it before. A bus had stopped, and people were getting out. She didn't notice them, either, and when the driver finally pulled the door shut in disgust, she didn't realize he had been waiting for her.

If she hadn't been taught to understand the plan, if she hadn't learned all about why things like this happened and what they were used for, she would have broken down right on this bench and cried for an hour.

2

Anne Ross Wyler had been depressed and jumpy all morning, long before she heard the news about her sister-in-law. Morning was not the best time in this neighborhood. Even in the half-light of a grey and overcast day, it was too easy to see the buildings around Adelphos House as what they really were: abandoned, or worse; haunted the way houses can only be haunted if their ghosts are still made of flesh and blood. Besides, Anne thought, getting herself coffee in the Adelphos House kitchen while she pretended not to look at Ryall Wyndham's column left lying faceup on the kitchen table, there was nobody around. The whores and the junkies were all night people. So were the pimps and dealers. Even the pawnshop didn't bother to open until noon. Annie had gone in there once to see what it was like. She'd ended up disappointed. She'd expected sin and sexuality, some kind of apocalyptic vision. She'd always secretly suspected that the people who lived on the streets lived more exciting lives than the one she had been brought up to live. They had adventures, and passions, and pasts. The truth was a thin layer of grime on the glass of display cases and mundane articles—class rings, ancient typewriters, gloves with the fingertips worn almost to nothing—waiting for buyers who would never materialize. Except, Annie had realized, that they would have to materialize. Somebody had to buy these things, or the pawnbroker would make no money.

She poured coffee into the first mug she could find in the first cabinet she opened. She never noticed what she ate and drank from, any more than she noticed what she wore. She put the mug on the table and sat down in front of Ryall Wyndham's column. It was illustrated by three small pictures, all murky, of women in evening dress. *Mrs. Carter Lindford at the Philadelphia Opera Gala*, one of them said. She remembered Mrs. Carter Lindford as a girl named Abigail Hull Drake, who used to spell out her whole name like that on English essays when they were both at Madeira. People went on doing the same things over and over again, without thinking about why they were doing them. They went to school where they were expected to go. They went to college where they were expected to go. They went into law or banking or university teaching because that was the kind of thing the people they knew did. They thought they believed in God, but except for the one or two of them who converted to

Catholicism or got born again and caught up in Bible study, most of them really didn't.

The first story in Ryall Wyndham's column was a progress report on the investigation into Tony Ross's murder. It said less than similar stories that had appeared in print and on television in the last few days, but it said it with an air of insinuating archness that was meant to indicate that its author knew much more than he was telling. All of Ryall Wyndham's writing sounded like that. It was what he sold to the people who read him, the illusion that they were on the inside of a world they were sure was barred to them forever, secret, out of sight.

The second story in Ryall Wyndham's column was about a dinner party at the house of somebody Annie had never heard of. If Wyndham had to stick to real Philadelphia Society for his columns, he'd make it into print about once a month. She looked at the picture of Ryall Wyndham himself up at the top near the headline and the byline. The picture was almost vanishingly small, and even more murky than the others, and she could get no impression of the man beyond what her memory served her. She tried to imagine what he had looked like in the back of a car being sucked off by Patsy Lennon, and couldn't do it. She couldn't imagine any man like that, and she had seen a few in the act.

The coffee was terrible. She didn't care. She had long ago learned to live with it. She was hungry, but it was too much trouble to go looking through the refrigerator to see if there was anything she wanted to eat. There might be, or there might be just the raw vegetables Lucinda liked to stock up on for making chicken soup. She wondered why she couldn't make herself sleep later. There was nothing to be done this early in the day, and by the time she got to the point where there was something to do, she was exhausted. She fiddled with her *Freedom FROM Religion* button. There was a part of her that was terrified that she would one day accidentally wear it upside down. Then she turned to the paper's front page.

It was a bad picture of Charlotte, one of those posed portraits women had taken when they were chairwomen of charity committees. The pearls were fake—Annie knew the difference between Charlotte's fake pearls and her real ones, but she would have suspected even if she hadn't—and Charlotte's skin looked sallow, as if she had recently been ill. It was not the picture Charlotte would have chosen if she had known she would appear on the front page of a newspaper, but Charlotte would never have wanted to appear on the front page of a newspaper. Seeing that picture, anybody who didn't know her would assume that Charlotte was a grade-*A* bitch. They would be right.

The problem, Annie thought, was that she felt a little too sick to her stomach. She was sure that if she'd had something inside her to throw up, she would have done it. Instead, she licked her lips, and then bit them. Something had happened to the nerve endings under her skin. She *had no* nerve endings under her skin. Her head hurt. Her body ached. She couldn't read the words on the page. Everything was blurry.

Outside, it started to rain. Annie could hear the drops hitting the panes of the kitchen windows, harder in that section of the wall where the gutter had collapsed and not yet been replaced. She got up and took her coffee with her. The house felt too quiet around her, just as the street felt too quiet around the house. Sometimes they had one or more of the girls staying over, waiting for a ticket home or to go to a treatment program, but this was not one of those times. Later on there would be scheduled activities and events: an encounter group; a self-assertiveness class; a class on how to use a computer. Annie wanted noise, distraction, company. Even the gunfire of a gang war in the street would have been better than this silence.

Lucinda was in the front parlor—the living room, she called it, and Annie tried to call it that too. The curtains were pulled back to let in what little sun there was. The glass of the windowpanes shone, newly polished. Lucinda had been working. She had taken all the books off the shelf so that she could dust.

"Well," Annie said.

"Did you just get up?" Lucinda asked her.

Annie came into the living room and sat down on the couch. It was an exceptionally long couch, big enough to fit half-a-dozen people. She remembered thinking, when she bought it, that Adelphos House would have crowds of young women on the premises all the time. They would need some place to sit.

"You left the paper on the table," Annie said. "You had it open to Ryall's column."

"Did you read it?"

"Ryall's column?"

"The paper."

"I read the front page," Annie said. "Why didn't you wake me up?"

Lucinda had finished dusting the shelves. She put her dust cloth and the Pledge on the floor and began to pick up books and put them back. "I didn't see any point," she said. "You can't do anything about it. It wouldn't have changed anything if I'd made you get up even earlier than usual and you ended up even more tired than usual when tonight came. And I didn't want to leave it, right there, where you'd just sort of walk in on it, without warning. It wouldn't seem right, somehow."

Annie wanted to say that she had walked in on it without warning. Whatever else could she have done when she wasn't expecting what she eventually saw? She looked over her shoulder at the street. It was empty. The three houses that faced this one directly had all lost all the glass from their windows. One of them leaned, slightly, backwards.

"I didn't actually read the front page," Annie said. "I read the headline. Then things got blurry. Did you read it all?"

"Most of it."

"Do you want to tell me what it said?"

Lucinda stopped working. "What do you think it said? She was killed."

"Shot? The way Tony was shot?"

"With a rifle, yes. Or police believe with a rifle. Like that. You know they're never very specific in the paper."

"When?"

Lucinda blinked. "Last night."

"No," Annie said. "What time last night?"

"Oh, I don't remember. Six, I think. Or the police arrived at the scene at six. Or something like that. Why is the time important? Are you worried about being a suspect?"

"No." This was true. There was no reason for anybody to suspect her of anything. She had none of the usual motives. She would inherit nothing because Tony had died. She most certainly would inherit nothing because Charlotte had. She hadn't spent enough time with her brother or her sister-in-law in recent years to hate them. She turned her face away from the street. Lucinda had gone back to putting books back on shells.

"There's a lot in the article about domestic terrorism," Lucinda said. "And there's a sidebar on the inside page, all about acts of violence by domestic terrorist groups. About this murder of an FBI agent out in Indiana or somewhere. Some group that called itself a posse."

"The Posse Comitatus," Annie said. "It's this obscure provision in a law. I remember them, vaguely."

"I don't."

"They were another one of those groups," Annie said. "The United Nations is evil. Any day now, it's going to take over the U.S. and we'll all be part of a One World Government. The world is secretly run by a cabal of the Vatican, the Freemasons, the British monarchy, and the Kremlin. Like that man who's been sending us that newsletter every once in a while."

"Michael Harridan."

"Whoever." Annie still had the coffee cup in her hand. It was nearly empty. She had forgotten all about it. She put it down on the coffee table. "The thing is," she said, "I don't think the police are going to buy that explanation anymore, the domestic terrorist one. Why would domestic terrorists want to kill Charlotte?"

"Because she raised money for the UN?"

"Lame," Annie said. "That's not the way those people

think. They'd choose something about the government, or somebody like Tony, somebody with influence."

"There's that priest who was here the night it all happened," Lucinda said. "His church was bombed. Doesn't that sound like domestic terrorism?"

"It sounds like religious bigotry and violence, but I don't know if it sounds like domestic terrorism. He had some little church on a side street. Why would a domestic terrorist bother to blow it up?"

"Because he thought it was part of this One World Government?"

"It's more likely some half educated idiot who's never heard of the Eastern churches and thinks they're practicing witchcraft on Cavanaugh Street. And there's no reason to think the incidents are connected, just because they happened on the same night. There must have been a dozen acts of violence in Philadelphia and on the Main Line that night."

"It doesn't make sense that they wouldn't be connected," Lucinda said. "Or maybe I've just seen too many crime shows. On crime shows, they would have been connected."

"Maybe they would have been."

Lucinda started taking things off one of the side tables. It was, Annie thought, what she did when she was nervous.

"The thing is . . ." Annie said.

"What?" Lucinda said.

"Nothing." Annie got up. She took the coffee cup off the coffee table. The bottom of the cup was muddy where some of the instant crystals had failed to dissolve. "It doesn't matter. I'm going to go for a walk."

"It's freezing out there."

"Yes, I know. I'll wear a coat. I won't be cold. Why do you think it got cold so early this year?"

"Global warming," Lucinda said.

Annie only half-heard her. She went down the hall to the kitchen and put the cup in the sink. She got her coat off the peg near the back door and put it on. She went back to the front of the house and out the front door. She did not stop in the living room again. She did not listen to hear if Lucinda was cleaning.

It was truly cold out, freezing, bitter, harsh. It was the worst she could ever remember it being, ever, no matter how far back in her memory she searched. She had reached that stage in her life when her entire childhood seemed to have existed only in summer. She wished she could see some signs of summer now.

Eventually, everything became known. Sometimes it became known quickly, and sometimes it became known only after a long time, but it wasn't true that people could keep secrets. In the long run, everything you'd ever done would be on display for all the world to see.

3

It only took a good night's sleep for Father Tibor Kasparian to realize there were drawbacks to staying in Bennis Hannaford's apartment. He'd never been able to sleep well in hospitals, and he'd been dreading coming back to Cavanaugh Street as well. He hadn't been sure how he'd react to the sight of Holy Trinity as a bombed-out mess. Then the people had just been too much. There had been too many of them at once, and too much food, and too much talk about things he knew nothing about, like this murder in Bryn Mawr. By the time Gregor had finally shown up, he'd been drooping. By the time he'd been left alone in the apartment for three minutes, he was on his way to bed. He noticed nothing, at the time, except that Bennis or somebody had put clean sheets on the bed and supplied it with enough quilts to manually thaw the polar ice caps. If he tossed and turned in his sleep, he didn't notice it. If he called out in his dreams, there would have been nobody to hear him. Years ago, in Armenia, his Anna had complained that he talked constantly in his sleep, nonstop, but never about important things. He shouted instructions at cats. He worried out loud about the number of cans in the pantry, and they didn't have a pantry. They had nothing. When he stayed with the faithful who wanted him to pray with them in their living rooms, they thought he was giving evidence of sanctity. If Tibor had been living in the West at the time, where such things were possible, he would have bought a tape recorder and run it while he slept. As it was, he had to take everybody's word for it, and to remind himself that no matter what else he might be, he was not a saint.

The first problem with Bennis Hannaford's apartment was in the bedroom, where the funerary urn containing her sister Anne Marie's ashes still sat on top of the low dresser near the window. That in and of itself would not have bothered Tibor much, in spite of the fact that Anne Marie had not been the best of people, except that the urn and the dresser top beneath it had been deliberately left out of whatever cleaning had gone on in anticipation of his arrival. He knew the oversight was deliberate because the urn and the dresser it sat on didn't have just a little dust. They had a monumental amount of dust, nearly half an inch of it, and it had been undisturbed for some time. It was as if Bennis had both wanted to do the right thing about Anne Marie and not wanted to do it at the same time. The urn was brass and had those big curving handles like sporting trophies had. The brass had never been polished that Tibor could tell. On the taller dresser on the other side of the room, there were family pictures in sterling-silver frames of Bennis and her brothers and sisters at her father's house, Engine House, in Bryn Mawr. In none of them was Anne Marie included.

The second problem with Bennis Hannaford's apartment was in the living room, where, Tibor noticed as soon as he got up, the only actually *real* furniture was the big wooden worktable with Bennis's computer and papers and books on it, pushed up against the window looking out on Cavanaugh Street. The sofa and chairs and coffee table they had all been using the night before were gimcrack and upholstered in odd colors that didn't match. Either Bennis had gone downtown in some haste and picked up whatever she could find that could be delivered immediately, or she had pulled these pieces out of other people's houses. Tibor thought the latter was probably true. Bennis's own furniture was upstairs in

Gregor's apartment. Gregor's furniture—which she had pronounced not fit for drunk muskrats—was in storage. Tibor remembered all this from when Bennis and Gregor had decided to move in with each other. It wasn't that anybody had told him, flat-out. They wouldn't. It was just that everybody knew, and if you sat long enough in the Ararat or in old George Tekemanian's apartment or at Ohanian's Middle Eastern Food Store, you heard anything you needed to hear.

He got dressed and went to the kitchen, which did have furniture in it. Maybe Bennis liked Gregor's kitchen furniture better than her own. He looked in the refrigerator, which was stocked for a long siege of bad weather. He could survive the blizzard of the century and its ensuing floods with what he had in there. He looked in the cabinets and found them overstuffed as well. Somebody had thoughtfully left him three big boxes of coffee bags, the kind you put in a cup and poured water over like you poured water over tea bags to make tea. Theoretically, it was impossible to make bad coffee with coffee bags. He didn't take any out. He was depressed, not sick. Depression was not cured by having coffee alone in an otherwise empty kitchen.

He went out to the foyer, got his coat, and went downstairs. He knocked on old George's apartment just in case, but he wasn't expecting to have much luck. It was nearly seven-thirty. Old George and everybody else would be at the Ararat already. He went out into the street and looked up and down. Howard Kashinian's youngest daughter, having been expelled from her fourth college in three years, was standing with a boy next to the Ararat's front windows. If she didn't watch it, the neighborhood would have her married, pregnant, and well on her way to grandmotherhood before lunch.

The first order of business was to look at Holy Trinity Church, in daylight, the way it was now. He went down the street, across the intersection, to the middle of the next block. From here, with the width of the street and the far sidewalk between him and the church, it looked strangely hopeful. In spite of the pictures he had seen in the papers, and once on the news, he had somehow expected to find it completely a pile of rubble. He crossed the street and went up the stone steps to what had once been the door. The door was gone, and so was most of the vestibule beyond it, although he could tell where it had been from the variations in the floor. He stepped through into the sacristy. This close to the street, there was no roof. Farther down, there was, but he thought it might be dangerous. Roofs were not meant to hang in free suspension over floors. He sat down in the last pew at the back in the set just next to the center aisle. The pews were beautifully carved wood, given by Howard and Sheila Kashinian when the church had been renovated in 1985. They were covered with dust and debris and they had been rained on more than once. They were not going to survive. He got up and went down the center aisle toward the altar. It was still standing, although the wall of icons that had once stood in front of it mostly was not. That didn't bother him so much. That was one of the things that should have been changed decades ago, because it was in the Greek churches that the altar was shielded by an iconostasis. In Armenian ones, there was supposed to be a curtain. Tibor suspected that the priests who had come before him had felt as he did. The iconostasis was a beautiful thing. They hadn't wanted to destroy it.

When we rebuild the church, we'll rebuild it to Armenian specifications, he told himself. He couldn't reach the altar. There was just too much in the way. He wondered what had happened to the icons. It was too much to hope for that somebody had taken them down and preserved them. Even if they weren't proper to shield the altar in an Armenian church, they could be given away, to a Greek church or a museum. They could be reframed to hang in the reception area of the new church when it was built.

He went back down the center aisle to where the vestibule had been. Nothing he was doing felt entirely real. He might have been an actor, so caught up in his role he'd ceased to notice the audience just beyond the lights. He went down the front steps to the sidewalk. Then he went around to the side. He didn't have to go very far into the narrow side alley to get the eerie feeling that he'd been transported back in time. Nothing here looked changed, or damaged, or in danger of falling over at the first rude jolt. He had to remind himself to be careful. The blast had done "structural damage" to the entire building, and the wall that lined this alleyway and his own small apartment at the back were part of the building. Still, when he got into the courtyard and looked around, everything looked exactly as it had. The little carriage light next to his front door was still burning, just the way he'd left it when he'd gone to Adelphos House on that night. He got his keys out of his pants pocket and went up to the front door. He unlocked and stuck his head inside. Everything was normal here too, and there was another light burning. That was the table lamp next to the big couch in his living room. He left that one lit day and night because he didn't like to be entirely in the dark.

He propped the door open, just in case the building started to collapse and he had to run for it. He went in through the little foyer and the living room to the kitchen. The chief change was in the books, which were mostly gone. Usually, this apartment had books stacked everywhere, floor to ceiling against all the walls, on all the furniture, even in the bathroom. He wondered where Bennis and Donna and the others had put the boxes they'd packed the books away in. He left the kitchen and went down the little hall on the left to his bedroom. The hallway was twice as wide without books stacked against the walls on either side. It was easier to navigate, but he didn't like the effect.

He was in the bedroom, making a small pile of pictures and letters, when Bennis came in. He knew it was Bennis because he could hear her muttering under her breath as she walked. He sat back on his heels and waited. Next to him on the floor, with nothing stacked on top of it, because he would never stack anything on top of it, was the largest and clearest photograph he had left of his wife.

Bennis came up to the door of the bedroom and said, "What do you think you're doing? Don't you know the building is unsafe? The roof could collapse on you and you could get killed."

"The roof didn't collapse on you," Tibor said. "You didn't get killed."

"We were being careful."

"I'm being careful too," Tibor said. He waved his hand at the pile on the floor. "There were some things I wanted to get. There is no point telling me that you could have gotten them for me. I wouldn't have been able to explain what to look for. And you don't read Armenian. Not very many people do, here."

"So what's that?" Bennis said. "That's your wife, isn't it?"

"My wife, yes, Anna. Close to the time when we were first married. She wanted to come to America much more than I did. I didn't really want to come. I wanted to live in a free Armenia. But Anna wanted to come to America even if Armenia became free."

"She died, didn't she?"

"Yes." Tibor looked down at the picture. "She was shot trying to run away when we were raided celebrating the liturgy. We were not allowed to celebrate the liturgy except in government-approved churches. The clergy in those churches were all spies. Nobody respected them. We would celebrate the liturgy in places where it was not licit, in people's houses, in basements. We took liberties so that people could worship God and not be spied on, and then one day we were given away, and that was that. When Anna died, she was already out of the house, running down the street, running away. The other two people who died were right there in the room, backed against the wall together. When they reported it in the press later, they said we were armed and had explosives. But they did not report it much. It was only another incident."

"What happened to you? How did you get away?"

"I didn't get away. If I could have gotten away, I would have gone with Anna. I was arrested. Then for a while I was in prison, in Armenia and later in the Soviet Union. Then eventually I was released. Don't ask me why. People were arrested and released on whims, almost. There were sentences, but they didn't mean anything. In my case there wasn't even a trial. So I was in prison and then I was released and taken back to Armenia, and when I got there I found some friends and began to make my way out. For a long time, I felt very guilty, being here. It didn't seem right to me that I should be here and Anna could not be. Then I was called to Holy Trinity, and the rest you know."

"What are the papers?" Bennis asked. "They look old."

"They're crumbling to dust. Everything does. I just hate the thought of losing them. They're letters, from Anna to me, the ones she wrote me when we were not married and I was studying to be a priest. But I wasn't studying in the ordinary way, in the government-approved theological college. We had to be careful."

"You know, there are ways to preserve old letters like those. If you don't mind not being able to touch the paper itself, you can have them sealed in plastic and that keeps the air from them and keeps them from disintegrating."

"This is expensive?"

"I don't know," Bennis said. "Why don't you let me have one of them later, and I'll get it done and we'll see."

"I have been thinking that they would wear away, and then I would have only the picture. It would not be the same. It is her voice I miss. Sometimes I can hear her talking to me, but it gets fainter all the time. It's only a trick the mind plays, I know. I am not being ridiculous. I just need to hear her voice."

"Well, in the meantime, let's get you and this stuff out of here. Go down to the Ararat for breakfast. Most everybody will be gone, but Gregor will be there because he's waiting for John Jackman. You can talk to them. I think they're going to go over what the police have on the bombing. And then something happened yesterday with a gun."

"Yes," Tibor said. He stood up and then leaned over to get his papers and his picture. Anna smiled up at him in black and white, posed with head tilted like a forties movie star.

"He has told me something of this yesterday. I wasn't paying enough attention. It seems to me, a little, as if—I feel all the time I am in a play, not a reality. Maybe I am becoming an adolescent in my old age."

"Come on," Bennis said. "If you've got to be up and about, it will do you good to be up and about among cheerful people. If anybody is cheerful these days. Oh, there was another murder out in Bryn Mawr. Have you seen the papers?"

Tibor had not seen the papers, and he had not watched the television news, and he found that he didn't really care. There was another murder out in Bryn Mawr. The church was a mess. His letters were not only old but written with cheap Soviet-manufactured ink, so that the words on them had faded almost to invisibility.

Somehow, this morning had not accomplished what he wanted it to.

THREE

1

Gregor Demarkian had always wondered if John Jackman minded eating at the Ararat, when he was almost always the only African American there, but if he did he'd never said, and the Ararat certainly seemed to like him. By the time Tibor came in, John was sitting happily in front of a gigantic platter of scrambled eggs, toast, sausage, bacon, and hash browns, as well as coffee and orange juice. Even Gregor didn't have the guts to eat that way in front of Bennis, who was prone to delivering lectures on short-term increases in blood cholesterol and long-term risk factors for heart disease. Of course, unlike other men entering middle age, John didn't seem to be thickening in the waist, or anyplace else. He was still a tall, thin, aristocratic man, except for the skin color more WASP-looking than most of the WASPs who lived in the great houses on the Main Line where he had started his career. When Bennis was in one of her better moods, she liked to point out that John might *be* more of a WASP than some of those people, considering the penchant of husbands for keeping mistresses of any color and of wives for having something on the side with the help. Gregor never knew whether to take her seriously.

By the time Tibor came in, John had pushed all their plates aside to write on a large sheet of scrap paper, actually the back of one of those flyers advertising car washes that appeared on the streets from time to time with no known provenance. The paper was already a mess, full of circles and lines and arrows. It all meant something to John, but no matter how often he tried to explain it, it did not make that much sense to Gregor. Tibor saw them at the table and hesitated. John looked up and saw Tibor there and waved him over.

"Father, Father," he said, standing up in the way he had been taught to stand up when priests entered the room by the nuns in his very strict Catholic elementary school. "It's good to see you back. I hope you're feeling better."

"I am feeling all right," Tibor said. Gregor made room for him on the bench. Tibor slid in and shrugged off his coat. "I was never sick. I was only—" He threw his hands in the air.

"In the hospital for observation." John sat down. "Yes, I know. Code for enough money to stay for a while because somebody is worried about you. Still. You got a good slam in the shoulder, if I remember. It couldn't have hurt to have a few days rest."

Tibor looked down at his hands, and then away. Gregor felt himself getting nervous. "Well," he said. "John was explaining to me the intricacies of conspiracy organizations in the city of Philadelphia."

"Not just in Philadelphia," John said. "They're all over the place. And if you go overseas, you get versions of them with twists. There are Islamic ones. America is the great Satan. There are African ones. There are Russian ones. There aren't too many Western European ones. Maybe their educational systems are as good as they're supposed to be."

Linda Melajian came over and put a coffee cup in front of Tibor. Then she filled it with coffee. Gregor thanked her. Tibor seemed to be a little distracted.

"So," Gregor said. "We've been going over the state of the investigation of who blew up the church."

"Yes," Tibor said. "I know. And Bennis says Mr. Jackman comes every morning before work, and you discuss this. It is progress that is being made?"

"Gregor showed me that letter you got," John said. "I'll turn it over to the investigating officers when I get in. I wish things fit together the way they should. Did Gregor tell you that a man came to him last night with a story about having been given a gun?"

"A little, yes," Tibor said. "Late last night, when he got in. Very late."

"I saw the light in your window when I came home," Gregor said. "I was worried."

"Let's try to make sense of this," John said. "Of course, it's way too early to tell. We're going to have to do checks from one end of the city to the other, and we're going to do more than that. The detectives don't like it, but even they've had to agree with me after this. We've called in the FBI for help."

"Not every special agent is like Walker Canfield. In fact, most of them aren't. If they were, the country would collapse." Gregor shook his head.

"Well, we're going to talk to Canfield too," Jackman said. "And yes, he's still around. I don't know what his status is. I talked to the cops in Lower Merion, and they don't know what his status is, either. But I thought it would be a good idea if we got pictures of the people in this group Canfield and his partner were investigating, and showed the pictures of the women to Andrechev. Just to see if he can make them."

"As in the woman who brought him the gun?" Gregor said. "Good idea. Doesn't it bother you, though, that whole incident? Why did she bring him a gun?"

"Maybe she didn't," Jackman said. "That must have occurred to you as well as to me. Maybe he had the gun and made up the story."

"Why?"

"Because he's connected with one of these conspiracy groups, maybe the very one that caused the bombing, and now he's trying to cover his ass," John said. "It's not a great explanation, I know, but it's a possibility. These people are *not* very bright. Or at least the rank and file aren't. Some of the movement stars have better imaginations than Stephen King."

"It's a terrible explanation," Gregor said. "But you should be able to tell if at least some of it's true. Do you know about fingerprints yet?"

"Only unofficially."

"And?"

"There aren't any," Jackman said. "Not any at all."

"Which means the gun was wiped," Gregor said patiently, "which Andrechev could have done himself. But you just said these people aren't very bright. Even most bright people don't think of all the places on the gun where there might be fingerprints."

"Well, whoever wiped this one did," John said. "It still doesn't prove that he's telling the truth. Don't worry about it. I'm not trying to hang the man. I'm just trying to make the incident make sense. Why *would* some woman come up and hand him a gun like that?"

"He said she said she was trying to make sure he was armed against devil worshipers, or something of the kind," Gregor said.

Tibor stirred in his seat. "It is ridiculous, this about devil worshipers. Where do they think of such a thing?"

"I don't think you can call what they do 'thinking' in the conventional sense," Gregor said.

"What's more important," John said, "is that all this talk about devil worship doesn't really fit with America on Alert, which is not a religious organization. Some of them are, of course. They think the whole plot is about the Antichrist. But America on Alert is not one of them."

"Did the woman who gave Andrechev the gun talk about the Antichrist?" Gregor asked. "I don't remember him saying she did. He said something about how she kept calling him a good American, and then I don't remember."

John reached into his jacket pocket and took out his notebook. "According to Andrechev," he said, "she told him that there were people on this street who thought they worshiped the Devil, but that Andrechev knew like she did that they were really doing something else. That's ambiguous enough."

"What about that stack of literature he had? There was *The Harridan Report*, but there were other things too," Gregor said.

John looked through his notebook again. "They hadn't finished going through it by the time I talked to them. It's going to take a few days. There was a lot of it, and from what they could tell, it seems to have come from all over. A-albionics, have you heard of them?"

"I have," Tibor said. "They have a Web site. You must pay to be a subscriber, and then you can have their information. So I do not have their information. But they have a few free essays, and these I have read."

"And?" Gregor said.

Tibor shrugged. "The usual thing. There is a plot to make the United States subject to one big New World Order and take all our freedoms away and have all our laws be the laws of the UN. Tell me, Krekor, because this I do not understand. What do these people have against international law? Do they think it is a good thing that when two countries have a border dispute, they shoot at each other? When they have a dispute with their neighbor, they don't shoot him. They go to court. When somebody commits a crime against them, they don't buy weapons and go down to this person's street and shoot up his house, and then hide behind concrete when the man's family comes and shoots their house to retaliate. They call the police, and the police bring the man to court. I have lived in places where there was no law and where there was war and I can tell you that that is not better than the Commonwealth of Philadelphia."

"Maybe they would shoot up their neighbor's house," John said. "Some of these groups have engaged in a lot of violence over the years. Others of them just put out newsletters and self-published books and that kind of thing. As if they were giant role-playing games for middle-aged sad sacks in midlife crisis."

"And?" Gregor said. "What was America on Alert?"

John laughed. "The reason Canfield and his partner were

up here investigating was that they'd got information that America on Alert was stockpiling weapons. Big-time."

"So? Why didn't they get a warrant and search?"

"According to Canfield, because they didn't know where to search. They could have searched all the houses of all the members they'd come across, and they tried doing that. The judge wouldn't buy it. After Ruby Ridge and a couple of other well-publicized fiascos, the federal courts are not exactly eager to grant more warrants on incomplete information. And they'd never met the head guy, according to Canfield."

"This would be Michael Harridan?" Gregor asked.

"Right," John said.

"Are they sure he exists?" Gregor said.

John shrugged. "I don't think anybody got into it that far. Not a bad question, though. It would be a cute trick, inventing a shadowy mastermind who didn't exist and making yourself look less important and feel more safe. Still, you'd have to wonder how it was done. Think of the difficulties."

"Like what?"

"Like the fact that you'd have to find a way to communicate without tipping off the rest of the group that one of them is never there when the contact happens," John said. "And you couldn't do it all by letter or e-mail, because people don't bond to text, they bond to other people. There would at least have to be a voice, every once in a while. So now look how it works. You take off to make the phone call to be Michael Harridan, that means you're not at the meeting as yourself. And that happens every time? It would be damned near impossible."

"It is also silly, yes?" Tibor said. "It is a lot of work to no purpose."

"If you really believed all the stories you told about conspiracies," Gregor said, "you might think that it had a very important purpose. Keeping you alive."

"Krekor, be sensible."

"I am being sensible," Gregor said. "You've got to try to

think in the same terms as the people involved. If I believed that America was being ruled by a secret government that had managed to invade the private lives of all of us, and that that secret government was ready, at the first hint of rebellion, to do what it had to do to shut the rebels up—including, remember Waco and Ruby Ridge, kill them—well . . ."

"*Tcha*," Tibor said.

"Whatever," John said. "The bottom line is that they couldn't get the warrants. Now that there's been a shooting, they might be able to, but I wouldn't count on it. John Ashcroft may talk a good game about expanding police powers, but the judges have responded to it by digging in their heels, at least out here."

"Good," Gregor said.

"There's no better way to know that you've finally turned into a civilian," John said.

"Get back to America on Alert," Gregor said. "Canfield and his partner must have information on at least some of the members, right? They went to meetings?"

"The partner did," John said. "Canfield stayed in the background and did backup."

"Canfield still has names, though, doesn't he? And you don't need a warrant to talk to people. Granted, they don't have to give you any information, but you can talk to them. I understand that Canfield was concerned about blowing his partner's cover, but that can hardly be an issue with the Philadelphia police."

"You mean you want me to ask my cops to go talk to the people at America on Alert," John said.

"I don't see where it would hurt," Gregor said. "There has to be some connection, even if it's only that the people who committed those murders in Bryn Mawr and whoever blew up Holy Trinity Church both seem to read either *The Harridan Report* itself or material very much like it. That's what the woman gave Krystof Andrechev along with the gun."

"Assuming she gave him anything at all," John reminded him.

"Assuming she gave him anything at all," Gregor agreed.

"But he had the material. I saw it. And among other things he had copies of *The Harridan Report*. Charlotte Ross was actually mentioned in *The Harridan Report*. I saw the issue. Every time we turn around, no matter what we do, we get *The Harridan Report*. There must be something going on."

"You can't really think the two cases are connected," John said. "That's ludicrous."

"I agree. It's ludicrous," Gregor said. "But if the two cases aren't connected, then somebody is going to a lot of trouble to make us think they are. I'm beginning to feel like I'm reading an Agatha Christie novel and she's doing that thing where she bangs people over the head with a two-by-four pointing out the solution and nobody ever pays attention. Except that I am paying attention. If you see what I mean."

"No," John said.

"It's all right," Tibor said. "He gets like this. He has enthusiasms. He reminds me of someone I knew when I was growing up, who always had a new invention that was going to change the world."

"I don't think it's a matter of having enthusiasms when you just want things to make sense," Gregor said.

2

When Gregor Demarkian had first come back to live on Cavanaugh Street—when he'd still expected to find it as he had left it, ethnic and economically marginal—he had been convinced that the last thing he was interested in was any more involvement in crime, criminals, law enforcement, or investigations. He knew many men who had left the Bureau and gotten private investigators' licenses, or hung out their shingles as consultants, but they seemed to him to be almost entirely pathetic. If you wanted to stay in the game, then the sensible thing was to stay in the Bureau. If there was some reason why you didn't want to stay in the Bureau, and he could think of several, then the sensible thing was to get a job with a real police department or some sort of state investigative agency. Hanging out a shingle was admitting to the worst sort of amateurism, the dream of being Philip Marlowe or Sam Spade, the kind of thing only civilians imagined had anything to do with the real work of handling cases. It was also admitting to the fact that the game had swallowed you whole. You had no other life. You had no other interests. If you couldn't file case reports and keep yourself awake thinking about the way in which that last piece of evidence might fit a pattern that didn't otherwise want to accommodate it, then you were as good as dead.

For those reasons, and more, Gregor had been careful over the years *only* to work as a consultant. He questioned witnesses if the police brought him along when they were investigating themselves. He looked at the evidence other people had collected. He did not go out on his own and do the footwork required of any decent investigator. The game had not swallowed him whole, and he did have a life. He would not be distraught if no one ever asked for his help on a case again. He refused to allow himself to be sucked into the all-consuming totality of the work. If there was legwork to be done, somebody else could do it.

Sitting in his living room after breakfast with John Jackman and Father Tibor, he decided that all rules had exceptions, and this was going to be the exception to this rule. He was glad that Bennis was off doing something with Donna Moradanyan Donahue. That way, he didn't have to explain himself until he was ready to. He got the cell phone and punched in a number he knew by heart, in spite of the fact that before a week ago, he hadn't dialed it for ten years. He got past the director's secretary with a heartening lack of resistance and laid out his problem, in detail. Then he hung up and waited until the call came telling him what he wanted to know. The call was not, of course, from the director himself, but it came because of him, and Gregor was very satisfied.

"You're all set," the man on the phone said. "I've told him you're coming. I've read him the riot act. You should be fine. Christ, he hasn't heard anything but the riot act all week."

"If it was up to me, I'd fire him."

"We'll get around to that, don't worry. First we've got a missing agent, right now presumed dead. Good luck. He's a pain in the ass."

"I know."

Gregor got his coat, took the paper he'd written down the information on—hotel, hotel room number, hotel room direct line number, cell phone number, pager number—and went down to the street. He started walking up Cavanaugh Street toward a busier intersection, up beyond Krystof Andrechev's store, but didn't make it all the way there. The cab appeared out of nowhere, as if summoned by fairy godmothers. He thought he could use a fairy godmother. He got in, gave the address of the hotel, and sat back. Then he tried to clear his mind of everything having to do with the case, and most especially of everything having to do with Walker Canfield. The problem with thinking about Walker Canfield was that it made him do something very much like mental frothing at the mouth.

The hotel was a mid-level one, built in the forties, right in the middle of downtown. The lobby was pleasant but dark. The furniture was newish, modern, and without character. He gave his name and was told he was expected. He got into the elevator—paneled, but not with good wood—and rode up to the fifth floor. Walker Canfield was waiting for him when the elevator doors opened on five.

"Mr. Demarkian," Canfield said. "I got a call—I mean, the director—shit."

"Where's your room?"

Walker Canfield gestured vaguely down the hall. He no longer looked nervous, which was how he'd looked when Gregor first saw him. He no longer looked scared, either, which was how he'd looked by the time Gregor had been through talking to him on that first meeting. He looked dead.

"Let's go," Gregor said. "There's no point conducting this conversation in a hotel hallway. Even if it is empty."

Walker Canfield turned on his heel and walked halfway down the long hallway to the left of the elevators, looking like a sleepwalker. Gregor followed him to the door of room 525. Canfield got out one of those plastic card keys and shoved it quickly in and out of the slot. The door buzzed. Canfield pushed it open and gestured Gregor inside. Gregor went. It was not a hotel room with character.

"So," Gregor said. "Is this where you've been since you got to Philadelphia, you and your partner?"

"Steve Bridge," Canfield said. "They think he's dead. I think he's dead. Or maybe I don't. I don't know. What would they have done with him? You can't just make a body disappear. It's got to be someplace. Even burning it doesn't get rid of it entirely. Hell, even putting it through a wood chipper doesn't get rid of it entirely. Do you remember that case, out in Newtown, Connecticut? What a thing."

"Yes," Gregor said. "I remember it. Let's try to stay on subject, shall we? What I'm trying to figure out is how exactly the FBI got interested in America on Alert. You don't monitor all these groups, do you? There are hundreds of them, as far as I can tell."

"Well, there are hundreds of Web sites, anyway," Canfield said. "I don't really know if there are hundreds of groups. It's more like—when I was a kid, I used to be a big science fiction fan. It's like that. You've got lots of people, some groups, but mostly individuals. They all know each other and keep up with each other and go to each other's stuff and buy each other's books. There are stars and groupies—the stars are the writers and the lecturers, the groupies are the people who follow them. It's like this whole alternative little world. They've got their own publishing companies—really small ones, you know, run out of post office boxes and people's basements, but you can do that these days. With desktop publishing, it's easy to make a book that looks like a real one. If you know what I mean. And if you didn't know what you had and you didn't know anything about the movement, you'd think you were seeing real scholarly work done by a professor somewhere. It's only when you start looking into the references in the footnotes that you realize they all only quote each other, or they quote outside sources out of context. It's like an alternative universe."

"All right. But that still doesn't answer my question. What got the Bureau interested in America on Alert, rather than in one of the others?"

"They were buying guns."

"Yes," Gregor said patiently. "But how did you know they were buying guns? Unless you *are* monitoring all the groups out there, which has got to be expensive as hell and mostly useless, since most of these people are no more going to kill anybody than they're going to lay eggs. *Something* must have tipped the Bureau off to the gun buying."

"Oh," Canfield said. "Yeah. I know that. There was a tip."

"An anonymous tip?"

"Yeah. I mean, we have those all the time. You have to listen to them. You have to check them out. You can't—"

"Yes, I know," Gregor said, "I'm not criticizing you. When did you get this tip?"

"Five, six months ago—no, wait. I can tell you exactly. July third. It's my niece's birthday. It stuck in my head when I saw the file."

"Exactly what did this tip consist of?"

Walker Canfield looked blank. "I don't know what you mean."

It was, Gregor thought, like trying to get molasses out of a squirt gun. "What did the tip *consist* of? Did somebody call in and say, 'you'd better take a look at America on Alert'? Did they say 'Michael Harridan bought six guns under six different names at six different gun shows last month'? What?"

"Oh." Canfield brightened. "I see what you mean. It wasn't that specific. It was—just a minute. Let me get my notes." He ran around to the side of one of the big double beds and came up with his briefcase. "I spend a lot of time going over this stuff these days. I'm going crazy, sitting in this room, waiting for something to happen. But that's what they want me to do, you know, the Bureau. They've sent up a couple of other guys to look into things. Here it is." He drew out a sheet of paper and brought it back across the room to Gregor. "It's only a copy, but you get the picture."

Gregor got the picture. The paper was a copy of a letter. At first glance, it looked like a business letter. The format was perfect—headings and addresses in the right places, paragraphs carefully blocked out with a space between each one, closing and signature centered. *To the Federal Bureau of Investigation*, it started, and then, *This is to inform you of the activities of an organization called America on Alert, centered in Philadelphia, Pennsylvania. According to its own literature, the purpose of this organization is to "save America from being oppressed under the One World Government of a New World Order." According to its president, Michael Harridan, "the day will soon come when good Americans must arm themselves and take to the hills and the side streets to save our nation by force of arms." I have reason to believe that that day is now here, and America on Alert is getting ready to commit a significant act of violence.*

"Very nice," Gregor said. "Nothing at all to indicate that whoever wrote it is a nutcase. It could have come from a bank."

"It's a mistake to think these guys are all illiterate yahoos," Canfield said. "I thought that too, before I got involved in this. You'd be amazed at how professional some of their material can sound. That's what makes what they do so insidious. If they wrote in bad grammar and exclamation points, nobody would listen to them."

"Was any attempt made to trace this letter?" Gregor asked.

Canfield nodded. "We looked into it, yeah. It was mailed in Philadelphia. We got one of those profiles done on the sender, if you want to see that."

"No." Gregor had no use for the psychological analysis of mail—"the writer is a middle-aged male with a deep neurotic attachment to his mother"—and it wouldn't tell him anything he wanted to know at the moment even if it were accurate. He gave the copy of the letter back to Canfield. "I want to get this straight. The Bureau got the letter. The Bureau assigned you and Steve Bridge to investigate it—"

"Well, there were about four of us at the time, back in Washington. They assigned Steve and I to come out here and do something about it."

"Okay, what made them decide to send the two of you out here? And to send Bridge undercover?"

"We checked it out," Canfield said. "We looked into the organization, sort of sideways. We went to their Web site. That kind of thing."

"And?"

"And it was true. This Michael Harridan really was saying that the time was near when the black helicopters would be coming and we'd be taken over by the UN and all the rest of it. But you've got to watch it for a while to see what's happening. They just don't leap out at you and start acting like complete lunatics."

"No, I'm sure they don't. So you checked out their material, and that—"

"No, not that alone," Canfield said. "It was something else. We checked out Michael Harridan."

"And?"

"And it's even more than I told you before. There is no Michael Harridan. Not anywhere in the country. At least, not anywhere that would fit somebody involved in America on Alert. There's a Catholic priest in Oregon, but he's been in Rome for the past two years. There's an eighty-five-year-old guy in a home for people with Alzheimer's in Texas. That's about it. You'd think it was a common enough name. It isn't. And there's no Michael Harridan in Philadelphia or on the Main Line. At all."

"So he's using an alias," Gregor said. "Is that all that surprising? These groups are the epitome of paranoid. Half the people in them must use assumed names."

"No, that's where you're wrong," Canfield said. "You see, the thing is, the whole movement is really hyped on trust. They're very suspicious people. They're convinced that everybody is lying to them. They put a lot of emphasis on the people they deal with being open and aboveboard and trustworthy."

"And are they?"

"Well," Canfield said, "a whole lot of them are lying their heads off. This is really fertile ground for running a scam. You have all these people afraid of the government, afraid of their television sets. I mean, what do you do with people who think magic wands and witches' spells are real? Critical thinking is not their strong suit here. There's this guy out there who's got a whole little thing going—he claims to have been a Catholic priest, a Freemason, a Mormon, and a priest in the Church of Satan. Sit down and try to add up the times and places and dates, and he'd have to be a hundred-and-fifty-years-old. But when people do add up the times and places and dates, he just says he did all this stuff at once and nobody thinks to question him. He sells books and tapes and lectures. People send him money."

"Then there isn't really anything odd about Michael Harridan not being named Michael Harridan," Gregor pointed out.

"No, but it was a compilation of things. The more we checked, the odder it got. We got hold of their mailing list and did gun checks. Practically everybody on it had at least one gun license. The more we looked into it, the creepier it got. And Harridan himself, that newsletter, it was so—"

"So what?"

"So targeted," Canfield said. "Most of these newsletters just give you big long lists of names. These are the people who were at the Bilderberger retreat this year. These are the people who work for David Rockefeller. That kind of thing. But *The Harridan Report* was always talking about specific people doing specific stuff. Charlotte Deacon Ross giving that party. That kind of thing."

"Okay," Gregor said. "So you got assigned to come up here, and you came. Then what?"

"Then we came," Canfield said. "And Steve went to one of their lectures, and then he went to another one, and then he joined up and started going to meetings."

"And?"

"There isn't much else. It's like I said. Nobody ever sees Michael Harridan, and nobody ever claims to have seen him except this one woman, Kathi Mittendorf. She says she went to a lecture Harridan gave personally. Steve and I didn't know whether to believe her or not. She could be telling the truth, but she could just be, you know, making herself hot. She doesn't have much else going for her to make herself hot. She's middle-aged. She works on the floor at Price Heaven. Part-time, by the way. Hell, she might not even have that for a while. From what I can tell from the papers, Price Heaven seems to be exploding."

"Did you check into Kathi Mittendorf? Or any of the others?"

"Of course we did," Canfield said. "Mittendorf and this other woman, Susan Hester, went to gun shows a lot, and sometimes they bought, but not usually. Steve and I were both convinced that they were buying on the black market, but we couldn't prove it, and until we could—" He shrugged. "You know how that is."

"How did Harridan keep in touch with the group?" Gregor asked. "Did he send letters? Send e-mail? Set up chat rooms?"

"He made conference calls," Canfield said. "Steve was there for one. They set up a speakerphone so that everybody could hear. Sort of a low-tech virtual meeting."

Gregor thought it over: the letter to the Bureau; the meeting-by-speakerphone; the gun shows. He tried not to think about Walker Canfield.

"All right," he said. "I'm going to want some contact information on a couple of people, if you have it. And if you don't have it, I'm going to need to know where to get it."

3

He began by going to the Price Heaven on Altaver Street, a small store without distinction crammed into a row of other stores, not the sort of place he associated with Price Heaven at all. Maybe this was what the papers meant when they said that Price Heaven had made the mistake of hanging on to older, outmoded stores that they would have done better to close down in order to give themselves more resources to compete in the suburbs. At least the people going into this store looked as if they needed a bargain outlet. The kind of people you saw going into Price Heavens in the malls often looked as if they'd been just as comfortable at L.L. Bean or Coach. He looked around inside for a while, noting a few things that made no difference. Most of the shoppers were African-American or Latino. Most of the saleswomen were white. All of the managers were white. The clothes hanging on the racks in women's wear were stretched against their hangers. The wide-open plan of the store made it feel oddly empty, in spite of having far too many small and inconsequential things crammed into it. He did not intend to question Kathi Mittendorf in Price Heaven. He didn't even intend to introduce himself to her. Doing something like that could get someone fired, especially from a place like this. All he wanted to do was to get a look at her.

Gregor went to the two departments where she was supposed to work, but saw nobody answering to her description, and nobody wearing a name tag with her name on it. In toys, a very small boy was sitting on the floor, having a screaming fit over something his mother would not let him have. In housewares, a rickety old woman was pawing through box after box of blue ceramic dinner plates, as if the next box she found would contain something else, like a dinner plate. The longer he stayed, the more depressed he became. The very air in the store was depressing. The saleswomen were all wearing dirty aprons. The cashiers all looked bored.

He went back out onto the street to look for another cab. It took him four blocks to find one, by which time he was in another neighborhood entirely. He gave the second address on the list Walker Canfield had given him and sat back to think. He didn't recognize the street, but that wasn't necessarily significant. He didn't know much about Philadelphia anymore. Since he'd come back from Washington to live, he'd restricted himself to Cavanaugh Street, a few neighborhoods in the center of the city where there were restaurants he liked and things he liked to do, and crime scenes. With crime scenes, he was never 100 percent sure where he was. Streets full of brick and stone houses went by, the kind of places that had either been cut up to make cramped apartments or renovated and restored by rich people who didn't want to live in the suburbs. Those turned into streets full of clattering industrial equipment, doing Gregor did not know what.

The street Kathi Mittendorf lived on might have been in the city of Philadelphia proper, or it might not have. It was in that grey area of small wooden frame houses and small stores and strip shopping centers that made the transition between the city and its suburbs, so that there was never a place where the city actually stopped. It just petered out. Gregor looked at the meter and winced. He'd have to find a cash machine after this was over. Either that, or call Bennis to rescue him. The cab pulled up to the curb in front of a small grey house with a porch that sagged slightly in the middle. The porch had a glider on it, but the glider was pushed into a corner, out of the way. There was a driveway, of sorts. Two thin strips of concrete vanished out of sight between this house and the one next door. No car was visible. Gregor got out, took the fare from the money in his wallet and added a very generous tip, and looked around. No children were playing in the yards. No housewives were washing their front windows. This was a neighborhood where people worked. In the daytime, it would tend to be deserted.

Gregor climbed the porch steps and crossed the porch. He rang the bell and waited. He didn't expect Kathi Mittendorf to be home. Just because he hadn't found her at Price Heaven didn't mean she hadn't been there, on her break, or in the back inventorying stock or putting away boxes. Even if she hadn't been there, it made sense that she would use her day off to do errands. He only wanted to make sure he had done everything he could to find her.

Behind the narrow front door, locks came undone. There were a number of them, including one bolt. Gregor knew the sound of a bolt being drawn back. He straightened up automatically. The door opened and a middle-aged woman stood framed in the doorway, her too-blond hair pulled back in elastic so tightly her hair looked ready to scream. The skin on her face sagged. There were frown lines around the corners of her mouth. Her eyes were heavy and had too many bags under them. Her body was shapeless in the way the bodies of women in their fifties got if they hadn't been very diligent about working out.

"Yes?" she said.

"I'm looking for Kathi Mittendorf," Gregor said.

Kathi Mittendorf stared back at him, placid but suspicious. Gregor was sure she was Kathi Mittendorf, even though she hadn't said so. She fit the description perfectly. What he would do if she decided to say she was somebody else, Gregor didn't know.

"Who are you?" she said instead.

"My name is Gregor Demarkian. I work, sometimes, as a consultant to police departments."

"Are you working as a consultant to police departments now?"

"Not officially, no. Unofficially, yes."

"And is that what this is about? Something to do with police departments?"

"Something, yes," Gregor said. "But mostly I'm here on my own. Nobody knows I came. This is not official. I'm trying to find a man named Michael Harridan."

"I don't know anybody named Michael Harridan."

"You told someone that you did."

"Who?"

"A friend of a friend of mine. It's not important. I know you're a member of America on Alert. That's Michael Harridan's organization."

"That's public information," Kathi Mittendorf said. "Our

membership lists aren't secret. We place ads for our lectures. My name is on them most of the time."

"So tell me something about what's public information," Gregor said. "I don't know much about this kind of thing. I don't even know what I'm looking for."

"I thought you said you were looking for Michael Harridan."

"Yes, I did. I am. But I don't think that's as straightforward as it sounds."

Kathi Mittendorf seemed to look up, past Gregor's shoulder, to the distance. It took everything Gregor had not to turn around to see if somebody was behind him. He was cold as hell. The wind out here was really wicked, unbroken by the tall buildings and the traffic in the center of the city. Kathi Mittendorf looked down again and then backed up, away from the doorway.

"Come in and sit down," she said. "It's not like I can tell you anything."

Kathi Mittendorf's living room was what Gregor had expected from his view of the porch: small, box-like, and claustrophobic. He was sure the ceiling was lower than the now-standard eight feet. He was sure the room could be no more than ten feet across. There was too much furniture, and it was too shabby, worn away in some places, stained in others. The walls had not been painted in a long time.

"Don't bother to tell me what a nice room it is," Kathi Mittendorf said, closing the door and throwing a few of the locks. "I know it isn't."

"I was going to thank you for being willing to talk to me," Gregor said.

"Sit down. I'm not willing to talk to you. I want to hear you out. I want to know what you're going to say that you think is going to work on me."

"I don't know that I'm trying to get anything to work on you." Gregor sat down on the couch. It was too soft. He sank into it. "I don't even know what I'm really looking for. And I'm not an official police presence, as I said. You don't have to talk to me."

"I don't have to talk to your official police presence, either. I don't have to talk to anybody. You're not used to people who say that to you, are you?"

"People say it to me all the time."

Kathi Mittendorf seemed not to have heard. "The biggest problem is that people don't really know what their rights are. They think they do, but they don't. They see these cop shows. Everybody talks all the time. All the criminals. They think that's what criminals are. A lot of lowlifes in dirty clothes. That's what they're supposed to think criminals are. They're not supposed to realize that criminals are people just like them who get on the wrong side of the secret government."

"That's Michael Harridan, isn't it?" Gregor asked. "He writes about the secret government. I've seen a couple of copies of *The Harridan Report*."

"Everybody's seen copies of *The Harridan Report*. We distribute it all over the city. It's free. And it's up on a Web site."

"And I want to know something about the man who wrote it," Gregor persisted. "I want to know what he's like."

"You want to know where he is," Kathi said, "but I can't tell you. I can't tell you anything, just that you'd better understand it. It's not going to last forever. People are getting wise to the people you work for. We know what's going on now. We aren't fooled. Anthony van Wyck Ross was a Mason, did you know that?"

"No," Gregor said. "And I'd be very surprised if it were true. People on that level don't usually belong to the Masons. It's—well—it's not considered a good thing to be. The people who belong to the Masons are small-time lawyers and doctors and that kind of thing."

"That's just the Masons you know about," Kathi said. "Those are the low-level Masons. They're just a front. The real Masonic organization is made up of the men who reach the thirty-third degree. They're the ones who understand. The Illuminati. Have you heard of the Illuminati? They're the ones who run the Masons."

"I don't know much about the Masons," Gregor said.

"It's hard to understand at first, because it looks like there are so many different organizations. The Masons. The Vatican. The Bilderbergers. The Trilateral Commission. Even the governments. It all looks separate, but it isn't. It's all one thing. They decide who will be in charge of the banks and the corporations and the governments too. They're the ones who decide who'll run for president and all that kind of thing. They make it look like you have a choice, but you really don't. It's a closed circle. That's why they founded America. They wanted a base of operations and they knew that Europe was too old. People were too suspicious of it. That's why they came here."

"Who?" Gregor asked. "The Masons?"

"Did you know that all but four of the signers of the Declaration of Independence were Masons?" Kathi said. "George Washington was a Mason. He was master of his lodge in Virginia. They were looking to create the New World Order. *Novus Ordo Seclorum.* It's right there on the things they wrote. Thomas Jefferson said it. Thomas Jefferson was a Mason. He was a member of the Illuminati. They wanted to create a New World Order and they put Masonic symbols on all our money."

"But that isn't what it means," Gregor said, dredging up the Latin he'd learned in high school, so long ago he could no longer remember the name of the woman who taught it to him. "*Novus Ordo Seclorum.* It doesn't mean "New World Order." It means "A New Order of the Ages." That's what they thought they had, people like Jefferson, because they were getting rid of monarchy for democracy—"

"They didn't get rid of monarchy," Kathi corrected. "They only pretended to. The world is still run by the same thirteen families it's been run by for a thousand years. Maybe longer. They're the real Merovingian dynasty. It's supposed to have died out, but it didn't. It's still around. Anthony van Wyck Ross was a member of that dynasty. So are George Bush and George W. Bush. So is Al Gore. They never give you a choice between one of them and a real person. They don't want you to have a choice. They're the only ones who arc cver allowed to be in control. They look like people, but they aren't really. They're reptilian. They're the offspring of humans who mated with a reptilian race and now they can do things nobody else can do. They can learn faster than real humans. They can remember more. They can invent things. You don't think people could have invented space travel, do you? We're not that intelligent. We're not that creative. But they can't just do it on their own, because they want to. They need us. They need to have us subjugated."

This was, Gregor thought, *the talk she gave people who were already slightly involved in the movement, the ones who had the specifics down and only needed somebody to put them together.* Since he knew nothing at all about any of this, it wasn't making sense. The Merovingian Dynasty was, he thought, something from the early Middle Ages—Pepin the Short, and a line of kings so incompetent they had collapsed under the weight of their own stupidity. What exactly that had to do with the Masons, or a race of reptiles, or George W. Bush, he wasn't sure. He wasn't completely convinced that Kathi Mittendorf was sure.

She had been standing in front of him, rocking back and forth on the balls of her feet. Now she turned abruptly and walked out of the room. A moment later, she was back, carrying a thick book and a small sheaf of papers.

"Here," she said. "Read it all. You'll be able to understand if you let yourself. There is no such thing as a coincidence. Everything is orchestrated. Everything. We're already more than halfway to a One World Government. Once that government is in place, they'll have what they want. They'll be able to control everything, even people who know them for what they are. Look at what's happening around you. The United Nations. All those appeals to 'international law.' There is no international law. They only want you to think there is, so that they can talk you into letting them run your life and everybody else's. So that they can have control."

"Why?" Gregor said.

"Some of the people in the movement think they're really

Satan," Kathi Mittendorf said. "They see that the Illuminati subject their own children to satanic ritual abuse and they think that means the Illuminati are in league with Satan. They see that the Freemasons worship Satan and they think the same thing. But it isn't true. There is no Satan. Religion is something they invented, the Illuminati, to make it easier to control ignorant people. But it doesn't matter. We make common cause with the Christian freedom fighters. They *are* freedom fighters. They've just accepted the metaphor as the reality. And they're looking for the bodies."

"The bodies?"

"The bodies of the infants," Kathi Mittendorf said. "The Illuminati make their children participate in rituals. They sacrifice infants. They've sacrificed hundreds of thousands of them in the last twenty years alone. Then they subject these children to ritual sexual abuse. It's the MKUltra mind control system. It was invented by the CIA. Do you know that the FBI doesn't even bother to track the numbers of children that go missing every year."

"That's not true," Gregor said. By now, he was beginning to feel desperate. "There's an organization called the Center for Missing and Exploited Children. There's a special agent of the FBI attached to it. They collect all the figures every year, how many children are missing, how many children are found, what happened to them—you can get that information on-line any time you want to. They publish it."

Kathi Mittendorf seemed to hesitate for a moment. Then she smiled. "Don't be ridiculous," she said. "They probably make it all up. They don't dare collect the real figures. Then they'd know that there is no such thing as False Memory Syndrome. The memories are all real. The children really did see infants sacrificed and small animals mutilated. It happens all the time. It happens in day-care centers. It happens in schools. They have to get to as many people as possible to make sure that they're brainwashed. They can't afford to leave any serious opposition. That's why they're trying to kill us."

"What?" Gregor said.

This time, Kathi Mittendorf's smile was wide and glittering. "That's why they're trying to kill us," she repeated. "That's what you're here for, isn't it? To see if you can get the information out of me. And if you don't, you'll go back and tell them, your reptilian masters, and they'll send somebody out to kidnap me. They'll bring me in and torture me. And when they're finished with me, they'll kill me, because they know that as long as I'm alive, I'm a danger to them. I'm as much of a danger to them as somebody like Michael, because I'm just an ordinary person. I'm not some kind of nut. People will see me and realize that you don't have to be a lunatic to see the conspiracy. And they'll start to think. I know who you are, Mr. Demarkian. I pretended not to know when you got here, but I know. You're one of them. You live with a reptilian master, with that Bennis Hannaford woman, whose bloodline goes all the way back to the Merovingians through the British monarchy. You know I'm telling the truth. And you can't let me get away with it. But watch out. This whole house is wired. Cameras have been taking down this entire conversation and sending it to people I trust. They won't let you get away with it. They won't let you win. It doesn't matter if you stand there right now and shoot me dead."

FOUR

1

By early afternoon, Ryall Wyndham was as wound up as he ever thought he could be—too wound up to function, really, but he wasn't as worried about functioning as he used to be. It was a big day. Murder or no murder, the Philadelphia social season was in full gear. In the next few weeks, there were enough hunt balls to make you think foxes were about to become an endangered species, and that in spite of the fact that this wasn't the big season for hunting. Then there were the private debutante balls, the really important parties that marked a girl's "honest" coming out, in contrast to the mass presentation balls, which were tacky, but everyone "did" them. Ryall would never have admitted it in public, but the truth was, he liked new-money debutantes more than he liked old-money ones. Old-money debutantes had no sense of fun. Half of them got their ball gowns at Sears, and he knew at least one, only two years ago, who had arrived at the Philadelphia Assemblies with a pair of sneakers on under her dress. New-money debutantes liked to make a splash. Ryall was all for splashes. He liked to make splashes himself. This year, the big status symbol for new-money debutantes was to have two dresses for every ball. They danced until midnight, then repaired to the powder room or a convenient bedroom and changed clothes: dress, shoes, gloves, jewelry. It was not only extravagant, but utterly mindless.

That was the way it was supposed to be. Cary Grant and Katharine Hepburn would never have made a go of *The Philadelphia Story* if the general public had ever known what really went on in those big old-money houses on the Main Line.

Today, the important thing was to look solemn, and to make sure not to say anything stupid while on the air. He was due to tape at four-thirty. He was going to be expected to say something about the murder of Charlotte Deacon Ross, and the trouble was that he had a lot to say. Which was that the old cow deserved to be dead, for one thing—God, how he hated those patronizing people, the ones who treated him as if he were their personal publicity agent, but too damned dumb and uncultivated to know the difference between Shakespeare and Dohnanyi. But it wasn't just that. It was the attitude, that half-distracted look that told you you weren't really on the same planet with this great, good, and important Goddess. She listened to you like she listened to the stereo when she'd put it on as background music. She'd notice if you were annoying, and she'd do something about you too, but otherwise you might as well have been in the next state. It was too bad he still needed to be careful about what he had to say about these people. He could tell the world a lot about Charlotte Deacon Ross: her rages, smashing crystal and dinnerware on hardwood floors when she wasn't getting exactly what she wanted exactly as she wanted it; the way she fired help without cause or warning, sometimes in batches of twos and threes; her relationship with her oldest daughter, which resembled the relationship Medea might have had with *her* children if she'd allowed them to grow up. The only thing Charlotte didn't do was screw. That made her infinitely different from most of her friends, who engaged in adultery the way they kept up their tennis, but it was mostly a matter of intelligence. Ryall Wyndham might have been a bug on the wall as far as Tony Ross was concerned, but he'd known that man well enough to know that if Charlotte ever gave him cause, he'd be out of that marriage in a shot. *There* was something for the tabloids and the infotainment programs. Men like Tony Ross do not get divorced, not ever. Men just a rung below them on the ladder sometimes did, but men like Tony did not. It was too damned dangerous, and too expensive. Still, Tony was looking for a reasonable excuse to get a divorce from Charlotte, and even Charlotte knew about it.

Ryall fixed his bow tie. He never wore ordinary ties, because they made him look even more like Porky Pig than he usually did. He checked his cuff links. He'd learned long ago that only French cuffs would do with the people he cared most about talking to. The self-buttoning kind were for middle managers and people who had jobs teaching in community colleges. He went to the door of his bedroom and looked down the short hall to the woman pacing back and forth across his living-room carpet. Then he made a face. God, how he hated these women who pretended not to have money when they did. There was something beyond snobbish about an American upper class that prided itself on looking as if it were sleeping in Dumpsters, or worse. He wondered where she had gotten that stretchy tunic thing she was wearing: Price Heaven, Kmart, Wal-Mart, Marshall's. Even when he was flat broke and eating ketchup in hot water for lunch, Ryall Wyndham had bought his ties from Asbury's and his shoes from John Lobb.

He checked himself out in the mirror one more time. If there had been plastic surgery to make you taller, he would have had it. He considered liposuction. He could get it done, but he would have to be careful not to let it get out. He really *did* prefer the nouveau riche in some ways. They wouldn't have given a damn if he'd got himself sucked, and some of them would have sympathized.

He brushed off his jacket—a good tweed from J. Press—and went out toward the living room. She heard the door open and stopped where she was to wait for him. She had a copy of *Town and Country* in her hands, one of the ones he kept on the coffee table because they contained stories he had written, or pictures of himself in the parties columns. She put the magazine down and straightened up.

"So sorry to have kept you waiting," he said. "I'm afraid I really do just kick back and pay very little attention when I'm at home. I shouldn't, really. It gets me in the *most* difficult situations, and more often than you'd like to know."

"There's nothing difficult about this situation," Anne Ross Wyler said calmly. "I surprised you. That happens. I should have called first."

"No, no. Drop in any time. Really. I love to have company. And at a time like this, I find it perfectly understandable. You must be *awash* in grief. I know I am. Charlotte was one of my oldest and dearest friends."

Ryall caught the sharp uptick of the left eyebrow. He'd been expecting it. Annie Wyler was famous for her eyebrows. He ignored it. He did not ignore the fact that he got a deep and abiding sense of satisfaction from the fact that he'd anticipated it.

"Sit down, sit down," he said. "You look positively exhausted. And I don't blame you a bit, of course. Two family funerals in the same week. I don't know what's happening to the Main Line. Even a few years ago, it was the safest place on earth. You could go anywhere there, even at night. Of course, Charlotte and Tony had security, but that was because of Tony's position. He had to worry about international terrorists. I don't know what I'm going to do if it turns out that international terrorists have begun to target Society. I'll be scared to death to go out in the evenings, and it's my life's work."

Anne Ross Wyler sat down, without looking behind her to see if a chair was there. Ryall felt his mouth purse up and did what he had to do to straighten it out again. He hated this about these women too. He hated the way they just expected things to be where they needed them to be, and the way the things were always there. Any normal person would have looked around to make sure she wasn't about to fall on her ass.

"So," he said. "What can I get for you? Coffee? Tea? I've got some excellent Ceylon, just arrived. I order it from a company in Bangkok. It's the only place on earth you can still get decent Ceylon, I don't care what anybody says."

She was staring at him, placidly, waiting. Why didn't she talk? God, he hated this about them too, the way they never got wound up, the way they just let you go on until you'd made a complete fool of yourself. Somebody ought to be appointed to teach some manners to the women of the old Main Line.

"Well," he said.

Anne Ross Wyler took her tote bag off the floor and put it down on her lap. She reached inside it and came up with a long manila envelope. She opened the envelope and came out with a small handful of snapshots. Whatever was she going to do? Ryall didn't think she would be bringing him family snaps of Tony and Charlotte to use in the column. She didn't like the column, and she hadn't seen too much of Tony and Charlotte over the last few years. She couldn't stand Charlotte. There was something *else* he'd love to tell the world: how these old families stuck together in spite of the fact that they found each other's company poisonous; the way Charlotte Deacon Ross had alienated even Tony's long-suffering relatives. Surely, Anne Ross Wyler was long-suffering. She was also that creature he despised most in the world: the victim of social conscience guilt. She probably thought she was so damned holy, running a house for prostitutes, giving up on parties and expensive clothes just so that the rest of the people she knew would feel utterly and irredeemably inadequate.

She took the handful of snapshots and leaned over to put them down, one by one, on the coffee table. Ryall leaned over to look at them and stiffened.

"Do you know what these are?" she asked.

"They're very murky snaps," Ryall said. "It's not possible to see much of anything in them, is it?"

"It is if you blow them up." She reached into her tote

bag again and came up, this time, with an eight-by-eleven glossy.

"It's still murky," Ryall said, after he'd had a chance to get a look at it. Still, it wasn't as murky as the other one. It was just—but not absolutely—identifiable. "Maybe you ought to take lessons on how to operate your camera. You seem to need instructions on using a flash."

"I was there, you know. I took these pictures myself. I stood just three feet from you on the night my brother Tony died and watched you take Patsy Lennon into that car."

"I don't know anybody named Patsy Lennon."

"I'm sure you don't. God only knows what name she's using on the street these days. Did you know she was just thirteen?"

"I still don't know what you're talking about," Ryall said. "If you're insinuating that these are pictures of me, I'll ask you to leave right this minute. I don't think I've ever been this insulted in all my life."

"I'm not going to leave," Anne Ross Wyler said, "and you're not going to throw me out. I was there. I stood on that stretch of sidewalk and watched you pick up a minor—more than a minor, what's technically a child—and get her into your car to blow you. I moved in and looked through the windows and saw her."

"I don't have a car."

"You had a rental car. Don't bother to whine. I checked."

"You didn't find my name on a rental agreement," Ryall said. "I assure you, I did not rent a car."

"Do you mean you did it under an assumed name? That won't be hard to unravel. Maybe I'll ask that Mr. Demarkian to do it for me. Don't bother to protest, Mr. Wyndham. You're not James Bond. I'm sure you've left traces a backward four-year-old could follow."

"You've got nothing at all but a lot of murky pictures. It's impossible to identify anybody in them, except of course the girl, who, I'll admit, looks very young. But if you seriously think you can get me arrested on that kind of evidence—"

"Oh, no," Anne said. "I don't want to get you arrested. What would be the point? I followed you afterwards, you know. I followed you right up to the gate of Tony's house. I know what you saw."

"What are you trying to do? You know what would happen in books at a time like this, if what you're alleging is true. I'd kill you now and dump your body in the incinerator."

"You won't kill me. And this building doesn't have an incinerator."

"Well, Mrs. Wyler, I really don't see the point to your visit here. You don't want to get me arrested. You're not trying to get me to kill you. What do you want?"

"I want you to keep your mouth shut."

"About what?"

"About everything that happened on the night Tony died. About who else you saw there. About what was going on at the gate when you arrived. About all of it. I saw it too. And I want you to do the one thing you've never been able to do in your life. I want you to shut up. Because if you don't, I'll use these pictures."

"There's nothing in those pictures to use."

"Not for the police to use, no," Anne said. "But I can think of a few other venues where they might be useful. I could, for instance, file suit against you for endangering the safety of a minor. Patsy Lennon has spent quite a lot of time at Adelphos House, did you know that? She's a very troubled and fragile girl. The court might not grant me standing, or it might, but it wouldn't matter, because I'd have made the charge a matter of public record. Then all I'd have to do would be to make sure it's reported."

"You couldn't get a charge like that reported. The papers would be afraid of lawsuits. And besides, they'd find it trivial."

"They'd find it trivial that their new media star and prominent witness to the Tony Ross murder is being sued on charges that he enticed a child into sex?"

"She wasn't a *child*," Ryall said, and bit his lip.

"She was thirteen," Anne said. "And don't kid yourself that the newspapers wouldn't be interested, or the television news shows, either. Even the ones I don't own significant stock in would be interested. The ones I own significant stock in might see some reason to make the story a priority. Did you know that I still had all that stock?"

"People like you always do, don't you?" Ryall said. "You make a grand show of being Mother Teresa, but you never let go of the money and you never let go of the power. I ought to do a nice little exposé on you. Just so that the city of Philadelphia can see that you're not anything at all like a saint."

"I've never pretended to be a saint. Please get me all the publicity you can. Adelphos House can always use donations."

"For all you know, I've already told the police whatever it is you don't want me to tell them," Ryall said. "I've already been questioned. I spent four hours at the police department the day after your brother was murdered. It was disgusting. But I told them everything I know."

"Fine. Then it's possible that you don't know what I think you do. No harm done. But if you get some bright idea in your head, keep it to yourself. Don't tell the police. Don't tell Larry King. Just calm down and shut up. Because if you don't, I'm going to take these pictures and shred your life, from the bottom up."

"You're such a bitch," Ryall said. "You always were, even when I first started the column. You were probably a bitch in grade school."

"I make a point of it." Anne Ross Wyler stood up and took the snapshots off the coffee table. "You can have these, you know. I have the negatives. And I have copies. It doesn't matter."

"I want them out of here as fast as you can make them go."

"Fine. Here's one more thing. Stay away from Patsy Lennon from now on. And stay away from that street and all the rest of the girls on it. I'm out there almost every night. I'll be watching for you. If you have to fuck children, take a sex tour to Thailand."

"What wonderful language. All of you have completely foul mouths, have you ever noticed that? Do they teach that kind of thing in dancing classes?"

Her tote bag was packed up and back over her shoulder. Her coat was in her hands. Ryall didn't remember her getting either. She was not a tall woman, but she was very trim. He didn't think she went on diets or worked out to keep herself that way. Why was he thinking about Anne Ross Wyler on a diet? He thought he was losing his mind.

"I don't understand how you can live the way you do," she said, looking around the living room. Then she turned her back to him and walked off, out of the living room, into the foyer so tiny it wasn't much more than a breathing space shoved against the door. He didn't think she'd been talking about the living room, but he couldn't be sure.

What he could be sure of was that he was sick. If he didn't get up and get to the bathroom immediately, he would soil himself. All his muscles felt completely out of control. Everything was twitching. And the worst thing was, he had no idea what she was talking about. He really could have told the police already. He couldn't remember what he had told them. He'd talked and talked and talked. He'd said whatever had come into his head. The same was true with what he'd been doing on television. He'd just *talked*.

He thought of himself, just through the gates when all hell had broken loose, the shouts of the security guards, the running of men in dark clothes. It had been like watching a movie. If there had been some secret there that he was supposed to have witnessed, he couldn't begin to imagine what it was.

2

David Alden was getting extremely tired of the game. It wasn't that he wanted to stop playing it, exactly. No matter what Annie Ross said, he was not, at heart, an emotional dropout from hypercapitalism. He'd always liked his job when Tony was alive. He'd liked being the one who knew everything, all the projections, all the risks, all the secrets. He'd liked being the one who made the decisions. Tony was supposed to make them, but in nine cases out of ten Tony left it to him, and they were both satisfied. Being Tony Ross's second in command was like being the chief clerk to a Supreme Court justice. You were the one who had the expertise, who did the work, who made the changes happen. You weren't the one who got the blame for it when things went wrong. *Well,* David thought, *not quite.* If things went wrong enough, you could end up with plenty of blame, but it would be private blame, meted out in secret, not the kind that appeared on the op-ed page of the *Wall Street Journal.*

Of course, when things went right, you didn't get quite as much of the credit as you deserved, but David was finding he minded that less than he thought he had. Nobody in the bank seemed to know what to make of him anymore. They couldn't get along without him. He was the only one who knew what Tony had known and who could explain it to them. They didn't want to have to get along with him at all. Two murders had made him seem more than a little jinxed, and he could tell that some of them were beginning to wonder if he had committed them, or if he had somehow brought them on. Maybe there was a jealous husband out there aiming for his back. Maybe the jealous husband had less-than-perfect aim. Maybe the nuts had found out who he was and were using him as a pilot fish. Maybe he was a pilot fish by choice.

Now he looked out at the early morning downtown New York traffic and felt almost infinitely tired. He hated staying overnight in Philadelphia in the middle of the work week. He hated the morning commute, even on the Amtrak express. He hated not being able to get to his own things in his own closet in the only place he'd ever called home without ambiguity, the apartment he kept on Riverside Drive that had exactly one bedroom, no room for guests, no room for family, no room for expansion. Mostly, he hated the feeling of disorientation it gave him, so that his timing was off for the rest of the day. Maybe that was his problem. Some part of him was back there with Charlotte dying in her own driveway and Marianne shrieking like a gored pig and the police sirens in the distance, all of it seeming so familiar that he thought he would never be able to think of Tony's place again without those sirens. He was, he decided, going slowly crazy. He looked up and down the street, which still seemed tense and cramped to him in the wake of September 11. He went into the building and across the high-ceilinged prewar lobby and into the ornate elevator. There were too many people in the halls, rushing in late to work, rushing around trying to get set up for the day. He rode the elevator to the twenty-fifth floor and got out again. He went down the hall to his own office and put his attaché case on his desk. He seemed to be the first one here besides the secretaries. He usually was. The secretaries were all hushed and agitated, and he didn't blame them.

He unbuttoned his coat, but didn't take it off. He walked over to the wall of windows and looked out on the financial district. He'd always liked this view. He still liked it, in spite of the fact that it had been . . . altered . . . somewhat in the destruction last year. He heard the door open behind him but didn't turn around to see who it was.

"I saw you come in," Adele said. "You didn't have to come in. God, David, we'd all have understood if you'd wanted to take a day off."

"I've still got Price Heaven up the wazoo," he said. The view was altered, but not altered enough, that was the problem. He couldn't see enough. "Get a coat on and come for a walk with me. Just for ten minutes."

"A walk? Where are we going? The office just opened—"

"There are other people to handle the phones. You don't do much of that anyway. Come take a walk with me. I want to go see it."

"See what?"

"Ground Zero."

"Good God, David, why?"

"I haven't seen it yet, did you know that? Everybody else has been over there to take a look, but I never have. On the day it happened, the first I knew that there was something going on was when the windows blew out. All these windows. They just popped, suddenly. I was sitting at my desk going over the risk cost figures for the loan to the government of Peru, and suddenly *snap snap snap*. It was the oddest thing."

"I think you should have stayed home," Adele said. "I don't think you've got your head on straight this morning. I know you didn't like her much, none of us did, but that doesn't mean you aren't affected by the way she died. You knew her a long time."

"Do you know Tony's sister, Annie Ross?"

"Mrs. Wyler? I've met her a few times, why?"

"She thinks I'm turning on, tuning in, and about to drop out. She thinks I'm emotionally detached from banking."

"Are you?"

"No. At least I don't think so. At least, it's not the banking. I know how this looks to people, you know. I hear all the jokes on Leno. Here we are, the heartless bank, making Price Heaven fire six thousand people right before Christmas. And I'll admit, the timing is not stellar. If it were up to me, the physical year would end on August thirty-first and then these layoffs wouldn't always coincide with the holidays, but Adele, the thing is, they'd still happen. They'd have to happen. And getting that damned fool CEO of theirs to take a cut in salary and bonuses wouldn't keep a single extra person on the job."

"I thought the idea was to get that damned fool CEO of theirs to resign."

"It is. We're going in on that today. But do you know what you get when you don't have people like me, people like Tony, people like the bank—when you don't have us coming in and forcing these things? Everything just jogs along getting worse until the business collapses completely. Or they get themselves a government bailout and then it jogs along even after it's dead, and the money that could have been used to put life into a new and viable enterprise isn't available, because we're putting it into keeping a gigantic dinosaur alive and for what? For sentiment? It's not even good sentiment. The collapse is going to come, no matter what. Staving it off just makes the mess bigger when it's over."

Adele cleared her throat. "David? You're preaching to the choir here."

"Yes," David said, "I know. I know. Come take that walk with me. I want to move around a little before I start the day. And I want to see it. Just this once. Have you been?"

"We went—the whole bunch of us, all the exec assistants and most of the typists—we went the day after the observation platform was opened."

"Why?"

"To see it," Adele said.

"See?"

"Yes to see," Adele said. "But we haven't been back. None of us, that I know of. I think we wanted to see it because we're all afraid of it. We're still afraid of it."

"You're afraid the terrorists will come back?"

"No," Adele said. "Not of that. I don't know how to put it. The terrorists don't bother me at all. They just seem like jerks."

David turned his back to the window and sat on the sill. "You're right. They seem like that to me too. Any loser can destroy things. They do it all the time. They get knives and guns and mug old ladies on Broadway. They set fire to buildings."

"It's—" Adele looked uneasy. "It's just, you know, you hear all these things, about how we should appreciate other cultures for what they are, that every culture is great in its own way. And after that I couldn't help feeling it wasn't true.

Their culture isn't great. If it was, they wouldn't have done that, and their people wouldn't have cheered it. And I shouldn't say that in the bank. We have a lot of clients from Islamic countries. Stewart Markham down in development will call me an imperialist."

"At least," David said wryly. "Annie wants to blame it on religion—all religion, everywhere, leads to violence. Christianity had its religious wars and it burned its heretics and hanged its witches. The Hindus kill the Muslims in India and Pakistan. The Muslims make war on the World Trade Center. We should go to work to abolish religion."

"How can you abolish religion?"

"I think it's all an excuse," David said. "All of it. Religion. Politics. Love. Hate. Rage. It's all an excuse for the fact that some people love blood. They love destruction. They hate everything about themselves so much. They hate what they are. They hate their humanness. And mostly they hate other people's humanness. They hate the fact that other people are human just the way they are, but they do so much more, they accomplish so much more. That's what they have to get rid of. The fact that there's no difference between themselves and those people, the people who do things, who make things instead of tearing them down. I think every murder ever committed on the face of this planet has been committed out of guilt."

"I'd like to say I know what you're talking about, but I don't," Adele said. "Maybe you should take your coat off and sit down. I'll bring you some coffee."

"Maybe you should get your coat on and come with me. I'm going to go look at it. When we come back, we can take a break from Price Heaven and look over the setup for the foundation Annie wants to endow for Adelphos House. We can write up the specs and send it down to Carver to hammer out the details. I want to go, Adele. I'd like you to come with me."

"All right," Adele said. "My coat's right out in the hall. Let me get it. Are you sure you shouldn't be home in bed with a tranquilizer?"

"I'm sure."

"You're behaving the way some of us did right after it happened. Post-traumatic stress syndrome, they call it. Some of the younger men walked around for days looking like they'd just been shot, and not being able to remember where they put anything. Tranquilizers do help, you know. And nobody would think worse of you for taking a day off when two of your closest friends have been murdered within sight of you in less than a week."

"I don't need a day off. Get your coat. Let's go."

Adele hesitated. Then she shrugged slightly, turned on her heel, and went. She left the door open. David stared through it for a moment. The outer offices looked busy. They always were at this time of day. In an hour or two, the men on the Asia desk would pack up and go home. They worked reverse hours to be in touch with the Tokyo market. He didn't think he had been exaggerating. He really didn't. Every murder was committed out of guilt, the guilt of knowing that you were less than you ought to be. That was what had happened on September 11 and that was what had happened to Tony and Charlotte. It was counterproductive to attempt to make something huge and special and enormous out of a terrorist attack, as if to be a terrorist was to be something more than human, or less. To be a terrorist was to be exactly human. To be a murderer was to be exactly human. No matter what the excuses were, at the bottom, the motives were always the same.

Less than you ought to be, David thought, turning to look out the windows again, through the narrow streets around Wall, toward the towers that weren't there anymore. He thought about Charlotte on the walk in front of the house, the back of her head gone, the grey-pink spatter of brains on the windows next to the front door. He thought about Tony with his face blown away. He should have known at the very beginning. All the signs were there. It simply hadn't occurred to him.

Now that it *had* occurred to him, he had no idea what to do about it.

3

Lucinda Watkins finished doing the dishes at eleven. The house was still almost as quiet as it had been in the early morning, except for the thumps and giggles coming from the second-floor drawing room where there was an encounter therapy session in progress. The day outside was grey and getting greyer. The kitchen was cold. One of the things Lucinda wanted to do, as soon as they had the money to do it, was to completely overhaul the heating system. It didn't make any sense to her to keep the house freezing cold when so many of the girls came here to get in out of the weather. If it was always warm and glowing and comfortable here, maybe more of them would come.

She went down the narrow hall to the front of the house where the living room was and looked out the front windows at the street. That *was* deserted. Even hookers didn't walk here, no matter what the time of day or night. She wondered if it was ever possible to find a hooker in the morning, on a business basis. She'd never thought about it before. They were so concentrated on the night in this place. Annie went out at night. Those pictures she was always bringing back were always taken in the dark. The windows of the cars that cruised the strip were sometimes tinted black too, although that was only for the men who could afford that sort of thing, or had the foresight to rent it. She wondered how many men rented cars to go trawling for tail. Then she winced at the phrase, even though she hadn't spoken it out loud. It was Annie's phrase. It sounded all right when Annie said it, just as it sounded all right when Annie said *fuck* or *cunt* as if she meant them. Annie could get away with anything. Lucinda didn't think even Grandma Watkins would have disapproved.

She was restless, and agitated, and tired. She knew she had to go out, but she hesitated to do it. She didn't want to leave and not get back by the time Annie did. She didn't want to wait until Annie got home, either. She wondered how many people out there, how many ordinary, everyday people, really knew what people like Annie were like. Before she'd come to Adelphos House, Lucinda had been like everybody else. She'd only been able to guess, and her guesses had been made up of too many viewings of *The Philadelphia Story* and a few desultory forays into the fiction of Dominick Dunne. She'd been convinced that people like Annie—that people like Tony and Charlotte—were "all prim and proper," as the saying went in her childhood, and that they only listened to classical music and went to Shakespeare plays. The truth was, she'd never heard anybody swear the way Annie did on a regular basis. Even the greaser boys of her adolescence, who'd made a fetish of their motorcycles and their violence, had had mouths less foul than Mrs. Wyler's over breakfast and the morning paper. She thought of Charlotte, dead on the walk in front of her house, but it was hard to get a clear picture of the woman. Lucinda hadn't known her very well. The few times they'd met, they'd said very little to each other, although it had been easy for Lucinda to see what Charlotte was thinking: *trailer trash, cheap flash, vulgar*. It was all well and good for Annie to fret over how paranoid and ridiculous *The Harridan Report* was, but it had a point, all the same. Those people really were different from you and me, if not different in the way the movies portrayed them as being. They didn't watch television. They didn't go to malls. They didn't play the lottery. Of course, Lucinda didn't do any of those things either, but that was different. She didn't do them because she was here, working, and it was too expensive to keep more than two televisions on the premises, with cable, so there always seemed to be somebody using the one she wanted to use to watch *Friends* or listen to the news. And she didn't play the lottery because she had sense. Every time she went home, or anywhere near it, she found her family and all their friends knee-deep in lottery tickets, hundreds of dollars of lottery tickets, and all of them losers. *Learn to count*, she wanted to scream at them—and then another happy-happy television commercial would come on for the Pennsylvania lottery, and it was like watching an ad for fairy dust. The girls all played the lottery too, of course. They bought their tickets at the convenience stores they passed on their way downtown to work. They hid them where they hoped their pimps wouldn't find them. Well, Lucinda knew, if one of them won, her pimp would find her soon enough. There was something *The Harridan Report* got exactly right. If the lottery wasn't a plot of the rich to drain the blood of the poor, Lucinda didn't know what it was.

She paced around the living room, aimless. She stopped at the window again and looked out again and saw nothing again. She thought about getting out the prospectus for the foundation Annie was setting up to fund Adelphos House. It was only a draft prospectus. The banks and the lawyers were still haggling over the details. Once the provisions were in place, Adelphos House would have a constant stream of income that would pay the bills and pay the taxes and pay the salaries of herself and two other full-time people, complete with benefits. Lucinda didn't understand why it was taking so long to put it all together. Couldn't you just take your money out of the bank and do what you wanted with it? There was something else *The Harridan Report* got exactly right. The money the rich had was different from the money ordinary people had, and not only because there was more of it. She wondered how banks stored their money. Were there vaults with gold under the rubble of the World Trade Center? Were there secret passages in Switzerland full of silver and precious stones? Surely, at some point, money would have to stop being paper for *somebody*. It couldn't all just be a matter of blips on a ticker tape or pulses on a computer screen or those green oblong things everybody carried in their wallets and nobody thought about. Lucinda had seen French paper money once. It was odd how obvious it was that "money" was just paper when you looked at foreign currency, which you weren't used to considering real.

Marvelous, she thought. *I'm not only losing my mind, I'm working overtime at it.* She didn't want to look at the draft prospectus. She didn't understand it, except for that bit about Adelphos House finally being set up to run independently of Annie's writing checks. Of course, it would still be a matter of Annie's having written a check, but a big one, so that they wouldn't have to go back to her for more checks two and three times a week. She didn't want to think about *The Harridan Report*, either. It gave her a headache, and then it made her feel a little resentful for being what it was. On one level, she couldn't help thinking it was a work of genius. Only somebody truly plugged in to the way people think could have produced it, and that meant plugged in to the way they *all* think, the Annies as well as the regular people. She didn't want to think about Adelphos House, either, which this morning felt like an oppressive weight. Sometimes it was like that. The whole history of human misery was wrapped up inside it and given a new name every hour: Patsy Lennon; Amy Margerbrad; Susie Kell.

She went back out into the hallway and back down to the other end of the house and got her coat out of the closet there. It was a big, heavy, thick wool thing that she'd bought at Price Heaven after a long summer of saving up. Annie would have given her the money to buy a better one. She'd have called it an "advance on salary" and then forgotten all about it. Lucinda had had no intention of asking. It was the kind of thing Annie did where she meant well, but it only made people angry.

Lucinda went back down to the front of the house. She could hear the encounter group rollicking away upstairs. Sometimes they screamed and cried for the whole two hours, but today they were laughing. She let herself out onto the street and looked around. Before she'd come to this place, she'd never believed that a city street could be utterly and irrevocably deserted, as if no human beings existed anywhere anymore, anywhere on the planet. She tried the door to make sure it locked. She turned left and began to move up the block as quickly as she could manage it with her weight. The wind was coming down between the abandoned buildings like swiftly flowing water through a shunt. It whistled and rattled and moaned. What glass was left in the windows around her shimmered in the very faint sunlight that emerged once in a while from the blanket of clouds. Annie said that she could feel the vampires who were buried here. Annie may have thought she was exaggerating for effect, but Lucinda knew she was exactly right. This neighborhood was full of vampires, and werewolves, and the shape-shifters that lived where no living thing could—and it had been a mistake for them to put Adelphos House here. They should have bought a building on a better street, closer to the action. They could have been right around the corner from the strip. Being where they were meant they were miles away from everything, even their own work—miles away emotionally, if not physically. Most of the time when they wanted to go anywhere, they had to use a car. That meant they had to keep two, just to make sure there was always one available at the house when Annie wanted to do her photographing. The wind sounded like children crying. The cold felt like glass. Lucinda knew there was no danger of it getting dark. It was still only late in the morning. She picked up speed anyway. The last thing she wanted to do was be caught on this street on foot after nightfall, when the vampires came out to feed and the werewolves began to wait in the shelter of the empty buildings that were just one small step from being shape-shifters themselves.

She made a right, past two vacant lots and a big building that might once have been a factory or a warehouse. She made another right, into the first faint stirrings of what could be called a neighborhood. She felt the muscles of her back ease a little, but only a little, because she knew she couldn't stop here. She was too close to home.

In another three blocks, there was a street with some life on it. People sat on stoops. People went in and out of stores. People minded their own business. There was a big pharmacy there with pay phones in the back near the candy counter, old-fashioned ones with wooden booths. She would feel much better once she had made her call. History was an engine. It ground everything in its way to dust. If she wasn't careful, they would all be dust too, and blood and skin and bone, lying out on the pavement, like those two people in Bryn Mawr.

FIVE

1

Murder, Gregor Demarkian had been told, when he was in training at Quantico, is the one crime without a reliable perpetrator profile. Every other crime—robbery, rape, assault, embezzlement—had its attractions for a certain segment of the population, a certain personality among all the possible personalties occurring among Americans in the twentieth century. Only murder was a wild card. *Some* murderers could be profiled. That was what the Behavioral Sciences Unit was all about. Serial killers were a definite personality type, more alike than different across the spectrum, and predictable, to a certain extent, because of it. The ordinary murderer was something else again. Go to any death row in any large state—go to Texas, Gregor thought sourly—and what you found was a hodgepodge of motives, social classes, educational backgrounds, religious convictions, car makes, tastes in books and coffee. The majority of the prisoners awaiting death would be what would be expected by anybody who spent significant time watching Bruce Willis movies. They would be poor, male, violent, senseless, addicted, the kind of people for whom nothing would ever be a deterrent if it required thinking. They would have killed their victims in robberies that hadn't required anybody to die, or beaten their girlfriends or their girlfriends' children into insensate pulps in an anger they were no longer able to explain. They were really rapists, or batterers, or thieves.

The murders were side issues they never could quite figure out how to explain. Somewhere on that death row, or somewhere else in that prison, blessed with life instead of death because of their age or youth or status, there would be other murderers—the Diane Downses, the Charles Stewarts, the Jean Harrises, the middle class and the well-off, the envious, the resentful, the hateful, the cold. That was what they'd meant at Quantico when they told agents-in-training to be very careful about murder. It was far too easy to ignore the true perpetrator in a futile search for a mythical criminal type, hulking and monstrous, as if real human beings never hurt each other at all.

Gregor felt the taxi pull up to the curb and looked out to see that he was right in front of Le Demiurge, where he was supposed to meet John Jackman for lunch. His watch said that it was barely noon, and Jackman, being Jackman, was always at least a little late. That had been true even when he hadn't had the excuse of being commissioner of police to explain the habit away. Gregor got out a small clutch of bills and handed them to the driver. He got out of the cab and looked around at a pleasant but mostly unassuming neighborhood. He had no idea where John found these places. Even Dennis, who looked on eating out as a sacrament, hadn't heard of most of them. This one had one of those arched canvas awnings stretched out across the sidewalk. Gregor had always wondered what the procedure was for getting the city to allow you to put one of those up. It was the kind of thing he thought about when he wasn't able to get to sleep at night and he didn't want to wake Bennis by getting out of bed and starting up the computer. Of course, she never worried about that sort of thing when it came to him, but she never woke him up, either.

The problem with Quantico's dictum on murderers was that it was only about 90 percent right. Even those murderers who seemed to have nothing in common did have something in common, if nothing else the fact that they'd killed someone. It went deeper than that. Gregor thought he could say with certainty that virtually all murderers actually killed the person they had intended to kill. Those plots that showed up in crime fiction sometimes, where bodies were strewn across the landscape by mistake until the perpetrator finally got it right, were implausible. The key was to pay attention to who had actually died. In this case, that meant paying attention to Charlotte Deacon Ross, and not just to Tony Ross alone. The danger was in the possibility that they would find an explanation they liked so much for that first murder that they would do whatever they had to do to shoehorn the second one into it. It didn't do to assume that all murders after the first, if there were more than one, occurred because somebody or the other "knew too much." It happened. Gregor had seen it happen. Most of the time, it didn't happen. If Charlotte Deacon Ross *and* Tony Ross were dead, it was because somebody had a reason to want Charlotte Deacon Ross *and* Tony Ross dead. That seemed to leave out America on Alert. Gregor was sure that Kathi Mittendorf considered Charlotte Deacon Ross to be a mind-controlled sex slave of the Illuminati, but he'd have been very surprised to find out that she thought Mrs. Ross was one of the people who ran the world. It also seemed to rule out a whole host of motives, like sex and jealousy. The kind of lover who might want one of them dead would be unlikely to want them both dead. The most obvious avenue of investigation would be the daughters. Gregor was sure they must stand to inherit something, and possibly a great deal. The problem was that Gregor couldn't remember a case of murder for inheritance on the Main Line—except for one, and that had been an extremely odd and bizarre situation brought on by a paterfamilias who had a mind as warped and paranoid as Howard Hughes's had been at the end. No, now that he thought about it, it was really remarkable. With all that money floating around, there should have been a fair amount of violence at the edges of that group of people, but as far as he knew, there had not been.

The other way in which all murderers were alike, every single one of them, was in that odd tunnel vision that allowed them to see only themselves as human. *Me me me*, Gregor thought. Then he looked around at where he was. He hated people who stood on sidewalks talking on cell phones, but he wasn't really happy with the ones who sat at restaurant tables talking on cell phones, either. Bennis said that in London, bums on the street sat in doorways and talked on cell phones. Gergor went into Le Demiurge and gave his name to the hostess at the desk. She checked him off a list and began to show him to a table. John was not, of course, there. John would not be there for at least another fifteen minutes. A waiter came by to ask him if he wanted something to drink. Gregor ordered a Perrier and lime and asked where the pay phones were.

"I could bring a phone to the table," the waiter offered helpfully. "Most of our patrons these days prefer their own cell phones, of course, but—"

"No, no," Gregor said. "I don't want to have this particular conversation in the middle of a restaurant. Are there pay phones?"

There were pay phones, in the narrow back hall near the men's and ladies' rooms. Gregor hoped to find the kind with a booth that could be closed, but had no luck. This restaurant was too new. It had only those weird wall cubicles that were supposed to surround the speaker's ears, but were always too low on the wall to manage it. Gregor went into the men's room and looked around. Nobody was there. He got out his phone and dialed Bennis's number.

"Live goat escort service," Bennis said, picking up. "We supply the billy to suit your lifestyle."

"Jesus," Gregor said. "What do you think you're doing when you pull something like that?"

"Scaring off telemarketers," Bennis said. "The national ones don't faze no matter what you do, but the locals just freak. We've had three calls from some company trying to sell us vinyl windows. Where are you calling from?"

"It's called Le Demiurge. It's one of John Jackman's restaurants."

"That ought to be good. If you like it, we'll go. Tibor's out with the architect Russ Donahue hired, walking over the rubble and outlining the requirements for floor plans. Russ thought it would cheer him up, to be doing something about all this instead of just brooding."

"Is it working?"

"Hard to tell," Bennis said. "He looks solemn enough, but he walked out of here telling the architect that he'd have to lend him a copy of *The History of the Theology of the Church in Armenia*. I've seen it. It weighs about forty pounds."

"It *is* working," Gregor said. "I want to ask you something. Why aren't there more murders on the Main Line?"

"What? There are murders on the Main Line. You said so yourself. You said—"

"No, no. I don't mean those kinds of murders. I mean murders among people like your family. All those rich families out in Bryn Mawr and Sewickly and Radnor. Millions of dollars at stake. Sometimes hundreds of millions of dollars. The sheer law of averages says there should be a certain number of murders for the inheritance money, and I don't believe that Main Line debutantes are any less rapacious than anybody else—"

"They're probably more," Bennis said. "But they wouldn't kill for the inheritance money. I mean, what would be the point? Most of them wouldn't inherit anything."

"Are you trying to tell me these people don't pass their money down to their children? Or are you just saying that your father was typical, and they don't give their daughters anything?"

"My father was never typical, on any point. No, I mean that if you've got serious money, you don't leave it around in bank accounts or whatever to be handed over to your children when you're dead. One of these days, George W. Bush or somebody will manage to get the estate tax repealed, but in the meantime, dying with a lot of money in the bank just means your heirs are going to hand a whole lot of it over to the government. So you don't do that. You take care of that before you die."

"You give your money to your children before you die? What do you live on yourself?"

"You give your money to your grandchildren before you die," Bennis explained patiently. "You live on the income until you die. It's called a living trust. I think. Ask somebody who knows about this stuff. But anyway, that's what you do, and then you put other money in regular trusts so that your children have something to live on themselves. But most of these people die with very small estates, relative to what they were actually worth, or in control of. And the children and the grandchildren have their money affairs set up so that they don't usually see any significant change just because somebody died. If you see what I mean."

"Vaguely," Gregor said. "Is that what the Rosses did? They've got four daughters."

"Are you thinking that one of the Ross girls killed her parents? Well, I suppose the oldest one could do it, but the other three have IQs like miracle golf scores. I couldn't see them doing the planning."

"But they can all shoot, can't they?" Gregor said. "You told me that—or somebody did. They weren't talking about the girls, but what I remember was that all these people belong to some gun club—"

"I'm sure they all shoot," Bennis said patiently. "I'm sure they're all good at it too. They'd make a point of it. They probably all ride, as well, and they're probably good at that too. Have you ever paid attention to who competes in the equestrian events at the Olympics? But that still doesn't mean that they're capable of planning a rifle murder in the middle of a charity ball. I should think that took an enormous amount of planning and forethought."

"Maybe."

"Only maybe?"

"I think we've been putting too much stress on the planning and forethought. There are other explanations. It might have been a matter of opportunity. Somebody happened to be there and saw his chance—"

"And where did he get the gun?" Bennis sounded impatient. "That place was crawling with security that night, and not just the firm Charlotte hired. And it's a good firm. It had to be, given Tony's position. But the secret service was there, for God's sake."

"I know. But something tells me there had to be a way. There were guns in the house, weren't there?"

"I'm sure there were, but I'm also willing to bet almost anything that they were locked away in gun cabinets. They were at Engine House when I was growing up, and even after we all grew up. It's just common sense."

"Still," Gregor said. "It keeps bothering me. That there's something obvious, or close to obvious, and I'm just not getting it. What about the sister? Would she be likely to inherit money when her brother died?"

"Her brother, yes, but not Charlotte," Bennis said. "Not unless something very dramatic has taken place in that family without anybody telling me about it. Charlotte and Annie hated each other practically as a matter of principle. Charlotte thought Annie was ostentatious. Annie thought Charlotte was a twit."

"I've met Mrs. Wyler. She didn't look ostentatious to me."

"When you buy your clothes at Price Heaven and wear them to places where everybody else has Chanel, you might be accused of being ostentatious. I don't see why you're so off the original theory. I thought it made a lot of sense that they'd been killed by some conspiracy group who thought Tony was bringing on a one-world satanic government, or whatever it is this week."

"And killed Mrs. Ross—why?"

"I don't know," Bennis said.

"I don't know either," Gregor said. "And that's my problem. Never mind. I'd better go find out if John has arrived, or if I'm going to be left drinking Perrier at the table until almost dinnertime. There *is* something about all this, though.

Some organizing idea. I must be asking the wrong questions. I wish I knew what the right ones were."

"Just don't order everything with cream sauce," Bennis said. "Are you all right? You sound depressed."

"I'm not depressed, I'm annoyed. I'll talk to you later. If you think of anything, write it down. Maybe this place serves that crème brûlée stuff you got for me a few weeks ago."

"I'm never again in my life going to feed you anything but steamed vegetables," Bennis said.

Gregor switched the phone off. The men's room was still empty. No one had come in in all the time he'd been talking to Bennis. He put the phone away in his pocket and then— for no reason he could have put in his words—washed his hands. *Remember who actually died*, he thought, and then, *me me me*.

There was something there, right at the edge of his mind, and he couldn't get hold of it.

2

Always, in the detective novels Father Tibor Kasparian insisted on pressing on him when he had a cold, the detective—usually a professional private investigator, but sometimes a little old lady living on her own in a village or a haute cuisine caterer active in the gay rights movement or a cat—would sit down halfway through the book, outline the details of the case, and know, immediately, not only who had done it and why, but how to catch the murderer in the way most likely to result in either an arrest or a suicide. Gregor did not remember a book in which the detective had arrived at the halfway point without actually knowing what the crime was. He had no idea if he was now at what would be the halfway point if this were a book, but he did know that the only thing he was sure of was that he wasn't sure. Tony Ross was dead. Charlotte Ross was dead. Holy Trinity Armenian Christian Church had been half-destroyed and rendered completely unusable. All those things might go together or not, might say something about each other or not, might help find a solution or not—but he had no way of knowing, because he had no way of organizing all the elements into a coherent whole. It would have been much easier if he could have assigned the Ross murders to a straightforward money motive. The daughters wanted the money. The sister wanted the money. Then he could have put the bombing of Holy Trinity definitively aside, separate and not in need of being included in anybody else's mosaic. As it was, he was going around in circles. If he'd been asked to explain the case to someone coming into it new, he would have had to say: which of several possible cases are you referring to?

John was not, of course, at the table when Gregor got back to it, so he drank Perrier poured over lime and looked around for something to scribble on. He couldn't scribble on the napkins here. They were cloth, and elegantly monogrammed. It was no wonder that great books were always conceived in bars and cheap diners. They had paper napkins their patrons could write on. Gregor went through his pockets and came up with another issue of *The Harridan Report*. He seemed to have dozens of them, stashed all over himself and his apartment back on Cavanaugh Street. He got out his pen and started to write names and draw lines and arrows. He filled up one sheet of paper and went on to another. He was on the third by the time Jackman did show up, and he was no better organized. On the third sheet of paper he had a list, although not a definitive list. His head hurt.

John sat down and asked the waiter for a Perrier of his own. Gregor thought idly that if they were in Italy, John could have had a glass of wine at lunch with nobody thinking anything of it. John looked at the paper upside down.

"What is that?" he said.

Gregor shrugged. "It's a list."

"A list of what?"

"I don't know."

"That won't do, Gregor. It can't be a list of 'you don't know.' You're not allowed not to know anything."

Gregor pushed the napkin across to him and shrugged. John Jackman picked it up.

"Tony Ross," he said. "Charlotte Deacon Ross. Father Tibor Kasparian. Ryall Wyndham. David Alden. Anne Ross Wyler. Michael Harridan and people connected to Michael Harridan. Krystof Andrechev. All right. Everybody who has anything to do with either of the cases you're looking into at the moment. That's what you were making a list of."

"In a way," Gregor said.

The waiter was back. John already knew what he wanted, which made sense, since John did not suggest restaurants for working lunches unless he was already comfortable with them. Gregor ordered something that sounded as if it might have beef in it.

"Why do you always go to these places where you can't identify the food?" Gregor asked. "What's the mania for cooking things in pastry crusts?"

"You'll love it. Don't worry about it. What else can this be if it isn't a list of everybody connected to the two cases you're looking into?"

"Well," Gregor said, "for one thing, I doubt if it's everybody. It's just the people who have surfaced in connection to the two. There may be dozens of others."

"Right," John said, "that's true enough. So?"

"So, then there's the question of Michael Harridan. Who he is. If he is—no, no, don't say it. I know there must be at least somebody who is playacting at being Michael Harridan, but it would be nice to know if there's somebody who's Michael Harridan full-time, or somebody who is someone else on this same list who is Michael Harridan only for publication. I talked to that woman today. Kathi Mittendorf."

"And?" John looked interested.

"And it was like talking to a schizophrenic, although she obviously isn't one," Gregor said. "Everything was the script.

But I'd bet my life that she was hiding something in that house."

"Like what?"

"Guns, explosives, something like that," Gregor said. "I could just smell it. And yes, I know you can't get a search warrant on the basis of just smelling it. But she exhibited all the signs. If I had to guess, I'd say they were stashed in the basement somewhere. That's what she couldn't stop looking at. Not at the basement, you know, but at the floor."

"You know, Gregor, it's a whole different ball game if we can prove they're armed. It's one thing to be a kook living off conspiracy theories, but the feds do not take kindly to large caches of weapons and explosives. Almost nobody collects that stuff without intending to use it."

"I know. What can I say? Get some decent intelligence in there and check it out. Except that decent intelligence has been nearly nonexistent in this case almost from the beginning. I talked to Walker Canfield too."

"Who's Walker Canfield?"

"One half of the team the Bureau sent out to infiltrate America on Alert," Gregor said. "I told you about him. And his partner, who has now been missing for almost two weeks. It was almost like talking to Kathi Mittendorf. Is it just me, or have people become less and less rational in the last ten years? Or maybe I mean in the last ten days."

"Well, your Mr. Canfield is not my problem. He's Lower Merion's problem, and from what I've heard, they're welcome to him."

"Except that, just like us, he's concerned with America on Alert. Everybody is concerned with America on Alert. Have you noticed that? And that idiotic newsletter is everywhere."

"That idiotic newsletter has been everywhere for months," John said. "You haven't noticed it because it's not the kind of thing you notice, but those things have been floating around forever. And there's a Web site too, that's been up for a while. And some of the guys who say the same things have been at it for years. David Icke. A-albionics. In spite of all the hysteria these groups put out about storm troopers and black helicopters, we don't usually pay much attention to them unless they shoot somebody, and most of them don't."

"I'd have noticed if somebody stuck one of those things in my mailbox," Gregor said, "or if Tibor had them piled up in his apartment. I do pay some attention to my environment. My point isn't that *The Harridan Report* hasn't been around for a while, only that it's suddenly become far more intrusive into the lives of people who aren't exactly its target audience. Charlotte Ross had an issue of it in the room she was sitting in right before she went out on the walk and died—and then there's that. Why did she go out on the walk?"

"I don't know," John said. "It's not my case, remember?"

The food was arriving. The waiter put a large plate of something that looked like fish buried under grapes in front of John Jackman. Gregor seemed to be staring at a gigantic beef rose on a celery stalk. The waiter murmured anxious wishes for their satisfaction, half in French, and then disappeared.

"You're a sensible man," Gregor said. "I really don't understand your attraction for this sort of thing."

"Maybe it's scar tissue from a legacy of discrimination and oppression. Maybe, deep down, I need to go to all those places that wouldn't have served a black man at lunch even if he had a million dollars. Maybe—"

"Can it," Gregor said.

"The fact remains," John said, "that it really *isn't* my case. There's nothing I can do about the death of Charlotte Ross. There's nothing I can do about the death of Tony Ross, either. I can probably get you information, if you think the Lower Merion police are holding out on you, but that's about as good as it's going to get."

"Could you do something else? Could you follow through on that idea of yours and get one of your people to get a good picture of Kathi Mittendorf that we could show to Krystof Andrechev?"

John looked surprised. "Sure. Do you think that's the explanation for that? I've got to tell you that our people are inclined to believe that there was no mysterious woman with a gun, that Andrechev—"

"Is somehow involved with the bombing of the church," Gregor said. "Yes, I know. And it's a sensible first impression. But there was no need for Andrechev to come to me with that story. There was no need for him to do anything but sit tight and keep his mouth shut. We might never have noticed him."

"We would have noticed him eventually," John said. "The investigators on that case have interviewed most of that neighborhood already. They'll get to everybody before they're done."

"Did they check out the gun?"

"They're working on it."

"My guess is that they won't find anything on it. It'll be completely clean. New. Never used for anything. Which brings us to the question of why Kathi Mittendorf went all the hell way across town—way, way across—to deliver it to Krystof Andrechev."

"You're that sure it was Mittendorf?"

"Yes," Gregor said. "The description fits. And, I don't know how to put it, it sort of fits the kind of thing I'd expect her to do, under the right circumstances."

"What are the right circumstances?"

"Michael Harridan telling her to," Gregor said.

"Why would he tell her to?"

"I don't know," Gregor said.

"Look," John said. "This scenario has the same problems as the one where she just shows up and gives him the gun. There's no reason why. Especially if the gun is clean. If the gun had been used in a crime, we could say she was trying to ditch a piece of material evidence. But as it is, there's no reason at all—"

"Don't you wonder what would have happened if Krystof Andrechev had actually said something?"

"What do you mean?"

"Well," Gregor said, "they're all hyperpatriots, aren't they? America on Alert and all its members. And Andrechev is a Russian. He's ashamed of his English, so he doesn't talk much, and he was listening to this woman give him a lecture on how evil foreigners were, so he didn't talk at all while she was in his store, but—and it's not a small thing—if he *had* said something, she would have known immediately that he was an immigrant, and given his accent, she'd have had a fair chance of knowing he was Russian. Maybe she would have taken the gun away without giving it to him."

"And?"

"I don't know," Gregor said.

John threw his fork into his plate. "You're impossible this afternoon, do you know that? Look, you've got a problem on the home front. Somebody blew up your church. We're going at it in the way most likely to find the perpetrators, and the chances are that the bombing has nothing at all to do with what was going on out in Bryn Mawr. Is going on, I should say, since people seem to still be falling like flies. But it just doesn't make sense to put them together the way you're doing. What happened out in Bryn Mawr has all the characteristics of a professional job, and you know it. Professional-grade marksmanship, for one thing. Carried out under conditions of tight security—"

Gregor straightened up a little. "Maybe not," he said.

"What? You told me yourself—"

"Yes, I know, but—" Gregor said. "Sometimes I think we've all read too many Tom Clancy novels."

"I've never read a Tom Clancy novel in my life."

"Seen too many Harrison Ford movies, then," Gregor said. "Never mind. Did you clear your afternoon the way I asked you to? I want to get out of here."

"Technically," John said, "I shouldn't be going anywhere. I live behind a desk now, and a big desk. So—"

"Did you?"

"Yes."

"Fine," Gregor said. "The best instructor I ever had at Quantico used to tell us, nonstop, that the worst enemy we had was the things we thought we knew. And it's true. Let's go."

"I haven't finished my lunch."

"That isn't lunch," Gregor said. "That's performance art."

"Well, it's performance art made with Dover sole, and I'm fond of it."

3

By now, Gregor Demarkian had heard so much about Adelphos House—from Father Tibor, from John Jackman, from the newspaper articles Bennis and Donna had taken to leaving for him after the church decided to provide volunteers for Anne Ross Wyler's project—that he thought of himself as having already been there. As soon as they turned onto the six-block stretch of street that Adelphos House called home, he knew it wasn't true. There was nothing unusual in the fact of neighborhoods changing quickly in Philadelphia. Turn a corner, and you might go from ethnic Italian to upscale shopping to African-American to something very much like a strip mall. What surprised him was the utter and unrelieved devastation of this place. This was not a rundown street in a city with too many of them. This was not the kind of area urban renewal claimed. This was a burned-out hulk. Better than two-thirds of the buildings he saw were abandoned. Windows were gaping holes without glass. What glass there was was on the streets. The buildings that were inhabited had boards put up over theirs, almost as if they feared that disappearing windowpanes were a communicable disease. Bricks were everywhere, along the sidewalks, even in the street. It was a good thing they had John Jackman's driver to take them where they wanted to go. Gregor didn't think there was a cab driver in Philadelphia who would be willing to come here, even in broad daylight. He couldn't imagine what it would be like after dark. The vision he got was from one of those old *Twilight Zone* episodes that were supposed to take place after a nuclear holocaust. Whatever would hunt you here might not be human. Gregor could see no signs of humans. The abandoned buildings gave every indication of being empty. There were no homeless people pushing carts of clothes and debris along the blocks. There were no empty soda cans or bottles in the gutters. There were no bus shelters. There were no stores. There weren't even any television antennae. Gregor supposed that these days everybody who had television had cable, but lots of buildings in other parts of the city had antennae on their roofs left over from the days when cable hadn't yet been heard of, and he didn't think it was likely that the cable people would be willing to come out here to hook somebody up, even if their agreement with the city said they had to.

"Tell me Adelphos House isn't really on this street," Gregor said. "Tell me we're just driving through on our way to someplace more sane."

"Nobody drives through this neighborhood," John Jackman said. "Except the cops. And they're armed. I wouldn't come out here myself at night without backup."

"Well, now I understand something Annie Wyler told me. She said they had two cars at Adelphos House because they *had* to have cars. I remember thinking at the time that it was a typical rich-girl attitude. Nobody in Philadelphia *has* to have a car. There's always public transportation."

"Not out here, there isn't."

"Yes, I see that. Why is Adelphos House here? Surely there have to be other neighborhoods, closer to what Adelphos House does. They couldn't all have been too expensive. Do hookers work this street? Who do they sell to?"

"Hookers do not work this street," John Jackman said as the car began to slow up. "From what I remember—I was working out on the Main Line at the time—she tried to buy something closer to the strip where the girls work, but she ran into all kinds of trouble. Zoning problems. Permit problems. Building code problems—"

"This sounds like a setup."

"It probably was. I don't have to tell you that there have indeed been some members of our esteemed city government who have been known to patronize underage prostitutes. Not that they admit to knowing the prostitutes are underage, you understand. But that hardly matters. And Anne Ross Wyler was a pain in the butt to those people before she ever opened Adelphos House."

"Was she taking pictures back then too?"

"Uh, yeah," John Jackman said. "She even landed in the hospital for it once. I don't know how many cameras she's lost over the years. This is it. Notice the windows—no boards. We've tried to tell her that junkies have no consciences because they aren't really conscious, but she won't listen. We haven't told her that the people she annoys aren't above and beyond taking potshots at her at home, but she probably already knows it. She won't listen to that, either."

"Has anything ever happened at Adelphos House?"

"From the outside, no. There have been a couple of incidents of the girls losing it. She lets girls stay if they want. She puts them back in touch with their families if they want. That isn't always possible. Sometimes, the families sold the girls into prostitution to begin with. Don't you just love junkie culture?"

"I think it's wonderful," Gregor said.

"That's why I think we should end the drug war," Jackman said. "Make it all legal. Let them kill themselves with it. I don't give a damn. But free up police resources to go after things like child prostitution. We spend millions of dollars every year in this city chasing potheads, and there isn't enough left over in the budget to even try to put an end to the people who put eleven-year-olds out to peddle their asses on the street."

The car had pulled to a stop at the curb. "I never thought

of junkies having a culture," Gregor said. John Jackman climbed out onto the sidewalk. Gregor climbed out too.

"Everything has a culture these days," Jackman said. "Mollusks have a culture. They probably also have an indigenous language they're trying to protect from the cultural imperialism of the squid."

Adelphos House was in one of those brick buildings— like the one Gregor lived in on Cavanaugh Street—that was built right up next to the sidewalk, so that all it took to get from the street to the front door was to go up a few small steps. Gregor went around the car to join John Jackman on the sidewalk. As he did, Adelphos House's front door opened and a gigantic woman stepped out, her hair pulled back in a bun, her flowered dress floating in the stiff cold wind. For a split second, Gregor was confused. His first impression was that he was looking at Kathi Mittendorf again, but that passed, and then he didn't know why he'd thought it. Kathi Mittendorf was lumpy, but this woman was obese. Gregor wondered how she managed to get up and down even this small set of steps every day. Kathi Mittendorf had hair dyed so falsely blond it hurt to look at it. This woman seemed to be content with her salt-and-pepper natural hair, pulled back against her skull and pinned untidily at the back of her head. Besides, Gregor thought, Kathi Mittendorf would never have been caught dead in a neighborhood like this one. It would have been far too threatening, far too close to being the thing she was most afraid of happening to her life.

"Lucy," John Jackman said, holding out his hand. "Go back in the house. It's got to be nine degrees out here. You're going to freeze."

"I've been freezing for an hour," the woman said. "The heat's out. We've got the oil company wheezing and whining and trying to get out of coming out here, even though they know they have to come out in an emergency, and this is surely an emergency. Is this Mr. Demarkian? Annie told me all about you."

"I'm Gregor Demarkian, yes," Gregor said.

"Lucinda Watkins," the woman said.

"Let me get to a phone," John Jackman said, "and make a few calls. Maybe we can straighten out your heat problem for you while we're here."

"That's why it's good to know an honest policeman," Lucinda said. "Too bad they're not all like you."

Gregor cocked an eyebrow. Jackman shrugged. "Some of the men on the force have been known to, ah—"

"You know you've got men on your force who are visiting child prostitutes?" Gregor said.

"No," John Jackman said sourly. "Once I know who they are, I find a way to get rid of them. But I know there are always some. Christ, Gregor. How do you think that strip keeps operating?"

Lucinda Watkins had retreated into Adelphos House's front hallway and left the door open. John Jackman followed her and Gregor followed John Jackman. Inside, the ceilings were high, but the house itself was not impressive, and never had been. This had not started out as a fashionable neighborhood, the way so many poor neighborhoods did. The people who had lived here had not always been poor, but they had never been the kind of people to go regularly to the opera or to art museums. If Gregor had had to peg it, he'd have said turn-of-the-century and mostly in the possession of Catholic immigrants, Italians and Poles. There was a discolored place on the wall of the front hallway in the shape of a cross. Gregor had no problem imagining a crucifix hanging there, with a shallow cup of holy water underneath it.

Lucinda scuttled behind him and shut the door. "I'll go get Annie. She's having a nap. She's up all night with that stuff, and then she's up early in the morning. It's insane. She runs herself down. She gets a dozen colds every winter. And she won't let anybody help."

"I thought you were getting some volunteers," John Jackman said.

"Oh, she'll let people help with that sort of thing," Lucinda said. "It's the trawling the strip I'm talking about.

She's out there every night, rain or shine, it doesn't matter what the weather is. She won't let me go because she says I'll be too conspicuous. I *am* very conspicuous, I know that. I know what I look like when I look in the mirror. Last time I had a physical, I weighed three hundred pounds. But still. I'm fast. You've got to admit I'm fast. And nobody would pay any attention to me out there. Nobody ever pays attention to middle-aged fat women. They pay attention to *her*."

A door along the hallway popped open, and a young woman dressed in jeans and a heavy cotton sweater came out. Lucinda looked up and smiled.

"Melissa," she said. She turned to Gregor and John Jackman. "This is Melissa Polk, one of our volunteers from Bryn Mawr College. Bryn Mawr provides us with a lot of valuable help during the school year. Melissa, listen, this is Mr. Jackman and Mr. Demarkian. Mr. Jackman is the commissioner of police. Mr. Demarkian—"

"Is the Armenian-American Hercule Poirot," Melissa said politely.

Gregor winced. Lucinda ignored it. "Would you mind running up and telling Annie they're here?" she said. "She's lying down for a while. I'll take them into the living room."

"No problem," Melissa said.

Lucinda began shooing them toward a door. Gregor had forgotten how houses used to have all their rooms walled off from all the others, with doors that shut. He allowed himself to be pushed through this door into the smallish living room. He walked over to the bay window and looked out on the abandoned street.

"I'm surprised nobody's ever broken this," he said. "I'd think it would be the perfect target for a certain sort of person in a certain kind of mood."

"What sort of person in what sort of mood?" Lucinda Watkins said. "There isn't much of anybody on this street anymore. What little population there is is junkies, bad junkies, the nearly dead ones. They can't work up the energy to throw rocks, not even when they're out of dope. They just collapse."

"Somebody broke the other windows," Gregor pointed out.

"Years ago," Lucinda said. "When this neighborhood was disintegrating, but before it actually died. When you had buildings full of angry young men with nowhere to go. You've got to wonder why they threw rocks at the houses in their own neighborhoods. If I was in their position, I'd go out to Society Hill or Chestnut Hill or the Main Line—"

"It's not so easy to get out to those houses on the Main Line," John Jackman pointed out.

"There are trains," Lucinda said. "There are cars to steal. It wouldn't take so much. I've driven out there myself a few times. It's not that complicated. You have to wonder—"

"What?" Gregor said.

Lucinda shrugged. "Oh, don't mind me. I'm always on a tear. Just ask Mr. Jackman. There's just a part of me that doesn't understand why all this stays up. All those people out there, like Annie's brother, living in thirty-thousand square feet when the girls we serve don't have a room to themselves and the space they do have has cockroaches crawling all over it. Thomas Jefferson thought that the country should be made up of farmers and artisans, small businessmen, small craftsmen. He thought that the country would be ruined if there were any men richer or more powerful than that. Maybe he had a point."

"Thomas Jefferson was a rich man who owned a plantation and slaves," John Jackman said drily. "What's this all about, Lucy? I didn't realize you'd gone Communist on me while I was busy elsewhere."

"Oh, Lucinda would never go Communist," Anne Ross Wyler said, coming into the room with her hair so completely a mess that it looked like she'd put a wig on backwards. "She thinks the Communists are as bad as the capitalists, they just put a different name on doing the same old stuff. Hello again, Mr. Demarkian. Hello, John. Is there a reason for this visit in the middle of the day?"

"Ask him," John Jackman said.

"I wanted to get a look at the place," Gregor said. "And I wanted you to show me the cars. Where they're kept. How they get in and out of the property. It hadn't occurred to me before I saw this place up close, but you must have a certain amount of worry with the cars. You have two, don't you?"

"Two, yes," Annie said. "A station wagon and a two-door. Why?"

"Which one did you have on the night your brother died?" Gregor asked.

"The two-door," Annie said. "The deal is to park inconspicuously, although I'm not very inconspicuous anymore. Still, a small dark car isn't very intrusive."

"They painted her trunk orange once while she was in some convenience store," Lucinda said. "Annie likes to pretend it was just kids, but I know better. They were trying to mark her. They managed it for about a day."

"Less than that," Annie said. "Why did you think we'd have trouble with the cars?"

"With people stealing them," Gregor said. "It's one thing to break windows or not to break them, but a car is a valuable piece of property. And there are car thieves all over this city who wouldn't think twice about coming into this neighborhood if they thought they could get a decent vehicle without much trouble."

"Maybe," Annie said, "but they haven't yet."

"We keep the cars in a little garage around the back," Lucinda said. "We've even got a driveway. She bought a house just around the corner and had it demolished. She cut the driveway through and had the garage built. You wouldn't believe what trouble we had getting all the permits."

"It wasn't as if anybody was ever going to live in that house again," Annie said. "There wasn't much more left of it than stray bricks and loose asbestos. This whole neighborhood is full of asbestos. And no, we don't lock the garage, Mr. Demarkian. There isn't any point. In the middle of the night, when we sometimes have to go out, we tend to be in a hurry."

"They pick up the girls if they call," John Jackman explained. "The ones who get scared by a john or who've just gotten beaten up by a pimp."

"They go back, though," Lucinda said. "You wouldn't believe it. It's like they've been brainwashed."

"What kind of car is the station wagon? What kind of car is the two-door?"

"The two-door is a Honda," Annie said. "I don't know what kind of Honda. I don't pay attention to that sort of thing. The station wagon is a black Volvo Cross Country. I know because we just bought it maybe six months ago, and the guy who sold it to us insisted on giving us the brochure."

"He was just doing his job," Lucinda said.

"I don't know why everybody on earth seems to think his job is to sell me something," Annie said.

There was a faint buzzing. John Jackman stuck his hand inside his jacket and came out with his cell phone. "Excuse me," he said, retreating back into the hallway.

Gregor looked around the living room. It was a pleasant space, not too large, not too small, newly painted, newly carpeted, dusted to within an inch of its life. On one wall, there were bookshelves. On another, a plain brick fireplace. The furniture was serviceable and comfortable, but not extravagant.

"How big is this place?" Gregor asked. "How many bedrooms? How many square feet? And how many people stay here full-time?"

"Only Annie and I stay here full-time," Lucinda said, "although there's usually somebody or other spending the night. And we've got, what, six bedrooms?"

"Seven, if you count what's in the attic," Annie said.

"Well, yes, but we never use the attic," Lucinda said. "And that's jury-rigged anyway, except for the bathroom, which is nicer than any of the other ones in the house."

"What about the night Tony Ross died?" Gregor asked. "Was anybody staying in the house then?"

"I don't remember," Lucinda said. "There was somebody or other doing something—a group, or something like that. There was a meeting. I remember that, because Annie here went out to take photographs while it was going on and we had Father Kasparian coming, and I was worried there wouldn't be anybody to talk to Father Kasparian while he was here."

"You could have talked to Father Kasparian while he was here," Annie said.

John Jackman came back into the room. "Gregor?" he said. "That was my office. We've got to go."

"All right," Gregor said.

Lucinda and Annie were both staring at Jackman, curious. "That doesn't sound right," Annie said. "What's the matter, John? Has somebody shot the mayor?"

"No," John said. "They've found somebody Mr. Demarkian has been looking for. Unfortunately, they've found him dead."

PART THREE

In Germany, as in the United States, a virtual
government was conceived with the trappings of
democratic rule by the engineers of the Holocaust.

—FROM "PREAMBLE: ON THE ROAD TO A
FOURTH REICH" FROM *VIRTUAL
GOVERNMENT: CIA MIND CONTROL
OPERATIONS IN AMERICA*
BY ALEX CONSTANTINE

ONE

1

It was not the middle of the night, but the police cars and the evidence vans and the ambulances were lit up as if it must have been. In the end, it didn't matter who among the civilians may have died. The town drunk and the president of the United States got differing levels of response, but neither got the response accorded to the lowest level of police officer. Even the death of police officers that other officers didn't like rated a full-court press investigation. Even the deaths of police officers from other jurisdictions, or on vacation, or undercover, or in disguise—Gregor couldn't remember when he'd known the death of a police officer *not* to bring out the visceral animal in the department who got the call. That was part reaction and part insurance. The safest course for any police department was to let it be known on the street that hurting one of their own would bring down the wrath of God and worse. The reaction was, Gregor supposed, inevitable. When you train men and women for months at a time and then make them work together for years under pressure, they begin to feel like part of a single organism. *Crap*, Gregor thought. Maybe it was none of these things. Maybe it was just the obvious, which is that people don't like to feel personally attacked, and police officers always took the murders of police officers personally.

The odd thing, Gregor admitted to himself, was that the city police had been so quick to assume that Steve Bridge was one of their own. Not only did most local cops have very little use for the FBI—and often for good reason, Gregor had to admit—but Bridge had had the kind of job that local cops had the least use for. He was going undercover, but only to spy on a group whose ideas he and his bosses didn't like. Gregor knew there had been a time when local cops had been just as zealous in the hunting down of Communists as they were at the hunting down of sneak thieves. In the Red scares of the twenties and the McCarthy-inspired witch-hunts of the fifties, local police had gone out of their way to aid and abet first the paranoia of the United States Congress and then the Bureau at its worst; breaking up "radical" meetings, locking people in holding cells for attending union organizing drives, shutting down printing presses to make sure no "subversive" pamphlets got out onto the street where somebody interested might read them. That was a long time ago. Somewhere in the sixties, a sea change had come. The Bureau was still too often preoccupied with "subversives," and Gregor was sure there were sheriffs out in Omaha and Kansas City who were preoccupied with them too, but the local cops had come to their senses and decided to leave well enough alone. If it was armed, you had to worry about it. If it wasn't armed, it didn't matter if it was preaching the eventual second coming of the Great Banana, it made no sense to do anything except leave it alone.

Unless you were the police department of Penryn, Pennsylvania, Gregor thought, who had refused to direct traffic at the annual YMCA triathlon because, it said, the YMCA was encouraging witchcraft by reading Harry Potter books aloud to children in its after-school program. Maybe Tibor was right. Maybe the world really was going crazy. Maybe he himself was going crazy, standing next to John Jackman's big black limousine and looking out across this rundown backstreet neighborhood as if this was all supposed to be making some kind of sense.

"What's wrong?" John asked, coming back from a low conference with two of the uniformed cops now watching the scene. He looked around at the sky and the neighborhood and shook his head. "God, this is awful. Have you seen him yet?"

"Briefly."

"There are maggots in his eyes," John said. "I've seen a lot in my time, but that was unbelievable. Christ, you'd think whoever it was could have buried him."

"Here?" Gregor asked.

They both looked around again. John shrugged. "Okay, maybe not here. But wouldn't it have made sense to move him?"

"I don't think so," Gregor said. "Assuming we're dealing with the same person who murdered Tony and Charlotte Ross, and assuming one person murdered both of them—"

"I think we can assume," John said drily. "At least about Tony and Charlotte Ross. I admit this makes something of a mess of things. At least it's within the city limits."

"Why at least?"

"Because now I have control of it," John said. "I don't want to say anything against the Lower Merion police, because they do a good job and they mean well, but they don't deal with the real trouble out there and you know it. They don't have the experience. And we do."

"You ever heard of Penryn, Pennsylvania?"

"No."

"Last fall sometime, a year ago, the police department there refused to do its usual duty at an annual YMCA event because it said the YMCA was encouraging children to engage in witchcraft because it was reading them the Harry Potter books."

"And?" John Jackman said.

"Well, John, what the hell? Is that usual? Does that sort of thing happen so often that it doesn't surprise you? Let me ask you a question Tibor asked me. When did we get to the point that we forgot that witches are pretend?"

"Does this have something to do with the case? With any part of the case? With the bombing of Holy Trinity Church? With the death of Steve Bridge? With anything?"

"I don't know," Gregor said. "Except that I want to answer yes, because it does, just not in the way you think you mean it. I get embarrassed for what's happening to this country, I really do. It's like we all took acid at a showing of *Alice in Wonderland* and now we think we're really all the way down the rabbit hole."

"Maybe you ought to go home to bed," John said. "Maybe you're coming down with something. Because you sure as hell aren't making a lot of sense."

"I want to go over there and take a better look," Gregor said. "Can I do that without screwing up everything from fingerprints to footprints to DNA samples?"

"Sure. Tell the boys I sent you. Wear gloves."

John Jackman meant latex gloves, which Gregor didn't have, although he was sure one of the officers over at the scene would. He walked over and nodded to the uniformed man on duty. His progress was not challenged. By now, everybody at the scene probably knew he'd arrived in the company of the commissioner of police. The scene was a vacant lot between two small frame houses, overgrown with the kinds of vegetation that grow on vacant lots: a lot of grass, brown and dead in the cold; some small shrubs; too many boxes and crates and piles of debris. The police had put a wooden plank down leading from the sidewalk to the body itself, so that officers needing to come and go wouldn't muck up the scene any more than they already had, but Gregor didn't think that it was really needed. The closer he got, the stronger the smell got. It was a wonder someone hadn't noticed it long before now—or maybe they had, and maybe they had complained, but the city had dismissed it as just another mess from a pile of garbage left on a postcard-stamp bit of land nobody wanted or wanted to claim.

Gregor came to a stop about a foot behind the two plainclothes detectives who were standing directly over the body. Right here, the stench was overwhelming, and the body itself was still visible and uncovered on the ground. Gregor didn't know if it had maggots coming out of its eyes, but it was badly decomposed, and at that stage of decomposition that made the most impact. The skin was black and had rotted away from the muscle and bone in several places along the jaw and the top of the hands. The skin along the nose was wet and oozing. Gregor shook his head. The plainclothesman closest to him turned around and nodded.

"It's Mr. Demarkian," he said. "The commissioner's friend."

Gregor had no way of knowing if that was being said sarcastically or not. He decided not to worry about it. "How do you do?" he said, nodding as well to the other plainclothesman, who had turned around when he heard Gregor and his partner talking. "I don't mean to get in your way. I was just wondering how you knew this was Steve Bridge."

The first plainclothesman shrugged. "I don't guess we do, absolutely, just yet. We'll have to take the body in for identification and DNA samples and all the rest of it. But we've had a heads-up on him for days—"

"This complete asshole of an FBI guy lost contact with his own partner and didn't call the disappearance in for days," the other plainclothesman said. "Can you believe it? I mean, who in Christ's name—"

"I wish you wouldn't do that," the first plainclothesman said. "You know how I feel about taking the Lord's name in vain."

"Christ," the second plainclothesman said. "You've got no idea what a pain in the ass you've gotten to be since you got born-again."

Gregor cleared his throat. "Steve Bridge," he said, directing their attention back to the problem at hand. "How did you find him? Who found him?"

"We don't know," the first plainclothesman said. "The precinct got an anonymous call about, maybe, two hours ago. Body in the vacant lot. You could smell the stench for blocks. That kind of thing. They didn't think anything of it, because you *couldn't* smell the stench for blocks—"

"That's because of the cold," the second plainclothesman said. "The damned thing has been out here refrigerated for however long it's been. A couple of weeks. But you know what it's been like. There hasn't been a day with temps over thirty-five since October."

"Yeah, well," the first plainclothesman said, "that only does so much. It's not like he was frozen. That would have been different. But the local precinct sent somebody out, just in case. And he walks in here and finds this."

Gregor nodded. "I'm surprised he wasn't visible from the sidewalk."

"Too much in the way of shrubbery," the first plain-clothesman said, "and then there's all the garbage around here. If people saw anything, they probably thought some old bum had come and ditched his clothes."

"Then I'm surprised some kid hasn't run in here and dis-covered this before now," Gregor said. "Kids play in vacant lots, don't they? They did when I was growing up."

The first plainclothesman shrugged. "Maybe that was the cold too. Maybe it's been too cold to play outside. I don't know. Maybe there aren't that many kids on this block."

Gregor looked around. A small crowd had gathered, in-evitably, on the road and on the far sidewalk from the place where all the vehicles were parked. It seemed to consist al-most entirely of women—old ones, young ones, middle-aged ones—all wrapped up in heavy woolen coats and scarves and gloves. There were no children that he could see. He turned back to the body.

"So your man got here and found the body and called in for help. Then what?"

"Then the usual," the first plainclothesman said.

"Think of it as escalation," the second plainclothesman said. "First, the uniforms got here, and the vehicles, and the ambulance, and then they called us in. One of the uniforms thought he recognized him. Although how anybody could do that is beyond me." He looked down at the body and shud-dered. "Jesus Christ, but you see bad things on this job."

"How about cause of death?" Gregor asked. "Or is it too early to tell? Have you checked the body at all?"

"He's got a bullet hole in the side of his head," the second plainclothesman said. "If you go around to this side, you can see it. Small hole. We're talking a rifle, I'd guess, maybe fired from some distance away. But you can see it. Come and look."

Gregor did come and look, very carefully, not getting off the plank. It was true. The bullet hole was clearly there, and it just as clearly could not have been anything else, but it was small. He looked up and around. There were buildings on every side, some of them close. The only really open space was the vacant lot itself, and the short stretch of sidewalk that separated it from the road.

"You're going to have to do a door-to-door around here," he said. "Especially if forensics tells you what you're expecting to hear, and the shot was fired at a distance. You'd think somebody would have heard something. Even if it took place at night."

"What makes you think it took place at night?" the second plainclothesman said.

"Day is too risky," Gregor said, not wanting to point out that the other two murders he'd seen something of in the last week had both taken place at night, or at least at early evening. There was no reason for these men to assume that the three deaths were automatically connected. Gregor wasn't even sure why he was so sure they were. "Thank you," he told both the men, suddenly catching sight of the tiny fish pin tacked to the first plainclothesman's suit lapel. The first plainclothesman was wearing a heavy coat, unbuttoned but still wrapped tightly against his chest. The lapel hadn't been visible before.

Gregor turned away and went back down the ramp to John Jackman, who was leaning against the side of his limousine and watching the action. Somebody had brought him coffee. Gregor wished somebody would bring him coffee too.

"Well?" Jackman asked when Gregor got back to the car.

"Bullet hole in the right side of the skull, small but obvious. The detectives are guessing a rifle. I would too. Still, you won't know until you know. Definitely fired at a distance."

"That you know?"

"If it hadn't been, the entry wound would have been a lot

larger," Gregor said. "The bottom line, though, is that it's the same M.O. Virtually identical. Of course, we have no way of knowing the time of day, but I'd be willing to bet we're talking about evening or night, probably evening. It's dark enough."

"And that would be in keeping with an identical M.O.?"

"Something like that. Listen, John, where are we, exactly? Near Adelphos House, yes. It didn't take us too long to get here. What about Kathi Mittendorf's place?"

"Nearly two miles in that direction," John said, pointing at the horizon. "I don't know, Gregor. What are we near? It's an inner-city minority neighborhood, mostly Spanish now, working-class, not a war zone. The schools suck, but then all the schools in Philadelphia suck, except the private ones and a few of the charters. There are dozens of neighborhoods like this all over the city. They're not really 'near' anything except maybe each other, and sometimes they're not even near each other."

"Kathi Mittendorf lives in a neighborhood like this," Gregor said. "The same general atmosphere. Frame houses, some of them three-deckers, all of them run-down. I doubt if it's a minority neighborhood, though."

"Ethnic, then," Jackman said confidently. "The kind of place that revolves around the local church. Catholic, Lutheran, different churches for different neighborhoods. It's all going, Gregor. Even the poorer people are beginning to move on out to the Main Line. In a few more years, there'll be nothing left but the very poor and the very rich. And not very many of the very rich. This isn't New York. They move on out to the Main Line too."

"In New York, they move on out to Westchester and Connecticut."

"Yeah, well. They still have Fifth Avenue and Park Avenue and the Upper East Side. I'm sorry to be such a pessimist, but I don't like what's happening. I haven't liked it for a long time. And you put this other stuff in it, this stuff like America on Alert and, yes, God help me, all the stupidity surrounding the Harry Potter books, you put that mental set into the mix and you're going for real trouble. I keep waiting for something to happen. I'm not sure what."

"Riots?"

"No," Jackman said. "I'm embarrassed to say it, but when I saw the World Trade Center thing, I thought it was that. I thought it was one of our own, another Tim McVeigh, a whole rash of Tim McVeighs, and the whole thing was about to crash down on our heads. And then the anthrax thing *did* turn out to be a Tim McVeigh, didn't it?"

"I think it turned out to be a lone nut," Gregor said. "Not Tim McVeigh so much as the Unabomber."

"Whatever. The landscape's changed. Policing's changed. Everything is caught up in this crap, and that includes a big chunk of the guys on the force, and I'll be damned if I know what to do about it. Never mind me. You want to go home?"

"Yes," Gregor said. "I think I do."

2

There was one advantage to being driven around in a limousine, in spite of the fact that it made Gregor a little uncomfortable, and especially uncomfortable when he was with John Jackman, who loved the experience out of all proportion to its significance. The advantage was that he had his hands free to write, and that he was far enough in the back of the vehicle not to need to mentally apply the brakes every time the driver did something that made him want to cringe. All drivers made Gregor Demarkian want to cringe more often than not. Bennis and Donna caused him to feel grateful for traffic lights.

As soon as they had pulled away from the scene, Gregor pulled out his notebook and started jotting. John Jackman sat on the other side of the seat and watched him.

"I could never figure out what you were writing down all the time," John said. "You never seemed to read those notebooks. Why do you write in them?"

"It helps me remember things." Gregor finished the page

and looked it over. It wasn't true that he didn't read what he'd written. "This is what I need somebody to do. First, that idea of yours about the picture of Kathi Mittendorf. Can we get one fast and get it out for Krystof Andrechev to see?"

"Sure. Have it done in a couple of hours."

"It may be harder to get a picture than you think."

"No, it won't. She was being watched by the FBI, remember? They've got surveillance pictures, and our department has copies."

"Fair enough," Gregor said. "I just want to know, as soon as possible, if she was the one who brought the gun to Cavanaugh Street."

"Do you think she was?"

"Yes. If she wasn't, my whole theory goes to hell, so let's hope I'm not wrong. I hate having to start again this late in the day. It wastes time."

"You think Kathi Mittendorf bombed Holy Trinity Church? Or you think she murdered Tony and Charlotte Ross? And Steve Bridge, if they're all connected."

"They're all connected," Gregor said, "unless, as I mentioned, Krystof Andrechev doesn't identify Kathi Mittendorf, at which point I don't know what's going on. As for the other things . . ." Gregor shrugged. "I don't think she's killed anybody, no. About Holy Trinity Church, it depends. My guess is not. I don't think he would have entrusted her with anything that important. Not, as it turned out, that it made much difference."

"I love it when you're being inscrutable. It satisfies my need to explode ethnic stereotypes. Who's 'he'?"

"Michael Harridan."

"You've found Michael Harridan? I thought you said Michael Harridan didn't exist."

"No, I never said that. Obviously, Michael Harridan exists. He writes a newsletter. He writes a lot of editions of a newsletter. Here's something I'd like to know, just for curiosity's sake. How often does that newsletter come out? I'm willing to bet almost anything that it's started coming out a lot more frequently in, say, the last six months."

"He's been planning all this for the last six months?"

"At least. Maybe longer."

"So where is he?" John Jackman said. "You can't just say he exists and committed a bunch of murders and not tell us where he is. We want to talk to him. The Lower Merion police want to talk to him. After what we saw back there, the FBI is going to want to talk to him too, and big time."

"We *have* talked to him," Gregor said. "Or at least I have. I have no idea what your people have been doing about him one way or the other. The problem is, proving he's himself, so to speak. Or rather, proving he's not himself, part of the time. Do you know off the top of your head when the bomb went off in Holy Trinity Church?"

"I think it was just about eight-thirty," John Jackman said, "or a little before. Why?"

"I was thinking about the principle of calculated risk. He calculates a lot of risk, Mr. Harridan does. If he wanted to be as sure as he could be that he wasn't going to kill somebody—and he could never have been one hundred percent sure—he'd have had that bomb go off at midnight, when there was a good chance nobody at all would be in the church and nobody at all would be on the street. That's a very conservative neighborhood in some ways."

"I've noticed. Why did he want to make sure nobody would be killed? I thought that that's what these guys did. They went out and murdered a bunch of people in the name of home, the flag, apple pie, and an interpretation of the United States Constitution so wrongheaded it could qualify for the founding document of a totalitarian space colony."

"Very nice. But he didn't want to kill anybody that night. He just wanted to make a mess. A very big mess. And distract my attention."

"Distract *your* attention?"

"That's right. Do you know of any celebrity murder anywhere on the Main Line or in Philadelphia that I haven't been involved in in the last ten years?"

"I think you've got delusions of grandeur. No matter what *The Philadelphia Inquirer* may tell you, you're *not* the Armenian-American Hercule Poirot. You're not better than the police. And one of the things I always did like about you was that you never considered yourself better than the police."

"It's not because he considers me better than the police," Gregor said patiently. "It's about perspective. And, of course, about setting the terms of the debate. That's what Michael Harridan does, you know. He sets the terms of any debate he's in, and the fact that nobody ever sees him only makes that outcome more certain. It's amazing the way that works."

"I now have absolutely no idea what you're talking about."

"Maybe I don't either," Gregor said.

They had pulled onto Cavanaugh Street. It was very late in the afternoon, almost evening, and the storefronts had begun to light up in the gloom. Ohanian's had a sandwich sign propped up on the sidewalk in front of its door, advertising stuffed grape leaves and something Gregor couldn't make out. The Ararat was still in its daytime mode, with all its lights blazing. When the dinner hour officially arrived, Linda Melajian would dim all the lights and put candles out on the tables. It was, Gregor thought, a perfectly ordinary, unassuming neighborhood, six or seven blocks of town houses and small apartment buildings and stores, of no interest to anybody but the people who lived on them. The car moved forward, and it began to be impossible to ignore the gaping hole where Holy Trinity's facade used to be.

"You all right?" John Jackman asked.

"I'm fine," Gregor said. "Get that picture over to Andrechev's place, as fast as you can, today if possible. All right?"

"All right."

"Then get me what you can on the forensics for Steve Bridge, as soon as you can. I need to know what kind of gun it was. Because he can't be carrying a rifle around with him."

"It's almost certainly going to be a rifle," John Jackman said.

"Oh, yes, I know. I know the murders were all done with a rifle. I'm just convinced they couldn't all have been done with the same rifle. And rifles are a problem. Because they're not like handguns. You can buy a handgun on any street corner in America. Rifles are a little harder to get."

"Well, you know, Gregor, we're not talking about an Uzi here. I don't think we're going to find that Steve Bridge was killed with a military assault weapon. I don't know what they've got in Lower Merion, but I saw the wound here close up, closer up than I ever want to see another one, and I've seen a lot of wounds in my life. And I don't think—"

"No," Gregor said. "Neither do I. That isn't what I meant."

"What did you mean?"

"I meant that wherever it is he's getting these guns, it can't be the way people usually get guns they don't want traced to themselves. It's the guns, you know, that I can't figure out. He must have used at least two different ones. The question is, where is he getting them?"

"Maybe he has them," John Jackman said. "We don't register all weapons, after all. If he's using small rifles, he may have had them for years, for deer hunting, whatever. There probably wouldn't be any record of the sale, or of his possession of them. If he's been keeping them under the bed for years, how would anybody know he had them?"

"But he hasn't been keeping them under the bed for years," Gregor said. The limousine stopped short in the street, next to several parked cars. It would be wrong to say that Jackman's driver double-parked, since he didn't kill the engine, but the effect was the same. Gregor got his gloves out of his pockets. "Never mind me," he said. "I'll call you tomorrow. Just, get that picture to Andrechev and see if he can identify it. And get me the lab results on those bullet wounds. Do we know if there were any bullets found on or near the body?"

"Not yet."

"Well, maybe we'll have a little luck for once. They do have the bullets found at the scene at the Tony Ross murder. I don't know about the murder of Charlotte Ross, but my guess is that they found those too. It will be interesting to see if they match."

"I thought you said they wouldn't match," John Jackman said.

"I said that at least two of them wouldn't match," Gregor said. "It's possible that the ones from Tony Ross's murder would match the ones from Charlotte's, or that the ones from Charlotte's would match the ones from Steve Bridge's. But unless Mr. Harridan can walk on water and raise the dead, he couldn't have committed all three of those murders with the same weapon."

"Why not?"

"Because on the night of the party, he couldn't have gotten a rifle onto the Ross property to save his life, and he didn't have the time or the opportunity to hide one there earlier and come back and get it when he wanted to use it. It would have been too risky, anyway. They were doing security sweeps right and left. There's only one place he could have gotten the weapon to kill Tony Ross, and he had to get hold of it on the night of the murder."

"What's the one place he could have got hold of a rifle on the night of the murder?" Jackman actually looked curious.

"From Tony Ross," Gregor told him. Then he popped the door—he refused to wait for the driver to open it for him—and climbed out onto the street. The two younger Ohanian girls had come out onto the sidewalk to watch the show. When they saw it was Gregor, they giggled and went back inside. Nobody on Cavanaugh Street thought anything at all of anything he did anymore. They had long ago decided he was crazy.

Gregor stuck his head back into the car. "We should have thought about that at the time," he said. "About the security at the party. I'm not saying that the security was as tight as the media has been making it out to be. It isn't that tight for the president himself, and he wasn't coming. Still, it was tight enough, and that left us with two choices. Either the murderer was a professional, or he was somebody considered practically part of the wallpaper. And I know he isn't a professional."

"Try to remember," Jackman said, "that I'm not concerned with the Tony Ross murder. Or the Charlotte Ross murder, either. That's Lower Merion's problem. I'm here to help you out with the bombing of Holy Trinity Church, and to look into the murder of Steve Bridge, except that I don't look into murders anymore these days. I'm a desk jockey."

"It doesn't matter," Gregor said. "It's all the same thing. Did you ever read a murder mystery where the butler did it?"

"No," Jackman said.

"Neither did I." Gregor slammed the door of the limousine shut and went around the back of it to the sidewalk. He climbed the steps to the front door to the building that held his apartment and went inside. There was a light coming from under old George Tekemanian's apartment door, and laughter coming into the hall from the other side of it, but Gregor didn't turn in that direction. He checked his mail— three bills; a frantic letter about how President Bush was destroying the nation from some Democratic Party fundraising committee; a frantic letter about how liberals were destroying the nation from some Republican Party fundraising committee; a Levenger catalogue—and went upstairs. For just a little while, he didn't want to talk to Bennis, or Tibor, or Donna, or anybody else on Cavanaugh Street. He wanted to make more notes for himself, and then he wanted to make some phone calls. He'd need to talk to the director again, because that was the fastest way to FBI information that he knew of. He'd need to talk to Margiotti and Tackner again too, because there were some details he needed to work out about what exactly had happened on the night Tony Ross had died. Most important, though, he needed to sit down with as many editions of *The Harridan Report* he could find, and read them.

Gregor Demarkian was not a conspiracist. He did not be-

lieve that everything that happened in the world—or much
of anything—was being controlled and directed by any central force. He did not work himself into a sweat over the possibility of a coming One World Government. In fact, he
vaguely liked the idea, at least in principle. Tibor was right.
Who *wouldn't* prefer to see the Arabs and Israelis suing each
other in an international court rather than doing what they
did now? When it came to things like MKUltra Mind Control, and the CIA running a project that was systematically
brainwashing half the population of North America, he
wanted to laugh hysterically. The CIA were the same people
who had managed to fail to assassinate Fidel Castro in the
middle of a civil war. Secret rituals held in the basement
dungeons of rich New Yorkers where thousands of babies a
year were sacrificed in orgies of satanic ritual abuse.
Catholic Mormon Freemasons who were the real power behind the spread of communism. A secret government made
up of Rockefellers and Roosevelts who made all the decisions that only seemed to be made by people like the president and the United States Congress. The content of these
ideas was ludicrous, but the content was not the point. It was
the atmosphere they created that was the point. Tibor
seemed to think that that atmosphere had somehow sprung
into being with the disasters of September 11. In reality, it
had been around a long time, making its way around the
American South and Midwest in waves throughout the twentieth century. It had existed before then too, in Europe. *The
Protocols of the Learned Elders of Zion* was a conspiracist
holy text, entirely fabricated but fervently believed by that
wing of the movement that saw the Jews as the cause of all
the world's problems. *The Turner Diaries* was a conspiracist
holy text too, but only in the United States, among people
who had given up anti-Semitism in favor of the imminent arrival of the apocalypse. If you tried to undo the strands and
make it all make sense, you'd go crazy.

Gregor let himself into his apartment. Bennis wasn't
home, which was just as well, since he didn't want to talk to
anybody but the people he needed to call. Upstairs, Grace

Feinman was pounding away on one of her harpsichords. Gregor thought he remembered someone saying that she now had three up there, plus the virginals. He put his coat on the hook of the coat stand and went into the living room to sit down on the couch. He pulled the phone to him and started dialing.

Later on, when he was finished with these, he would have to find a way to talk to Kathi Mittendorf again.

3

It wasn't until it was over that Gregor Demarkian admitted to himself that it was a relief to talk on a regular phone, rather than a cell. Not only couldn't you be intercepted out of thin air—he had visions of vans roving throughout the city, randomly snatching messages in mid-flight in the hopes of being the person who picked up the next phone call from Monica Lewinsky—but you didn't have to worry about the sound quality fading out on you or disappearing altogether. Gregor did not remember either of those things ever happening to him. Bennis was too much of a stickler for getting exactly what she wanted and too willing to pay lots of money to get it to be saddled with inefficient cell-phone service. Still, that sort of thing was always happening to Howard Kashinian, and Gregor was sure that if something could happen to Howard, it could happen to him.

He looked down at the notebook he'd been jotting things down in for the past hour of phone calls and hoped he'd be able to decipher it when the time came. He had very neat handwriting, but he'd not only written lists and words but drawn arrows and made symbols, all in an attempt to straighten out the complexities of just who could or could not have fired a rifle at Tony Ross on the night of the party. The short explanation was that anybody who had already been on the grounds at the time and who had already had access to a gun there could have committed the murder. That was less helpful than it seemed, because although the secret service had screened the area early on in the day, they hadn't been able to keep it absolutely secure because of the right-of-way granted to the riding club. Besides, the secret service simply didn't apply the same level of scrutiny to the arrangements for the first lady as they did for the president himself, unless there was some indication that the first lady was in direct and immediate danger. They had provided near-paranoid security for Hillary Clinton, because the media had been full of furious denunciations of her almost from the day her husband began running for office. *This* first lady was far less controversial. She was also far less interesting, but Gregor had to admit that interesting people were more likely to be vilified than uninteresting ones. The simple fact was that the secret service had not been all that concerned about a party given by Charlotte Deacon Ross. It was unlikely to be dangerous. The first lady didn't have legions of enemies hoping to get rid of her at the first opportunity. Charity balls were a regular feature of a first lady's life, and if they had to do a full security sweep on every one of them, they'd have to double their numbers and never do anything else.

The problem, Gregor decided, was not how the murderer got on to the estate. He—or she, he amended, for the sake of the voice of John Jackman in his head—could have managed that any of a number of ways, including simply walking in through the front gate. The problem was how the murderer got out again after the murder, which was by no means an easy thing. The first lady had not arrived and never did arrive. The secret service had turned the car around and taken her right back to Washington. The security already in place on the estate had locked into place only seconds after the shots were fired. It wasn't as good, or as tight, as the secret service would have been, but it would have made just strolling out the front gate a near impossibility. It would have meant strolling out the bridle path a near impossibility too, because there had been a man stationed at that entrance. That left only a very few options for escape, and he understood why Michael Harridan hadn't liked any of them.

He folded the notebook up and put it back in his pocket. It was after six. He wondered where Bennis was. He grabbed his coat from the coatrack in the hall and headed out down the stairs. He could still hear laughter coming up from old George Tekemanian's apartment, but Grace was no longer playing her harpsichord. Maybe she'd gone to rehearsal, or to play a concert. He went down one flight and knocked on Bennis's door. He would always think of that apartment as Bennis's apartment, even though she never went there anymore except to work. They really ought to knock the two apartments together and make a duplex, even if it did mean confirming in public what everybody on Cavanaugh Street already knew.

There was a shuffling sound on the other side of the door and then it was pulled inward. Tibor stood in the doorway in a pair of black trousers, a white shirt, a tie, and an expensive, thick cotton sweater that looked both very new and very orange. Gregor raised his eyebrows. Tibor shrugged.

"Bennis sent for it for me from Land's End," he said carefully. "She thinks I do not have enough clothes. She thinks the clothes I have are too depressing. Come in, Krekor. I have been trying to pay attention to blueprints."

Gregor went in. The apartment looked the way it always looked. Tibor was not doing much in the way of redecorating it for his stay. The papier-mâché models of Zed and Zedalia had been taken off the end tables in the living room. The coffee table had been cleaned of trays and now held only a single cup of coffee and a small plate of butter cookies. They looked like very good butter cookies. Gregor had to restrain himself from taking one.

"I thought I'd come along and get you to go to the Ararat for dinner with me," he said. "Bennis is missing in action, I have no idea where. And you've barely been to the Ararat since the explosion. Maybe I think you're depressed."

"I have only been to the Ararat once or twice," Tibor said. "I find it difficult to walk by the church. I try to look on the positive side, as Bennis tells me to. We'll have a new church. I'll have a new apartment. And this church will be built just for us. It will not be something we take over from somebody else. Still. I have made arrangements today for preserving the icons."

"Are they the kind of icons that should be preserved? I have no idea where Orthodox churches get their icons. I supposed I always half-thought that there were factories someplace."

"I don't think so, Krekor, no. And especially not a hundred years ago, when Holy Trinity was first built. They would have had to send to Greece for them, to be painted by artists who specialized only in icons. There are still such artists now, but perhaps there are factories too. I was thinking that the people who first built this church worked very hard to have the icons here, and we should not destroy them, or put them in storage where nobody can see them. Isn't it too early for the Ararat?"

"A little." Gregor took a seat on one of the big black leather chairs. "I thought I'd ask you about something first, if you're up for it."

"About something that has to do with the investigation? Because if so, Krekor, I will not be of a great help. I went to Adelphos House. I stopped at that man's newsstand and bought something. I walked down the street to the Ararat to get coffee and the building exploded behind me. If I had had any kind of real information, I would have told you about it long ago. I know what to worry about. Did I see any unusual person around the church at any time in the month or so before the bombing? No, I did not. Did I see any unusual person around the church on the day of the bombing? No, I did not. Did I see any unusual person—"

"That's all right," Gregor said. "I'm not worried about your seeing unusual people. It's a theory I wanted to ask you about. Or maybe you could get on the Internet and ask the people at RAM."

"You want to know which mystery novels to read when you take your vacation?"

"I didn't think RAM ever discussed mystery novels," Gregor said. "Last time I checked into there, you were all discussing the War on Terrorism and responses to September eleventh."

"Everybody was discussing that then. Grace's harpsichord newsgroup was discussing that then. Now we are discussing formula in crime fiction. It's very interesting."

"I'm sure," Gregor said. "I want to discuss One World Government."

"Oh," Tibor said. "Please no, Krekor. It gives me a headache. The people who are always harping on it give me an even bigger headache."

"There are people who harp on it on RAM?"

"One or two."

"Anybody named Kathi Mittendorf? Or Susan—wait, I'm going to have to look up the last name—"

"Don't bother," Tibor said. "There are no women. Only men."

"How about Michael Harridan?"

"*Pfft*," Tibor said. "What do you take me for? If I had seen that name on RAM pushing conspiracy theories, I would have told you about it. But no. These were just two, maybe one and a half—they would get on and talk about satanic ritual abuse, and how the FBI was covering up this abuse of children. And for a while I tried to check that out, Krekor, because of course you never know. It is not a good thing to trust government agencies. But it turned out to be craziness. The FBI keeps numbers on all the missing children. There are only a hundred or so a year who are not accounted for. The files are all open and public knowledge. And when you say that to these people, the ones who have the conspiracy theories, they say that the infants who are killed in sacrifices are not recorded anywhere because they have been born especially for this and their births have not been registered. It is a truly crazy thing, Krekor."

"I agree with you," Gregor said. "But I want to understand it. There seem to be a lot of people out there who believe it."

Tibor shrugged. "Believe what? There is more than one version of it. There is the Islamic version of it. There is the

fundamentalist Christian version of it. There is the secular
version of it."

"Are the versions substantially different?"

"Not so different as you'd think," Tibor said. "And with
the fundamentalist Christians and the secular conspiracists,
there's a great deal of overlap. They read each other's material. They believe each other's 'evidence,' except it isn't really evidence. Krekor, these things—"

"Start from the beginning," Gregor said, giving up and
snagging one of the butter cookies. Whoever made them
must have used pounds of the stuff. "There's a conspiracy to
bring the United States under the aegis of a One World
Government—"

"No, no," Tibor said. "You must start from the beginning.
First, a race of aliens came to earth and mated with human
women. To the fundamentalists, it was Satan and his angels
who did this. They mated with human women, and produced
offspring who looked human, but were really reptilian."

"Reptilian as in snakes?"

"And lizards and that sort of thing," Tibor said. "Yes. And
this race was very powerful, because they were smarter and
more ruthless than real human beings. They were geniuses.
They had better memories, and they could create things that
we could not, and they had access to the technology of their
home planet, and the advanced science there."

"So far," Gregor said, "there's nothing so very odd about
this. Oh, it's odd enough to think the world is full of people
who are half-human and half-reptile, but you can find
dozens of societies through the ages who have looked on
more technologically advanced societies as practicing
magic, because they can't imagine actual people being capable of that kind of creativity. That's a persistent theme in human history."

"Very nice," Tibor said. "This is a persistent theme
among truly insane people, except they're not the ordinary
kind of insane. Now, listen. There arose this race of half-
human, half-alien or satanic whatever you want. And they
intermarried only with each other. And they formed the

world's thirteen richest families. And they spread throughout Europe. First, they founded the Merovingian dynasty, which was a dynasty in Europe in the area that is now Germany and Austria. And this is where it begins to get truly insane, Krekor, because there was a Merovingian dynasty in Europe, in the seventh and eighth centuries. And they were not a race of superbeings. They were idiots. Complete and utter idiots. I am not joking here, Krekor. There are factory chickens less stupid than the Merovingians were, especially at the end. They died out in the ninth century. But not according to this theory, of course, where they only pretended to die out. Do you know that we have nearly complete records of monarchical succession throughout that period of the Middle Ages, right down to our own day in some places. But when you tell these people that they tell you that these are only the fake records, the real records are hidden from sight or have been destroyed so that the conspiracy is not derailed by an outraged populace. How do they know this? They know it because once a mayor of a town in France had the basement of his town hall dug up and in that basement people say he found papers that were the real succession records of the Merovingian dynasty."

"What people say?"

"People," Tibor said. "That's it. Not any people in particular. And there are no records of these people or of what exactly they were supposed to have said. But if you try to explain that this means you should not believe them, they tell you that it would be close-minded not to say that it's at least possible that these were the real records of the Merovingian dynasty. Can you see this rule applied to logic everywhere? Your mother's uncle's cousin's aunt heard that 'people say' the Liberty Bell is made out of Roquefort cheese, so you should ignore all the reports of all the people who have actually seen the Liberty Bell and think that it might just be made of Roquefort cheese. I could think better than this when I was in primary school, Krekor."

"Stuffed animals could. How do we get from the Merovingian dynasty to now?"

"Ah, well. The years went on and all these people wanted was control of the earth, but the technology had not reached a stage where that was possible. The reptilians were the ruling families of Europe, and they were in control of their territories, more or less. They founded all kinds of institutions to recruit people to their cause and to keep their power in place. They founded the Catholic Church and put the pope and the cardinals in the Vatican and sent bishops everywhere to keep the people under control. They founded the Freemasons, where they recruited men to their causes and swore them to blood oaths to advance the reptilian hegemony. Then, in the eighteenth century, there came the great danger to their rule: the English colonies in America, which were threatening to establish a society based on the freedom of the individual human person. The reptilians went into action. They put their own people, high-level Freemasons, into positions of power in the new rebellion. And in 1776 they formed a special section of Freemasonry called the Illuminati, who were the most powerful of all the Masons and who were always real reptilians, not just recruits. And they got together and made their plans to bring the whole world under a single world government, controlled by them. In this, America was supposed to be key. America is supposed to be a Masonic country. There are supposed to be Masonic symbols on our money. And all of America's presidents are supposed to have been Freemasons, including George Washington."

"Were they?"

"George Washington was, Krekor, yes, but that is not all that surprising. The Freemasons were a group of men who ascribed to Deism, which was a religious idea that said that God existed, but all He did was make the universe, establish the laws of nature, and then completely ignore His creation ever afterwards. It was really atheism for people who did not know enough about science to find atheism plausible—they knew nothing about the big bang, you know, or about evolution. In most places, it was dangerous to be a Deist. It was considered heresy, and you could be fined or imprisoned for it, or ostracized by your neighbors. So George Washington went every week to an Episcopal church and he was a Mason in his private life, because that was prudent. If he had been outspoken in his Deism, he would have had a lot of trouble. The same was true of John Adams and James Madison and John Quincy Adams. If you think the United States was founded as a Christian country, you should read what some of these people had to say about Christianity, in private, in their letters, where they did not expect to be overheard. Of course, Thomas Jefferson *was* outspoken in his Deism, and he still was elected president, but they called him a lot of names."

"All right," Gregor said. "So we get the Freemasons, and a special inner group of them called the Illuminati. Then what?"

Tibor threw his hands in the air. "Then, who knows? There are books and books of this sort out there, Krekor. These people have their own magazines. They've founded their own publishing houses. They have Web sites. In the end, what it comes down to is that the conspiracy is in place, and everybody is in on it. It looks like the world is being pulled every which way by opposing forces, but that is only a delusion. Everything is working to the same end, to bring the world under a single man's rule. For the Christians, this is Satan, and we are headed for the apocalypse and the end of the world. For the secularists, this is just a dictator to give the reptilians complete power over all people. Everything we think we see is a sham. Democracy is a sham. Always, in the United States, both of the candidates running from the major parties will be chosen by the Illuminati. Nobody the Illuminati does not control will even be able to run. Everything else that happens, like plant closings, or nuclear plant accidents, is part of the same all-controlling plot. There are no coincidences, and there are no accidents. Three Mile Island was planned and carried out by the agents of the Illuminati. The September eleventh attacks were planned and carried out by the agents of the Illuminati. Alan Greenspan is an agent of the Illuminati."

"And nobody but this group of conspiracy theorists ever notices?"

"They cannot notice," Tibor said, "because they are mind-controlled. There were secret CIA experiments called MKUltra Mind Control to brainwash as many Americans as possible into thinking they were in favor of the Illuminati's plans. Did I tell you that everybody at the UN is supposed to be an agent of the Illuminati?"

"No," Gregor said. "But if I'd thought about it, I could have guessed."

"In Illuminati families and families closely connected to them, they control the children through ritual abuse," Tibor said. "They breed infants for sacrifice, and then take their own children and make them take part in these sacrifices and then abuse them, over and over again, until they're unable to think for themselves. Don't ask me how such children are supposed to grow up into adults who can rule the world, Krekor, because I don't know. I don't think they know either."

"So," Gregor said. "Where does Holy Trinity come in? Why blow up the church?"

"You think it was these people who blew up the church?"

"Not exactly. It's a little complicated. Still, the question remains. Why blow up the church? Why this particular church?"

Tibor shrugged. "For the Christian fundamentalist conspiracists, we are devil worshipers. That's what the notes say. To the secular ones, devil worship is just a ploy by the Illuminati, a cover for really heinous doings, like plotting to make the United States part of the International Criminal Court. Krekor, it doesn't do to look too long at what it is these people are thinking. It's not only that it doesn't make sense. It's that it's all about fear. They fear change. They fear the future. And they are disappointed people, most of them. They feel insignificant and as if their lives are out of control. So they look for a way to be important, and this is it. It is not true that Alan Greenspan doesn't know who they are or care about what they do. Alan Greenspan cares desperately. So does the president of the United States. So does the pope. So do all those shadowy people who run the international banks. Those people know the names of every conspiracist, because conspiracists are the one true danger to their rule. You can change the scenario a little for each of the different kinds of conspiracists. The Muslim conspiracists know that they do not really come from cultures that have failed to develop technologically and scientifically—rather, their inventions and discoveries have been stolen by the Conspiracy and ascribed to other people, to Jews, mostly. The Christian conspiracists know that they are not the last gasp of a dying religious culture. Instead, they alone hold the power of Christ up to a corrupt and satanic world, and in the end at the great battle, it is the believers and not the Conspiracy who will win. It goes around and around. Some of them commit violence, and then we hear about them. Most of them just go to each other's lectures and buy each other's books and visit each other's Web sites and we don't hear about them at all. I wonder sometimes if men and women always felt so little in control of themselves and their world. Because I think really, Krekor, that we have more control over it now than we did three hundred years ago, but more people are anxious and afraid now than were then."

Gregor tilted his head back and looked at the ceiling. It had been washed, and recently. The women must have come in to make sure that Tibor was "comfortable." "All right," he said. "It's got to be about time to go to the Ararat now, isn't it? Let's go get something to eat. Just tell me one thing. Do you think the people who peddle this stuff, not the rank-and-file believers but the people like Michael Harridan—do you think they believe all this, or do you think they're conning?"

"Some of them believe it," Tibor said. "It's obvious from the way they write. But go look at the Web sites, Krekor. A lot of them are conning. They make their money this way. Sometimes the rank-and-file believers, as you call them, catch them at it."

"Then what happens?"

Tibor shrugged. "Some of the rank-and-file believers

desert them. Others stay on and defend them. It's like it is with mediums and people who claim to be able to speak to the dead. Sometimes, it's so damned important to some people to believe, they'll do whatever they have to do to go on believing. I know what this is, Krekor. I've seen it before. It's what happened with the hard-core Communists. The Stalin show trials. Genocide. Decades of support for dictatorships. Decades of indulgence in repression, torture, and summary execution. The fall of the Soviet Union. To some people, it made no difference. They would not see, or they would explain it away. Maybe we all do that with what we believe. Maybe we all need not to be forced to let go of our delusions."

"Let's go get something to eat," Gregor said again. "I don't care about my delusions. I just want to know what Michael Harridan thinks he's up to."

TWO

1

David Alden understood that there was no way he could stay in Philadelphia nonstop and indefinitely, no matter how much he might want to in order to follow the investigation into the deaths of Tony and Charlotte Ross, or how much the police wanted him to because they feared he might suddenly abscond to Switzerland and completely remove himself from their control. The simple fact of the matter was that he wouldn't be able to follow the police investigation even if he stayed put. He was not Gregor Demarkian. Nobody was in the least bit interested in giving him information. He learned what he knew about weapons, and bullets, and the way the police were thinking from the newspapers and the television news, just like everybody else. He didn't know much, and he wasn't likely to know much more, no matter what he did, until the case was solved or abandoned. As for police fears that he was planning to jump ship to Europe or South America, they were ludicrous. He had far too much work at the office. The Price Heaven mess was becoming an utter meltdown, complete with competing sets of lawyers, competing sets of accountants, and competing sets of board members at the bank, with everybody pointing fingers at everybody else and nobody making any sense. David had no idea if things would have gotten this bad if Tony had lived. He had a gut feeling that they wouldn't have, because Tony was the kind of man who commanded both obedience and respect. Since he himself was not that kind of man, he would have to go with what he had. That amounted to relentless common sense and all the facts, laid out in thousands of document pages that he alone had read every one of. By now he knew more about the inner workings of Price Heaven than the executives of Price Heaven did. It was more than possible that he had known more than they knew all along. Just thinking about it gave him a headache. When he remembered that the regulators would be descending—why was it that whenever there was a serious bankruptcy, the U.S. Congress felt it necessary to hold hearings into matters they didn't understand, couldn't be made to understand, and didn't want to understand?—it was more than his head that ached. Maybe he was lying when he said that what he really wanted was Tony Ross's life, with Tony Ross's job to go along with it. This was like a dress rehearsal, and it was awful. He wanted to go to bed for a week. He wanted to take all these papers and stuff them in a bonfire somewhere in the darker reaches of Central Park. He wanted not to read anything but the collected works of Elmore Leonard until it was at least July.

Instead, he shifted slightly on the seat of the limousine that was taking him in to New York and watched the dawn come up outside, glaring and orange. Out there it was cold. When they passed people in their yards, taking garbage cans out from behind their houses or going to their garages to get their cars, the people were always well wrapped up in parkas and hats. He found himself wondering what it was like to live in a house that backed directly onto the interstate, so that you had to have a tall chain-link fence around your property to make sure your children didn't run right out into the sixty-five-mile-an-hour traffic when they were playing in the yard after school. He had, he realized, absolutely no idea how "ordinary" people lived. Even though his family had never been really rich—or never in this century; they had been rich enough in the age of the robber barons, and before that in the Colonial and Revolutionary eras, when to be rich in America meant to be a prosperous lawyer in one of the better cities—even so, they had always been oriented toward the rich. It had no more occurred to David's parents to send him to public school than it had occurred to them to serve toasted grubs at their cocktail parties. In one way or another, they had done what they had to do to make sure he got through good private elementary schools, a good prep school, and, of course, the Ivy League when the time came, all without student loans or any other encumbrance on his future or career. They had managed all the things that had to go along with it too. He hadn't seen a television set until he was six. His parents owned only one, which they kept in their own bedroom for emergencies, like major assassinations. He hadn't eaten in a fast-food restaurant, or a popular restaurant chain, until he was in prep school and out for the weekend on senior privilege with friends. Then he'd had a single Big Mac and never gone back for another. It hadn't been all that popular a pastime in Boston and New Haven anyway, where his friends tended to be drawn to small ethnic restaurants featuring the cuisine of countries only very rich and very pampered people could go to. Sometimes, the things that he had never done in his life truly astonished him. He had never been shopping in Price Heaven or Kmart or Wal-Mart. He'd never spent any time in a mall except to look it over for the bank when they were considering loaning its owners money. He'd never had a car loan. He'd never been to a prom, or even to a school that gave a prom. He'd never been late paying a bill. He'd never had to apply for a mortgage. He'd never had a summer job. He'd never been inside a T.G.I.Friday's, a T.J. Maxx, a Marshall's, or a Bradlees.

It was more than money, he thought now, feeling more and more uncomfortable as the landscape changed inexorably and they were not only out of Philadelphia, but nearly out of Pennsylvania. Tony used to harp on this point all the time, because he was extremely worried about it. Too many of the people at the bank—too many of the people at all the banks, and in Congress, and on the boards of all the institutions from the Metropolitan Museum of Art to the Red Cross—lived in a kind of parallel universe that rarely intersected with what most Americans would call normal life. They wore ties and blazers to school as early as first grade. They spent first Friday afternoons, then Friday evenings, then Saturday evenings at the formal "dancing classes" that taught them not how to dance but how to behave. They spent their summers in Martha's Vineyard or Greece. They went to the opera instead of the movies and to museums instead of the mall. They played lacrosse and squash instead of football and basketball. They went to coming-out parties and expected to have to wear a dinner jacket at least four times a week between Thanksgiving and Easter every single year.

"The reason the men who create great business empires always seem to come up from the bottom," Tony used to say, "is because those are the people who know what most Americans want to buy. The reason the business empires fail when those men die is that they're taken over by people like us, who know nothing of the kind. No prep-school boy could have created Wal-Mart. No prep-school boy could even have conceived it. And it works the same way in art. Steven Spielberg makes the movies he wanted to see when he was growing up in a subdivision in Southern California. Stephen King writes the books he wanted to read when he was growing up poor in rural Maine. And don't kid yourself thinking that there's something called Great Art going on in all those books we read that sell two thousand copies and that they'll be rescued from obscurity after their authors are dead. One or two might be, but most of them will just disappear. In the meantime, this culture, the culture of the whole world, is determined by the very people you and I have nothing to do with most of the time and probably wouldn't like very much if we had. The only thing I can't figure out is if this is a flaw in capitalism or a virtue. Maybe that's the way it is to ensure that nothing like a real and stable aristocracy will ever exist again."

Dozens of Price Heaven papers were spread out across the seat next to him. The window between the passenger compartment and the driver's compartment was firmly shut. Maybe Tony had been right all along, and he was constitutionally incapable of solving the Price Heaven mess, because he didn't understand enough about what the business needed to run, or to appeal to people. Maybe he should have done what Tony had urged him to do months ago and tried to live "normally" for a month or two, rent an apartment, put himself on a budget, shop at the very places Price Heaven's customers liked to shop. Now it was too late. He was too aware of the fact that Price Heaven was his test. If he solved it, he would go on at the bank, or at another bank. He would have the career he had been trained to have. If he did not solve it, he would be shunted off to the sidelines. They wouldn't fire him right away. It would look bad, and give the regulators ideas about who should be investigated in the Price Heaven collapse. Still, they'd fire him eventually, and when he found himself out on the street with his pockets out, he'd also find himself without an open sesame to other banks or to brokerages or to any of those places where someone like him expected to work. He was fitted to do nothing else but what he did. His accent would disqualify him for a job in any but about two-dozen firms. His taste in clothes would make him conspicuous in any retail operation.

He looked out the windows again and saw that they were going through country now. Great rocky outcrops rose up on either side of the road. On this part of the interstate, it was as if America were largely uninhabited. Everything was country. Everything was pristine. He didn't know what he was worried about. It was true that the very idea of living the kind of life Tony had suggested he sample made him break out in a cold sweat. He didn't want to eat at McDonald's or buy the kind of clothes that could be bought at Price Heaven. He didn't want to see movies about aliens from outer space or Hobbits or vigilante heroes who machine-gunned the landscape to save the damsel in distress. He didn't want an SUV with a Britney Spears CD in the CD player. He didn't want "entertaining" to mean a big Thanksgiving dinner with a thousand relatives in attendance and all the women in the kitchen afterward, cleaning up. He didn't want to set his table with Martha Stewart Everyday dishes and glassware bought in big cardboard-boxed sets at the local warehouse store. He didn't want . . . to know any of those people, who were impossible to talk to, and who seemed to care about nothing he understood.

But then, he thought, he didn't have to. Even if he was eased out at the bank, even if he made such an utter disaster of the Price Heaven fiasco that he would never be hired by another financial institution anywhere, he still didn't have to. He had money in the bank, and money in investments, and a decent severance package that wasn't quite a golden handshake, but came close. He didn't care what people said about the virtues of ordinary life or the deep inner nobility of the common man and woman. He liked living the way he lived.

He got his cell phone out and punched in a number. The sound system was working, but the radio was tuned to NPR and the announcer's voice was so low, David couldn't make out the words. The police had discovered the dead body of an FBI agent who had gone undercover to infiltrate one of the conspiracist organizations. David wasn't worried about it. It was the kind of thing FBI agents undercover were likely to have happen to them. He was worried about the deaths of Tony and Charlotte Ross, but that was entirely natural. Tony had been his friend. Charlotte had been, if not a friend, an acquaintance of long standing.

Adele picked up on the other end. He must have gotten her at home. She sounded sleepy.

"Adele?" he said. "Sorry to wake you."

"You didn't wake me. I'm having coffee. Where are you?"

"On the road back from Philadelphia."

"You're spending a lot of time on the road."

"I've been going home, that's all. And Tony and Charlotte—"

"Yes," Adele said. "Do they know anything about that yet? Everybody is upset. Tony was bad enough, but with Charlotte on top of it, people are getting paranoid."

"I think they think it was one of those conspiracist groups. You know the kind of thing I'm talking about."

"Yes, I do, and I don't understand why you think that's going to make me feel better. Or make anybody feel better. Those people are nuts."

"I agree."

"They're dangerous nuts."

"I agree with that too, but at the moment they're beside the point. We've got to make some decisions on Price Heaven today. I've been over all the paperwork a million times. How could they possibly lose thirty million dollars in eighteen months and not notice it?"

"Think of Enron," Adele said solemnly.

"Enron was fraud. This was not fraud, at least as far as I can tell. This was sheer stupidity and incompetence. Except you know what the regulators are like. They won't like that. They'd prefer fraud. It makes them feel safer."

"Maybe you ought to do what you were talking about doing. Shut them down and close them out and stop throwing good money after bad."

"If we do, we'll sink dozens of pension funds and hundreds of four-oh-one K's. And Tony didn't want to shut them down. Did you get the notes for the refinancing schedule I left on your desk?"

"Absolutely."

"Good, let's work with that. Let's get copies of that out to everybody concerned by noon today, and then let's call a meeting for tomorrow morning to go over it. Only I want to talk to Mark Corvallen before that. He was Tony's closest ally on the board. Maybe I can convince him to back me on this so I'm not fighting an uphill battle against a bunch of vice presidents who are all scared to death that they'll get tarred and feathered with a meltdown. Somehow or other, there's got to be a way to keep this company afloat."

"If you say so."

"I say so. It's either that, or the bank takes a loss in the hundreds of millions of dollars. Which would you prefer?"

"I'll get Mr. Corvallen for you. But, David? Try to get some rest, will you please? You're beginning to sound very tightly strung."

"I'll calm down when this is over."

"You'd better calm down before noon, because you're supposed to go on television at a press conference about all this. And don't complain. They all want you to do it, so you're going to have to do it."

"Hell," David said. "All right. Never mind. Get Corvallen. Get copies of the rescheduling out to everybody who needs them. I'll be in in another half hour."

"Right," Adele said.

David switched off. Any minute now, he knew, they would begin to see the small houses and low warehouse buildings that announced the approach into the city. Ages ago, he had been able to look out and see the twin towers of the Trade Center in the distance. If there was one thing he wished for, it was that he could go back to before that date and rethink everything he was doing in the six months that preceded it. He had no idea if he would change any of it. Nothing was ever that simple.

At the very least, he wanted somebody to assure him that nobody else would die in that tight little circle in which he lived his life—not now, and not in the next few months, and maybe not ever, although he knew that was impossible. He was tired of the dying. He was more than tired of the nightmares he had of blood spreading out across the slate tiles of the walk in front of Tony Ross's house.

2

Father Tibor Kasparian had come to a conclusion, over a long night of sitting in Bennis Hannaford's apartment listening to a CD by a Portuguese neo-fado group called Madredeus. He could go on sitting by himself, feeling immobile and useless and hopeless and depressed, or he could get out and get on with his life, even if he didn't yet know how he was supposed to get on with it. Looking back, he could see whole periods of immobility. When he had first made it out of the Soviet Union, he had spent nearly six months in Israel. He had nothing against Israel, but he had been there by accident. It was the place he'd been able to find a safe haven in when he'd been without all his proper paperwork and not yet recognized as a dissident by the United States. He'd known from the start he wouldn't be able to stay there. He had felt so leaden, he hadn't been able to move himself to do anything about finding another place to go. He hadn't even been able to deal with the American embassy, where he had contacts dedicated to getting him to New York. If it hadn't been for those contacts, he might have stayed in the Middle East forever, or been sent back to Armenia when his ability to stall ran out. He'd been lucky. The contacts had had other contacts. He might not be moving, but they were. They sent him to Paris, where he proceeded to vegetate for another four months, going out every morning for coffee in a little café at the end of the block where his dismal small hotel took up the center, reading newspapers, wondering what he was supposed to do now that he no longer had to worry about being arrested at every minute of every day. It was only after they had finally gotten him to New York that he had begun to snap out of it. Even then, it had taken him weeks, and that peculiar energy that was New York's alone, coupled with the friendship of a very nice young woman in blue hair and safety pins. He wondered what had happened to her. He'd always worried that the safety pins would infect, or that the holes in her skin that they were stuck through would, but they never seemed to, and she never mentioned them.

What he needed, Tibor decided, was to get back into a routine, and to begin planning his week in an ordinary way, including planning to celebrate the liturgy on Sunday. He was not sure what he would be able to do about that, but he thought there must be a way. They couldn't use the church, but surely, throughout the history of Christianity there must have been many times when there was no church to use. There were a few large spaces on Cavanaugh Street: Lida Arkmanian's living room; the first floor of Donna and Russ's apartment. He would need permission from the

bishop, but he thought he could get that without too much
trouble. What he didn't want was for the people of Cavanaugh Street to go looking for another church to celebrate
in before this one was rebuilt. There was a very large Armenian community in Philadelphia. There were plenty of
other churches. Tibor thought it would be the worst possible
thing if the people of Cavanaugh Street had to go to them,
instead of staying home, and behaving as if this nutcase did
not exist.

He was up too early, so he waited. He took his shower and
got dressed and spent half an hour on the computer, answering e-mail from people on RAM wanting to know how he
was and what the progress was in finding the people who
had blown up his church. Then Bennis's little clock
chimed—it was a beautiful thing, all polished brass and
crystal dome so that you could see its works moving if you
weren't in need of the time—and he got his coat and went
out to the landing.

He considered going upstairs to see if Gregor was coming to the Ararat for breakfast, but decided against it. Gregor
always came to the Ararat for breakfast, usually with Bennis
in tow. He could meet them both there. He listened for
Grace's harpsichord but didn't hear it. Maybe she didn't get
up early. He was astounded at how fond he'd become of the
sound of that instrument. It was much better for him than the
neo-fado Portuguese group, and much less melancholy. He
went downstairs and knocked on old George Tekemanian's
apartment.

Old George must have been standing just inside the door.
Tibor still had his hand in the air to knock for the third time
when the door opened and George nearly hopped into the
hall, all enthusiasm and morning vigor.

"Father," he said. "Father. I wasn't expecting you. I
thought Grace had come down and we'd go out to breakfast
together."

"Is Grace coming down?" Tibor asked.

They both looked toward the stairwell, as if it was normal
to find apparitions on it. A second later, far above them, a

door slammed open and then slammed shut again, and they could hear Grace humming something that sounded like a polka.

"Does she play polkas, do you think?" Tibor asked.

"I don't think so," George said.

Grace clattered down the stairs. She came so fast, Tibor found himself anxious that she would fall. She didn't. The closer she came, the less the song she was humming sounded like a polka, but Tibor wasn't sure what else it sounded like. It was quick. It was lively. It was not rock and roll.

"Father," Grace said, as she reached the ground floor. "This is wonderful. Are you coming for breakfast? I bet you haven't been eating right at all since you got back. They bring all kinds of food, but it isn't breakfast food, if you know what I mean."

"I just wanted to get out of the apartment and move around," Tibor said.

"Well, come to the Ararat with us," Grace said. "Gregor and Bennis probably won't make it for another half hour. Gregor was gone half the night. I know. I heard him come in. I saw the news at eleven too. There's been an FBI agent murdered, actually murdered a long time ago or something, and they just found his body. Decomposed."

"Ugh," old George said.

"In a vacant lot," Grace said. "But I don't know. That doesn't seem right to me. Does it seem right to you? You'd think people would have found it in a vacant lot a long time before this. The news said he was probably out there for more than a week. Kids play in vacant lots. They'd just love to discover a body."

"I wouldn't have loved to discover a body when I was a child," old George said. "But maybe I'm being old-fashioned again. These days, children go to the movies and watch aliens blow up the White House."

"And dinosaurs eating San Diego," Tibor said.

They went out the front door onto the street. It was just starting to get light. Tibor truly hated the late fall and early winter, when it was dark until late in the morning and dark again early in the evening, so that the light seemed to be an intruder in something sinister. Now there was a small smear of pink just above the tops of the houses and the air seemed illuminated—but not illuminated enough—from within.

Lida Arkmanian was just coming out of her own house, with Hannah Krekorian in tow. When Tibor saw them, he waved tentatively, not sure how they would respond to seeing him out. He didn't want to be hustled back into Bennis's apartment and told to rest.

Lida and Hannah came over, the tall and thin and the short and squat, and fussed at him.

"You're getting out," Lida said. "That's a good thing. You can't spend the rest of your life in Bennis Hannaford's apartment."

"Especially not the way she keeps it clean," Hannah said.

"She has a cleaning lady come in," Lida said.

"It's not a very good cleaning lady, then," Hannah said. "Besides, you can't trust cleaning ladies. They do the least work they can get away with for the money. And you really can't blame them. I wouldn't want to clean somebody else's house."

"I have a very good cleaning lady," Lida said.

Tibor cleared his throat. This could go on forever, and it was cold. "I was thinking," he said. "We should find some place to have a liturgy on Sunday."

"We went to St. Paul's last Sunday," Lida said. "You don't have to worry about that. We won't be missing church."

"We won't," Hannah said. "But some people will. Not that I mean to speak ill of Sheila. She's got her troubles just like I've got mine. But—"

Tibor began to move purposefully down the street. They really could be here forever. "No," he said, once he was sure he had them moving. "I mean we ought to find a place to have a liturgy here. Not go to another church. Be here."

"But where?" Lida said, bewildered. "We're not supposed to go into the church, even though there's a lot of it left. The police came and gave us all a warning about how dangerous it could be because the structure isn't stable—"

"I know the structure isn't stable," Tibor said, and suddenly he did know, immediately and unmistakably. They had reached that part of the sidewalk directly across from the church. They could all see it for themselves, the gaping hole where the facade used to be, the roof beginning to cave in toward the center far in near the altar. "It is clear we are not able to use the church. But we do not have to use the church. The Christian community has often not had churches. We have celebrated the liturgy in fields, in caves, in living rooms. Where Christians are persecuted, where Christianity is outlawed—"

"But Christians aren't persecuted here," Grace said. "And Christianity isn't outlawed. Could you just—what—say Mass—"

"Celebrate the liturgy," Hannah said.

"The Catholics say celebrate the Mass," Lida said. "My son's girlfriend said—"

"Stop," Tibor said. "We need only a space large enough to fit in all the people who want to come. Possibly we will have more than usual, since it will be the first time since the explosion, unless people are worried about there being another explosion—"

"*I'm* not worried about there being another explosion," Lida said. "We could use my living room. I get nearly everybody in the neighborhood in there at Christmas. I mean, granted that's a buffet, but—"

"Well, we're not exactly looking to stage a sit-down dinner, are we?" Hannah said. "Honestly, Lida, the fuss you can make over the simplest—"

"I'm just saying we could use my living room," Lida said. "It would be a good thing. And then, because it's the first time, we could have a potluck. I could make some finger food and people could bring what they liked and then after the service we could spread out over the whole house and everybody could eat—"

"You'd better not forget the children will be there," Hannah said. "If you're going to hold a potluck afterwards, you're going to have to do something serious about all that china you keep all the hell over the place. Although what you want with china eggplants and china lily pads is beyond me. Really, some people don't have enough to spend money on—"

"What's this?" Sheila Kashinian said, coming up from the other side of the street.

They were almost at the Ararat. Old George and Grace looked shell-shocked, the way people got when they were suddenly exposed to the women of Cavanaugh Street in full swing, planning something. Tibor hung back for a while and then retreated, up the street, across the little intersection, to that place on the sidewalk where he could stand directly in front of the church. Eventually, he thought, you realized it was only what it was, a building, made of steel and mortar and brick. Buildings came and buildings went. They were destroyed by fire and earthquake and flood and time. They were not important in themselves.

He looked up over the sagging roof to the rest of Philadelphia, beginning to come alive with the arrival of the sun. Then he turned away and went back up the street to the Ararat. Old George and Grace were waiting for him on the sidewalk. Lida and Hannah and Sheila Kashinian had gone in and taken a table. Tibor could see them through the Ararat's big plate-glass front window, writing things down on napkins.

"They're discussing coordinated serving silver," Grace said. "Are they always like this?"

"Worse," old George said morosely.

Tibor pushed the Ararat's door open and shooed them inside.

3

It wasn't that she had been laid off that bothered Kathi Mittendorf. She had expected to be laid off, all the way back to the day she had first heard what was going on with Price

Heaven. It was so hard to figure out what was happening with the Illuminati at any one time. Even really brilliant people, like Michael, got confused. She was more and more aware these days that she was not a brilliant person. She would very much like to be, but in the end she was just herself. She could man the blind end of a wire without too much difficulty, and do the scut work of buying and storing and hiding weapons, but when it came to tactics and strategy, she was hopeless. What was worse, she had no real self-control. She couldn't appear passive on the outside. She only managed glassy-eyed and tense. She couldn't appear calm in a crisis. She was never calm, even when she should be. In the middle of a major action, she was a mass of raw emotion, excitement and hysteria, fear and bliss. Sometimes she wished she had learned to do crafts when she was younger. Maybe it would be some help to her if she could knit.

What bothered Kathi Mittendorf was that, *because* she had been laid off, she had nothing to take her mind off what she had to do in the next twenty-four hours, and nowhere to go to get away from the house and all the potential it held for her to make a really serious mistake. She was fretting, and along with fretting she was fussing with too many of the details on the edges of the project she had committed herself to carry out. She was in the same state of mind she had been in just before the night Tony Ross died and that satanic church had been blown up. If she breathed in the wrong direction— if she so much as twitched at an inopportune moment—she would destroy them all and everything they'd worked for, but she couldn't stop breathing and she couldn't stop twitching. She also couldn't stop hating the sight of Susan in her living room, sitting on the couch with a big glass of Diet Coke in front of her on the coffee table, looking smug. She would rather have left Susan out of it. She would rather have left everybody out of it except herself and Michael, but that was the kind of thing she never said with full clarity to herself, even just inside her head.

"I still say we ought to be careful," Susan said, flipping her blond hair from the front of her shoulders to behind. She had had the top of it cut short and curled into ringlets. She reminded Kathi of Tonya Harding at her worst. "I know Michael is a genius, and I know he's in charge of this operation, but we're talking about a serious weapons charge here—"

"There won't be any weapons charge," Kathi said. She was trying to sound patient. She only sounded panicked. "There won't be any arrests. We're not supposed to be arrested. We're supposed to end up dead."

"Then maybe the smartest thing for us to do would be to run," Susan said. "Let's take off. We've got those fake identities—"

"What if they've been found out?"

"We've got them," Susan insisted. "And from what I understand, it isn't that hard to get more. Why don't we take off and go into hiding? You may look forward to an all-out gun battle against the United States government, but I don't—"

"We can't run," Kathi said. She was feeling not only panicked, but desperate. "They know who we are. They know what we look like. They know we were involved—"

"I wasn't involved. I had no idea 'we' were involved."

"Do you think it would matter?" Kathi said. "Do you think they care who really killed Tony Ross or blew up that church or did any of the rest of it? Or that—FBI agent? Did you know he was an FBI agent? Michael knew."

"Yes, Michael knew," Susan said. "And he told us. And we expelled him from the group. And now they've found his body. That's a problem in and of itself, don't you think?"

"They don't care who does what," Kathi repeated stubbornly. "It isn't about law and order. It isn't about truth and justice. It isn't about murder. It's about control of the world and a One World Government that will put an end to freedom once and for all. They're moving in. You can see it. They're not just moving in on us. They're moving in on the whole country. The homeland security czar—they even call him a czar. And those people in Washington. They think they have the country fooled, because they call themselves Republicans, and people think only Democrats want to turn the United States into a police state."

"How did we get to homeland security from this?" Susan asked. "I'm talking about this. I'm talking about the simple fact that if we do what you're suggesting we do—"

"I didn't suggest it. I don't suggest anything. I'm not smart enough to plan. It's Michael who suggested this."

"Fine. It's Michael who suggested this. I think Michael is smart too. But I don't think he's God, and that's what you're treating him as. I think this is nuts, and so would you if you thought about it for only a couple of minutes. What have we actually done that could get us in trouble? Nobody is going to believe that a couple of middle-aged women—"

"Ethel Rosenberg was a middle-aged woman," Kathi said. "They gave her the electric chair. That woman who died after the assassination of Lincoln was a middle-aged woman—"

"We haven't been collaborating in the assassination of a president," Susan said. "We haven't been doing much of anything except going to lectures and listening to speeches and, okay, working with a couple of wiretaps. But they don't execute you just for wiretaps."

"It's not the wiretaps, and you know it. It's Anthony Ross. And his wife. And that—the FBI agent."

"Right. Yes. I understand. They like to pin their own crimes on the people because that keeps the people divided, and we're it at the moment because we're here and available and—"

"And because we're dangerous to them," Kathi said. "Never forget that. We're dangerous to them."

"Yes, right. We're dangerous to them because we tell the public what they're doing, the way they're all subverting the Constitution, the Republicans and the Democrats both, the way they're trying to stamp out freedom and make us all part of a single dictatorship that will rule the whole world. We know what the UN is really for and what they're doing. We know the way the courts really run. We know who they are. But what good do you think it's going to do if we get blown away on some backstreet in Philadelphia and they can go on the network news and tell everybody how we were a bunch of domestic terrorists plotting to blow up churches from one end of Pennsylvania to the other? What good did it do Timothy McVeigh?"

"Timothy McVeigh is a martyr. He was a plant, but he was a martyr. They sacrificed him."

"Yes," Susan said. "He's a martyr. He's also dead and a dirty word to practically every ordinary American. Make sense for a little while, will you please? What is it that you think you're playing with here?"

"I'm not playing."

"No," Susan said. "And neither are they. They've got tanks, and mortar, and nuclear bombs. We talk about the Second Amendment and about how the right to bear arms means that we'll be able to defend ourselves against the government if they ever come after us, but that's not true. They've got stuff we couldn't get our hands on if we tried, and couldn't conceal if we got our hands on it. Howitzers. Grenades."

"We've got grenades."

"We do? Good. But it doesn't change anything. They can put together an army to storm this place if they want to. How are we going to protect it? How is Michael going to protect it? I'm not saying he's completely wrong. I can see his point. That—FBI agent. Yes. I can see how that's going to get us into a lot of trouble, but the smart thing to do in that case is to run, take off for Idaho or Montana or one of those places where we'd be impossible to find. Go to Alaska. Go to Canada—"

"I've got a headache," Kathi said. "I've got to get an aspirin."

Susan leaned forward and picked up her Diet Coke. The curls on the top of her head looked fake. The thin chain bracelet around her left wrist made her arm look too plump. Her eye shadow was smeared. She had not been laid off her job. She had taken a sick day to be here now. Kathi walked away from her, through the small dining room, into the kitchen. It was the middle of the morning now, but the world was still grey. She had begun to feel that the world had been grey nonstop all her life. Even when she was growing up, there had never been any sun. That was ridiculous. She had to be careful. It was far too easy to go off the rails when you were under this much pressure.

She went to the cabinet next to the refrigerator and got out her bottle of aspirin—generic, bought at Price Heaven for half the price of name-brand aspirin. That was one of the ways Americans could figure out what was going on in their country, if they were willing to pay attention. The health-care crisis was a sham, cooked up by the insurance companies and the hospitals and the big government health-care centers to make Americans think they had to have socialized medicine if they were going to have health-care at all. It was just one more thing, one more signpost on the way to tyranny. Once they got control of the health-care system, they would be able to impose all kinds of rules. Never mind the rules against smoking, which were unconstitutional and tyrannical as they stood. They could force people to change their diets to grains and rice instead of meat and potatoes. They could make daily exercise a requirement for every citizen. They could fine people for doing things like eating at McDonald's or sleeping in on Sunday mornings. *If society pays for it, society should be able to make the rules for how it is used.* How would Americans feel when *that* little precept was applied to the very food they ate and the hours they spent asleep in bed?

Kathi got a glass from another cabinet and went to the sink and filled it with water. Then she went to the wall phone. She didn't need to look up the number. She knew it by heart, and had for over two years. It was really true that she was not good at planning. She was not good at making decisions, either. She never liked to do anything drastic without consulting somebody with better information. The phone on the other end of the line rang and rang. Her head ached. Suddenly, the line was picked up and a recorded voice said,

"We're sorry. The number you have called is not in service at this time."

Kathi hung up and stared at the phone. She was sure she couldn't have dialed a wrong number. This wasn't a number she had to look up. Still, she was nervous. She could have made a mistake. She dialed again and listened to the ring again. The line was picked up and the recorded voice repeated,

"We're sorry. The number you have called is not in service at this time."

Kathi hung up again. She got two aspirin out of the bottle and took them. She bit her lip and tried to think. Everything was on the move, now. Michael was on the move too. He must have canceled his phone service and started to go into hiding already. By tonight, they would all be in hiding. There was nothing to worry about. She just hadn't realized it was all happening so fast. Even though she'd been stressing speed and urgency to Susan, somewhere at the core of her she had still been tied to the old rhythms, when there had been no emergency. She had still been thinking the way she thought before Anthony Ross was dead.

She put the cap back on the aspirin bottle and the bottle back in the cabinet. She went to the big drawer she kept hammers and screwdrivers in and opened it up. She had a .357 Magnum pistol in there. It was twenty-years-old, but it had never been used, and it was fully loaded. She had put it in there only last night, when the word had come from Michael that they were about to be attacked and that she had to start getting ready for what was likely to be a very messy operation. She'd lain in bed for an hour, wide awake, thinking about all the guns and the explosives and the ammunition stored all around the house. None of it was easily accessible. She hadn't even left herself a handgun for self-protection. Finally, she hadn't been able to handle it. She'd gone down to the basement and opened up one of the wall panels and found herself the gun and loaded it. Then she'd had second thoughts—Michael had been adamant; she was not to start getting ready until the morning; she was to leave everything in place until then—and left the gun down here. It had felt safe where she'd put it. She had no idea why.

I'm really not good at making decisions, she thought now. Then she took the gun out and took it off its safety. It felt heavy and cold in her hand, very different from the way it had felt when she'd been handling it before. She had fired similar weapons on firing ranges. That hadn't felt like this, either. *Everybody has to grow up sometime*, she thought, and then that didn't make much sense, so she let it go. She was all grown up. She was part of an underground organization whose purpose was to defend the freedom and sovereignty of her country against the forces of darkness. She was, in a way, really more of a soldier than a civilian.

She felt the weight of the gun in her hand. She went out of the kitchen and through the dining room. She stood in the arch there, watching Susan sipping Diet Coke.

"I'm just trying to be reasonable," Susan said.

Kathi Mittendorf raised the gun in both her hands and fired.

THREE

1

It was a question of making lists, and making sure everything was in its proper place in line, and not getting blinded to the obvious by the obscure but interesting. Gregor Demarkian didn't think he would have expressed it like that to anybody, but that was how he felt. The first thing he did when he woke up on the morning after the Philadelphia police found the body of Steve Bridge was to get on the phone with the Lower Merion police, and for once he did not feel guilty for getting anybody out of bed. The whole thing was beginning to feel more and more wrong to him, not because he expected another murder—he was fairly sure that this murderer would not kill again, unless something very unusual happened, or unless he was cornered in the wrong way, which Gregor prided himself on knowing how *not* to do—but because some of the elements in motion there were not under anybody's control, and never had been, no matter what they'd looked like a week ago. He did not examine the fact that he got a great deal of satisfaction out of waking the director out of a sound sleep to get information that he could have gotten by asking Walker Canfield. He never had examined his feelings for directors of the Federal Bureau of Investigation generally. It would have been embarrassing to admit that he had never entirely recovered from his deep, abiding, and well-founded hatred of J. Edgar Hoover. It would have been even more embarrassing to admit that he now somehow held the office of director as tainted, as if Hoover was haunting it.

"I could have faxed you this from the office if you'd waited an hour," Frank Margiotti had complained as he reeled off the one list Gregor really cared about.

Gregor hadn't answered him. There was no point. He wrote the list down carefully. He made notations next to two or three of the names. Then he hung up.

By ten o'clock, when Bennis came back from Donna's house after a morning of consulting on What to Do About Tibor—as far as Gregor could tell, Tibor was doing fine, and busily involved in planning the building of a new church, which is what he ought to be doing—Gregor had sheets of paper full of lists spread out all across the kitchen table. His coffee was in a mug on one of the kitchen counters, because he didn't want to spill any. He'd put together a plate of toast and forgotten about it. He heard her come in and grunted in her direction. A second later, it occurred to him that he was behaving as if they were married.

"So," she said, "what exactly is this?"

He took the paper out of her hand. "This is a list of all the people on the grounds at the time the gates were closed just after the shooting."

"Not at the time of the shooting?"

"No, there's no way to know that. If the secret service had already arrived in force, we'd be in better shape, but as it is we have to rely on Tony Ross's security, which was goodish but not really what I'd call professional. Also, it wasn't blanket, and wouldn't be until the federal officers got there. That means that the shooting happened and there was a window of about three minutes when all kinds of things could have happened."

"Three minutes isn't very much time."

"It is if you just want to step back across a gate you're not very far from, especially if the guard was distracted."

"Was he?"

"Well," Gregor said, "according to Margiotti, he wasn't. The guard says he wasn't. Which is what the guard is going to say. And I haven't talked to him myself. However, I do have something else here—the times people say they came in."

"And that would be accurate?"

"No," Gregor said drily, "that would indicate that there was, at the time of the shooting, a fairly heavy load of traffic coming through that gate. I thought rich people were supposed to be fashionably late."

"Really rich people are never late," Bennis said. "Punctuality is the courtesy of kings." She picked up the list. "All these people were there? Why didn't I see them?"

"They weren't there, as in at the party," Gregor said. "They'd either just come in at the gate or were on their way down the drive. That's my point. If you were really going to control who came in and who came out of that place on the night in question, you didn't need a guard on the gate. You needed six, and you needed a couple of backup people to police the perimeter."

"Oh, Gregor, for God's sake. They've got one of those fancy Victorian gates out there, wrought iron with the arrow spikes on the top for decoration. There's no way to climb them except maybe to throw a mountain-climbing rig over the top horizontal bars and pull yourself up, but if you tried it you'd probably pull the gate over. It wasn't meant—"

"To protect against serious danger, I know," Gregor said. "You still would have needed some people policing the perimeter, because you have no idea the kinds of things people can think up to get around security."

"Well, did anybody think of anything this time?"

"I haven't the faintest idea. You forget, the problem isn't just with the murderer. Lots of other people might have had reason not to want to be at that place in the middle of a police investigation, or what was going to become a police investigation. Even perfectly innocent people are often very anxious to stay out of the way of the police or to make sure their names aren't connected with a scandal or a crime, even as innocent bystanders."

"Does it *matter* that somebody might have got in or out of the gates?"

"It depends on how the prosecutor presents the case in court," Gregor said. "A rich man with a rich man's lawyer might be able to argue that the place was a sieve and for all we know the real murderer could have been climbing over the gate and on his way to Canada while the Lower Merion police were annoying his client. Which, of course, was the reason for all this incredible nonsense. I should have realized that the times didn't match up."

"What times?"

"Let me ask you something," Gregor said. "Look at this list. Is there anybody on it you don't know?"

Gregor sat back as Bennis took the paper back again, and frowned.

"Well," she said. "It all depends on what you mean by 'know.' I mean, there's you and me. Obviously, I know us. And there's Charlotte and Tony. And I know them. Knew them. Ryall Wyndham. I know him slightly. Margaret and Hamilton Cadwallader. Lee and George Foldenveldt. Alison and William Pomfret. Virginia Mace Whitlock. David Alden. Martin Cameron. Where were all these people? I don't remember any of them at the time Tony died, and as for later—"

"As for later, there were a lot of people milling around and you weren't paying too much attention," Gregor said. "Most of the people on that list had just come through the gates and were headed down the drive to the party. Do you know them?"

"Slightly," Bennis said. "You know what I mean. I've been to parties where they've been to parties. I ran across most of them while I was growing up. God, the Main Line doesn't change much, does it? I never did understand how all those people could stand it to see nobody else but each other. I mean, you'd think you'd get bored seeing the same faces day after day without a break for fifty years."

"Of course, there's one person who isn't here," Gregor said. "But I'm willing to bet she was inside the gates when the shots were fired and just managed to get out again in the ensuing confusion."

"Who?"

"Anne Ross Wyler."

"Annie? Oh, Gregor. You can't really think Annie shot her own brother. I mean, for goodness sake, it's not like she needed his money, at least not unless she's been incredibly stupid over the last thirty years, and I don't believe it when it comes to Annie."

"No," Gregor said. "I don't think she killed her brother. I think she thinks she knows who did."

"Who does she think it was?"

"Lucinda Watkins." Bennis was obviously drawing a blank. Gregor shook his head. "You never pay attention when I talk to you," he said. "Lucinda Watkins is—"

"The social worker at Adelphos House," Bennis said suddenly. "I remember her. She's a very strange woman. I mean, to look at her, you'd think she was—" Bennis flushed.

"Trailer trash," Gregor said firmly. "I know. I think she was, once. That that's what her family was. And I agree with you. In some ways, she's a very strange woman. My guess is that, philosophically, she isn't much different from Kathi Mittendorf. But she didn't kill Tony Ross."

"But Annie thinks she did? Why?"

"Because at the time her brother was killed, Anne Ross Wyler was following Ryall Wyndham into that party. She says she only went as far as the gate and stopped, but I'm about ninety-nine percent certain that wasn't true. You see that name on the list—Virginia Mace Whitlock?"

"What about it? She's a real pain in the ass, but I don't think she's sinister. I mean, she's just trying to be a legend in her own time, if you know what I mean. Buys her clothes at Price Heaven. Makes a fetish of being cheap. There are always people on the Main Line like Virginia, they're just—"

"The reason why there's a star next to her name," Gregor said, "is that at the time of that party, Virginia Mace Whitlock was in the hospital in Boston having a hip replacement."

"Oh," Bennis said.

"My guess is that Anne Ross Wyler simply gave the wrong name at the gate. Like I said, the security was very uneven, and there were a lot of people arriving, and I'd guess that the single guard on wasn't being all that careful. It's easy to look back now and talk about how important it was for Tony Ross to have real security in place, but you know what life is like. None of us think we need real security in place. Most people get annoyed with security in no time at all, unless they're very fearful people. Would you say Tony Ross was a fearful person?"

"Of course not," Bennis said.

"What about Charlotte Deacon Ross?"

Bennis snorted. "She was one of those women who would have offed the burglar in a split second if there had ever been one stupid enough to enter her house. And she probably had the arms in that place to do it."

"So," Gregor said, "trust me, neither one of them would be likely to put up with anything like real security for long, because real security is a pain in the ass. And in fact they didn't, and we know they didn't. Margiotti and Tackner commented at the time on the fact that there was less of that sort of thing than they'd expected there to be, although I don't see why. I can't imagine that most of those houses in Bryn Mawr are tricked out with a full array of security devices. Three quarters of an hour later, of course, it would have been different, because the first lady would have arrived and the feds would have been there in force."

"But you still haven't said," Bennis said. "Why does Annie think Lucinda Watkins killed her brother?"

"Because at the time of the shooting, the murderer was wearing Lucinda Watkins's clothes, or something very much like them."

"What?"

"And standing in a tree," Gregor said. "I didn't realize what was going on until I actually saw Lucinda Watkins. And heard her. I'd expect Annie Ross has spent a long time listening to Lucinda's tirades about the evils of the upper class, or however it is she puts it when they're alone and she can really let loose. With me, she was a little strained."

"I can bet. Where did the murderer get Lucinda Watkins's clothes?"

"From Lucinda Watkins's closet."

"So who's the murderer? Annie Ross?"

"Michael Harridan," Gregor said.

Bennis sat down. "Listen," she said. "You've spent the last week telling me that Michael Harridan doesn't exist—"

"Not exactly."

"And that the killing of Tony Ross had nothing at all to do with America on Alert and domestic terrorism and conspiracy nuts—"

"Not exactly," Gregor said. "It's like that thing you said about 'knowing' the people at the party. What does 'know' mean? Well, what does 'have to do with' mean?"

"I'm beginning to think you need medication."

"What I need is my coat," Gregor said. "Jackman is due to pick me up in five minutes."

2

Even with Bennis there to keep him company, Gregor couldn't sit still in his apartment to wait for John Jackman. It was odd how that worked. He'd been in situations where time really mattered: where there were hostages; where the murderer was waiting to strike again; where evidence would be destroyed if it wasn't secured quickly. As far as he knew, there was now no urgency. He was a little concerned about Kathi Mittendorf and the other strongly committed members of America on Alert, but not very, because as far as he could tell, they never did anything without Michael Harridan's having commanded it first. He didn't think Michael Harridan was in the mood to command any more murders, or church bombings, or violence. In fact, he was willing to bet that Michael Harridan did not usually think of himself as a violent man. It always amazed him how many men *did* think of themselves as violent, though—as if violence were the hallmark of virility, or a kind of merit badge. The

Michael Harridans of this world tended to sign on to Asimov's famous dictum. *Violence is the last resort of the incompetent.* It was true too. The people who blew up churches, the people who gunned down other human beings, the people who flew commercial airliners into the sides of skyscrapers on sunny late-summer mornings, were marked first and foremost by their inability to cope with the day-to-day necessity of practicing decency in ordinary life. Michael Harridan wouldn't see himself in that, either, but it was as true of him as it had ever been of Charles Manson. People who were able to earn money and respect and position did not need to kill for it.

Gregor went downstairs and onto the street in a frenzy of sheer restlessness. He walked up to the church one more time, but the scene had ceased to have the power to depress him. Maybe it was because he had seen Tibor this morning and it had become obvious that the scene had ceased to have the power to depress Tibor too, and all along it was what was happening to Tibor that had most concerned him. He stood for a while and looked at the rubble and then through the rubble to the icons and the pews and the ceiling that really was going to come down in a day or two. Then he walked up the street a short ways and bought a copy of the morning paper at Ohanian's Middle Eastern Foods. If Mary Ohanian had been manning the cash register, he would have stopped to talk. Mary, however, was away from home at her freshman year at Harvard, and the cash register was being manned by her younger brother Jared, who gave new depths to the word *surly.* Gregor could not remember if he had been that morose and sullen at the age of fifteen. Psychologists and women's magazines were always harping on the idea that sullenness was natural to teenaged boys, but Gregor had the idea that if he'd behaved in public the way Jared was now behaving, his father would have beaten him to a bloody pulp and his mother would have followed that with a month of guilt trips, resulting in a teenaged Gregor with all the hearty cheeriness of Mickey Mouse greeting visitors to Disney World. He took the paper and looked without much interest at the front page. There was a story on the finding of the body of Steve Bridge, but it had been beaten out from the top spot by the story on the Price Heaven collapse, which seemed to be total and threatening to put a thousand people out of work in the Philadelphia greater metropolitan area alone.

He walked back up the street, past the Ararat, past the church, to his own front steps. The Ararat was mostly deserted. It was too late for breakfast and too early for lunch. The church was still what it had been when he'd looked at it a few moments before. He thought about buying one of those posters of the Twin Towers lit up at night and having it framed, the way Bennis had had one framed for Tibor. He was in the oddest mood, and not one he trusted. He felt as if he had arrived at the unified field theory of all existence. He knew not only the meaning of life, but the combination code to unlock its intelligibility.

It's a good thing I don't drive, he thought, letting himself recognize that the mood he was in was very much like being on a drunk. It had been years since he'd been on a drunk, or even been a little bit tipsy. Drinking was the kind of thing you did in the army and then were a little ashamed of afterward, mostly because it was hard not to recognize what an idiot you'd been while indulging. He wondered if things would be different if young men were required to go into the army as a matter of course, the way the men of his own generation had been. He wasn't really in favor of a peacetime draft, or of any draft. He wasn't sure that a draft did much of anything for the country except give the worst of its leaders the means to wage war when no war was necessary. Still, he wondered what would have become of Michael Harridan if he'd had to spend two years practicing military discipline, in an environment where, in the best cases, there were neither distinctions nor excuses. Maybe the answer was that Michael Harridan would have become exactly what he did become. Tim McVeigh had been in the military. It hadn't recruited him to the defense of civilization.

John Jackman's car pulled onto Cavanaugh Street—not

the official limousine this time, but the black Cadillac two-door he kept for personal use. It was a tribute to Jackman's finely tuned political sense that it was a Cadillac and not a Mercedes. Gregor grabbed the passenger-side door as soon as the car began to ease up along the curb. He had the door open and was climbing inside before Jackman had actually stopped.

"What's the matter?" John said. "We can't go up to your place and talk in peace?"

"I'm too antsy for my place."

"How about the Ararat?"

"For Christ's sake," Gregor said.

John pulled the keys out of the ignition and dropped them in his pocket. "I never understand you when you get like this," he said. "Why not just tell us who it is and get it over with? Let our guys pick him up, or let Lower Merion pick him up—"

"I don't have the faintest idea where he is this morning," Gregor said. "But what I said to you on the phone holds. I'm ninety-nine percent certain. I want to clear up the other one percent. Did you bring what I asked you to?"

"A picture of Kathi Mittendorf, a picture of Susan what's-her-name, and four more pictures to create a diversion, yes. You could have waited for this, you know. I told you yesterday that I would get the boys on it and I had gotten them on it, they were just—"

"Doing business as usual," Gregor said. "Yes. I know. I'm not criticizing. I'm just in a hurry. What about the rest of it?"

Jackman reached inside his coat and took his notebook out of his pocket. "One, yes, Ryall Wyndham owns stock in Price Heaven. It's registered with the Securities and Exchange Commission and he votes in stockholder elections. Oh, and he's taking a bath. A big one. He bought at a hundred and two. The stock is now trading at seventeen. There's no indication he got out in time on any of it."

"Excellent," Gregor said. "What about Anne Ross Wyler?"

"Lower Merion did that one. Sent that guy, Frank—"

"Margiotti."

"Yeah, him. Sent him out there in the middle of the night last night. Not to Lower Merion, he was already there, but out to the Ross estate. Did *not* go over too well with the eldest daughter, Marianne. Anyway, Margiotti found the guard and showed him the picture. He ID'ed it. Sort of. It was dark. He was busy—way busier than he should have been. Like that. But we got a tentative positive that it was Mrs. Wyler in at least one of the cars. He doesn't specifically recall which one. He doesn't really remember what the woman calling herself Virginia Mace Whitlock looked like."

"In other words, that one's a wash," Gregor said. "Of course he can identify Anne Wyler. She was Tony Ross's sister. She was probably on the premises a number of times. All right. I don't think that will matter too much. I wasn't really convinced he'd have noticed her anyway. She must have done at least a little to disguise herself, since there was always the chance he'd recognize her then. I just hate not having the loose ends tidied up. What about the clothes?"

"That one we're going to need a search warrant for," Jackman said. "According to Margiotti, the eldest daughter is a cross between Medea and a nuclear warhead. Anyway, she isn't having any. No police in the house. Nothing. You've got to wonder what these people are thinking sometimes. Her parents are dead, killed within a week of each other, and she won't cooperate with the police? It's a good thing she was well out of town at the time of that first murder, because if I were still on the force in the ordinary way, I'd be ready to suspect the hell out of her right now."

"Maybe we can make this part a little easier for everybody," Gregor said. "I don't think it's necessary to send detectives in to do the searching. Ask Ms. Ross to ask her laundress if she's found anything that doesn't belong to the house in the wash. My guess is that we're looking for a black skirt, long, jersey-knit, that kind of thing, something cheap and in a very large size. Also maybe a black cardigan, or some other kind of button-up top, also in a large size, also cheap."

"So what did Michael Harridan do?" Jackman asked. "Stuff the clothes with pillows so that he looked like Lucinda Watkins?"

"No, of course not. That would have been unwieldy as hell and it would have taken far too much time. He wasn't trying to look like Lucinda Watkins. He was just concerned to wear something dark, so that he couldn't be spotted, and large, so that he'd be well-covered, and belonging to somebody else, so that it couldn't be traced back to him. It was just an accident that Annie saw the clothes and thought she'd seen Lucinda as well. If the two of them had been physically closer or the light had been better, Annie would never have made the mistake. My guess is that there's a little nugget of doubt in the back of her mind even now."

"There's a little nugget in the back of *my* mind," Jackman said. "It's not just that you're crazy. It's that every time I have to work with you, everybody is crazy. I hope to hell that this guy has a motive that won't sound idiotic to a jury."

"He's got the best motive in the world," Gregor said. "Don't worry about it. And there's always the chance that somebody on Cavanaugh Street will recognize him. He was here, after all. I realized when I was talking to Kathi Mittendorf that he must have planted the bomb in Holy Trinity Church all by himself."

"Why? I thought you said she was a complete true believer conspiracy nut."

"She is. But even complete true believer conspiracy nuts have their codes of ethics, and in this case she's got an interior image of herself, and of America on Alert, that tells her quite firmly that they are not the kind of people who bomb churches. I wonder how long it took him to discover what somebody who'd run into these people before would have known all along. They may be irrational, but they're not illogical. They may be some of the most logical people on earth."

"Right," Jackman said. "Yes. You've said this before. Lots of times. Over the years. I've always thought it was proof positive you were nuts."

"I'm not nuts. I'm not nearly logical enough to be nuts. Get those pictures and let's go see Andrechev."

Gregor popped his door open and climbed out of the car. He hated bucket seats. Jackman got out on the driver's side and carefully locked up. Jackman was always careful about cars. The only reason he didn't park them across two spaces was because he knew how angry it got people and how prone angry people were to scraping the sharp edges of their car keys across the paint of offending cars. Jackman put his notebook back in the inside pocket of his coat. He got the pictures out and held them in his hand.

"Okay," he said. "Here they are. If he doesn't identify any of them, we're screwed."

"Don't worry about it," Gregor said.

He was right too. They went down to the far end of the next block where Krystof Andrechev had his newsstand and, less than three minutes later, came out again, with a positive identification. Andrechev made the identification so quickly, he didn't even have time for his usual struggle with the language. Jackman laid the pictures down across the counter, one right after the other. As soon as Kathi Mittendorf's picture went down, Andrechev picked it up.

"That one," he said.

To Gregor, all the pictures looked more or less alike, except the one of Susan, which was there only in case he was wrong about which of the two women Harridan used to throw his smoke screens. Jackman put the rest of the pictures down on the counter and insisted on Krystof looking at them all. Krystof looked, but he didn't change his mind. He pointed again and again at Kathi Mittendorf, as if he'd memorized her face.

"It is not a thing you forget," he said, "when a woman comes and puts a gun down in front of you and is not for robbing you."

Jackman picked the pictures up again. Gregor thanked Krystof Andrechev. Jackman and Gregor went outside.

"Now what?" Jackman asked. "You want to go out to see Kathi Mittendorf again?"

"Yes," Gregor told him. "Absolutely. But I want to make one more stop along the way."

"As long as it isn't a stop at the zoo," Jackman said. "If it is, I'm going to be very tempted to have you locked up."

Gregor said nothing to that, and got back into Jackman's car. It felt good to be doing something, anything, that was not brooding on the evils of human nature.

3

Gregor Demarkian had no sense of direction, and he never drove, so explaining to John Jackman how to find Henry Barden's town house could have been a challenge. It wasn't because Jackman had been a beat cop in Philadelphia before he'd been a detective there—and in other places—and before he'd risen to the exalted heights of commissioner of police. It also wasn't difficult to find because it was not an obscure address.

"Australian Aborigines have heard of Rittenhouse Square," Jackman said, as he pulled the car into an open non-spot only feet from Henry Barden's front door. Gregor guessed they were more in the hydrant's territory than outside of it. "Who is this guy, anyway?"

"Somebody I used to know at the Bureau. Do you realize you're illegally parked?"

"I'm on official police business." Jackman punched the side of his fist against the glove compartment to open it and got out his police parking card. He hung it over the back of his rearview mirror. "Knew in the Bureau, how? He was a special agent or somebody you picked up for bank fraud?"

"He was an analyst with a specialty in subversive groups."

"Oh, marvelous. Subversive groups. You know how I feel about the FBI and their subversive groups. They thought Martin Luther King was the head of a subversive group."

"Yes, I know, I agree with you. Henry Barden would agree with you. That's why he ended up quitting. However, he does know a lot about how to analyze and investigate nut groups, real ones. And I see him on and off since we've both been retired. And he's here and is willing to help and probably spent last night drowned in America on Alert paper, so would you like to talk to him or do you want to wait in the car while I do?"

Jackman got out. Gregor got out too, and as he did he saw the door of the small town house open and Henry Barden, short and round and cheery-faced, step out.

"How does a retired FBI agent afford a place like this in Rittenhouse Square?" Jackman asked.

"Family money," Gregor said. Then he sprinted a little to get to Henry in the doorway.

"Gregor," Henry said. "Good to see you. This must be your Mr. Jackman. I'd be dead under the paper, except that Cameron agreed to help me out. You've met Cameron, haven't you, Gregor? He came to pick me up that time we went to lunch near Independence Hall."

"I've met Cameron," Gregor said.

A young man appeared behind Henry Barden in the doorway, tall and elegant and aristocratic in the extreme, like one of those pictures of the moles in MI-5 at the end of the Kim Philby affair. Henry Barden smiled. "Mr. Jackman, this is Cameron Reed, my partner. Mr. Jackman is commissioner of police for the city of Philadelphia."

"How do you do?" Cameron said. He did not have a British accent.

"Come in, both of you," Henry Barden said. "This really has been very interesting, Gregor. I've got to thank you for sending it my way. I don't know if Gregor told you, Mr. Jackman, but since my retirement, I've made something of a hobby of collecting the really far-out conspiracy groups. I probably know more about most of them than the federal government does. It makes me nervous sometimes. Some of them are very paranoid."

"Some of them are very violent," Cameron said.

"Yes, yes. I know. Some of them are violent. But most of them aren't. Most of them are just confused, I guess. And fearful. And addicted to magical thinking. Why do you think that is, that so many people are addicted to magical thinking?"

"Because so many people find life hard," Cameron said, "and can't see any way out of their difficulties."

"He's a novelist," Henry said. "A published one."

"That's just to indicate that I'm *not* some pathetic case he picked up and decided to call his protégé," Cameron said.

They had been proceeding into the town house all this time, down a long narrow hall next to a steep flight of steps, to the kitchen at the back. Gregor stepped into the kitchen and saw that the large table at its center was full of papers. Some of them were copies of *The Harridan Report*. Gregor was impressed that Henry had been able to get so many on such short notice. Some of them were printed pages of what looked like something Henry had done himself on the computer.

"Sit down, sit down," Henry said. "I'll make coffee. Let me make a little room here. You asked me when it started, and what it's been doing, and I think I can give you a timetable."

"Good," Gregor said. He found a chair and sat down. There was no debris on the chairs. Jackman found a chair and sat down too.

Henry did something to the large coffeemaker. Then he came to the table and sat down himself. "Now," he said. "The first you see of Michael Harridan was two and a half years ago, almost exactly. That's when the Web site went up, and two weeks later, I found the first notice I could find of *The Harridan Report* going out in the mail. In case you want to know, there's no mention of Harridan before that in any of the other groups. Which is very unusual. In fact, it's nearly unheard of. Most of these guys belong to one or the other of the established groups before they set out on their own. It's a classic case of progressive delusion, for some of them—"

"Only some?" Jackman said. "What about the rest?"

Henry Barden smiled faintly. "For a small segment of the population, it's simple fraud. There's a fair amount of money to be made at this stuff. Oh, you won't get as rich as Bill Gates, or rich at all in any serious sense, but you can do fairly well in an upper-middle-class sort of way if you're good at spinning the theories and good at organization and willing to work hard. I do want to emphasize, though, that the out-and-out frauds are few and far between. For one thing, it's very difficult to commit to the time and energy you need to run an organization like this if you don't really believe in what you're doing. For another thing, it's fairly difficult for most people to spin the theories in a convincing way if they don't believe them. There are, of course, other people."

"What about Michael Harridan?" Gregor asked. "Would you say he's one of the other people?"

"Oh, definitely," Henry Barden said. Something was happening with the coffee. Cameron went to get it. "And it's not only that he hadn't had any presence in any of the other organizations before starting his own. For one thing, his stuff is much too precisely targeted—"

"Excuse me," Jackman said. "I've seen that stuff. It isn't targeted."

"I mean relative to the stuff these organizations put out. You see, the usual procedure is to produce a comprehensive overview of your version of the meaning of world events. Go look at the sites sometime. Quite a few of them start their explanations with the dawn of civilization. Most of them go back at least until nineteenth-century Bavaria, with the founding of the Illuminati. Did you know that? There really was an Illuminati, a group of Bavarian business and professional men who founded an offshoot of the Freemasons that lasted maybe two-dozen years. They were political radicals in the context of their time. They disappeared, but their name has proved nearly irresistible to the anti-Masonic conspiracists, and especially to the Catholic Church, which has been using them in anti-Mason propaganda for more than a century now. Although, of course, the anti-Masonic propaganda these days is much more sophisticated. You'd be surprised at how unsophisticated some of the stuff is from the late nineteenth century. Conspiracy nuts in high places. And, of course, in this country, conspiracy theories in response to rising numbers of Catholic immigrants and rising hysteria among anti-Catholic natives."

"But Michael Harridan doesn't go back that far," Gregor said.

"No." Henry Barden returned to the subject. Cameron began passing out cups of coffee. "He makes no attempt to produce a comprehensive explanation at all. He publishes *The Harridan Report*. He non-gives a few lectures—"

"What?" Jackman said.

"—and he maintains the Web site, that's it. He hasn't written a single book. He doesn't have a single publication for sale. Most of these guys have several of each. Most of them sell all kinds of things. Audiotapes, videotapes, pamphlets, books, you name it. It's like I told you. These are businesses. Their owners may be intellectually and emotionally committed, but at the end of the day they get paid for what they do and they have to get paid to keep on doing it. Michael Harridan doesn't seem to have to get paid for what he does and he isn't even trying to."

"What did you mean about giving non-lectures or whatever it was you said?" Jackman asked.

"Well," Henry said. "It's very interesting. Not only are these businesses. They're part of a circuit, a subculture with its own rules and members and events. Most of these guys give lectures to the same people in the same places. There are groups all over the country that sponsor speakers. Michael Harridan isn't on the circuit, although I'd bet he's been asked."

"Why?" Gregor said.

"Because there's a little notice up on his Web site explaining why he can't accept speaking engagements in 'outside' venues," Henry said, "which means, I'm sure, venues where he isn't in control. With any other group of people, this might have been suspicious, but we're dealing here with people who make paranoia a profession. At any rate, he doesn't accept those, but for a while he did do talks and speeches, sort of. I say sort of, because he never actually appeared at any of them. People would come in, sit down, and listen to an audiotape. That lasted for"—Henry checked his papers—"seven months. At the end of that seven-month period, what we find is that the talks are being set up by one Kathi Mittendorf, and all requests for lectures are being routed through her."

"So, do you mean to say that Kathi Mittendorf is Michael Harridan?" Jackman asked.

"No," Henry Barden said. "I think that what happened was that Michael Harridan managed to recruit Kathi Mittendorf, to get her to do things for him so that he didn't have to be physically present himself. Probably, when he first started, he would be in the audience himself when he non-gave his lectures. He'd set up and sit back and pretend to be one of the audience. Or maybe he'd stand up and say he was somebody else. But I'm also guessing that this wasn't very safe for him. My best guess here is that he had reason to be concerned that somebody could recognize him, if not at the time he started then later. He didn't want somebody seeing him as himself in the newspapers or on television and leaping up to say, 'I know that man! That's Michael Harridan!' "

"So he recruited Kathi Mittendorf and she did his scut work for him," Gregor said. "Then what?"

"Well, then he put out his newsletter," Henry said. "And that's a very interesting artifact too. Most of these things take on everybody and everything. The World Bank. The United Nations. George W. Bush. And there's some mention of that stuff in *The Harridan Report*, but not enough of it. Everything I could find, everything on the Web site, everything you gave me, ninety percent of it was targeted at Anthony Ross and his bank. Specifically, *his* bank. Not Morgan. Not Citigroup. Not Chase. Not banks in general."

"What was the other ten percent targeted at?" Gregor asked.

Henry shrugged. "Everything and nothing. The usual mix, except that you were quite right. For at least a month before the murders, there are small but persistent mentions linking the Russian Orthodox Church and the other Orthodox Churches in the Soviet Union to the KGB and the 'worldwide conspiracy for One World Government.' Etc. Armenia and the Armenian Church are mentioned directly several times."

"Wonderful," Gregor said.

"Why the Armenian Church?" Jackman said, bewildered. "What did the Armenian Church have to do with Tony Ross? What does any of this have to do with Charlotte Ross?"

"There's just one thing," Henry Barden said. "If you're right in your theories, and I'm right in mine, then he's got to get rid of Kathi Mittendorf and he's got to do it as quickly as possible. And he can't do it himself. Not now. Not under the circumstances. So—"

"So what?" Jackman said.

"So we have to get to Kathi Mittendorf," Gregor said. "But I told you that already."

FOUR

1

Ryall Wyndham knew, as well as he knew anything—better than he knew how to enter a ballroom when he was sure to be the poorest person there, or how to ride a horse, or how to shoot a rifle in a way that would make sure to not have people laughing at him—that the one thing he could not do in the situation in which he was in was to let people see him sweat. Unfortunately, ever since Annie Ross had showed up at his apartment door, he had been doing nothing but sweating, and sweating was the thing that made him most like the Italian-peasant ancestors who lurked back there in his family tree. Hell, they did more than lurk. They dominated. You could forget the genealogical chart that hung on the wall next to his desk in the corner of the living room, the one the photographers so liked to catch when they produced pictures of him for the publicity shots that would appear in the papers on the day he was due to appear on *Dateline* or *Larry King Live*. Ryall was beginning to think he should not have allowed those photographers to see him in his apartment at all. By now, they all had to be as suspicious as hell. He would be if somebody claimed to come from one of the most important families in Philadelphia but lived in a dump like this, and a messy dump at that, without so much as a glance from a cleaning lady. The one thing he wanted, the one thing that really mattered to him, was that he not have to go back to being nothing but Philadelphia's "most important" society gossip columnist. That was like being Akron's "most important" cultural reporter. Forget Katharine Hepburn. Forget the Main Line. Society was worse than dead. It had metamorphosed into an octopus of excess, and what it cared about these days was not the venerableness of family lines or the purity of generational commitment to High Culture. What it cared about was money. Thirty years ago, he would have said this was impossible. Money was a New York thing. Now he knew that, when the really rich people in the country paid any attention at all to the Main Line, they did so in the way they paid attention to old movies. They found it quaint, and somewhat endearing. It was only those people—like Tony Ross—who meant something in the great world outside, who were powerful in the institutions that were centered in New York and Berlin and London, who "counted" outside the very rarefied small circle of Old Philadelphia Families who still talked only to each other. Ryall used to think they only talked to each other because they were too careful of their associations ever to let outsiders in. He now knew they talked only to each other because nobody of any importance was interested in talking to *them*.

It was a bad idea to start thinking of Tony Ross, or especially Charlotte Deacon Ross. It made his face flush and his blood pound in his ears, as if he were the hero of a paperback thriller being chased through the city by the personification of Civic Malignity. He still hated them, though. He hated both of them. He hated Tony for thinking that he was nothing but a clown, a buffoon who need not be listened to courteously, never mind taken seriously. Not that Tony had ever been anything but courteous. Tony would have been courteous to Satan if he'd encountered him on a street corner. Tony was courteous to homeless women asking for spare change. Ryall thought it would be difficult to exaggerate the extent of that man's condescension. That was what they were all like—condescending. They talked to him as if they were talking to a child.

Still, they were better than the people like Charlotte. At least Tony had an excuse. He really was Important, in objective terms, in the real world. What had Charlotte been, but an aging postdebutante and Main Line matron, the sort of woman there were dozens of at every reunion of Agnes Irwin and the Madeira School. It was amazing the way these women took on their husbands' auras as if they deserved them. *My husband runs a very important international investment bank, therefore I deserve more respect and deference than the president of the United States.* Unlike Tony, Charlotte was not always courteous. Ryall would have thought her also less condescending, except that she wasn't. She was very out-front and straightforward about her condescension, and her contempt. There had been times when he had wanted to take her neck between his hands and snap it off—except, of course, that he couldn't have done it. He was not strong. He was no danger to anybody without a weapon in his hand, whether it was a pen or a gun. But that didn't work either. He couldn't write what he wanted about them. If he did, they would do to him what people very much like them had done to Truman Capote. They'd cut him off, and then where would he be? He wondered if it had been like this for the great social chroniclers of the past, the "powerful" columnists who had played right-hand man to people like Mrs. Astor and Mrs. Vanderbilt. He was willing to bet that it had been exactly the same. They would have been careful when they were required to be careful. They would have flattered and attended and lied to keep their place. Ryall didn't understand why people like Charlotte and Annie were so surprised at the kind of things they stumbled on in *The Harridan Report*. He was sure half the country secretly thought the kinds of things that were written there. They might not believe in an alien race of reptilians who only pretended to be human, but they did believe in a conspiracy, because there was one. There was a conspiracy of the already important to make sure the unimportant never forgot their place.

For no reason he understood, he had a vision of Tony lying there on the ground with the bullet in his head, the blood on the sidewalk, the perfect aristocratic face half gone. The result was a sexual desire so immediate and intense, it almost made him stagger. The next thing he saw was the girl, the one he had picked up that night, but only that night. He never liked to have them more than once. Once he had seen them bending over his penis, struggling to stuff it as far down their throats as Linda Lovelace had done and still not gag—once he had seen that, he never wanted them again. He couldn't take them seriously. Somebody ought to shoot Annie Ross, he thought. She was interfering in things she didn't understand. None of these women understood. They were too old for any man to be interested in them as anything but broodmares. Ryall wasn't interested in a broodmare. He couldn't afford one. When he could afford one, he would get one. Then he would be like all these guys, the ones at the Society parties, the ones who provided the talking heads on television shows. He'd have his broodmare and his eleven-year-old doxy on the side, set up decently in private, so that he didn't have to run the risk of exposure every time he wanted to get laid. Yes, somebody ought to kill Annie Ross. Somebody ought to blast her head to pieces, just like Tony's, just like Charlotte's. He knew exactly how Charlotte's head had come apart there on the drive in front of her front door, the blood and skin and bone falling over the thick molded cement rim of the planter near the door, the wind blowing cold wet darkness through her hair. He hoped she had lain there writhing in her own blood for many long minutes and only expired when the ambulance arrived. He hoped the same thing happened to Annie Ross, whose only purpose in life was to destroy men for doing what was natural to them.

The phone rang. He straightened up a little and tried to breathe. He was sweating all over now. He could feel wet heavy sweat soaked into the back of his jacket. His hands were so slick, he had to wipe them against the knees of his pants in order to pick up the phone. He was going to have to change all his clothes before he went out. He was going to have to take a shower. What if she had been lying to him? What if she had gone to the papers already, or the police? What if everybody in town knew what he did in his car in the darkness of the early evenings before he had to go to another party or another opening or another wedding? They all did it too. He knew that. They all did it too, but they wouldn't admit it.

He took one more deep breath and picked up the phone. He was sure he was going to hear Matt Drudge at least, somebody who specialized in real gossip, somebody with the clout to get the news out on an international scale. They all said they didn't read Matt Drudge, but they did. They read him first. Ryall wondered if he could be Matt Drudge himself. He knew he couldn't. It was the Porky Pig thing, again. No matter what he did, he still looked like Porky Pig. Sometimes he expected Warner Brothers to sue him for copyright infringement.

He picked up the phone. It wasn't Matt Drudge. It wasn't the police. It wasn't even Annie Ross. It was only Nick Bradenton, sounding exasperated.

"Ryall? Ryall, where are you? You owe me a column. It should have been here an hour ago. Are you paying any attention to what we pay you for anymore at all?"

"I've been paying attention," Ryall said defensively. His chest hurt. This was what was wrong with letting himself get spooked. He got breathless. His voice squeaked. "I've turned in the best columns of my career over the last couple of weeks. I've even provided you with real news. You can't fault me for that."

"You've been late four out of the last six days," Nick said. "I know you like going to New York. And I know you like going to Atlanta. And I know you like seeing your face on the television screen. But if you expect to have a job here when this is over, you'd better get your act together."

"Of course I expect to have a job here," Ryall said. That was not strictly true. He expected to have the job, yes, but he did not expect to want it. He was sure it was only a matter of time before CNN would give him a spot in the same way they had once given Greta Van Susteren one. That was how these things happened. Just in case, though—in case something went wrong, in case the universe was as uneven and unfair as it had always been—it was best to play safe. "The column's done," he said. "I'll e-mail it as soon as I get off the phone."

"Yeah, well. Do that. But there's something else."

"What else?"

"There's some news. Not really news. It's not for publication just yet, if you know what I mean. We've got a source. Can you get to Anne Ross Wyler?"

"*Anybody* can get to Anne Ross Wyler," Ryall said. "She lives in that godforsaken settlement house. She doesn't even have servants."

"Well, neither do you, do you, Ryall? Our source says that she's the prime suspect out there in Lower Merion. That she killed her brother and his wife. For money, I presume, although we don't have any word on that. Maybe she's another one of those crackpot debutante Marxists. I don't know. We just want to know if you can go out there and talk to her. Get an interview about how she feels about her brother's death and that kind of thing, but be cool about it. Don't say anything that might tip her off."

"Hard news?" Ryall said, finding it difficult to breathe again. "I can't believe it. You're trusting me with hard news."

"Yeah," Nick said. "I'm not a hundred percent happy about it, if you want to know the truth."

"Oh, thank you."

"Be serious, Ryall. This is not the kind of thing you usually do. But the rest of the guys thought you'd be the best one because you know the territory and you know the woman. She's more likely to open up to you than she is to a stranger. Although, I don't know. She's always been so intensely loyal to Tony Ross. If that's been an act all these years, she can't be straight with anybody. Can you get over there right away?"

"To Adelphos House? Of course I can. How do you know she's there?"

"I don't, but that's where she usually is, isn't it? Maybe you ought to call first. There's a certain amount of hurry. We hear she's going to be picked up this evening. I have no idea why they're waiting so long. But there it is. You have to get to her before that."

"I'll get to her as soon as I get off the phone," Ryall said, wondering how long it would take him to get the hint. *Get off the phone. Get off the phone. Get off the phone.*

"You can get off the phone now," Nick said. "And send that column, ASAP."

There was a click and then a dial tone. Ryall put the phone back in the hook and stared at it. He didn't really have a column done. It was only half done. He could get it finished in, maybe, half an hour. He wondered if he would be able to concentrate on it. Maybe he should call Adelphos House first. Maybe he should stop off on the strip on his way to talk to Annie Ross. There were so many options, he didn't know what to do.

Then, abruptly, he sat down in the nearest chair and burst out laughing.

2

David Alden had always prided himself on being able to stay calm in a crisis. It was one of the things he was known for, even among the people who wanted to find some reason to get him out of the bank. And, truthfully, it wasn't that he was *un*calm, exactly. He wasn't running around in a panic. He wasn't having trouble trying to think. It was just that, since Charlotte had died, he'd been restless. It felt to him as if the things he was doing were ephemeral. There was this bank, this pre-war building with its high ceilings and marble floors and chandeliers that had to be cleaned six times a year by a company hired for just that purpose. There was Price Heaven, which was rapidly descending into the morass of an Enron scandal, with half the news stories devoted to the way in which Price Heaven's middle managers would lose all the money they'd saved for retirement if the company collapsed and its stock became worthless. There was Michael Harridan and his *Report*, which had been cluttering up his briefcase ever since that last day at Tony's house and that even now took up more of his time than it should. All he wanted was that people should start out making sense and go on making sense. He didn't want them to wander off on tangents and confusions. Sometimes it seemed to him that people operated on an entirely symbolic level. The bank was not a temple and it did not house the body of a God, living or dead, no matter what its vice presidents thought. The middle managers at Price Heaven would not be in the midst of losing their savings if they'd taken the sensible advice most of them admitted to having been given and diversified their portfolios instead of keeping everything they had in one company's paper. And as for Michael Harridan—

There were five copies of *The Harridan Report* spread out across his desk, including a copy of the one Charlotte had shown him just before she died. David didn't think he had ever known anybody, real or imaginary, as solemn and humorless as Michael Harridan. It was frightening to think of that man in the world. Maybe that was because that man wasn't in the world. He was part of all of us. He was part of the people who ran the banks and the people who hated them. He was part of the pundits and part of the audience that checked their stocks online every day at lunch when they had a little free time at the office. He had gone out to the Trade Center with Adele and looked at the rubble there. Then he'd come back to the office and found a picture on the Internet of that church that had been bombed in Philadelphia. In the end, it came down to the same thing, it all came down to the same thing, too many people taking too many things seriously when they didn't mean anything at all. Nothing meant anything at all. You worked and worked. You stayed up late and came in early and canceled dates and family dinners. You did all the things you were supposed to do and then it ended here, with you feeling like a piece of tired fruit suspended in Jell-O.

That was it, David thought. He wasn't feeling panicked. He wasn't losing his head in a crisis. He was simply passing into another phase, where nothing was urgent except the need to shut out all the noise that cluttered up his life.

Next to the copies of *The Harridan Report* on his desk

were the summary sheets of his report on Price Heaven. The type on their pages was smaller and less bold than that of Michael Harridan's rag, and far more difficult to read. Here was the skinny on Price Heaven: It was an old and venerable company, probably too old and too venerable. Its image was antiquated. Its facilities were Stone-Aged. Two years ago, it had come to the bank with a cash shortfall and a need to modernize. Six months after that, it had begun to hemorrhage money. It was still hemorrhaging money, although not quite in the same way as it had been, since the bank had stopped all payments to creditors, even itself. Now it was only hemorrhaging money in its stock price. He could write the facts down in a hundred million different ways, but they would always come down to the same thing, and they would always result in the realization that there was nothing anybody could do now about Price Heaven. The board had a decent argument when they said he should have seen this coming when he first recommended the loan. There was nobody better suited to seeing it coming besides himself. He had a decent argument when he said that he had not been responsible for granting the loan, and that it wasn't his recommendation, but Tony's, that had swayed the board. It wasn't an argument they wanted to listen to, because Tony was dead. He had this terrible, ugly urge to tell the truth, the kind of urge he knew he must never give in to, if he expected to have a life when the dust settled and Price Heaven had finally gone out of business.

There was a knock on the door and Adele came in, bustling. "They're almost ready downstairs," she said. "Are you absolutely sure you want to hold this in the lobby? I know the conference room is too small, but that lobby looks so much like a stage set for a Depression movie about evil bankers. I wish you'd let me get somebody to take down the chandelier."

"It would be a waste of money to take down the chandelier," David said. "And the lobby is the only place big enough. We won't be completely screwing up anybody who wants to come in and out, will we?"

"No, of course not. We've got one newsstand that's going to be out of business for the duration. And there are a lot of people down there. That surprises me a little, do you know? I didn't think the Price Heaven collapse was that big a story."

"Tony's dead," David said. "Charlotte's dead. Maybe the press has finally made a few connections."

"Do you think they're dead because of Price Heaven?" Adele asked. "That doesn't seem right to me. I mean, what did Charlotte have to do with Price Heaven?"

David gestured to the copies of *The Harridan Report* on his desk. "She didn't have anything to do with it rationally. These people aren't rational."

"Oh, that thing. I found some of those in the wastebasket a little while ago and read them. Complete lunacy. Is that what the police think, that Tony and Charlotte were murdered by somebody like that?"

"I don't know what the police think."

"No, of course you don't. I don't know why I should think you would. Maybe it's just that I always think you know everything. Are you *sure* you're all right? You've been behaving in the oddest way all day, as if you were sleep-walking. And with a press conference due to go off in less than fifteen minutes—"

"I'll be fine with the press conference," David said.

The phone rang. They both stared at it. David turned away and stared out the window. Adele's voice was a low hum, sprightly and not particularly solemn. She was talking to somebody she knew and didn't mind hearing from.

He was thinking about the Trade Center again when she tapped him on the shoulder. He wondered how many people who worked in the financial district stopped in the middle of their day and thought about the Trade Center. He wished they would clear the rubble and put the things back up. No memorials. No compromises. Put them back *up*.

"It's Annie," Adele said, holding the flat of her hand over the receiver. "I said I'd see if you'd talk to her. If it's too much with the press conference so close—"

"No, no," David said. "I'll talk to her."

"Good. Maybe she'll cheer you up. I'm going to go make sure we've covered all the details."

"Thank you," David said.

Adele handed over the phone. She stood up and straightened her skirt and left the room. David stared at the phone for a second.

"David?" Annie's voice drifted out at him, sounding tinny.

He put the receiver to his ear. "Hello, Annie. I've been thinking about you."

"I thought you might have been."

He didn't know what to say to that. He really was like a fruit suspended in Jell-O. "Sorry. I seem to be having an out-of-it sort of day."

"That's bad news. Tony used to say that people on his level could never afford to be out of it, even for an hour."

"I'm not on his level."

"You are for all practical purposes, aren't you? The Price Heaven mess seems to have been dumped in your lap as if nobody else had ever had any responsibility. Not that you necessarily dislike that. I know you've always wanted responsibility."

"I've got to go give a press conference in a few minutes," David said. "Exactly what it is they expect me to say is completely beyond me. There's nothing to be said that hasn't been said already. A million times. In a million other meltdowns. Do you remember the Kmart bankruptcy?"

"Not really. It's not the kind of thing I pay attention to, David."

"I know. Never mind. I feel the way you do when you wake up in the wrong part of your sleep cycle. Like I'm not quite connected. All I want to do is go home and go to bed for a week."

"Maybe you should."

"I can't. You know why I can't. We seem to be in nonstop crisis mode here today. We've been that way for a couple of weeks, now. Do you know what I was thinking about? I was thinking about what it was like in those five days after the attack on the Towers, when the Stock Exchange was closed. On one level, it was completely insane. We couldn't get into the building. We still had deals and relationships that couldn't be neglected. Some of our clients were willing to cut us a little slack, but a lot of them weren't. But the thing is, even so, it was the calmest period I can remember in all my time at the bank. It was as if we'd all been stripped down to the skin, and nothing mattered except what really mattered. Do you understand that?"

"I always told you it was a bad idea for you to stay in that job."

"I know."

"I always told you you'd end up regretting it. And you will, you know. If you don't already."

"I don't know if *regret* is the word I'd use."

"I'll let you go to your press conference, then. I didn't call for any reason. I just wanted to hear the sound of your voice. I was wondering how you were feeling."

"I'm feeling fine, I guess. There's nothing in particular wrong. There's nothing in particular right. You know how things are."

"Yes," Annie said. "I know how things are. I'll let you go now, David."

The phone buzzed. David pulled it away from his ear and stared at it. He thought that was the oddest conversation he had ever had. It might never have happened. It was like talking to a ghost.

He took all the copies of *The Harridan Report* spread across his desk, wadded them up into a single ball, and threw them in the wastebasket.

3

Annie Ross Wyler hung up the phone and stood for a long moment in the shelter of the pay phone cubicle, doing nothing. For a moment, she wondered what had happened to phone booths. One of her strongest childhood memories was of being let loose in a Woolworth's in Central Philadelphia while her mother was otherwise engaged at the jeweler's. Mademoiselle Chirac, who had been imported only a year before to teach French to both Annie and Tony, was supposed to give them a supervised afternoon in some park. Annie didn't remember which one, or where it was. Mademoiselle Chirac hadn't liked parks, any more than she'd liked American cheese, American television programs, or American wine. Her life was one long keening complaint, punctuated at unpredictable intervals by young men whom she seemed to think very little of but could not live without. Annie knew what was going on from the beginning: the clothes that were never put back quite the way they should have been; the lipstick smeared along the curve of the upper lip; the whispered calls in the middle of the night to plan trysts just out of sight of wherever the children would be. This afternoon, Mademoiselle Chirac was sitting at the fountain counter in the back while Annie and Tony ran wild—although, being Annie and Tony, their wildness probably looked like good manners to most of the nearby adults. Tony had found the telephone booths first, a whole line of them, all empty.

I'm no longer making any sense at all, Annie thought. She stepped away from the non-booth whatever-it-was-called— they had to call these contraptions something. She ought to ask. She had AT&T stock. They would have to answer—and looked up and down the nearly empty street. It had to be close to noon. She could have checked her watch, but her head felt too heavy. Her eyelids felt like lead. She went back to the car she had parked on the curb and took a parking ticket off the windshield. That must have happened while her back was turned. She didn't really care about the parking ticket. She'd always had more money than she knew what to do with. Now she not only had it, but couldn't think of what she wanted it for. Her whole life felt upside down and sideways, all at once. Maybe she would give a lot of it to Patsy Lennon and the girls like her, the ones she knew personally, just to see what they would do with it. Maybe she would give it to the Freedom from Religion Foundation, since she knew exactly what they would do with it, and she was in something like a fighting mood. She wondered what it would be like to live like an ordinary person for real, instead of just playing pretend at it, what it would be like to have no money to spend rather than to refuse to spend it. That didn't make much sense either, but it all went together on one level or another. It didn't help that the money was in trusts, where she could not touch the principal.

She got in behind the steering wheel and popped open the glove compartment. She took her latest bumper sticker out of there and propped it up on the windshield. *Religion Stops a Thinking Mind*, it said. She never left it when the car was parked, because when she did people vandalized the car. She got out the street map of Philadelphia and laid it out across the wheel. Then she gave up. She couldn't read maps without a magnifying glass anymore. Maybe she ought to spend her money on that new eye surgery that was supposed to restore your sight to what it had been before you'd reached middle age. She hated the thought of anybody or anything coming near her eyes.

The magnifying glass was in the pocket of her jacket. She never carried a pocketbook. In the neighborhoods she frequented, pocketbooks were an invitation to purse snatchers. Still, she thought, she'd trust herself with the pimps and the drug dealers and the teenaged whores with fewer reservations than she would trust herself with the kind of people she'd grown up with. Tony was the last of the good ones of them, and he was gone. She ran the magnifying glass over the map. She found the street. She checked it again. She took the tip of her fingernail—not much; mostly bitten off—and tapped down along the broken lines until she thought she'd found the right block. Then, just to make sure, she got the copy of *The Harridan Report* she'd brought with her and looked at the bottom on the back, where the address was. Her back ached. Her head ached. She wanted to lie down right here on the seat and close her eyes and sleep for a week.

Instead, she got the key into the ignition and the car started. She looked carefully into her rearview mirror and saw that there was no traffic coming in her direction. There was no traffic coming in either direction. She knew where the map said she was, but she didn't actually know where she was. She had never been in this part of the city before. It looked pleasant enough. There were a lot of narrow, tallish brick houses. There were trees. She put on her turn signal for the sake of the people who were not there to worry about what she would do next, and eased out onto the road.

Four blocks south, six blocks east, two blocks north—she had to be careful about the dead ends and the one-way streets. Why were there always so many dead-end streets in Philadelphia? She turned on the radio and caught NPR doing classical music. It was what she always listened to, but it wasn't what she wanted to hear. Why did the announcers on classical radio programs always sound as if they were announcers at a funeral? Was it really necessary to whisper the news that you were about to play Beethoven's *Emperor's Concerto*? Beethoven would have known better. His music was triumphal, the rock and roll of its day. She punched buttons but didn't come up with much she recognized. There was a lot of rap—hip-hop, they called it now. She'd never been able to get that straight. She punched more buttons and came to music she did recognize, but it didn't make her feel any better. The Beach Boys were playing "Surfer Girl." She wasn't sure, but she thought most of the Beach Boys were dead. Two of the Beatles were.

She made the next turn and began to slow up. The neighborhood was a little shabbier here than it had been where she started. She was getting close to the fringes of the city, where the landscape was neither city nor suburb. The houses here were not brick, but frame. Most of them were double- or triple-deckers. All of them had porches. None of them had been painted recently enough. Every once in a while, there was a storefront: convenience groceries; newspapers and magazines; hardware. In another few blocks, the pawnshops would start. The tattoo parlors would come quickly afterward.

She checked the address again. She had to drive nearly blind to do it, with the magnifying glass in one hand and *The Harridan Report* plastered against the steering wheel. She threw the magnifying glass and the newsletter down on the seat next to her and kept driving. She didn't have to check the address again. She knew the address. She knew the voice that was on the other end of that phone number too. She'd called more than twice in the last twenty-four hours. She'd called and hung up as soon as the woman began speaking, which was not polite, and had probably made the poor woman paranoid as hell, but she couldn't think of anything to say. She didn't know where to start. She didn't even know what she wanted to say.

She found an open space at the curb and pulled into it. It was almost certainly not a legal parking space, and she would get another ticket while her back was turned or she was safely out of sight in the house with this woman who might or might not have the answers she was looking for. She got out of the car and locked it, carefully. There was nothing in it to steal, and it was older than most cars that would interest car thieves, but you could never know. She put her keys in her pocket and walked back a little to the walk of the house at number 244. She went up the walk and stared at the front door with its black paint and shiny brass knocker. David was in New York. She knew that without question. She had called him at his office and on his office number and talked to him. It was a good thing that this was not a triple-decker house. She didn't know what she'd do if she had to put up with nosy neighbors.

She pressed the buzzer button and waited. She heard someone opening locks on the other side of the door, three or four of them, their bolts and tumbrils thudding open one after the other. All she needed was the answer to a single question, and she was sure, when she had it, that she would feel like a fool. This was not the sort of thing sensible people did. This was not the sort of thing they thought.

The door swung open, and Annie blinked. She didn't think she had ever seen anyone quite like this woman before in her life. She was a middle-aged woman, with all the sag and bag that entailed for someone who did not spend hours a day taking care of herself—but Annie was a middle-aged woman too. That wouldn't have bothered her. What bothered her was the hair, bright blond, almost lemon, and piled high on her head and falling down to her shoulders in giggling cascades of curls, teased up and splayed out, beyond Big Hair, almost something with a life of its own. What bothered her was the makeup too, which was much too vivid and much too thick. The red of the lipstick was the red of the nose on Bozo the Clown. The blue of the eye shadow was the blue of a computer screen right after a systems crash. It was like looking at a bad painting. Annie felt she had to be staring.

"I'm looking for Miss Mittendorf," she said, hesitating. "Or Mrs. Mittendorf, possibly. I'm sorry. I got your address—"

"I'm Kathi Mittendorf," Kathi Mittendorf said. "I've been waiting for you."

Then, just as Annie was about to say that there had to be some mistake, she hadn't said she was coming, nobody could be waiting for her, Kathi Mittendorf raised the gun. It was a gun-gun, not a rifle, and it was huge. Annie didn't think she'd ever seen a hand weapon that large, not even in the hands of the men who sometimes came to Adelphos House to get their hookers back.

"Come inside," Kathi Mittendorf said.

She's going to kill me, Annie thought.

And then, stepping through the front door as Kathi Mittendorf pulled it shut behind her, she saw that Kathi had apparently killed somebody else.

At least, there was the dead body of a woman on the sofa.

FIVE

1

All the way across town from Henry Barden's place, John Jackman kept reminding Gregor Demarkian that this was no longer his job.

"The whole point of ending up behind a desk," he would say, paused at a stoplight that was green, but of no interest to the driver immediately ahead of him, "was not to be shot at anymore, and I have a distinct feeling that by the end of this mess, I'm going to end up getting shot at. And where? Are we going out to Bryn Mawr?"

"No," Gregor said. "Do I sound like I'm giving you directions to Bryn Mawr?"

"How would you know if you weren't? You've got the sense of direction of belly-button lint. Let me try to rephrase this. Do you know who killed Steve Bridge?"

"Yes. So do you."

"Not that I can tell," Jackman said. "But Steve Bridge happens to be the only dead body we've got—or the only one connected to you—within the city limits at the moment. If we're going off to confront the murderer of Tony and Charlotte Ross, then I shouldn't be here, because it's none of my business. I remember when I was working as a detective, Gregor. I did not appreciate having outsiders come in and muck up my case, and your Detective Margiotti won't appreciate it either."

"He understands the problem. I called him. He'll be there."

"Where?"

"At Kathi Mittendorf's house."

"Why should he come to Kathi Mittendorf's house?"

"Because I asked him to," Gregor said, "and because it gets him where he wants to go."

"Even though Kathi Mittendorf didn't kill Tony or Charlotte Ross? Or Steve Bridge, either, I take it."

"She didn't kill anybody," Gregor said. "But I disagree with Henry on one very specific point. I think she saw who did."

"She was a witness to the killings," Jackman said.

"No," Gregor said. "She's seen Michael Harridan. Face to face. I know what Henry's getting at, but I don't think Harridan could have done what he's done if he hadn't let at least one person see him in the flesh. My guess is, she's seen him more than once too, although of course not any more than he could help it."

"Of course. You think you're making sense."

"I am making sense," Gregor said. "Look, let's say you wanted to steal a lot of money. I mean really a lot of money, not just a lot of money the way most people think of it. Let's say you wanted to steal thirty million dollars."

"Are you joking?"

"Of course I'm not joking," Gregor said. "What have we been hearing in the newspapers every day? What have we been hearing on the television news? When they aren't talking about the murders, what are they talking about?"

"I don't know. The Middle East? George Bush?"

Gregor wanted to hit something. "Price Heaven. We've been hearing about Price Heaven. Yet another icon company meltdown. First Enron. Then Kmart. Now Price Heaven. And what do we hear about Price Heaven? We hear that there's thirty million dollars missing from their operation—except we don't hear that it's missing. We hear that it was hidden. Do you notice that?"

"Maybe it was hidden," Jackman said. "I don't trust those

guys and you shouldn't either. I mean, look at Enron. They were hiding everything known to humans and siphoning money out of the business like it was lemonade."

"Yes, they were, but if you'd paid much attention to that story, you'd have realized that it took them several years to do it. Look, I don't know this for certain, because I'm not a forensic accountant and I don't know how to do that kind of paperwork, but with any luck the Lower Merion police will have access to one, or the city of Philadelphia will loan them one, because what I think happened was this. Price Heaven came to Tony Ross's bank almost two years ago. David Alden did the legwork on the loan they wanted, and made the recommendation to the board to take that loan—"

"How do you know?"

"He told me," Gregor said. "For goodness sake, you could find out the same thing by paying attention to CNN. David Alden did the legwork, and eventually he took over the management of the account. That's been on CNN too. My guess is, Price Heaven had a problem going in, bad accounting practices, leaking money, that kind of thing, but not a bad problem. And that, you see, gave David Alden his shot."

"So that's it? David Alden is our murderer? Are you nuts? When would he find the time? He's one of those idiots who commutes from here to Manhattan. Of all the self-satisfied, stupid pieces of snobbery—"

"Listen," Gregor said. "He's the only one who could have done it. Who could have killed Tony Ross, I mean. Because he's the only one of all the people who were there that night, besides the family, who had the run of the house. He could go upstairs to the second floor on his own and without permission and nobody would think anything of it. And that's the trick. The problem isn't who could have fired off a gun at Tony Ross in the middle of all that security. The security wasn't that good. People kept telling us that, but we all—you and me and Margiotti and Tackner as well—we all kept seeing a neon sign in our heads that said 'first lady.'

The first lady was coming, so security had to be tight. But it wasn't tight. It would have gotten tighter once the first lady arrived, but it was still early. The only people who were actually there yet were the people who were setting up and a few of the kind who have to get there first and stay until it's over, like Ryall Wyndham. But David Alden was there. He was there right after the shots were fired. He's on the list of the first set of interviews. And nobody thought anything of it."

"Why should they?" Jackman asked. They were now in one of those parts of the city that were all overpasses and four-lane roadways and chain-link fences. "It would make sense to me that Alden would be there. Why wouldn't it make sense to you? He was Tony Ross's assistant, wasn't he? Some kind of second in command?"

"A protégé, mostly," Gregor said. "Yes, I know. And that was the opportunity and the problem at once. Alden had complete control of the Price Heaven account, and that meant of Price Heaven's ready cash. He and Tony Ross were the only two people in a position to make use of that for personal gain. It's always possible that we'll find that Tony Ross was in on it, but I doubt it. He had too much money of his own. Thirty million doesn't mean as much to a billionaire three times over as it means to the ordinary guy on the street. I should have listened to Bennis. She said something the first or second day about how there were always people around the rich who weren't rich themselves but managed to live as if they were, and nobody knew how they did it. But you know, that's not quite true, either."

"I can't believe you think Bennis told you something that isn't true," Jackman said.

"I don't mean she lied," Gregor said. "I mean it's not quite true that they live as if they were rich. What they do is appear in public as if they live as if they were rich. That's Ryall Wyndham's whole thing. He has great clothes—"

"Too bad he looks so awful in them. He looks like Porky Pig, Gregor, have you noticed that?"

Gregor ignored this. "The thing is, I never went out to

Wyndham's apartment to see him, but I do have the address written down. It's not a good address. I know that neighborhood and I know the apartments you can get there. If his place is like everybody else's, it's a dump. He really can't afford to live as if he were rich, so he doesn't."

"So?"

"So," Gregor said, "David Alden does. Do you want to see the addresses I have down for him? The apartment in New York probably belongs to the bank. That's not a problem. But he's got a place in Rittenhouse Square, and that isn't cheap. It doesn't come close to cheap. So what's he paying for it with?"

"Family money?"

"According to Bennis, no," Gregor said. "That's how we got onto that discussion about living as if you were rich. His family used to have money. He has an old Philadelphia name. He's gone to the right prep school and the right college and all the rest of it. He's got the right job, and he gets paid well. But if he's keeping up that place on straight salary, I'll almost guarantee you that he's living paycheck to paycheck and that he's probably in debt. That's something you can check out, or Lower Merion can."

"Do you ever do the conventional thing and arrive at theories after you've collected the evidence?" Jackman said. "You're going to get yourself and whoever you're working for in a lot of trouble one of these days."

"Only if I try to make them act on what I don't know yet, which I won't. He's an interesting man, David Alden. You should talk to him sometime."

"If you're right about all this, I'll get my chance."

"No, you won't. You'll talk to him through his lawyer, and you won't get the measure of the man at all. But he is an interesting man. In a way, it's a shame he's a completely venal one."

"That's always a shame, Gregor."

"Sometimes it's more of a shame than it is at other times. Even if, as is usually the case, he isn't as smart as he thinks he is. He could have gotten away with it, you know. Don't think it's impossible to get away with financial fraud on a major scale. It happens all the time. If he'd been careful not to tip Price Heaven into bankruptcy, the chances are pretty damned good that nobody would ever have caught up to him. On one level, they're all alike though, these guys. The need for money is infinite. Anyway, once the bankruptcy was inevitable, Tony Ross would have been required to step in and oversee the proceedings. He was David Alden's superior. He would also, most probably, have realized without too much trouble that something was fishy about that account."

"So David Alden killed him. Fine. Why didn't he wait for a more opportune moment? Why not catch Ross at the golf club or somewhere? They had to be alone sometime, didn't they?" Jackman asked.

"Of course they did," Gregor said, "but David Alden knew he was going to kill Tony Ross from the first. He's been setting up that murder for over a year. That's why he became Michael Harridan. Don't you get it?"

"No," Jackman said.

They had reached a neighborhood of small frame houses. Gregor tapped on Jackman's shoulder.

"We're here," he said. "I'll go on explaining a little later."

"If you go on explaining, my head will explode," Jackman said.

He eased the car up against the curb. Gregor started to get out before the car stopped moving. It was a trick he had seen other people make look easy. It nearly got him killed. He caught his balance and stood up. He looked at the number on the house just ahead of him and started walking north.

"Right up here," he said to Jackman coming up behind him. "Let's only hope we got here before he did. Because I don't know how he's going to do it, but I do know—"

He had gone three houses up and stopped a moment to look at the sagging porch and the thin white lace curtains in the windows. He was not thinking of anything except the fact that the small black car parked up against the curb near the house looked familiar.

"Listen," he said, turning back to look at Jackman.

That's when the bullet caught him in the back of his right shoulder.

2

It occurred to him, falling to the ground in what felt like slow motion, that he had never been shot before. Not in the Bureau, not even in the army, although that might not count, since he had never been much of anywhere but the American South while he was in the army. Why was it that so many army bases were in the South, and in the rural South at that? Didn't it make more sense to protect, say, New York City or Washington, D.C.? Would the hijackers have been able to hit the Pentagon if Fort Bragg had been in Chevy Chase instead of wherever it was, which Gregor could not remember, because he was in an impossible amount of pain. He couldn't remember ever having hurt this badly in his life. He couldn't remember ever having felt so disembodied, either. His head was occupying space where his body was not. Or something. Or something. He wanted to scream, but his mind was not connected to his lungs.

He felt himself being pulled along the ground, and that hurt too, but it was a long way away. A moment later, he realized that he was lying next to a car wheel. The big black tire had treads that were much too worn for safety. He ought to leave a note for the owners. He could put it under the windshield, the way you put notes there when you'd dented somebody in a parking lot and couldn't wait around for however many hours it might be before the somebody got back. He was making no sense at all. He was listening for the sound of another gunshot. He didn't hear one.

"I can't be dead," he said, out loud. "I'm too cold."

There was movement beside him, and then the sight of a knee, encased in good black wool, far too thin.

"You're not dead," Jackman said. "I'm calling everybody on the planet. I'm not armed."

"Aren't policemen supposed to be armed?"

"The commissioner usually isn't."

Gregor closed his eyes, and then opened them again. It was very unpleasant closing his eyes. It made him want to throw up. Jackman's phone made those beeping and booping noises cell phones make when they're dialed, if *dialed* was the word you used for cell phones, when it really meant something that could only be done on a rotary phone, and rotary phones were out of date. He had gone beyond making no sense. He was no longer connected to linear thought.

"Listen," he said.

"Shut up," Jackman said. "You're not going to do yourself any good by wearing yourself out. They'll bring an ambulance. Bennis is going to kill me."

"Listen," Gregor said again. "Don't let them kill her. The police, when they come. Don't let them kill her."

"Armed standoffs are armed standoffs, Gregor, you know that. We don't kill anybody if we don't have to, but sometimes we have to."

"It's what he wants," Gregor said. Somewhere down there there was a point. Gregor even knew what it was. He could see it resting at the bottom, the way a cask of treasure rested at the bottom of a murky ocean pool. He just needed to bring it up. "He has to kill her," he said, "and he can't do it on his own. Don't you see that? This isn't his territory. This isn't someplace he's comfortable with and besides, he knows people are watching him. He knows. So he's got to find a way to kill her, and he wants to get the police to do it for him."

"That's quite a speech. When you die from loss of blood, will your ghost come back and protect me from Bennis?"

"Die from loss of blood," Gregor said. Then he looked down at his body—the body that didn't feel like his anymore; the body that seemed to be nothing and belong to nobody—and there was blood coming out of his shoulder. He tried to think about that. There might be an artery there somewhere. He couldn't remember. He didn't think the bullet had hit it if it was there, because his suit jacket was covered with blood but it wasn't pumping out of him like a spring. He could not keep himself thinking along any particular path to any particular point. His mind would not do it.

"I don't really think you're going to die from loss of blood," Jackman said.

In the distance, there were sirens—but not very far in the distance. They got louder and louder, and the worse they got, the worse they were for his headache.

"Listen," he said again, trying to shout. It didn't work. His voice came out in a croak. "Don't let them kill her. She's all you've got. If she dies, you'll never be able to tie him to America on Alert, or to Steve Bridge. Got that?"

"We'll discuss it later."

"It's the only direct evidence you've got," Gregor insisted, and by now he felt like he was swimming through a sea of noise. "Everything else is circumstantial. Don't let them kill her."

The sirens were right there now, right on top of them. Gregor felt the heat of the first vehicle before he saw it, which wasn't odd, since he was still lying flat on his back. He tried to sit up. Jackman pushed him down. He tried to sit up again. Nobody stopped him, because there was nobody to stop him. Jackman was off talking to somebody else. He got himself more or less upright and looked around at what was now a sea of cop cars. There were uniformed officers everywhere. There were detectives too. Maybe he only thought they were detectives. His head had reattached to his body just long enough to give him a splitting headache. He wanted to stand up. He tried, and felt somebody push him down.

"What's wrong with you?" Jackman said. "You're going to kill yourself. And she's still in there, and she still has a gun."

"Do you have any liquor?"

"Of course I don't have any liquor. In my car? What do you take me for?"

"I need a shot of something serious," Gregor said.

There was a sound like a gong ringing, and Jackman ducked. "Jesus Christ," he said. "There she goes again."

Somebody else crouched down next to them, somebody Gregor didn't know, or didn't recognize, at least at the moment. "How many are there?" the somebody else said.

"I don't know," Jackman said. "I've only seen one. She may be alone."

"Susan," Gregor said.

"What?" Jackman said.

"Susan," Gregor said again.

"Oh, yeah," Jackman said. "There's two of them involved in the organization. The one we think is shooting is called Kathi Mittendorf. There's another one, though, named Susan something. You'll have to get the details later."

"No men?" the somebody said.

"No," Gregor said. "Don't kill her."

"What is this guy, her husband?"

"No," Jackman said. "She's a witness in a murder case. In three murder cases. It would be a good idea if we didn't kill her."

"Yeah, well," the somebody said.

There was another ping, and another, and another. Gregor felt the ground shake—everybody was hitting the dirt, getting down behind the cars.

"Jesus Christ," somebody said. "That's a machine gun."

"Grenades," Gregor said.

"What?" Jackman said.

"Grenades," Gregor said again.

Then, suddenly, the people right next to him were wearing white and not talking much. Somebody was tearing the cloth away from his wound. It was one of his best suits and they were ripping it to shreds . . . but maybe it didn't matter anyway, because maybe the blood would never come out. They were ripping into his shirt. Somebody put a hard metal edge next to his skin and he screamed.

"For God's sake," Jackman said. "Give him something for the goddamned pain before you go digging into him."

"Don't let them *kill* her," Gregor said.

"Listen," Jackman said. "If she starts lobbing grenades,

we're going to kill her. This is a residential neighborhood. What's wrong with you?"

"You can see what's wrong with him," one of the ambulance men said. "He's got a bullet in his shoulder."

"Nah," the other ambulance man said. "It went right through. I'd bet anything."

"Jesus Christ," Jackman said.

"Listen," Gregor said.

There was another burst of gunfire, steady and staccato. How much ammunition could she have in there? They wouldn't be able to take him out to the ambulance as long as she was shooting. They wouldn't—

They weren't paying attention to him anymore. Gregor could tell. A new set of vehicles was pulling in. The whole scene was beginning to seem like something out of a Bruce Willis movie, and Gregor hated Bruce Willis movies. Still, it gave him his chance.

He held on to the door handle of Jackman's car and began to pull himself very carefully to his feet, inch by inch, molecule by molecule. He was in such pain he thought he was going to pass out, and the blood was coming out of the wound much faster now than it had been. He kept inching his way up, and then he was standing.

He made it upright just in time to see that Kathi Mittendorf had dropped the machine gun and put her hands on a body instead, and the body was coming through the door and down the steps at them.

It was Anne Ross Wyler, and she looked dead.

3

Later, when the shooting finally stopped, Gregor Demarkian would wonder exactly what had happened to him, and why. The sirens, the police strobes, the shouting—surely he remembered himself standing upright as Kathi Mittendorf staggered out the front door of her house, a gun in one hand

and Annie Ross in the other, and bullets sprayed in an arc over her head, breaking windows, chipping brick. When you were dying, everything was supposed to happen in slow motion. Since everything had speeded up, Gregor concluded he was not dying, although he didn't really conclude anything, because that assumed reasoned analysis. This was more like stream of consciousness, or stream of *un*consciousness. Once he was standing up, he didn't seem to be able to sit down. Everything hurt. He was dizzy. His eyes were watering. Kathi Mittendorf took Annie Ross's body and dumped it on the ground. Then she backed into her house again and slammed the door shut. Gregor felt himself swaying in the wind. The wind was strong and cold and everything was getting darker. The door opened and Kathi Mittendorf came out again. She was carrying another body, and for a moment, all the police shooting stopped dead while everybody tried to get a look to determine if this body might still be alive. Gregor knew at once that it wasn't. She wasn't. It was the body of a woman. It had a hole the size of a McIntosh apple in its forehead.

"Get *down*," John Jackman screamed into his ear, grabbing him by the lapel of his coat and pulling him.

Gregor had no idea why the pulling didn't work. He was upright, and he seemed destined to remain upright. He could see the ambulance men, all three sets of them, crouched down behind their vehicles. They didn't dare move from where they were. There were bullets everywhere. The sound of shooting was so constant, it had begun to feel like background noise. He wondered what Kathi Mittendorf was doing. She ought to be retreating into the house again. She wasn't. She ought to be surrendering. She wasn't. She had a gun in her hands, but she had stopped shooting it. Suddenly, everybody stopped shooting. The silence was so abrupt, it was like death. Kathi Mittendorf stayed were she was. The gun in her hand was a rifle, really. Gregor finally realized what it was she reminded him of: Sylvester Stallone in the Rambo movies, holding a machine gun in one hand and firing it. Did he do that? Gregor couldn't remember. He hadn't seen the movies. He'd only seen the commercials.

Jackman stood up himself, cautious. "Maybe," he said.

Somewhere in the crowd of police, ambulance, civilians, SWAT teams, whatever was out there, somebody stood up and pointed a bullhorn at the door where Kathi Mittendorf was standing. Gregor had no idea why. They were close enough for a shout alone to have worked as well as it needed to.

"Put the gun down," the man said through the bullhorn.

Gregor really wanted to sit down. He tried to bend his knees. They wouldn't bend. He tried to bend his waist. It wouldn't bend either. The pain in his shoulder was beyond belief. He didn't even feel it as pain anymore.

Up at the door, Kathi Mittendorf dropped her rifle to the ground. She stuck her hands in the pockets of her jacket. She looked out at the crowd. Gregor couldn't remember ever having seen anybody so calm. People in death were not this calm. Nobody was ever this calm. He searched her face for something in the way of emotion, but all he got was . . . amusement. Why would she be amused?

He thought of her sitting in her own living room only a day or so ago, telling him about the reptilian aliens who had taken over control of the planet, of the One World Government that was already more than half in place, ruling the world, destroying the lives and hopes and dreams of Good Americans. The words had rolled out of her like mercury rolling out of a broken thermometer, practiced and perfect. He remembered it like music. It made no logical sense and it made no practical sense but on some very basic level it made emotional sense. It was the truth of her. He stood there staring at her as the wind blew across his face and across hers, and finally it hit him. She was smiling.

If he'd been feeling better, his reaction time might have been better. On the other hand, it might not have been. She was smiling. The wind was blowing. She had something in her hand. *Fruit*, he thought, and then: *oh, Jesus*.

He still couldn't bend his legs. He stood where he was and watched her pull the pin out of the grenade and lob it in a high, wide arc over their heads into the street.

The first explosion came from behind him.

The second came from Kathi Mittendorf's head.

EPILOGUE

Current Working Hypothesis: "The Overt and Covert Organs of the Vatican and British Empires are Locked in Mortal Combat for the Control of the World."

> —ANNOUNCED AT A-ALBIONIC OVERVIEW
> ON MARCH 18, 2001
> HTTP://A-ALBIONIC.COM/A-ALBIONIC.HTML

1

Anne Ross Wyler decided to give 500,000 dollars to the Freedom from Religion Foundation. It was in the *Inquirer* on the first day Gregor Demarkian felt capable of sitting up in his hospital bed—and it was on the front page too, along with a picture of Annie and Lucinda, with Annie in her usual frumpy Price Heaven baggy clothes, jeans this time, and a big sweater that had not come from Price Heaven at all. The thing was, Gregor thought, moving his shoulder slightly to see if it still hurt, Annie couldn't disguise her face. The high cheekbones, the wide eyes, the chin-up back-tilt of self-confidence did not belong to the sort of person who usually looked, otherwise, as Annie looked. The headline didn't help either. *Billionairess Gives Gift To Atheists*, it said. Gregor had had no idea that Annie Ross was a billionaire. He wondered if she really was.

Outside in the hall, there was the clear sound of Bennis arriving, the Main Line accent drifting down the corridor, the shuffle and smack of clogs. His shoulder *did* hurt. In fact, it hurt a lot. He got the little electric gizmo from the utility table next to the bed and tried to get the bed to put him in a more upright position. He was apparently as upright as it was going to let him get.

Bennis came in, carrying two large canvas tote bags, but otherwise alone. This was something of a relief. At least once since he'd landed in the hospital as a result of Kathi

Mittendorf's last stand, they'd all arrived at once, and he thought he was going to die.

"Oh, good," Bennis said, putting the tote bags down on the floor next to the bed. "You're awake. And conscious. You have no idea how that makes me feel. *Are* you feeling better?"

"I must be," Gregor said. "I've been reading the paper."

He waved the paper at her. She shrugged. "Oh, that. Apparently, a whole bunch of people wrote her letters after she was hurt saying that they just knew that she'd accepted God now, because there are no atheists in foxholes. Anyway, this organization she gave the money to has a project called Atheists in Foxholes, where they collect stories of people who didn't get religion when they were in danger of death. Or something. I don't know, Gregor. It's just Annie Ross. Yesterday the paper was full of the foundation she's setting up for Adelphos House. She's giving it forty-five million dollars outright and a building closer to the strip where the girls are. A big building, too."

"The last time I saw her, I thought she was dead."

"She was barely even scratched," Bennis said. "I think she spent something like six hours in the hospital before she bullied them into letting her out. She got hit over the head, and that was about it. Although you'd think she'd be in danger of concussion. Well, no matter. She probably made the nurses nuts. She used to make the teacher at dancing class nuts too. She nearly got kicked out of Madeira twice. Why don't I have that kind of strength of character?"

"Is strength of character what it is?"

"It must be," Bennis said. "It's not like she's marrying ski instructors. She's helping the sort of people most of her parents' neighbors probably secretly wished could be wiped off the face of the earth."

"Tell me about David Alden," Gregor said.

Bennis bent down and got something out of one of the tote bags. "You're not going to like it," she said, coming up with a cookie tin and popping the top off it.

"What aren't I going to like?"

"He's disappeared," Bennis said, holding out a cookie tin full of honey cakes.

"Disappeared how?" Gregor asked.

"Disappeared," Bennis said. "While Kathi Mittendorf was shoving a grenade down her throat and blowing herself to pieces, he was getting on a plane to Switzerland. By the time the police started looking for him, he'd gotten to Switzerland and gotten out, nobody is quite sure where. He doesn't seem to be there anymore."

"How can nobody be sure where?" Gregor asked. "There are controls, there are passports—"

"There are cars, there are roads, there are fake identities," Bennis said. "I don't know. That man from Lower Merion, Frank Margiotti—"

"Yes?"

"He's coming in to see you as soon as they tell him it's safe. We've all been worried about you. But he can tell you more about this than I can. David seems to have done a lot of planning beforehand. And I mean a lot. The money was gone at least three days before, as far as anybody has been able to determine. It went to the Caymans, but that doesn't mean it's there now, and they're not cooperating. Oh, Gregor, I don't know. I should have saved you the papers. They were full of it. But that was nearly a week ago."

"I've been out of it for a week?"

"Just about. Oh, you were never in danger. At least that's what they said. But you were woozy and not well, and your shoulder is a mess. They're going to have to do surgery on it. And I haven't the faintest idea what's going on. I mean, I still don't understand this thing with America on Alert, except that David apparently started it, or something—"

"As a smoke screen for the murder of Tony Ross," Gregor said. "That took me a while to figure out. I thought that the murder was a last-minute thing. It seemed logical to me that an embezzler wouldn't want to kill anybody, and wouldn't get started embezzling if he thought he was going to get found out and have to kill anybody."

"But David knew he was going to have to kill Tony all

along? That just seems so odd. Tony was like a father to him. They'd been close for years."

"I rather think David Alden is one of those people who are never really close to anybody."

"All right. But America on Alert?"

"We should have seen it coming," Gregor said. "Not the murder of Tony Ross in particular, but that people like David Alden would use the new hysteria about terrorism to try to cover perfectly ordinary crimes. And that's what he tried to do. He set up a situation where it looked as if Tony Ross was being targeted by domestic terrorists. He put up a Web site, half-plagiarized a bunch of stuff from the conspiracist sites, and then set up some local meetings to see what would happen. And he sent that newsletter to the Ross house for months, so that the police would find them everywhere, so that America on Alert would look like the likely culprit. And we know what happened. Kathi Mittendorf happened. Do you think we could get the nurse or somebody to get me some coffee to go with all this food you keep unloading?"

"No coffee, only tea," Bennis said. "Ring the little bell thingee next to the bed. So Kathi Mittendorf came to one of the lectures."

Gregor tried the "little bell thingee" and hoped it worked. He had no idea how to tell. "We think that what he'd do was announce a lecture and then set it up so that his speech would be heard through a public address system. We think he told his listeners that he was being hunted by the agents of the One World Government and couldn't afford to allow his face to be seen. In the meantime, he'd be sitting in the audience as a supposed listener, keeping track of what was going on. Kathi Mittendorf probably came to a few of these lectures. Eventually, he decided to trust her."

"To tell her who he was," Bennis said. "I mean, not that he was David. That he was Michael."

"Yes?" the intercom squawked. "Can I do something for you?"

Bennis went to the wall. "This is Gregor Demarkian's

room. Do you think he could have some tea? The doctor said yesterday—"

"He should start taking sustenance as soon as possible. I know. We'll be right down."

"There," Bennis said.

"She sounds like a Morlock," Gregor said.

"He decided to trust Kathi Mittendorf," Bennis said. "Then what?"

"Then," Gregor said, "he started to build an organization. He started very slowly, and he built small. My guess is that, by the time he murdered Tony Ross, America on Alert had maybe half-a-dozen members, if that. That other woman at the house the day of the standoff was probably one of them—"

"Susan Hester," Bennis said. "She was. They searched her apartment after it was over and it was full of America on Alert stuff. Oh, and guns, and ammunition, and hand grenades, and I don't know what else. She was armed to the teeth."

"So was Kathi Mittendorf."

"We noticed," Bennis said.

The door opened and a woman in a green dress with a white collar came in, pushing a trolley. On the trolley there was a small metal pot of steaming water, a tea bag, a spoon, a pile of sugar packets, and a cup and saucer. Maybe, Gregor thought, there was a way Bennis could sneak coffee into his hospital room as well as honey cakes.

Bennis took the things off the trolley and thanked the woman. The woman went out, looking completely bored. Bennis put the tea bag in the cup and poured water over it. "I don't understand why they can never make tea properly in this country. I mean, what does it take to remember to pour boiling water over the bag?"

"What does it take to understand that I got my shoulder hurt, not my stomach, and there's no reason for me not to have coffee?"

"Back to America on Alert," Bennis said.

"Yes," Gregor said. "Well. It was simple, really. He had this organization set up, and he was producing those newsletters, lots and lots of them, really harping on Tony Ross and the bank, so that when the time came the first place the police would look would be at America on Alert. And that would be okay, because nobody would really know him, nobody would be able to finger him. If he'd been reasonably careful about the computers, which I can't imagine he wouldn't be, nobody would be able to trace him, really. And he could leave copies for Charlotte at the Ross house without being suspected. The only bottom-line problem he had was that Kathi Mittendorf had actually seen him, and that was something he could worry about later, if he had to worry about it at all."

"Okay. So then, what? This Steve Bridge person—"

"Yeah. Well, Kathi Mittendorf was amassing weapons, and she was an amateur. So, eventually, she came to the attention of the two most inept agents in the history of the Federal Bureau of Investigation—"

"Oh, I think that's harsh," Bennis said.

"Don't get me started on the deficiencies of Walker Canfield. At any rate, Canfield and Bridge were sent in to check out America on Alert, and when Bridge started to get too close, David Alden killed him and dumped his body in that vacant lot. Which was all right too, if you want to know the truth, because neither Canfield nor Bridge had ever laid eyes on him, and the vacant lot was in one of the worst neighborhoods in the city, the kind of place where you wouldn't be surprised to find the body of some white guy with all the money and jewelry stripped off it. It also, by the way, happens to be only six blocks from Adelphos House, which means that David Alden had a perfect excuse if anybody saw him in the vicinity, since he's been doing work for Annie Ross Wyler's foundation and he did visit her at Adelphos House on and off."

"Tea's ready," Bennis said. She took the tea bag out and laid it in the saucer. "It all sounds so complicated," she said.

Gregor tried the tea. It was Lipton. He didn't like tea. "It wasn't really," he said. "It was just a diversion. What got complicated was the endgame, when he finally hit the point where he knew he would have to kill Tony Ross. In the first place, he had to use a venue where he wouldn't automatically be the prime suspect, which, as Ross's second in command and general right-hand man, he was likely to be. In the second place, he had to create a diversion, specifically to get me out of the picture."

"You? Really? Are you flattered? It must be very gratifying to know that master criminal manqués now think you're a formidable master detective yourself so they—"

"Hardly," Gregor said. He tried putting three packets of sugar into the tea. Now it tasted bad, but sweet. "It was more in the way of supplementary insurance. Since I tend to get called in on major cases, it would be better if I was out of the way. So, he did a very sensible thing, given what he was thinking. He came down to Cavanaugh Street before he came to the party and left a bomb on a timer in the vestibule at Holy Trinity Church. He thought that if I was investigating the bombing, I wouldn't have time to investigate the death of Tony Ross."

"You'd think somebody would have seen him," Bennis said. "The Very Old Ladies see me every time I so much as sneeze in front of Ohanian's."

"They're looking for you. Cavanaugh Street is still part of the city of Philadelphia. It's a city street in the middle of a busy city. Strangers come walking through all the time. It wasn't much of a risk, either. And if somebody did see him, what would it matter? What would they have seen? A tall, young Caucasian man in a dark coat. All he had to do was pull up his collar and hunch into it for his face to be completely obscured, and it wouldn't have looked suspicious, either. The wind had been awful all week. It was awful that night."

"Could you prove all this?" Bennis asked. "If they bring him back, would you have enough for the city to bring charges against him for the bombing?"

"No," Gregor admitted. "The only way I know is that

there's nearly an hour's discrepancy in the times—when he says he was in New York, when he says he was in Philadelphia, when he got to the party. Agatha Christie notwithstanding, it's a hotbed of reasonable doubt. And, besides, he covered his ass on this one too, by sending Kathi Mittendorf to Cavanaugh Street to give that gun to Krystof Andrechev."

"Which is odd in and of itself," Bennis said. "Why Krystof Andrechev?"

"No reason," Gregor said. "Alden probably went into the shop, or looked in the window, and didn't talk to him. The only important thing was to get Kathi Mittendorf onto the street and have witnesses be able to attest that she was armed. He had a lot of luck. If Krystof hadn't been so embarrassed by his accent, if he'd actually said something to Kathi Mittendorf, everything might have been much different."

"You mean she wouldn't have put a grenade down her throat and blown herself up?"

"I wish you'd stop putting it that way."

"It's the way the papers put it," Bennis said. "There were pieces of her as far as five blocks away. They'd have gone even further except that there were buildings in the way, and—"

"*Bennis.*"

"What about Charlotte?"

"Piece of cake," Gregor said. "He was already in the house. All he had to do was go out a side door and come around by the bridle path. Blow her away. Go back the way he came, get in his car, come around to the front gate and go in as if he had no idea something had happened. He thought that by doing that, we'd all think the killings were about Tony and Charlotte. That they had to be America on Alert, which was railing against them both. That the murders couldn't be about Price Heaven, because Charlotte didn't have much to do with Price Heaven. He was wrong."

"Marvelous. Everybody on the Main Line is going to hire super security this week. We'll have to go through barbed wire every time we're invited to dinner."

"I doubt it. People don't work that way. I feel sorry about

Kathi Mittendorf, though. She wasn't wrapped too tightly, I'll admit, but she was essentially harmless, left to herself."

"Nobody with four thousand rounds of ammunition in her basement is essentially harmless," Bennis said. "And don't ask. That was in the paper too. Do you realize she set a bomb to go off to blow the house up once she was dead? Fortunately, she didn't seem to know what she was doing and nothing exploded, but if it had, she would have taken most of that block with her, and who was on the block? Families. Children. Nobody who was any danger of being part of the One World Government."

"I know, I know. I feel sorry for her anyway, Bennis. For all the Kathi Mittendorfs, the people whose lives have not worked out, who feel neglected and passed by and unimportant and helpless. There are a lot of them. More than you know."

"Most of them aren't attempting to blow up their neighborhoods."

"Did Lida and Hannah happen to send meatballs? Because I could really do with some meatballs just about now. And some coffee."

Bennis leaned over and pulled both tote bags off the floor and onto the bed. They weighed so much, they made the bed springs creak.

2

It was dark when Tibor arrived, and by then Gregor was feeling "better." At least, the nurses called it "better." Gregor called it "annoyed." His shoulder still hurt. The only thing he could do to stop it from hurting was take Demcrol from a hypodermic, seventy-five milligrams shot straight into his veins, and when he did that, he was a zombie for at least an hour. He was tired of not being able to think, and he was even more tired of being in the hospital. When they came to give him another shot, he turned it down and asked for a couple of Tylenol. He calculated the amount of time it would take for them to decide he was no longer in danger of relapsing and send him home. He was convinced that hospitals did not send you home when you still thought you needed serious painkillers. He wondered if it mattered that he didn't have an HMO. He wondered what he would have to do to get somebody to bring him a large porterhouse steak. He thought of calling everybody from John Jackman to Frank Margiotti. In the end, everything was too much effort. He found himself lying back in bed and watching the television hanging from the ceiling. He watched *The Jerry Springer Show* and thought it made sense.

By the time Tibor got there—after "dinner," which Gregor didn't eat; during the eight o'clock visitors' hour—Gregor was in so much pain he found it impossible to sit up all the way in bed, but his head was clear, and he told himself that was all he wanted. He had eaten an entire cookie tin full of honey cakes and another entire cookie tin full of some kind of hard cookie he couldn't remember ever having tried before. It was probably something very traditional all their mothers used to make when they were young. Lida would chop him up one side and down the other when she found out he didn't remember it. He watched the news and saw that Anne Ross Wyler was the lead story, ahead of something the Bush government was doing, he couldn't determine what. He tried not to doze off. Outside the big windows next to his bed, he could see the city lit up for night. Across the street, there was a cemetery. He tried not to find it symbolic.

"Why are hospitals always built next to cemeteries?" he asked Tibor when Tibor came in carrying an overstuffed tote bag that looked like one of the ones that belonged to Bennis.

Tibor put the tote bag on the floor and looked out the window. "Possibly because they have use of the cemeteries," he said. Then he turned his back to the scene and sat down in the visitor's chair. "So," he said. "You are better now? Bennis tells us this afternoon you are no longer babbling."

"I think I just missed some medication," Gregor said. "Maybe the nurses were busy. Anyway, I've started turning it down. It makes my head fuzzy. I can't think."

"This is a good idea, refusing to take your medication?"

"It's only the painkillers, Tibor. I'm not refusing to take antibiotics. I don't suppose they sent you with a steak."

"*Yaprak Sarma,*" Tibor said. "The meatballs are in the tin. The broth is in the Tupperware, which I'm not sure what that is, but Lida showed it to me. You put them together in the bowl, but this way the crust on the meatballs does not get soggy."

"Very nice." Gregor did manage to sit up. A pain like a stab went through his shoulder. He ignored it as much as he was able. "Let me have it. That's the first sign of decent food I can remember for days."

"I don't think you can remember much of anything for days, Krekor. You have not been so sensible."

Tibor put the tote bag up on the bed. Besides the tin and the Tupperware, there was also a good-sized bowl and a stainless-steel soup spoon. There was even a ladle. If the United States government were this well organized, it could afford to cut taxes by half. On everybody. Gregor managed to sit up without compromise. It hurt, but not as much as it had. He pulled the utility table across his lap and began setting up for dinner.

"Now if I could just get myself some coffee," he said.

"Bennis said to tell you the doctors say no coffee now for some time. You should drink Perrier. She has included a bottle."

Gregor took out the bottle of Perrier and made a face at it. If he wanted water, he wanted it without bubbles. "So," he said. "How are you? Bennis said you were better. And making plans for the new church."

"Yes, Krekor, I am making plans. We have designs and blueprints—not for this new church yet, that will take time, but blueprints from other churches that I can look at for comparison. We have an architect. Bennis hired him. We have to get permissions from the city, but according to Mr. Jackman, that should not be a problem."

"No, it shouldn't be. No mayor wants to go into an election hearing about how he wouldn't let some poor little parish priest rebuild his church."

"I am not some poor little parish priest, Krekor. I may be small in stature, but I—"

"I'm just trying to tell you how it would look in the papers if the city tried to turn you down. And I wasn't asking about the church, Tibor. I was asking about you. Bennis said that *you* were better. You were . . . a little depressed, for a while there."

"Yes, Krekor, I was a little depressed. I am now not so. I am only—more cautious than I was, maybe. Do you ever find that there are things in the world you do not understand?"

"Practically all of them."

"No, no. Be serious. I think, from what Bennis says to me, that this man who set the bomb in our church, he did it for a frivolous reason. To distract attention from the murder he was about to commit, or was in the middle of committing. That part was not so clear. But not because he had anything against our church in particular. Does this make sense to you?"

"Yes," Gregor said, pouring broth very carefully over the meatballs in bulgar crust he had already placed in his bowl. "The David Aldens of the world have always made sense to me. Money as a motive makes sense to me. So does love. And David Alden is just a man who loves money. For all the manic planning, he isn't even very original."

"And what about the others? This Katherine—"

"Was she a Katherine, and not a Kathleen or something? I never heard her called anything but Kathi. She spelled it with an *i* on the end. The way girls used to do in the sixties, when they were all pretending to be Marianne Faithfull."

"So I have been reading the papers on this woman, Krekor. And on this organization that wasn't a real organization. And then I go on the Internet and ask people on RAM about these people, these conspiracists. Do you know that's not a real word in the dictionary? When you type it onto the computer, the spellcheck yells at you."

"I'm not sure spellcheck should be the standard for English usage."

"Yes, I know. But here is what I don't know. Why is there

so much fear? Because it is all about fear, Krekor. All these people. This Kathi. These people who put up the Web sites and send the newsletters and write the magazines. That the CIA is running the government. The CIA. I have had acquaintance with the CIA in Armenia when there was a Soviet Union. The CIA could not run a newsstand and keep it secret."

"I wonder if Lida could send this stuff every day," Gregor said. "And yes, I know. The CIA couldn't assassinate Castro in the middle of a civil war. They even tried exploding bananas. It was like watching a children's cartoon about a superhero who can never do anything but screw up. You can't be worried about the CIA."

"I am not worried about the CIA, Krekor, no. But I am worried about the fear. When you see the people from the Third World do it, it at least makes some sense. America is the Great Satan. America is responsible for everything that happens. At least America is really strong, and the Third World is really weak. And when the Europeans do it, it is the same—they are not so strong as America is. But when people do it here and it is the same thing, a few of the names are changed but everything else is the same, there is a secret force ruling us all, we have no control over our lives or our destinies—we are being controlled by the thirteen richest families, or by the Soviet Union that only pretended to collapse, or by the British royal family. The British royal family, Krekor, where is the sense in that? A group of people with no expertise at all except in alcoholism and adultery."

"I think we've been over this several million times in the last few weeks."

"Yes, I know, but I wish to say that I do not understand it. What is it that people here are afraid of? These Kathi Mittendorfs. These people who read the Web sites and belong to the John Birch Society. What is so frightening? That we don't have complete control of our lives? We never have that. That we aren't the most important people in the world? Believe me, Krekor, I would prefer not to be. It is fear and envy and resentment without rationality, and I don't like it."

"If you're looking for rationality, I don't think you're going to find a lot of it," Gregor said. "I don't think there are answers for these things the way you want there to be."

"Does it make sense to say that some people are not really people, but are reptilians, the children of human women and aliens, only pretending to be humans among us?"

"I said you weren't going to find a lot of rationality."

"*Pah*," Tibor said. He went to the window again and shook his head. "We think we will make things better by being reasonable, but I am not sure that is so. What can you be reasonable about when fewer than twenty percent of the people in the Muslim world think that Muslims were responsible for the World Trade Center disaster? The rest of them blame the CIA, or they blame Israel. Kathi Mittendorf blames the CIA. It goes on and on like this, and it makes less sense by the day. How are we to make things better if the whole world is drowning in irrationality?"

"We've always managed before," Gregor pointed out—and that was true. They had always managed before. There was never a time when the world wasn't drowning in irrationality. Only some people escaped it, and they were the ones who moved the story forward.

"In New Mexico they burned Harry Potter books because the pastor said they encouraged witchcraft," Tibor said. "Right here in Pennsylvania, a police department said the same thing. I know I am harping, Krekor, but I am worried, and you should be worried too."

3

Gregor was not worried, although that might have been the result of his physical condition. He was expending so much energy pretending not to feel the pain in his shoulder, he had very little left over for anything else. After Tibor left, he lay down again in bed and looked out the window at the city lights, blessedly free of the sight of the cemetery, which was below his line of sight. He had a tin of those hard cookies he didn't know the name of. He was no longer hungry to the point of being light-headed. He wished he could call Bennis on the phone and have her take him home. There was music coming in over the intercom—NPR, he thought, or the local classical station, with people talking in hushed voices and music that had been written to soothe the savage beast.

He sat up a little again—God, that *hurt*; was he ever going to get to the point where that didn't *hurt*?—and rummaged around in the tote bag that still lay on the bed near his knees for the thing he had seen in there earlier, but not wanted to bring to Tibor's attention. He pulled it out and lay back to read it—not a newsletter this time, or a magazine, but a book, a well-printed book too. Most people would not be able to tell the difference between it and a mainstream book produced by a mainstream publisher. This publisher was called Feral House, and Bennis had stuck a Post-it note to the glossy cover of the book that said: *publisher seems to be post office box in California.*

Gregor looked at the book. *Secret and Suppressed: Banned Ideas and Hidden History*, edited by Jim Keith. He flipped open to the table of contents. "AIDS—Act of God or of the Pentagon?" "An Open Letter to the Swedish Prime Minister from a Survivor of Electromagnetic Terror." Gregor blinked. Sweden? He opened to the essay called "My Father is a Clone," by Gary Stollman. There was a brief biographical sketch, which was not promising. Then the essay started.

"The man who has appeared on KNBC for the last three years is not my biological father," it said. "He is a clone, a double created by the Central Intelligence Agency and alien forces. It is only a small part of a greater plot to overthrow the United States government, and possibly the human race itself. The CIA has replaced and tried to destroy part of my family, and those of my friends."

READ ON FOR AN EXCERPT FROM

THE HEADMASTER'S WIFE

By Jane Haddam

COMING SOON IN HARDCOVER
FROM ST. MARTIN'S MINOTAUR

1

Later, Mark DeAvecca would say that he could see the body from the moment he first looked out the narrow arched gothic window at the north end of the Ridenour Library's narrow catwalk—he could see it lying there, on the snow, under the twisted black branches of a birch tree that had died in an ice storm before the last Thanksgiving. It wasn't true. The body wasn't a body then. It was alive. If Mark had been able to stand next to it, he could have heard it breathing, in and out, in and out, in a ragged contrapuntal staccato that sounded a little like broken bells. He could have felt the fear, too—or maybe not, since his own fear was as all-encompassing as anything he had ever felt in his life. His head was full of fuzz. The muscles in his hands were twitching spasmodically. He was so tired, it was as if all the blood had been drained from his body. He kept closing his eyes and trying to think of the word. What came into his head were scenes from *Buffy the Vampire Slayer*. Bats with human heads and fangs seemed to be hovering around his head. They darted away to hide in the stone arches in the ceiling whenever he turned to look for them. He closed his eyes and counted to ten. He flexed his hands and felt the pain in his joints like needles under his skin. *Exsanguinated*, he thought. *That's the word I want.*

It was nine o'clock on the night of Friday, February 7th, 2003, and as cold as Mark could ever remember it being. It was so cold there was ice on the inside of the window he was sitting next to, and ice on the stone frame around it. The glass was leaded and heavy. That was supposed to mean something. He couldn't remember what. Usually, he came up here when he couldn't face one more person wanting to look into the deepest reaches of his soul. Today, he only wanted to read two short pages in *The Complete Guide To Family Health*, a book he had been carrying around with him for five days. It was big, and heavy, and awkward, and there was always the danger that somebody would notice it and ask what it was.

It wouldn't be so bad if they ever came up with anything except cliches, he thought. *What does it mean that they look into the deepest reaches of my soul and come up with cliches?*

The book was lying on the floor. He was sitting on the floor. The floor was made of stone and as icy as the stone frame around the window. He flipped the book open to the double-page spread on Huntington's Chorea and rubbed the side of his face until the skin under the stubble started to burn.

Depression, he thought. *Yes.*

Moon swings. Twitching. Inability to concentrate. Memory loss. Clumsiness. Forgetfulness. Nervousness. Mental deterioration. Yes and yes and yes and yes and yes.

The problem was, there was a single *no*, and it was the answer to the most important question.

Huntington's Chorea is caused by a single dominant gene.

Dominant, Mark thought. *Dominant means it always exhibits. If you have it, it exhibits. And you had to have a parent who had it, and the parent would have exhibited.*

Mark put his head down between his knees and tried to breathe. He had no idea why he wanted to believe he had Huntington's Chorea instead of a simple mental illness, schizophrenia, something. He was very sure he was going crazy. He had now been away at school for five months, and in that time he seemed to have managed a one-hundred-eighty-degree personality turn. He no longer recognized himself in the mirror. He no longer recognized himself as a human being. If he'd been allowed to have a cell phone, he'd have called his mother five times a day, just to hear her voice. After about a week of that, she'd probably have driven up here to Massachusetts to get him.

Maybe I should go home, he thought. *Maybe they're right and I just don't belong here.*

Out in the quad somewhere, the carillon was ringing. It did something or other every quarter hour, and tolled the hours when they came. It went on all night, so that if you lived in Hayes House or Martinson, in one of the rooms facing the chapel, it could wake you up from a sound sleep. Mark's hands were twitching. Sometimes his shoulders twitched, too, and sometimes the joints in his hands just felt so thick and out of sync that he found it hard to move them. It would be giving up to go home, and that much about him had not changed. He did not give up, not ever. The one time he had wanted to—in that first year after his father had died, when life had seemed like a tunnel without end—he had known, with the kind of absolute clarity most adults couldn't manage to save their lives, that to do it would be to die himself. He'd been less than ten-years-old.

There has to be something wrong with me, he thought. *It can't just all be in my head.*

But that wasn't true, and he knew it, and so he unwound his body and began to get up. There was nothing to do but go to work and salvage what he could, even if it wasn't much. He didn't understand a word of what he read any more. He finished a page and couldn't remember if he'd been reading John Donne or his biology textbook. He drilled himself for hour after hour in German, or got Frau Lieden to do it with him, and half an hour after he was finished it was is if none of it had ever happened. It was cold, but he was sweating like a pig. The sweat was pouring down his back as if he'd just run the Boston Marathon. He was tired, but he knew that if he lay down he would not be able to go to sleep for hours. He had had at least six cups of coffee since lunch, but if coffee was supposed to wake you up, it didn't work on him. He was the walking dead.

He looked out the window again and for the first time thought it was odd. There was a . . . person . . . lying there, in the snow, alone, under the tree. It was a person dressed in black, but there was nothing unusual about that. Half the school liked to dress in black and to pretend to be alienated from all things material and capitalistic. Maybe whoever it was had passed out. It was Friday, and the school was supposed to be drug and alcohol free, but Mark knew what that was worth. There was enough marijuana in Hayes House alone to supply a hospital full of terminal cancer patients. If you got caught at it, they sent you to intervention, and after a few months they asked you to write up the story of how you beat addiction for the *Windsor Chronicle*. Mark knew people who had beaten addiction three or four times, although they'd only been allowed to write about it once, at the beginning. It was like the pictures the *Chronicle* ran about the memorial service for 9/11. The real pictures had been ruined somehow, and so the school had had them all go back into the quad and pretend to be doing it again, so there would be photographs for the story about how sensitively the school was handling terrorism issues.

Everything about this place is fake, Mark thought—and he was almost himself again for that split second. Then the feeling faded, and the insight along with it, and he pressed his face to the glass and tried to get a better look at the person in black lying under the tree, not moving.

If he lies there long enough, he could freeze to death, Mark thought, but there was something wrong with that, something he couldn't quite put his finger on. There was something wrong with the body lying under the tree. Mark was sure that it wasn't a student, although he wasn't sure why he was sure. The person was big, but a lot of the seniors were bigger. He tried to imagine a Windsor School teacher getting smashed on vodka and grass and passing out on the ice twenty feet from Maverick Pond, but it didn't compute. The faculty drank mineral water they bought from a small local company run as a cooperative and talked about how important it was not to allow the liquor companies to invade the rainforest. They didn't wear black, either. They preferred earth tones and polo shirts and books most people found too boring to read.

Something wrong, he thought, but he was drifting in and out of consciousness again, in and out of coherency. If he didn't get moving, he'd find himself trapped up here after lights out. He'd already done that once this term, and been handed sixteen hours of work jobs because of it. They had been absolutely convinced that he'd done it on purpose, because they rang the bell three times and sent a librarian through the stacks calling out for anybody who might not be paying attention. He hadn't done it on purpose, though. He'd just zoned out. He'd just stopped existing in this body and been somewhere else, except not, because he couldn't remember anything else. If he'd believed in ghosts, he would have thought he was one.

He took another look out at the black figure under the tree, then bent over and picked up his book.

If he went the long way around back to Hayes House, he could stop to see if whoever it was needed any help.

2

Marta Coelho had been grading papers for four hours, and she still wasn't close to done. Her eyes hurt. Her arms hurt, too. Mostly, she found herself thinking obsessively about the fact that she had never spent a Friday night not working, at least not during term time, in this entire academic year. It was the kind of thing that, phrased in the right way, she would have thought of as a good thing about the Windsor School before she had come to it, but like most of those things—and there had been a lot of them—now felt egregiously wrong. She found it hard to believe that she had defended her dissertation only eighteen months ago, and that her dissertation committee—at *Yale*—had been absolutely certain that she'd find a faculty place within the year. If you couldn't find a university job with a degree from Yale, what did you need to do to find one? It was hard to remember, now, that this particular job had seemed like a godsend when it was offered to her, because she was up to her eyeballs in debt from college and grad school and close to being evicted from her apartment. It was hard to remember the things she had told herself when she'd written the acceptance letter and walked down Chapel Street to mail it. Bright, committed prep school students had to be better to teach than bored, not-so-bright college students stuck at a fourth-rate state college and wanting only to get through their core courses as quickly and painlessly as possible. A school committed to equality, diversity and truly innovative ideas in education had to be better than the routinely brutal mediocrity of the high school she had escaped for Wellesley and then the Ivy League. *Had to be, had to be*, she thought now. There was nothing that anything had to be. Life sucked, as the kids liked to say, and you couldn't even make yourself feel better about it by thinking about sex.

The office was a high-ceilinged room on the first floor of the Ridenour Library, the one building on campus that looked like it belonged on a campus. The lights above her head hung down on long dark poles and ended in wide globes that gave out too much light. She could see her reflection in the leaded glass windows in front of her desk, and her head looked as if it were encased in a helmet of light. *I should dye it a different color, one of these days*, she thought, absently. Then she tapped the stack of papers in front of her, the ungraded ones, ten to twelve pages each, researched and footnoted. It was impossible to explain to anybody who hadn't had to put up with it just how bone-numbingly boring it all really was, day after day with these kids whose lives had been so perfect they might as well have been produced by Disney. She'd heard all the stories about alcoholic mothers and absent fathers, but she didn't believe any of it. It was the kind of thing rich people liked to say about themselves in order to appear to be Suffering, and therefore all that much more Virtuous. She knew something about alcoholism and absence. Alcoholism was her father getting fired from the fourth job in two years. Absence was the ritual placement in foster care, three months here, five months there, over and over again, never the same family, never the same school bus, but always the same school—so that everybody knew, all the other students, all the teachers, and she would walk the halls very careful never to let her body touch another person or another thing. If she hadn't been a *truly extraordinary* person—far and away better than those boarding school girls she'd met when she first went to Wellesley—if she hadn't been unlike everybody and everything around her, she would never have ended up where she had. She'd have been waiting tables back in Providence, the way her sister still did. Marta couldn't remember how long she had gone on thinking of herself as a *truly extraordinary* person. She did remember when she had stopped. It was on that day she had walked down Chapel Street to mail the letter telling the Windsor School that she would be happy to teach American History and serve as a dorm parent in Barrett House for the next full school year.

She swivelled her chair around so that she could look through the open door onto the hallway. She always kept the door of her office open. When she closed it, she felt as if she were suffocating. She heard the sound of heavy footsteps in the hall and then saw, suddenly, the hulking figure of one of the students she liked least and respected not at all: Mark DeAvecca, looking as usual as if he had fallen off a garbage truck and was still wearing the odd banana skin. He said "hi" without looking at her. He was staring at the floor, something else that was usual. He either stared at the floor or over your left shoulder. He never looked directly at you, and his body was never completely still. She mumbled something in reply that could have been anything, except encouragement. He kept moving until he was out of sight. There he was, that bright, eager prep school student she had heard all about, a monumental mess who never did the reading, never handed his homework in on time and never studied for tests. He might as well have been playing football at some farm belt regional high school where all the kids wanted was to take over the family farm, except that he was no good at sports, either. He just had a famous mother and a rich father, and that was all he needed to get into a school that was supposed to be more selective than most American colleges. Marta knew, too well, what "selectivity" meant, when it came to schools. It meant that they were places that were very careful about who they let in of those people who could not be said to already belong.

For a second, she felt energy surge through her as if somebody had turned on her switch. She was suddenly purposeful and angry. She bolted out of her chair and across the office to the door. She stepped into the hall and looked both ways for Mark. She had no idea what she intended to say to him, or why she wanted to say anything. She only knew that she wanted to grab hold of him and do *something*. When she saw that the hallway was already empty, she felt angrier still—and then the door at the other end opened, and Alice Makepeace came in from outside, wearing that black hooded cape that fell to the floor and always reminded Marta of *The French Lieutenant's Woman*.

"Marta?" Alice said.

Marta did her best not to cringe. Alice was the headmaster's wife, and no matter how progressive and egalitarian the Windsor School was supposed to be, junior faculty did not piss off the headmaster's wife without expecting some repercussions from it. Marta bit her lip and looked in the other direction, the direction she had seen Mark go. Alice was . . . one of those people. She had an accent like William F. Buckley's. She was too tall, and she actually looked good in leather pants.

Marta had never looked good in much of anything. She was not fat, but her thinness did not make her attractive, or fashionable. If she had tried to wear black leather pants, she would have looked like a sausage in a natural casing.

"Mark DeAvecca just went by," she said. "I was trying to catch him."

"Ah, Mark," Alice said, shaking out her hair. She had long, wavy, thick hair. Marta didn't believe for a moment that the bright red of it was Alice's natural color, although she knew it had been, once. Still, nobody cared about that, natural or unnatural. Nobody cared about anything except the special effects.

"He's going to fail history," Marta said. "Or he's going to come damned close. I've talked to him and talked to him. Nothing seems to help."

"He doesn't seem to be adjusting well, no," Alice said. She pushed the cape back over her shoulders. Black cape, black leather pants, black cashmere turtleneck sweater, black boots—Marta couldn't look at her. She was too ridiculous. Except that she wasn't. She was perfect. It was hard to bear.

"I don't think it has anything to do with adjusting," Marta said. "I think he's irresponsible, that's all. He doesn't do anything. He has reading assigned every class. He's supposed to take notes. He never does it. I know. I've asked to see the notes. I don't think he's ever bothered to study for history. Even before he came here."

"He had excellent grades in history," Alice said. "He had excellent grades in everything."

"There are ways to get excellent grades without doing any work," Marta said. "You can have your mother do it, for instance. I don't suppose his stepfather would be any help, but his mother—well, there's always that. You could go to a school where it matters more who your parents are than what work you're doing. There's that, too. Everybody's so hyped on how rigorous this place is. If it's rigorous, he doesn't belong here."

"Doesn't he?"

Marta flushed. She had been ranting. Again. She was getting a reputation for ranting. She knew what Alice Makepeace said about her behind her back. *She's terribly earnest*, that was the line she used, to everybody, and now everybody used it, too. Marta was terribly earnest, and very dedicated, and of course a complete bore and an utter frump. It was, Marta thought, all true, and she didn't care.

She turned away, back towards the inside of her office, where the papers still sat stacked and waiting for her. It was Friday night, and she wanted to be in Boston with friends, out to dinner, at a silly movie about superheroes, in a dark club listening to a band no one had ever heard of. She didn't want to correct Mark DeAvecca's research paper, which would be a mess, badly argued, inadequately sourced, physically disintegrating. She didn't want to be at the Windsor School at all, except that she had no place else to be where they would pay her enough money so that she didn't have worry about it.

"Well," she said.

"You're not adjusting too well either," Alice said. "It's not uncommon, really, for people who are used to more structured and traditional schools. It's hard to get past the dominant paradigm and learn to experience something new."

"I'm fine," Marta said. She was still looking into her office. She didn't want Alice to see the expression on her face, which was not the expression of a teacher dedicated to progressive ideas and the encouragement of diversity in every aspect of campus life. She could, she thought, recite the entire text of the viewbook they had sent her when she'd first applied for this job. It had been written by a good PR firm in New York that specialized in "development" materials for academia.

"I'm fine," Marta said again, turning back to look at Alice's bright red hair. "You're all wet. You got snow on you."

"I should have. It's snowing again. We're supposed to get eight inches by tomorrow morning. Maybe you should knock off and get a little rest before you finish whatever you're trying to finish."

"Research papers. I've got a lot of them."

"Yes, I know you do." Alice shrugged. "I've got to knock off, though, or I'll miss the library. One of these days, I'm going to get organized well enough to remember to pick up my books in the afternoon. Are you sure you'll be all right by yourself?"

"Of course I will."

"Well, you only have to go back to Barrett House. There's that. Have a good time with your papers."

"I will," Marta said.

Alice shrugged a little and walked away, in the same direction Mark had gone, and Marta stood in the hall and watched her leave. The doors at both ends of this corridor were fire doors. They had air closures. They made a hissing sound when they fell back into place, if you listened for it.

Marta went back to her desk and sat down again. The first paper on the stack belonged to Sue Wyman. It would be serviceable and unimaginative, but it wouldn't require much correcting. She took the paper clip off and spread the sheets across her desk. She picked up her red pen and adjusted the glasses on her nose. She thought that she really should do something about getting contact lenses.

It was minutes later, when she had gotten to the point where Sue was arguing doggedly in favor of an "expanded understanding of the role of women in the American Revolution," when it suddenly occurred to her: it made no sense at all for Alice Makepeace to come in the door she'd come in and go out the door she'd gone out if what she was doing was coming in from the outside to go to the library. You could get in from the outside from that end of the hall. Just beyond the fire door there, there was a breezeway that connected the office wing of the library from the main part, but the main part *was* over there, in that direction. If you went out the door on the other end, the only way to get into the library was to go around the pathways to the front. It was like going from Boston to New York by way of Philadelphia. It made no sense.

Marta took off her glasses and put them down on Sue Wyman's paper. She rubbed the bridge of her nose and then her forehead, as if rubbing would wake up some faculty of discernment she'd never yet possessed. Did Alice Makepeace ever make sense? Was she supposed to? The answer was "probably not" to both, and it was all beyond anything Marta was capable of understanding anyway. If there were different kinds of intelligence, then she lacked the kind that fit well in a place like this.